SHEIKH,
DOCTO...

BY
MEREDITH WEBBER

SIX-WEEK
MARRIAGE MIRACLE

BY
JESSICA MATTHEWS

MIRACLE FAMILIES

A love that's meant to be

Whether it's in the arid sands of the desert dunes,
or under the fiery Latin sun of rural Mexico,
Dr Alexandra Conroy and Nurse Leah Montgomery
find that love can find you wherever you are.

Relax and sit back as Mills and Boon® Medical™
Romance takes you on an exhilarating journey
to find love, and watch as families are made in:

SHEIKH, CHILDREN'S DOCTOR…HUSBAND
by Meredith Webber

and

SIX-WEEK MARRIAGE MIRACLE
by Jessica Matthews

SHEIKH, CHILDREN'S DOCTOR... HUSBAND

BY
MEREDITH WEBBER

First published in Great Britain 2011
Harlequin Mills & Boon Limited,
Eton House, 18-24 Paradise Road, Richmond, Surrey TW9 1SR

© Meredith Webber 2011

ISBN: 978 0 263 88572 9

Harlequin Mills & Boon policy is to use papers that are natural, renewable and recyclable products and made from wood grown in sustainable forests. The logging and manufacturing process conform to the legal environmental regulations of the country of origin.

Printed and bound in Spain
by Litografia Rosés, S.A., Barcelona

Dear Reader

From an early age I have been fascinated by the folk tales and fairy stories of the Arab world. *The Seven Voyages of Sinbad the Sailor, Ali Baba and the Forty Thieves, Aladdin's Wonderful Lamp*—all the stories Scheherazade spun to the Sultan to save her life—were part of my childhood, and the illustrations, the images they evoked, have remained with me all my life. So writing sheikh stories seemed a natural extension of this childhood fascination. Having visited many of these areas, experienced the fascination of the markets, seen lamps just like Aladdin's, and touched the huge jars the forty thieves might have hidden in, my interest has become greater—which is why a sheikh story seems to bob into my head at least once a year.

This story was special, because I leave the intrigue and mystery of the cities behind and spend most of the book in a small remote village, devastated by an earthquake. Out of the devastation a special kind of love takes seed, grows, and finally blooms.

Meredith Webber

Meredith Webber says of herself, 'Some ten years ago, I read an article which suggested that Mills and Boon were looking for new Medical™ Romance authors. I had one of those "I can do that" moments, and gave it a try. What began as a challenge has become an obsession—though I do temper the "butt on seat" career of writing with dirty but healthy outdoor pursuits, fossicking through the Australian Outback in search of gold or opals. Having had some success in all of these endeavours, I now consider I've found the perfect lifestyle.'

Recent titles by the same author include:

BACHELOR ON THE BABY WARD*
FAIRYTALE ON THE CHILDREN'S WARD*
DESERT KING, DOCTOR DADDY

Christmas at Jimmes collection

CHAPTER ONE

He'd send for her!

No, he'd go himself.

Shouldn't there be someone else to handle things like this? Monarchs of their country shouldn't have to check out women who'd intruded themselves into the royal family.

His father certainly hadn't checked out Clarice.

Perhaps if he had, things would have been different...

His Supreme Highness Sheikh Azzam Ghalid bin Sadiq, newly anointed ruler of Al Janeen, groaned and buried his head in his hands as the random thoughts whirled around inside his head.

As if his father could have done anything to prevent his twin brother's marriage. Bahir had fallen in love with Clarice the moment he'd laid eyes on her, not noticing that Azzam had already lost his heart to the beautiful woman. But it was the way Clarice had transferred her attention from him to Bahir that had staggered Azzam, and her behaviour since, the pain she'd caused his brother, had left Azzam with a deep distrust of women.

That is a ridiculous bias, the sensible part of his brain told him. You're judging all such women by one example—totally unacceptable!

Yet deep inside he knew the hurt had never really healed—Clarice's betrayal had cut deep, leading to him shunning most female company over the last few years and seeking solace in his work.

Which didn't solve the problem of the stranger in their midst!

He'd see her himself. *He'd* handle it.

He left his office, his mind churning as he entered the wide colonnade surrounding the courtyard gardens, striding towards his mother's favourite sitting area.

Striding—but reluctantly.

He'd met his mother off the plane on her return to Al Janeen, but in the cluster of chattering women disembarking with his mother he hadn't noticed a stranger among them.

Had she deliberately hidden herself among the other women?

He tried to ignore the alarm bells ringing in his head but the parallels with Clarice's arrival in his country were just too strong to be ignored. Back then, it had been him, not his mother, Clarice had accompanied, him she'd fussed over on the flight, convincing him he'd need a massage therapist once the cast was off the leg he'd broken in a skiing accident.

Not that he'd needed much persuasion. He'd been attracted to the golden beauty from the first moment he'd set eyes on her, fallen in love with her within days, only to find that once she'd met Bahir and realised *he* was the heir, Azzam had been dropped like a smouldering coal.

Azzam couldn't say for certain his sister-in-law was responsible for his brother's death, although he knew her continual and extravagant demands had weighed his brother down. Then there was the talk of fights and arguments that was surfacing among the staff—one story in particular of a loud and bitter altercation before Bahir had driven off in his car that fatal day...

It could all be rumour-mongering, but Azzam had to admit that recently Bahir had been patently unhappy, though he, Azzam, had been too busy with his own interests—with his passion for the new children's hospital—to seek too closely into the cause.

The pain this knowledge caused outweighed all other—to have failed his brother, his twin, his other half! Although, could he have done anything? Interfered in his brother's marriage?

Azzam knew he had to stop groaning. Groaning achieved nothing. In fact, it was weak and wimpish—he was behaving like a fool!

He had to pull himself together and behave like the ruler of the country.

He had to check out this woman, for a start. His mother was particularly vulnerable at the moment, and he didn't want anyone taking advantage of her then upsetting her further by letting her down. That, too, had happened in the past...

Straightening his shoulders, he strode on towards the shaded area where his mother sat each afternoon with her friends and female relations.

What was she doing here?

How *had* she let herself be persuaded to fly off at a moment's notice to some foreign country?

What about her *jobs*?

The hospital had assured her, when Alex had phoned them, that they would always have her back. Doctors willing to work nights in emergency rooms were always welcome. But how long would the clinic keep her second job open? She'd thought maybe they'd pay her while she was away, as technically Samarah was their patient, but that idea had been slapped down, the manager telling her if she took time off to accompany Samarah back to her home, it would be without pay.

Pay she desperately needed. But when Samarah had wanted her help, she hadn't had the heart to refuse.

Alex pondered the situation for the hundredth time as she lay back on the silk-quilted bed. No answers were forthcoming so she looked around the sumptuous surroundings, trying to take it all in so she'd remember this part of the dream in which she found herself.

She was in a room with dark red walls, hung with what looked like very fine carpets—tapestries perhaps—woven into fascinating patterns with jewel colours of emerald, ruby and sapphire, and the shadows on the silk coverlet on which she lay were formed by fretwork across open windows, what looked like marble carved into patterns as intricate as those in the carpets on the wall. More carpets were layered on the floor, so when she stepped off the bed her feet sank into softness. Above her, silk sheets like those on which she lay were draped from a central point in the ceiling so she had the impression of being in an extremely luxurious tent.

Her journey had taken on the aspects of a magic-carpet ride to a fabled world, for here and there around the rooms were huge brass urns like the ones in Ali Baba's story, and strange-looking lamps Aladdin would have recognised!

It's an adventure, she told herself.

Enjoy it.

Work will wait.

Oh, how she longed to believe that—to relax and enjoy the thrill of the new—to see something of the world beyond this room, the wide, empty desert, the rising red dunes, the colour and scents of the markets and the noisy delight of the camel auctions Samarah had spoken of with such vivid words and obvious love.

Impossible, of course, Alex knew that much! The reason she worked two jobs wouldn't wait—not for long. Bad enough that her brother had cheated his bosses, but how could he have been so stupid as to get involved with dodgy money-lenders? With people who would have no qualms about threatening his wife and vulnerable daughter?

Alex sighed, then turned her attention to practical matters, like getting out of this country she was yet to see.

Apparently Samarah had a niece who was a doctor. As soon as she returned from overseas, Alex would be free to leave. Samarah's son, the king, was also a doctor, but Samarah was adamant it was not his highness's job to look after her.

In the meantime?

For a start, she should get up off the bed, find her way outside, possibly dropping breadcrumbs on the way so she could find her way back, and have a look around. Arriving in the dark of very early morning, she'd gained nothing more than the impression of an enormous building, more like a walled town than a house. She'd been led along dimly lit corridors, past shadowy rooms, then seen Samarah settled into bed, sat with her a while until she slept easily, then slept herself. Now daylight was nearly done and she'd seen nothing—

'Please, you will come.'

The young woman who'd been fussing over Alex since she'd woken up halfway through the afternoon was hovering in the doorway.

'Samarah? She's sick again?'

Alex shot off the bed as she asked the question, looked around for her shoes then remembered she'd left them in the doorway the previous night. She brushed back the stray hairs that had escaped her plait, and followed her guide.

'Samarah is there but it is the prince who wishes to see you.'

'The prince?'

'His new Highness.'

It was all too confusing, so Alex kept walking, trusting that a conversation with this august personage would sort out a lot of things, not least of which was when she could return home.

Her carer led her out of the building, into a covered colonnade that joined all the houses around a beautiful central courtyard, with fancifully shaped trees, and massed roses in full bloom and fountains playing tinkling music, the cascading water catching the sunlight in a shimmer of such brilliance Alex felt her breath catch in her throat.

What a beautiful, magical place...

'Come, come,' the woman urged, slipping on her sandals and motioning for Alex to do the same, but although Alex responded, she did so automatically, her mind still lost in the delight of her surroundings.

That all this lush beauty should be hidden behind the high walls she'd glimpsed last night!

They walked around the colonnade, passing another dwelling, eventually reaching the end of the rectangular courtyard. In front of her, Alex could see carpets spread, with fat cushions and a low settee placed on them. Samarah was there, and some of the women who had been in Australia with her, their low-voiced chatter reaching out to Alex, making her feel less apprehensive about this meeting with the 'new highness'.

But as she drew near, the women moved away, drifting lightly down into the courtyard, Samarah among them, so only a man in a white robe remained on the plush red velvet settee on the vivid carpets.

* * *

Azzam looked at the pale, tired woman who appeared in front of him. Not a golden blonde, more a silver ghost, slim and insubstantial, the shadows beneath her grey eyes the only colour in her face.

Was it the strain he read on her neat features—a strain he knew was visible in his own face—that made him pause before he spoke? Or did he have some fundamental weakness—some predilection for blondes—that clouded his judgement?

That suspicion, though he instantly denied it, strengthened his will.

'I am Azzam,' he said, standing up and holding out his hand. 'My mother tells me you have been good to her and I wish to thank you.'

'Alexandra Conroy,' she replied, her voice soft but firm, her handshake equally solid. 'And I've done no more for your mother than any doctor would have done. Adult onset asthma is not only very distressing for the patient, it can be extremely serious.'

She paused and the grey eyes, made paler by their frame of dark lashes, studied his face for a moment before she added, 'But of course you'd know that. You're the doctor, your brother was the lawyer.'

Another pause and he saw her chest rise as she drew in a deep breath.

'I am sorry for your loss. It is hard to lose a sibling, doubly hard, I would imagine, to lose a twin.'

The simple, quietly spoken words pierced his soul, the pain of losing Bahir so acute that for a moment he couldn't speak.

Had it been the wrong thing to say? Alex wondered. She found the man's silence discomforting, but more distracting was the glimpse she'd had of his eyes—a startling green, gleaming out of his olive-skinned face like emeralds set in old parchment.

'Please, sit,' he eventually said, his voice cooler than the evening air, making Alex certain she'd breached some kind of protocol in mentioning his brother's death. She eyed the cushions, then the settee, which had taken on the appearance of a throne as she'd approached. But he waved his hand towards it, so she sat, then regretted it when he remained standing, putting her at an immediate disadvantage.

'My mother's asthma? It came on suddenly?'

If a discussion of his mother's health was all he wanted of her, why was she feeling uneasy?

Because there's an undertone in his voice that sounded like—surely not suspicion...

She was imagining things.

Yet the sense that this man was judging her in some way persisted, making her feel uncomfortable, so her reply was strained-hurried.

'I work for a clinic that does—I suppose you'd say house calls—to hotels on the tourist strip of the Gold Coast. About four weeks ago, the clinic had a call from the hotel where your mother was staying. I was on duty and I found her breathless and fatigued, and very upset, which wasn't so surprising as it was her first such attack.'

'You treated her?'

An obvious question, yet again she heard some underlying emotion in it.

Putting her silly fancies down to tiredness, not to mention an inbuilt distrust of men as handsome as this one, she explained as concisely as she could.

'I started with an inhalation of salbutamol, then a corticosteroid injection. Her breathing became easier almost immediately, but I put her on oxygen anyway, and stayed with her. The next day, when she was rested, I talked to her about preventative measures she could take to prevent another attack. I explained about having a management plan for the condition.'

'I can imagine how well she took that,' the man said, and Alex thought she caught the suggestion of a smile lifting one corner of his lips. Unfortunately, it drew attention to his lips, so well shaped an artist might have drawn them. Something that *wasn't* apprehension fluttered inside her. 'Not one to take even a mild painkiller for a headache, my mother.'

Alex nodded, and forgot her suspicions, *and* the flutter, enough to smile herself, remembering the battle she'd been waging with Samarah to convince her that prevention was better than suffering the attacks.

'You're right, although after the second attack I think I was gaining some ground.'

Her smile changed her face, Azzam realised. It lifted the tiredness and smoothed out the lines that creased her brow, making her not exactly pretty but—

She was speaking again. He had to concentrate.

'Unfortunately, when the news of her son's death came, it triggered the worst attack. She was desperate to return home, but I couldn't in all conscience let her travel without medical care. A competent nurse could have handled it, but Samarah had come to know me as I'd called in most days over the weeks since I first saw her. I suppose she felt safer with me beside her, so I flew here with her and her friends. As you know, we broke the journey in Singapore, stopping over for the night so she could rest.'

'And now?'

Azzam knew he'd spoken too abruptly, his voice too cold, too remote, but once again the past seemed to be colliding with the present—Clarice's insistence she fly to Al Janeen with him—this woman coming with his mother.

The woman's smile gave way to a frown as she responded.

'February is our most humid month at home. Although your mother was in a hotel, she'd had the air-conditioning turned off in her suite and she insisted on walking on the beach beside the surf every day. I am assuming it was the humidity that triggered the attacks and now she's back in the dry air here, she should be all right, although with adult onset, the asthma could persist, and she did have a mild attack on the first stage of the flight.'

Again Alex paused. A woman who thought before she spoke…

'I believe she has a niece who is a doctor and who normally takes care of her health, but apparently she is away.'

Was she angling to stay on?

His mother would like her to—he already knew that—but previous experience suggested the sooner the stranger was gone the better. His mother would settle down with her friends, he'd get on with the mammoth task of learning his new role, and everyone would be happy.

No, happy was definitely the wrong word, but life could begin to return to normal—a new normal, but still…

'So?'

The word came out like a demand, unintended, but she was disturbing him in ways he couldn't understand. So quiet, so shadowy.

Insidious?

But if his mother needed someone to keep an eye on her, which she obviously did, then this woman…

'I suppose it's up to you,' she said. 'But I won't leave

Samarah without competent care. Is there someone else who could keep an eye on her until her niece returns?'

Alex wanted to suggest he do it himself, despite Samarah's protestations, but there was something forbidding in the stern features of this man.

And what features! They drew her mesmerised gaze as a magnet drew iron filings—the high sculpted cheekbones, the deep-set eyes, the slightly hooked nose—a face that looked as if the desert winds she'd heard of had scoured it clean so the bones stood out in stark relief.

Hard as weathered rock...

She was still cataloguing his features when he replied so she missed the early part of his sentence.

'I'm sorry?' She was so embarrassed by her distraction the words stumbled out and seemed to drop like stones onto the carpet where Azzam was pacing.

'I asked if you feel my mother should stay on preventative medication now she has returned home.'

Was it suspicion she could hear in his voice? Was *that* the note bothering her?

Or was it pain? He'd lost his brother, his twin—his world had been turned upside down...

Realising she should be speaking, not thinking, and relieved to have an easy question to answer, Alex now hurried her reply.

'Probably not in the long term, but for a while perhaps it would be best if she continued to take leukotriene modifiers. I've been monitoring her lung capacity with a peak-flow meter daily and prescribing preventative medication as needed, but she is reluctant to use the meter herself and to take control of the illness.'

To her astonishment, the man smiled. Smiled properly, not just a lip quirk. And it was a smile worth waiting for, because it lip up his stern face the way sunrise lit the highest peaks of a cold mountain.

Alex gave a little shake of her head, unable to believe the way her mind—not to mention the fluttering thing inside her chest—had reacted! Sunrise on a mountain indeed! She was losing it!

Tiredness, that was all!

She looked at a point a little above his right shoulder so she didn't have to see his face again, and concentrated on his words.

'You are asking her to do something against what, she believes, is meant to be. She would see, and accept, her illness as the will of God. Can you understand that?'

Alex nodded, then, for all her determination not to even look at him, she found herself returning his smile as understanding of Samarah's opposition became clear.

'Ah,' she said. 'I did wonder why she was so adamant about it, but if she feels that way, of course she doesn't want to interfere in what she feels should be beyond her control. Can *you* persuade her? Could *you* convince her that she is better off taking mild medication than having to take the really heavy-duty stuff when she has an attack?'

His smile had slipped away, and he looked darkly grave, as if, in his mind, *he'd* slipped away, and to a not-very-happy place.

'My brother could have,' he said quietly, and this time she heard the pain distinctly. 'My brother could have charmed the birds from the trees so my mother was easy work for him.'

He paused, looking out over the delights of the garden courtyard, and Alex imagined she could feel his pain, throbbing in the air between them.

'I will try,' he said, 'and in the meantime you will stay, care for her, until Maya, her niece, returns?'

Although the invitation sounded forced, as if the man felt he had no alternative but to ask, Alex's immediate reaction was to agree, for she'd grown very fond of Samarah and certainly wouldn't leave her without competent medical support, particularly while she was grieving for her son. But money, something Alex had never thought she'd have to worry about, reared its ugly avaricious head, and she hesitated.

As the full extent of Rob's indebtedness had became obvious, she'd promised her dying mother she'd repay his debts, clearing the family's name and restoring its honour, but beyond that promise was the fact that her sister-in-law, unable to work herself because of her daughter's special needs, was relying on her. No way could Alex let these much-loved people down.

An image of the money-lender's henchman rose up in her mind, clashing with memories of the promise. She'd met him only once and that had been enough. There was no way she could allow that man to terrorise her sister-in-law or her frail little niece.

Alex drew in a deep breath. It was useless. No breath could be deep enough for what she was about to ask, so she blurted out the words she hated having to say.

'I can stay. I'd be happy to, but personal reasons mean that I can't stay unless—'

She balked! She couldn't do it!

'Unless?' he prompted, and she knew the coldness and suspicion she'd imagined she'd heard earlier had returned to his voice.

She stood up and did a little pace of her own around the carpet, avoiding the man who now stood close to the steps that led into the garden.

'Look, this is an embarrassing thing to have to ask and I am ashamed to have to ask it, but if I stay, could I talk to you about some wages? Originally it was just to be two days—fly over with Samarah and fly back—then the stopover and now her niece isn't here to take over... We'd become friends, Samarah and I, and I was happy to be able to help, but I've this obligation—money that is paid out of my bank account regularly—and if I'm not working, not earning, if the money's not there—'

He cut her off with a wave of his hand, an abrupt movement that seemed to ward her off, although she was back on the settee now, embarrassed—no, utterly humiliated—by having to discuss money with a stranger.

'Money!' he snapped. 'Of course there'll be money. Do not worry, Dr Conroy, you will be well paid!'

He stalked away, his white robe swirling around him, and what felt like disgust trailing in his wake.

Not that Alex could blame him—she was pretty disgusted herself, but what else could she have done?

Anger pushed Azzam away from the woman. No, not anger so much as an irritated discomfort. At himself for not realising she *wasn't* being paid? No, the sensation seemed to have been triggered by the fact that she'd been so obviously uncomfortable at having to discuss it.

By the fact he'd made her uncomfortable?

Of course she should be paid, he'd arrange it immediately. Yet as her words replayed in his head he heard the strain behind them, particularly when she'd said 'obligation'. Now more questions arose. If the money for this obligation was paid automatically from her bank account, what good would cash be to her here?

He wheeled round, returning to find she'd walked into the garden and was moving from one rose bush to the next, smelling the blooms. The rose she held to her face now was crimson, and it brushed a little colour into her cheeks. For

a moment he weakened—his irritation slipping slightly—
because there was something special about the sight of that
slim, jeans-clad woman standing among the roses.

'You might give your serving woman your bank details.
If, as you say, payments are taken regularly from your account, it is best I transfer the money direct into it rather
than give you cash.'

'If, as I say?' she retorted, stepping away from the crimson rose and facing him, anger firing the silvery eyes. 'Do
you think I'd lie to you? Or are you just trying to humili-
ate me further? Do you think that asking a stranger for
wages wasn't humiliating enough for me? Do you think I
wouldn't care for Samarah out of fondness and compassion
if I didn't have financial obligations? Believe me, if I'd had
an alternative, I'd have taken it.'

She stormed away, her body rigid with the force of her
anger as she slapped her feet against the paving stones.

There'd been a ring of truth in her words, and the anger
seemed genuine, and for a moment he regretted upsetting her. But Bahir's death had brought back too many
reminders of Clarice's arrival in their midst, and suspicion
was a bitter seed that flourished in pain and grief.

She shouldn't have asked, Alex told herself as, on shaking
legs, she escaped the man.

She should have told him she had to leave immediately!

But how could she leave the gentle Samarah when she
was grieving and ill? How could she, Alex, just walk away
from a woman she'd come to admire and respect?

She'd *had* to ask, she reminded herself, so she may as
well stop getting her knickers in a twist over it. So what if
the man thought she was a mercenary female?

She kicked off her shoes with such force one of them

flew across the paving, disturbing the neat rows of sandals already there. Muttering to herself, she squatted down to restore them all to order and it was there Samarah found her.

'You will eat with us this evening?' she asked in her quiet, barely accented English. 'I am afraid we have neglected you shamefully, but I was tired from the flight and slept until late in the day. In our country we pride ourselves on our hospitality. It comes from the time of our nomad ancestors, when to turn someone away from a camp in the desert might be to send them to their death.'

'I would be honoured to eat with you,' Alex told her, standing up and studying Samarah's face, then watching her chest to check it was moving without strain. 'You are feeling all right?'

Samarah inclined her head then gave it a little shake.

'Hardly all right when my first-born is dead, but it is not the asthma that affects me. Only grief.'

She reached out and took Alex's hands.

'That you will understand for I read grief in your face as well. It is not so long since you lost someone?'

Alex turned away so she wouldn't reveal the tears that filled her eyes. It was tiredness that had weakened her so much that a few kind words from Samarah should make her want to cry. Weakness was a luxury she couldn't afford— like the pride that was still eating into her bones over her request for wages.

Samarah took her hand and led her into the building.

'I know I gave you little time to pack, but you will find clothes in the dressing room next to your bedroom and toiletries in the bathroom. We will eat in an hour. Hafa will show you the way.'

Alex thanked Samarah and followed Hafa, who had

appeared silently in front of them, back to the splendid bedroom.

Clothes in the dressing room?

Alex looked down at her serviceable jeans and checked shirt, then caught up with her guide.

'Samarah mentioned clothes,' she said to Hafa. 'Are my clothes not suitable here?'

Hafa smiled at her.

'Because you are a foreigner no shame attaches to you, but I think Samarah has chosen clothes especially for you—a gift because she likes you—and she would be pleased to see you wear these things.'

'Very diplomatically put,' Alex responded, smiling at the woman, worry over her request to the 'new highness' pushed aside by the kindness of the women she was meeting.

Not to mention the thought of a shower and getting into clean clothes. Packing in a hurry, she'd grabbed her passport, a small travel pack, underwear and two clean shirts, thinking her jeans would do until she returned home. At the time, all she'd intended doing was accompanying Samarah home, but the older woman's asthma attack on the flight had frightened both of them, and Alex had realised she couldn't leave.

So she'd *have* to send her bank details to the prince, though her stomach twisted at the thought, and she felt ill remembering the contempt she'd seen in his eyes.

The same contempt she'd seen in David's eyes when she'd told him about Rob's debt and offered him back her engagement ring, certain in her heart he wouldn't take it— certain of a love he'd probably, in retrospect, never felt for her.

His acceptance of it had cut her deeply—the one man

she'd been relying on for support backing away from her so quickly she'd felt tainted, unclean in some way.

But David was in the past and she had more than enough problems in the present to occupy her mind.

Inside her room, fearing she'd lose the courage to do it if she hesitated, she dug a notebook out of her handbag and scribbled down the information the prince would need to transfer the money. At the bottom she added, 'Thank you for doing this. I am sorry I had to ask.'

'This note needs to go to the prince,' she told Hafa, who took it and walked, soft-footed, out of the room, the roiling in Alex's stomach growing worse by the moment.

Forget it. Have a shower.

The thought brought a glimmer of a smile to her face and she pushed away all her doubts and worries. If the bedroom was like something out of the *Arabian Nights* then the bathroom was like something from images of the future. All stainless steel and glass and gleaming white marble, toiletries of every kind stacked on the glass shelving and a shower that sprayed water all over her body, massaging it with an intensity that had been delicious after the long flight.

She stripped off, undid her plait and brushed it out, deciding to try some of the array of shampoos that lined the shelves and wash her hair. The shampoo she chose had a perfume she didn't recognise, yet as she dried her hair she realised she'd smelt the same scent here and there around the palace, as if the carpets or tapestries were permeated with it.

She sniffed the air, liking it and trying to capture what it was that attracted her.

'It's frankincense,' Hafa told her when Alex asked about the scent. Frankincense—one of the gifts carried by the wise men! Again the unreality of the situation hit her—this was truly a strange and fascinating place.

By this time she was showered and dressed, in long dark blue trousers and a matching tunic top—the least noticeable set of clothing she'd found among an array of glittering clothes in the dressing room—and Hafa had returned to take her to dinner.

'I've heard of it, of course, but I don't think I've ever smelt it,' Alex said, and Hafa smiled.

'It is special to us,' she replied, but didn't explain any more than that, simply leading Alex out of the suite of rooms and along new corridors.

What seemed like a hundred women were gathered in a huge room, most of them seated on carpets on the floor, a great swathe of material spread across the floor in front of them, the material loaded with silver and brass platters piled high with fruit and nuts.

Hafa led Alex to where Samarah sat at what would be the head if there were a table. Samarah waved her to sit down beside her, greeting Alex with a light touch of her hands, clasping both of Alex's hands together.

'Tomorrow we will bury my son, my Bahir,' Samarah told her, her voice still hoarse with the tears she must have shed in private. 'You would feel out of place in the traditional ceremony so Hafa will look after you, but tonight we celebrate his existence—his life—and for this you must join us.'

'I am honoured,' Alex told her, and she meant it, for although she'd only known Samarah a short time, she'd heard many tales about this beloved son.

Serving women brought in more silver plates, placing one in front of each of the seated women, then huge steaming bowls of rice, vegetables and meat appeared, so many dishes Alex could only shake her head. Samarah served

her a little from each dish, urging her to eat, using bread
instead of cutlery.

'We do eat Western style with knives and forks as you
do,' she explained, 'but tonight is about tradition.'

And as the meal progressed and the women began to
talk, their words translated quietly by a young woman on
Alex's other side, she realised how good such a custom
was, for Bahir was remembered with laughter and joy, silly
pranks he'd played as a boy, mistakes he'd made as a teen-
ager, kindnesses he'd done to many people.

It was as if they talked to imprint the memories of him
more firmly in their heads, so he wouldn't ever be really
lost to them, Alex decided as she wandered through the
rose garden when the meal had finished.

She'd eaten too much to go straight to bed, and the
garden with its perfumed beauty had called to her. Now,
as she walked among the roses she thought of Rob, and
the bitterness she'd felt towards him since he'd taken his
own life drained away. At the time she'd felt guilt as well
as anger about his desperate act. She'd known he was convinced that finding out the extent of his indebtedness had
hastened their mother's death from cancer, but Alex had
been too shocked by the extent of the debt and too devastated by David's desertion to do more to support her
brother.

Forget David—subsequent knowledge had proved he
wasn't worth being heartsick over—but now, among the
roses, she found she could think of Rob, remembering
rather than regretting. Here, in this peaceful, beautiful
place, she began to reconstruct her brother in her mind,
remembering their childhood, the tears and laughter they
had shared. Here, among the roses, she remembered Rob's
ability to make their mother laugh, even when the burden

of bringing up two children on her own had become almost too heavy for her to bear.

'Oh, Rob,' she whispered to the roses, and suddenly it didn't matter that she'd had to ask the prince for money. She was doing it for Rob, and for the wife and daughter he'd so loved—doing it for the boy who'd shared her childhood, and had made their mother laugh...

CHAPTER TWO

THE last person Azzam expected to find in the rose garden was the stranger, but there she was, tonight a dark shadow in the moonlight, for her fair hair was hidden by a scarf. He watched her touching rose petals with her fingertips, brushing the backs of her hands against the blooms, apparently talking to herself for he could see her lips moving.

He stepped backwards, not wanting her to see him—not wanting to have to talk to anyone—but fate decreed he missed the path, his sandal crunching on the gravel so the woman straightened and whipped round, seeming to shrink back as she caught sight of him.

'I'm sorry, maybe I shouldn't be here,' she said, and her voice sounded muted—tear filled?

'There is no reason why you shouldn't be here,' he told her, and although he'd been certain he didn't want to talk to anyone when he'd sought the solitude of the courtyard, he found himself drawn towards her.

'You like the roses?' he asked as he came closer.

'They are unbelievable,' she said, voice firmer now. 'The perfume overwhelms me. At home it's hard to find a rose with perfume. The new ones seem to have had it bred out of them. Not that we can grow roses where I live—not good ones—the humidity gives them black spot.'

Azzam found himself smiling. How disconcerting was

that? Was it simply relief that all the details of the funeral were completed that he found a conversation about perfume and black spot on roses a reason to smile?

'The same humidity that triggered my mother's asthma?' he said, coming closer, smelling the perfume of the roses for himself, breathing in the scented air, releasing it slowly, relaxing, but only slightly, made wary by this unexpected shift in his mood…

She returned his smile as she said, 'That's it,' and made to move away.

He was about to put out his hand to stop her—though why he couldn't say—when she paused, turned back towards him.

'I had dinner with your mother and her women friends a little earlier,' she said quietly. 'I found it very moving that they all offered her their memories of Bahir, as if giving her gifts to help her grief. He must have been a very special person.'

Azzam knew the women gathered at this time, but offering gifts of memories? He hadn't thought of their behaviour in quite that way. He studied the woman in front of him, surprised by her perception, and caught, again, in his own memories of his twin.

'Bahir, the dazzling, the brilliant.'

The words slipped almost silently from his lips, while pain gripped his heart.

'The dazzling, the brilliant?'

The woman echoed the words and Azzam hauled his mind back into gear. He should have walked away, but perhaps talking to a stranger might ease his pain, whereas talking to his family forced him to carry theirs as well.

'It is what his name means in our language,' he told her, and saw her shake her head as if in wonder, then she looked up at him, her eyes a shining silver in the moonlight.

'And your name?' she asked. 'Azzam?'

'My name is less lofty, Azzam means determined, resolute.'

Her lips curled into a smile, and it was his imagination that the ground seemed to move beneath his feet.

'I am sure you are that,' she said. 'When your mother spoke of you, she made it sound as if you were the one who got things done—as if your brother might have had the vision, but you were the practical one who could make things happen. She spoke of a hospital you were building—a hospital for children.'

She was beguiling him—though it couldn't be deliberate, for how could she have known he'd seek refuge in the rose garden?

He set his suspicions aside as his disappointment about the hospital flooded his being and forced words from his lips.

'It was to be a special hospital for children, built to accommodate the families so they do not have to be separated from their sick child. It must be a frightening place, for a child, a large, impersonal hospital, although I know these days all hospitals try to make the children's wards bright and special. In my mind it needed to be more—low set for a start, maybe two or three levels, not a towering, impersonal, corridor-littered monolith.'

'It sounds a wonderful idea,' the woman said. 'But surely you can still achieve it.'

He hesitated, uncertain why he should be discussing his dream with a stranger.

Or was it because she *was* a stranger that he found it easy to talk to her?

'I had hoped to make things happen quickly with the hospital—to make my vision come true—but having to take my brother's place as ruler will put a stop to that.'

She touched his robe above his arm and he felt the heat of her fingers sear through the fine cotton material.

'You will do it,' she said quietly. 'Determined and resolute—remember that—and although I'm sure you'll have a lot of pressing duties for a while, surely once you're used to the job, you'll find time for your own interests.'

'Used to the job!' He repeated the words then laughed out loud, probably for the first time since Bahir's death. 'You make it sound so prosaic and just so should I be thinking. I have let all that has happened overwhelm me.'

He took her hand and bowed to kiss it.

'Thank you, Alexandra Conroy,' he said. 'Perhaps now I shall sleep.'

Definitely weird, Alex thought as she watched him move away, the swaying robes making it seem as if he glided just a little above the earth.

Not the burning on her hand where he'd dropped the casual kiss, although that *was* weird, but the way the man had treated her, like a friend almost, when earlier his voice had held a distinct note of suspicion, and later, when she'd asked about the wages, there'd been a faint note of contempt.

Yet out here in the moonlight it was as if the afternoon's conversation had been forgotten.

Poor man, he'd be devastated by his brother's death, and now to have to shoulder the responsibilities of the ruler—no wonder he was confused.

'*And* confusing,' she added out loud as she lifted her hand to her lips and touched them with the skin he'd kissed, the warmth his touch had generated still lingering in her body.

She smiled to herself, delighting, for a moment, in the fantasy in which she'd found herself, alone in a rose garden in a foreign country with a rivetingly handsome sheikh talking to her of his dreams…

What was she supposed to do? Alex had eaten breakfast in her room, checked on Samarah, who'd been pale but stalwart, then returned to what was coming to feel like a luxurious prison cell. Not wanting to get inadvertently caught up in the funeral proceedings, she'd stayed in her room until Hafa had explained that the ceremonies were taking place back in the city, nowhere near the palace.

Now she escaped, drawn by the compulsion of their beauty and perfume, to the rose garden. But wandering there, smelling the roses, reminded her of the strange encounter of the previous evening.

When he'd spoken of his brother, she'd felt Azzam's pain—felt it and seen it—recognising it because she'd carried a fair load of pain herself over the past few years.

Had that recognition drawn her to the man that he'd stayed in her mind, his almost stern features haunting her dreams? Or was it nothing more than the strange situation in which she found herself, making her wonder about the man and the country he was now ruling?

She wandered the courtyard, drinking in the lush beauty of it, freeing her mind of memories and questions she couldn't answer. One of the fountains spurted its water higher than the others, and she left the rose gardens to go towards it, ignoring the heat burning down from the midday sun, wanting to hear the splashing of the water and see the rainbows in its cascading descent.

As she approached it seemed to shimmer for a moment, or maybe she was still tired, for her feet faltered on the ground. Soon cries echoing from the buildings surrounding the courtyard and figures emerging out of the gloom suggested that whatever had happened wasn't tiredness or imagination.

'An earth tremor,' Hafa told Alex when she found the woman among the chattering crowd of servants who had remained at the palace. 'Sometimes we have them, though not bad earthquakes like other countries. Ours are usually gentle shivers, a reminder to people, I think, that there are powers far greater than humans can imagine. For this to happen today…well, there are people who will tell you it is the earth's response to Bahir's death—the death of a loved ruler.'

Alex considered this, wondering if it was simply accepted form that every ruler would be a loved one, or if Azzam's brother had been as dazzling and brilliant as his name.

Certain any hint of danger had passed, the women all returned to the buildings, Alex following Hafa.

'Samarah has returned,' the young woman told Alex. 'The women's part of the proceedings is done.'

'I should check on her. I still get lost—can you show me to her rooms?'

Following Hafa along the corridors, Alex felt a surge of regret that she'd probably never get to know her way around this fabulous place. Soon she'd be gone, and Al Janeen would be nothing more than a memory of a story-book bedroom and a white-robed man in a scented rose garden.

Samarah welcomed her, and although the older woman looked exhausted, her lung capacity was surprisingly good.

'See, I am better in my own land,' Samarah told her, then, to Alex's surprise, she turned and introduced a young woman who'd been hovering behind her. 'And now here is my niece, Maya. She arranged her return as soon as she heard of Bahir's death so she could care for me. But although she is now here, I would like you to stay for a while as my guest. I would like you to see something of this country that I love, and to learn a little about the people.'

Alex acknowledged the introduction, thinking she'd talk to Maya later about Samarah's condition, but right now she had to deal with her own weakness—the longing deep inside her to do exactly as Samarah had suggested, to stay and see something of this country. It was so strong, this longing, it sat like a weight on her shoulders but she couldn't stay if she wasn't needed—well, not stay and take wages, that wouldn't be right.

And she *had* to keep earning money!

Her mind was still tumbling through the ramifications of hope and obligation when she realised Maya was speaking to her.

'Adult-onset asthma?' Maya asked, holding up the folder with the information and treatment plan Alex had prepared.

'It could have been the humidity in Queensland. We've had a very hot summer and the humidity has been high,' Alex explained.

'That, and the fact that she's been debilitated since her husband's death a little over twelve months ago. I ran tests before I went away but found nothing, just a general weakening,' Maya replied. 'It was I who suggested a holiday somewhere new—somewhere she hadn't been with her husband. She was excited about it, and though I suggested a doctor should accompany her, she believed having a doctor in the group would worry her sons and, of course, *they* must be spared all worry.'

The edge of sarcasm in Maya's voice made Alex smile. Someone else wondered at Samarah's attitude towards her sons—the unstinting love that probably hid any imperfections they might have had.

An image of Azzam's striking features rose unbidden in Alex's mind.

'And now?' she asked, determinedly ignoring the image. 'Do you think she's strong enough to get through whatever will be expected of her in the weeks ahead? Is there much for her to do? Will she have duties she has to carry out?'

'More than she should have,' Maya replied, moving Alex away from the lounge on which Samarah rested. 'It is traditional that the wives of the dignitaries who have come for the funeral call on the widow, but this particular widow will make some excuse to avoid anything that might seem like work to her and Samarah will feel duty bound to take her place.'

'Perhaps the widow is just grieving too much,' Alex offered, surprised by a hint of venom in Maya's soft voice.

'Perhaps!' Maya retorted, more than a hint this time. 'But Samarah will find the strength to do what must be done. She is a very determined woman.'

They talked a little longer about the various preventative treatments available, until Alex sensed it was time to leave. She said good-bye to Samarah, promising to see her in the morning, knowing it would be a final good-bye because staying on would be impossible.

The only bright side was that she could send a note to Azzam telling him to forget about the wages, although she'd already been gone three days and if it took a day to arrange a flight and another day to fly home, that made six by the time she got back to work. One week's wages lost, that was all.

She sighed, thinking how little importance she'd once have placed on one week's pay. These days she knew to the last cent how much was in her account, her mind doing the calculations of credit and debit automatically. Knowing what went in each week and what went out made it easy, but losing a week's pay from the two jobs would eat into the small reserve she'd been carefully hoarding.

If the clinic *did* take her back, all would be well.

And if it didn't? If they'd replaced her?

She sighed and knew she wouldn't send a note to the prince. If the job was gone, she'd need a little extra to tide her over until she found something else...

Damn it all! Why was money such a difficulty?

Gloomily Alex followed Hafa back to her room. It wasn't only for the money she had to return home. Simply put, there was no reason for her to stay. But the thought of leaving the place Samarah had spoken of with such vivid words and so obvious a love without ever seeing more of it than a highway and the high-walled building in which she was staying caused disappointment so strong in Alex that it shocked her.

Not that she *could* go home! Not right now anyway. The prince—Azzam—had said it would be arranged, but he'd hardly be organising her flight home while attending the all-day ceremonial duties of his brother's funeral, and the state visits that Maya suggested would come after it.

Needing to escape to consider these contrary reactions—wanting to stay yet knowing she couldn't—Alex retired to her room. But once there, she was uncertain what to do. She didn't want to sleep again. All the rules of air travel suggested fitting into the local time patterns as quickly as possible, so she'd go to bed at the regular time—Al Janeen time—tonight.

Now the women and maybe the men as well were back at the palace. If she went outside again—to walk around the beautiful courtyard—she might unwittingly offend. So exploration within the walls of her suite was all that

remained to her. She opened cupboard doors, discovering
a small writing desk, and behind another door a television
set. Wondering if the funeral procedures might be televised,
she turned it on, not understanding any of the words but
guessing from the serious expression of the news-reader
that he could be talking of the ceremony.

Huge photos of a man so like Azzam he *had* to be Bahir
appeared to have been erected all along the street, and shots
of them were flashing across the screen, interspersed with
images of a crowd, no doubt lingering from the funeral.
White-garbed men and women, a sea of white, filled the
screen, and their cries of grief echoed from the television
set, filling the room with their pain.

With the voice droning on in the background, Alex sat
at the desk, taking up a pen and finding paper, determined
to jot down her meagre impressions of this country she had
yet to see.

And probably never would!

She'd barely begun to write when a change in the tone of
the talking head's voice had her turning back towards the
screen. Once again she couldn't understand the words, but
now a map was showing on the screen, apparently a map
of Al Janeen. The capital—given the airport and the lights,
Alex assumed they were somewhere near it—was shown
in the bottom right of the picture, and arrows pointed to
an area to the north.

'Great! They're probably being invaded!' she muttered
to herself. 'Don't coups usually happen when the monarchy
is unstable—when there's a change of ruler? Just my luck
to be caught in a war in a foreign country! What else can
happen?'

Wanting to know more—the timbre of the man's voice
suggested shock and panic—but still worried that if she
wandered beyond the building she might end up where she

shouldn't be, Alex left her room, wondering where Hafa disappeared to when she didn't need her.

Hafa was sitting outside the door, legs crossed, head bent over some intricate embroidery.

She smiled as she stood up and tucked the piece of material into her pocket.

'I wonder if you could explain something else to me,' Alex asked. 'I turned on the television in my room and the announcer sounded very excited about something happening in the north of your country. Is it a war?'

'A war?' the young woman repeated, looking more puzzled than anxious by the question. 'I do not think war. We are a peaceful country and we like and respect our neighbours.'

'Come and see,' Alex invited and led her back to her room where the television still showed a map of what Alex assumed was Al Janeen, with arrows pointing to a place in the north.

Hafa listened for a while, a frown gathering, marring her fine, clear skin.

'It is not war but an earthquake,' she said, still frowning. 'This is not good. The town is a not big one, more a village really, but it is a very old place of history in the north, between the mountains, and the reports are saying the quake was very severe.'

'That must have been the tremor we felt here,' Alex remembered. 'I was in the garden.'

The young woman nodded but she was obviously too engrossed in what she was hearing from the television to be taking much notice of Alex.

'Many people have been injured,' Hafa explained. 'There is a school that has collapsed with children inside. The town is in the mountains and landslides have closed the roads in and out, so it will be hard to get help and supplies to it.'

She paused as a new figure appeared on the screen, a familiar figure.

'It is His Highness, His new Highness,' she pointed out, her relief so evident Alex had to wonder at the man's power. 'He has left his brother's funeral. He says he will go there now. If the helicopter cannot land, he has been lowered from one before. He will assess the situation and arrange to bring in whatever is needed. He can also give immediate medical help.'

'Where will he go from?' Alex asked, as new excitement stirred inside her. This was what she'd been trained for, but it was some time since she'd done this kind of work, the need to earn as much as possible to repay Rob's debts taking precedence over all else.

'He will fly from here—his own helicopter is here at the palace. It is used for rescues as well as his private business so it has medical equipment on board. Sometimes it takes people to hospital if there is an emergency. It brought the other Highness, Prince Bahir, to the hospital after the accident.'

Alex had heard enough. What she had to do was find Azzam and offer her services—explain her training and expertise, not to mention her experience.

But finding Azzam might not be the best way to attack this situation. Better by far to find the helicopter and get aboard. Samarah was in good hands with Maya. The hospital would already be on full alert. Arrangements would be under way for other medical staff to get to the stricken area, but she knew from experience that such arrangements took time, while the sooner trained people were in place, the more chance there was of saving the injured.

She wrapped a scarf around her head—downdraughts from helicopters caused havoc with even braided long hair. The helicopter, if it was used for rescues, would have emergency equipment on board, but she grabbed a small plastic pack out of her hand luggage. In it she had water-less hand cleaner, a small toothbrush and toothpaste, a spare pair of undies and a tiny manicure set—experience in emergencies had taught her to be prepared. The pack fitted easily into the wide pockets of her loose trousers. Then she ran out the door, calling to Hafa to show her the way.

CHAPTER THREE

'YOU are doing what?'

Azzam stared in disbelief when he saw Alex already strapped into the back of the helicopter, adjusting a helmet over her pale hair.

'Coming with you to the earthquake region,' she answered calmly, adding, too quickly for him to argue, 'and before you get uptight about it, it's what I'm trained to do. As well as clinic work, I'm an ER doctor, mostly doing night shifts these days, but I'm a specialist major emergency doctor with experience of triage in cyclones, fire and floods. I also know how long it takes to get hospital personnel mobilised, and right now, for the people in that village, two doctors are better than one, so let's go.'

Was she for real?

Surely she wouldn't be lying about experience like that, and if she wasn't lying, she'd certainly be useful.

'Maya is with your mother, so she is in good hands.'

She *sounded* genuine, and he knew from his mother that she appeared to genuinely care, but he must have still looked doubtful for she hurried on.

'I've been lowered from helicopters. I've done rescues off ships. I *am* trained.'

'Cutting my legs out from under me—isn't that the expression?' he responded.

She smiled and he realised it was only the second time he'd seen a proper smile from her, but this one, in daylight rather than the dim light of the rose garden, was something special. Her generous lips curved in what seemed like genuine delight, while silver flashes danced in her eyes.

Disturbed in ways he didn't want to think about, he turned away from her, gave a curt order to his pilot, nodded to the navigator, who would act as winchman if necessary, and climbed into the front seat. He hoped there'd be a patch of flat land where the helicopter could land, but if there wasn't they'd have to be lowered on a cable.

'You say you've been winched down on a cable?' he asked, speaking through the microphone in his helmet as the engines were roaring with the power needed for lift-off.

'Onto the deck of a ship pitching in sixty-knot winds,' she told him, and he felt an urge to grind his teeth.

'Wonder-woman, in fact?' he growled instead.

She glanced his way and shrugged.

'No, but I believe if you're going to do something you should do it well.'

He believed the same thing himself, so it couldn't be that causing his aggravation. Was it nothing more than the presence of the woman in the helicopter?

Impossible question to answer, so he turned to practical matters, taking care to keep any hint of sarcasm out of his voice as he said, 'Well, you've probably had experience of this before, but unless the chopper lands a fair distance away, dust from the rotors can cause more problems for people who have been injured, or buried beneath the rubble. Dropping in a short distance away is usually safer and if we can establish a drop zone, medical supplies and water can be lowered into the same place as well.'

Azzam realised he'd mostly done training runs and

learnt from books and lectures the latest ways to handle mass disasters. He'd even written the hospital's policy papers for the management of such things. But he'd never really expected it to happen—not in his own country.

Driven by his need to see for himself, and his fear for the people of the northern village, he'd left the funeral feast and rushed straight back to his rooms, issuing orders through the phone to the hospital as he went, speaking to the police department and army officers as he changed into tough outdoor wear, making sure the emergency response teams he had set up, but never yet used, were all springing into action.

'I don't know how long the flight will take, but you should try to snatch some sleep.' Her voice broke into his thoughts as he went over the arrangements he'd already put in place.

'Sleep?'

He heard the word echo back in his helmet and realised he'd spoken a bit abruptly.

'I've found these emergency situations are a bit like being back in our intern years, and the rule is the same— snatch what sleep you can when you can.'

He realised she was right. There was nothing else to do until they were on the ground, where, together, they would assess the situation and call in whatever help was needed.

He wanted to tell her she was right and that he was grateful to her for being there, grateful that he'd have someone with whom to discuss the situation and work out best options, but it had been a long time since he'd shared any feelings with a stranger—and a female stranger at that.

Yet—

'I *will* sleep.'

At least he'd acknowledged her presence, Alex thought

as she looked around the interior of the helicopter. She sat in one of two seats fitted against the fuselage, a door beside her and another one opposite it. In the seat behind the pilot, directly opposite her, was another man, who apparently didn't speak English for he hadn't been involved in the conversation Alex had had with the pilot when she'd persuaded him to allow her to join the flight.

Alex assumed this second man would play multiple roles—second pilot, navigator, and winchman.

She hoped he was good at his job!

Secured to the walls were familiar-looking equipment backpacks. Some would hold emergency medical supplies, one a special defibrillator and vital-signs monitor. Next to them were two collapsible stretchers, also in backpacks, and she could see where these, once opened out, could be secured to the floor of the aircraft.

'I understood this was your personal chopper, so why the emergency equipment?' she said, forgetting she'd told her companion to sleep.

'It *is* the prince's aircraft, he flies it himself at times,' the pilot replied, 'but he believes it should have more use than a convenience to get him to and from work in the city, so he had it specially fitted out.'

Knowing how much money was needed to keep the emergency helicopter services afloat at home, Alex could only marvel that one person could have a private aircraft like this at his disposal. Her wages would be chicken feed to him, although even thinking about her request for wages made her stomach squirm.

Forget it! she told herself, and she did, turning instead to peer out the window, seeing for the first time what a desert looked like.

It was like flying over the sea at sunset, something she'd been lucky enough to do, seeing the ocean turned to red-gold, the row upon row of waves like the dunes beneath them now. But shadows were already touching the eastward sides of the dunes and the blackness of those shadows made the colours more vivid.

Up ahead she could see mountains rising from the sands—red mountains with deeper shadows below them, what appeared to be a road or track of some kind disappearing between two ranges.

Used to flying over coastal scenes and greenery and water, the endless red conjured up the magic-carpet image yet again, the patterns of the windswept sand and shadows like the patterns in the carpets back at the palace or whatever it was to which she'd been taken.

'Ayee!'

The cry came from the man behind the pilot and Alex peered forward, shocked by what had caused his cry. From the air it looked as if large white blocks had been tumbled down a hill but, as they drew closer, Alex realised they were houses.

'It is a narrow ravine,' Azzam explained, his bleary voice suggesting he had slept at least for a short time. 'It was a guard point on an ancient trade route—the frankincense trade, in fact. It was settled because of the oasis there at the bottom, the houses built on the sides of the hills because the *wadi*—the river bed—floods after rain.'

His voice faded from her earphones but not before Alex had heard shock and deep sadness in it.

Now Alex could see where the mountain looked as if it had sheared in two—as if some giant with a mighty sword had sliced through it. She was trying to make sense of it when the helicopter lifted in the air, turning away from the shattered remains of the town and heading back along the narrow valley.

'We could cause more disruption with the noise so we

will winch down further along the valley,' Azzam said to her. He had climbed into the back cabin and looked directly into Alex's face.

'There is no need for you to do this,' he said, the dark eyes so intent on hers she felt a shiver of apprehension down her spine.

'I didn't come along for the ride,' she told him, unbuckling her seat belt and standing as steadily as she could. 'Which backpack do you want me to take?'

His eyes studied her again, assessing her.

'The medical supplies and stretchers can drop safely, but I would appreciate it if you would take the defibrillator. I don't anticipate needing it but the monitor could be handy. The pilot will drop us in, lower what gear he can, then return to the capital to bring back more personnel and supplies. He will find a safe place to land further down the valley and the rescuers can walk in. For now I—we—need to assess the damage and get word out about the amount of damage done and the kind of help we will need.'

Alex took the small backpack he passed her.

'Strap it on your front,' Azzam told her. 'We will be winched down together.'

Alex stared at him.

'I've *been* winched down before, I *know* the routine!'

'Together,' the infuriating man repeated, while Alex added 'bossy and obstinate' to the meanings of his name.

It was an exercise drop, nothing more, she told herself as Azzam's strong arms closed around her. And she was only annoyed because he didn't trust her to do it on her own!

More annoyed because she felt uncomfortable about the way he was holding her, as if dangling on a line above an earthquake-wrecked valley was some kind of romantic foreplay!

Yet annoyance couldn't mask the responses of her body, which, through clothes and backpack straps and webbing, still felt the hardness of the man who held her clamped against him.

Still reacted to it, warming so inappropriately she wondered if she was blushing.

Would she have felt this reaction with David holding her? Or was it because she'd known him so well she'd never felt these tingling, tightening sensations along her nerves, or a strange heaviness in her muscles, when *he'd* held her in his arms.

David had only ever kissed her, nothing more. Anything extra was what he'd kept for the string of other women who, unbeknownst to Alex at the time, had drifted in and out of her fiancé's life.

'Ready to roll if we need to?' Azzam asked, his chin brushing her ear, the words so close she felt as well as heard them. She drew up her knees, unconsciously pressing closer to him so they'd roll together as they hit the ground. But the roll wasn't needed, the helicopter pilot holding the craft steady and the winchman easing them onto the ground so they stepped from the loop in the cable without even the slightest jar.

Azzam released the line and moved away from his companion, disturbed by the fact his body had responded to hers, not boldly or obviously but with a flare of awareness that was totally inappropriate. He'd not been with a woman for some time, preferring to keep his life distraction free as he'd pushed ahead with his plans for the children's hospital—*his* hospital. At first it had been little more than a wild idea—a hospital purely for children, staffed only by specialist paediatric doctors and nurses. He could have, as

Bahir had pointed out many times, simply built a special wing onto the existing hospital, but Azzam was certain the new hospital would provide a more peaceful and positive atmosphere for families from a culture that had an inbred fear and dread of being separated from their children.

The woman who'd been the source of his body's betrayal was looking up towards the cradle stretcher being lowered from the chopper, the basket laden with more medical supplies. She lifted her arms to catch it as it drew close and he stepped up beside her, taking it from her.

'Stand clear, I will do it,' he said—or maybe ordered.

She snapped a salute at him and said, 'Yes, sir!' in a derisive tone that would have earned instant retribution in his army. Did she not realise who he was?

The thought had no sooner swung into his mind—as he swung the stretcher to the ground—than he had to shake his head at the impertinence of it. There *were* some women in Al Janeen's army now, and he supposed it *was* his army, but *this* woman was here to help his country. He could hardly bust her for insubordination!

'I am grateful to you for coming here,' he said, straightening up and looking directly at her. 'I may not have said that before.'

She smiled, the smile that had struck him as unusual once before, and he caught the glint in her eyes again.

'No, you may not have,' she agreed. 'Now, shall we leave most of this gear here until we've seen what we're up against? I think even the defibrillator could stay and I'll carry the second pack of medical supplies.'

He took the defibrillator from her and fitted it onto his chest, then held the pack of medical supplies as she put her arms through the straps. He adjusted them for her slight frame and was about to secure them across her breasts when the inappropriate heat he'd felt earlier returned.

Tiredness, grief, concern over what they would find in the village...

No wonder his head was no longer in control of his body. And if he was going to be attracted to a woman, it certainly couldn't be to this woman. His brother's experience of marriage had been enough to convince Azzam to seek a wife—something, given the circumstances, he'd have to do before long—from his own country, someone who knew what would be involved in her duties and would carry them out without a fuss.

'Right, let's go,' said the woman to whom he wasn't attracted, the pack securely strapped across the breasts he'd come close to touching.

The downdraught from the helicopter as they were lowered had loosened her head scarf and she was retying it as she spoke. He watched as she covered the pale hair and wondered about a woman who would voluntarily come to help people she didn't know.

Of course, she was a doctor, but would all doctors have reacted in this way?

Might not some have offered to help out at the hospital?

What motivated such a woman?

She was here to help and then she'd leave, so all he could do was wonder.

He finished strapping his two backpacks into place and looked up, realising she was well ahead of him, striding out along the old track at the bottom of the valley.

And for some obscure reason the fact that he wouldn't get to know her well caused a twinge of something that felt very like regret deep inside him.

None of the buildings had been very big, Alex realised as she drew closer to the scene of devastation that lay before her, but as they'd tumbled down the steep-sided hills on either side of the valley they'd crushed the buildings below them.

Azzam joined her and she read on his face the same pain and horror she was feeling, although for him, she knew, it must go deeper, for these were his people.

'Daytime,' he groaned. 'The school would have been operating. It was there, tucked beneath the cliff on the lower level.'

He pointed across the rift.

'And the market, a little further on, would have been full of men and women, traders and customers.'

They were close now, opposite where he'd pointed out the school, and they could see dust-covered figures working in the rubble and hear the cries of panicked men and women, no doubt parents of the children who lay beneath the shattered walls and roof.

'You go on ahead,' Alex said. 'You need to see the whole picture before you can radio out for more help. I'll stay here and tend the rescued.'

He turned and frowned at her, as if he couldn't understand her words.

'Go!' she ordered. 'The sooner you report back to the services in the city, the sooner we'll have more help.'

'But I cannot expect you—'

Azzam was trying to work out which was the most important reason for his not leaving her—safety, danger from an aftershock, her lack of understanding of the language—when she spoke again.

'Go,' she repeated, and, knowing she was right, he went, his heart growing heavier and heavier in his chest as he saw the extent of the destruction and heard the wailing cries of the injured and bereft.

The village headman came to greet him, blackened

streaks of tears tattooed by grief and horror on his cheeks.

'Highness, you have come,' the man said, taking one of Azzam's hands in both of his, then, speaking quickly, he explained what was already being done, pointing to where a line of men and women lifted and passed back jagged rocks and pieces of mud-brick wall from the top of the debris, digging down to find the injured.

Azzam walked what was left of the village with him, before radioing back to the hospital at Al Janeen, which he'd already established as the control point for all services. The first necessity was for a helicopter to drop bottled water and more medical supplies, also paramedics and the small group of trained army rescue specialists. Heavy equipment should be sent along the road to clear the landslide there, so ambulances and supply vehicles could get through. In the meantime, they'd airlift out the most seriously injured people, but night was closing in quickly in this deep valley, the darkness making it too dangerous for a helicopter to come in low, so no more help would be arriving tonight.

The cries of the children beneath the rubble tore at Alex's heart and she dug into it, working as fast as the men and women already there, tearing away the rocks but careful all the time that they didn't cause any further collapse for the cries told them the children—at least some of them— were alive.

'Aiyiyi!'

The high-pitched wail startled her, but it had the quality of happiness rather than grief. She hurried to the man who was crying out, and saw him squat, pointing downward.

'Doctor—I'm a doctor—medico,' she said, hoping one of the words would ring a bell with someone in the group.

It must have, for the man moved to squat a little farther

away, passing Alex a torch so she could shine it into a gap that had appeared beneath a huge slab of wall.

The torchlight picked up two shining eyes, a grubby face and lips twisted in pain or fear.

'Talk to the child,' she said to the man. 'Do you understand me?'

'I know little English. I talk. What more?'

'Ask if there are other children there.'

The man took the torch and moved into her place, and Alex mentally congratulated him as his voice was calm and soothing as he spoke into the darkness.

'More children,' he reported back to her, 'but they can't get out.'

Alex studied the pile of stones and rubble they would need to shift, wondering just how stable it might be. Once they pulled more rocks off the top, might that not alter a precarious balance and cause the lot to collapse on the children?

Tentatively she moved a rock that was beneath the slab but not supporting anything, then another, until she had a hole she knew she could slide into.

'I will go down and pass the children up to you,' she told the English-speaking man.

He wailed in horror, throwing up his hands then passing on the information to the gathered men and women, who now clustered closer to Alex, speaking rapidly but whether in delight that she was going to rescue their children or warning her not to do it, she didn't know. She only knew they accentuated the danger.

'Tell them to keep right back—right off the rubble—and don't move any more stones until I get the children out.'

She wasn't sure if his English was good enough, but the man not only understood but obeyed immediately—waving the people back onto firm ground, yelling at those who hesitated even momentarily, moving them all back to a safe distance.

She removed her backpack and opened it, showing the man whom she'd appointed as her helper what was in it. She unwrapped the webbing from the pack, knowing the backstraps could be used as a rope, and indicated she would take one end down the hole as she went.

'I'd prefer to pass the children up to you,' she said. 'The rope might help the older ones climb. When they come out, there are three things you must check, ABC, airways, breathing, circulation. Clear the mouth and nose of dust or debris, make sure the child is breathing, or breath for him or her.'

Alex used a rock to demonstrate breathing into a child's mouth and nose.

'Then check the heartbeat and find any blood. If it's pumping out—' she used her hands to illustrate a spray of blood '—apply a tight pad and bandage over it.'

The man nodded, repeating 'ABC' as if the concept was familiar to him.

With the medical supplies set out and the agitated crowd safely out of the way—if there *was* a collapse she didn't want anyone else injured—she had to figure out the easiest way into the space where the children were trapped. Feet first for sure, but on her back or on her belly?

'Do not even think about it!'

Azzam's voice came from directly behind her, and she turned, sure he must be speaking to her because who else would speak such perfect English?

'You cannot go down there.'

'Of course I can,' she told him, irritated by the waste of time an argument would cause and knowing from his voice that argument was looming. 'Look at the hole—I'm the only one who will fit. Besides, you'll be more useful up here tending the injured—you can ask questions and understand the answers the injured people give you, which is more than I can do.'

She didn't wait for his response, opting to slide in on her belly, thinking she could remove any impediments beneath her without compromising what was above. Tremors of fear vibrated along her nerves as she knotted the wide trousers around her ankles so they wouldn't impede her. She reminded herself that one of the reasons she'd become involved in rescue work had been to overcome her fear of small, enclosed spaces—a fear she refused to acknowledge as claustrophobia.

Wriggling down a short tunnel that seemed to have the dimensions of a rabbit burrow, she finally reached a place where most of her body was dangling in the air, only her head still in the hole, with her arms above it, braced against the sides so she wouldn't plummet to the floor and injure some small child.

Above her she could hear Azzam's voice, still grumbling and growling, but her entire being was focussed now on what lay below.

Were there older children in the space? Would they have the sense to keep the younger ones out of her way when she fell?

She was still wondering about this when small hands grasped her leg and she found her feet guided onto something. A rock? Perhaps a desk?

Praying that it would take her weight, she released the pressure of her arms against the rock tunnel and eased herself out, turning on the torch she'd thrust into her pocket before starting her journey. She was standing on what must have been the teacher's table, a solid wooden piece of furniture that right now seemed like an enormous piece of luck.

Shining the torch around, she saw dark eyes, most red with tears, peering at her out of dusty, blood-streaked faces. She dropped down off the desk and held out her arms. The little bodies crowded against her, so, for a few seconds, they could feel the safety of an adult hug.

'English?' she asked, but there was no response, so she eased herself away from them and lined them up, running the torch over each child, checking for serious injury. She had reached the end of the line of nine when she saw the others on the floor, some sitting, some lying down, perhaps unconscious.

She was drawn towards these children that needed help, perhaps immediately, but instinct yelled at her to get the others out. Perhaps she could do both.

Checking the line-up, she chose the smallest child and, lifting the little girl onto the table, she climbed up, tied the webbing around her, and lifted her higher into the hole. Alex tugged the rope and felt an answering tug. The little one would suffer scrapes being hauled up the short but rough tunnel, but at least they were fixable.

Next she chose a sturdy-looking boy and, as soon as the feet of the small girl disappeared from view, she pointed to the tunnel and made climbing motions with her hands. The boy understood and as soon as she held him up, he grasped at stones on the sides of the escape route and climbed nimbly out of sight.

The children, realising what was happening, began to clamour, no doubt about who would be next. Another big child climbed onto the table as the rope slithered back down. He gesticulated to the hole and to the children then pointed at Alex and at the patients in the corner.

Without words Alex understood he would do her job of lifting the children while she tended the injured, so she climbed down, passed him a small child, and, not wanting him to think she didn't trust him to save his friends, turned her attention to the children on the floor.

Not all of them were children, she realised, for a man in a long, dark robe lay there as well, his body curled protectively around the smallest of the injured. He was dead, Alex saw at once, but the child beneath him was alive. He'd saved that child!

She'd left her torch on the desk so all the children had some light to lift their fears, and couldn't see what injuries these—four, she counted—had suffered. Not wanting to deprive the children of the light, she'd have to go by feel, and trust her hands to do the basic diagnosis. Chest first to check on breathing and heartbeat—rapid movement. This child was alive. Her hands felt their way to the head, seeking a tell-tale shift in the bony skull, feeling for blood spurting or seeping. No head wound but further exploration revealed this first child had an open fracture of the humerus, no doubt the pain of that contributing to the child's lack of consciousness.

Aware there could be spinal damage but more concerned about further injury should an aftershock bring down the wall above where they lay, she lifted the child and carried him across the small space, placing him beneath the table in the hope—possibly false—that its solidity might provide some protection.

One of the children waiting to be lifted out began to cry and knelt beside the child. No doubt a sibling, a bond so strong the able child was obviously insisting she stay too, settling beneath the table to hold the little boy's hand.

No time to argue! Alex shrugged at her helper on the table and passed another child up to him. Five to go, then him, then the injured ones. She'd need to work out how best to get them out.

The next child was conscious, anxious eyes peering at

her in the dim light, lips moving as he tried to tell Alex something. His breathing was okay, heart rate rapid but not dangerously so, no sign of bleeding, but when Alex pricked the small foot with a sharp shard of plaster she'd found on the floor, the little boy didn't flinch. Spinal injury. How was she supposed to handle that?

She crossed to the table again and took the torch.

'Sorry, kids,' she said, although she knew they wouldn't understand, and she swept the torchlight around the small space, searching for anything that might do to stabilise the injured boy's neck and spine. A tall stick stood in one corner. With these steep hills, maybe the teacher had used it as a walking aid. She grabbed it and returned the torch to the table so the evacuation could continue, but before she could break the stick, she heard a voice yelling down the tunnel.

'That was an aftershock! Are you all right? Come up out of there—we'll extend the hole.'

CHAPTER FOUR

AZZAM held his breath. How could he have been so stupid as to leave Alex on her own? Although he could hardly have known she'd decide to go down through an impossibly small hole into the ground below. She was either incredibly brave or incredibly foolish, but he could no longer hover here above her while she risked her life in an unstable hole beneath the ground.

Surely they could enlarge the hole.

'Nothing shifted,' she called up to him, sounding so calm and composed he regretted the momentary panic he'd felt as the ground had shuddered once more. 'But there is something you could do. There are no children in the tunnel right now so could you drop down some bandages, and a small neck collar if there's one in the pack, a couple of splints if you have them. Most of those men are wearing intricate turbans—could you drop a few of them down too so I can use them as bindings to protect the injured children as you pull them out?'

Calm and composed? She was more than that. Thinking ahead and thinking clearly—thinking medically.

'And another torch,' she called. 'That should provide weight for the other things as you drop them.'

'Get out and let me come down,' he ordered.

'As if you'd fit,' she retorted. 'Just get that stuff down

here so I can get the rest of these kids out. This space could disappear if there's another aftershock.'

The image she'd offered him stopped his heart for a moment, but he organised what she needed, grumbling to himself all the time, frustrated that this stranger was doing so much for his people—that *she* should be the one risking her life. She was a visitor to his country—a guest—and she had put her life in danger.

It wasn't right!

And yet it was. As she'd said, she'd trained for it—it was what she did—but the courage it must have taken for her to slide down that hole…

'Some time soon,' she prompted, and he bundled up the things he'd been putting together as his mind raced with worry. Thinking ahead, as she had, he realised she might need more than a few turbans. He slid off his gown and wrapped that around the bundle, and dropped it down.

Alex heard a lot of grumbling from above but eventually a bundle came down the hole, wrapped not in black turban material but in dirty white cloth which she suspected had once been Azzam's pristinely perfect gown. An image of the man ungowned—broad chest, toned abs—flashed into her head but was quickly banished. For all she knew, he could have a pigeon chest and a beer gut.

Obviously her brain was using these irrelevancies to stop her worrying about the situation. She lifted a little girl who had become hysterical and was flailing in her arms, making it obvious she had no intention of being thrust up into the hole above their temporary shelter. Using the dark turbans, Alex wrapped the little limbs so the child's arms were close to her body and her legs bound together, not too tightly but not loosely enough for the child to kick or hit out and injure herself against the tunnel wall.

Using the webbing, she tied her bundle securely then called up to Azzam.

'As far as I can tell, this child is uninjured but she's panicking so I've wrapped her in a bundle. Can you haul her gently? Are the children's parents out there? Is there someone who can soothe the poor wee thing?'

Azzam felt the tug on the webbing rope and pulled gently, finding, indeed, a bundle on the end of it. Alex had managed to swaddle the little girl so completely that even her face was covered with a thin layer of cloth through which loud shrieks of fear and anger could still be heard.

Anxious hands took the bundle from him, the child passed back from man to man until it reached the parents waiting on the solid ground at the base of the *wadi*. The loud wailing cry of a woman told him the child had found her mother, but again his attention was drawn back to the hole.

The work continued, bigger children scrambling out on their own, smaller ones wrapped and tied to the webbing.

'The boy coming up next is a hero,' Alex called to him. 'It is he who looked after the other children and then passed them up to the hole so they could get out. But I think he's close to exhaustion so if you could reach in to help him out, I would be grateful.'

'*You* would be grateful!' Azzam muttered, but mostly to himself as he flattened himself on the rough ground and eased his head and arms into the hole, hoping to feel for the boy's hands and haul him out.

The hands were smaller than he'd expected, a child still, this lad.

'You are all right. You have been very brave to help the others. You are only a boy but the doctor says you did a man's job down there.' He urged the boy upward, drew him out then held him close, soothing him as he spoke, because now he was out of danger the scared child inside the lad had begun to shake and cry.

'But I need more help from you,' he added as the boy calmed down.

Hearing the conversation, a woman called from the *wadi*.

'Help the man, Dirar. He is your prince.'

The boy looked up at him.

'You are the prince?'

There was so much wonder in the boy's face, Azzam had to smile.

'But I am only a man,' he said, 'and once I was a boy like you, but I doubt I was as brave. Now, tell me, Dirar, how many people are still trapped and what is the doctor doing down there?'

'Our teacher is there but I think he is dead,' Dirar whispered, tears sliding down his cheeks again. 'And Tasnim will not come because her brother is hurt. He is under the table. The woman put him there.'

Great! Just wonderful! Azzam thought to himself. The mountain could collapse and that insane female thought a school table might provide protection.

Yet inside the anger he acknowledged respect, for she was doing the best she could under incredible and horrific circumstances. It was frustration that he couldn't be down there himself that made him want to snarl like a wild leopard.

Leopards!

Night was coming and the leopards would smell the blood of the dead and injured…

He'd think of that later. Now he had to concentrate on what the boy was telling him. Four injured children and a loyal sister. Would he and Bahir have been less foolish over women—over Clarice—if they'd grown up with sisters?

'So you must get them out now,' the boy was telling him, easing out of Azzam's arms and running nimbly over the debris of the buildings towards the waiting arms of his mother.

A tug on the rope reinforced his decision to concentrate on one thing at a time.

'I've splinted this one's arm as best I could. I notice you sent morphine down but not knowing if the child has head injuries I didn't want to use it. He's unconscious anyway. Perhaps when he comes up, you should get my English-speaking helper back there and do some doctoring.'

Did she not want him here? Azzam wondered as he gently pulled the rope. He felt so drawn to stay—so held in place by the fear he had for her—he doubted he could move, although what she'd said made sense.

The child, again bundled like a mummy, emerged, and after the bundle a small girl scrambled out, glaring at Azzam as he unwrapped the turban from the injured child's face so he could breathe more easily.

'My brother!' she said, in such a possessive voice Azzam put out his arms and drew her into a hug.

'You are a good sister,' he told her in her own language as she wept against him. 'Your brother will be all right. I am going to pass him over to safe ground and I want you to go with him.'

The little girl nodded against his shoulder but even after she eased away he felt the imprint of her frail body.

Would the day ever come when he could put the past behind him, and hug his own children?

It would have to come. The country would need an heir...

'It'll be a while before I can move the rest,' a soft voice called, recalling him yet again to his duty. And loath though he was to leave the top of the escape hatch, he waved to the man who'd held the position earlier and they crossed paths as he made his way down to the *wadi* to see the injured child. Dr Conroy—he'd think of her that way—was right. There were already too many injured people to be tended by one doctor. He'd had no business to be wasting time in the rescue effort.

The villagers were lining the injured up on a grassy bank near where the *wadi* had been deepened and widened to form an oasis. On this section of the northern side there'd been no buildings to collapse so the area was safe from anything but a rock fall and he had to pray that wouldn't happen until the road was clear and all the injured evacuated.

Men had walked back to the helicopter drop and carried the cradle with supplies, and some of the women were carrying bottles of water to the men still lifting debris. Azzam concentrated on the victims, seeing first the little boy with the broken arm, checking the rough way Alexandra had positioned the splints and wrapped them, realising she'd been trying to immobilise the arms so the movement up the escape route wouldn't cause further damage.

What to do? The child was conscious now, asking for his mother, his sister by his side. He was breathing easily and didn't seem to be in much pain. He could be dealt with later—decisions made then about setting the arm.

He wanted to tell the little girl to find their mother, but what if their mother was trapped? Did he want to send the child on a search that could cause her heartbreak?

He patted her head instead, telling her to watch her brother—an unnecessary statement as she seemed to have attached herself to his good hand and had no intention of moving.

Azzam walked towards the other injured villagers, thinking only of lifesaving measures, knowing he needed to prioritise who would be lifted out first and who could be cared for here.

'Sir, sir!'

A call from the man at the school. Azzam hurried back and was handed a small form wrapped in his once-white gown. The child's pulse was faint, so Azzam carried him swiftly to the *wadi* and put him gently on the ground, carefully unwrapping the little form, finding not only a brace around the child's neck but three lengths of stick ingeniously bound into a firm stretcher, the little body tied to it with lengths of turban.

Azzam grabbed a torch from the pack and opened one of the child's eyes to shine the light into it. No response. Neither was there any response when he pinched a finger or a toe.

A woman dropped to her knees beside the child, demanding that he sit up, refusing to accept the child might be badly injured, berating Azzam for not helping her son to sit.

'Spinal injury or brain, internal injury, it's hard to tell,' a soft voice said, and he realised the rescuer had been rescued. She was filthy, her clothes torn and her hands streaked with blood, yet his heart gave a leap that he knew was relief that she was safe, for all it was an unusual response. 'I think he is the most severely injured, although there's a little girl who's comatose as well. I brought her out. Her father is with her.'

She hesitated, then added, 'The school teacher and another child are both dead. It would be good to get them out so they can be laid to rest by their families, but I thought I might be needed here.'

He could hear the anxiety in her voice and understood she'd fought a battle with herself before leaving those two souls behind.

'You did the right thing,' he assured her. 'And you saved the other children as well, remember that, although—' his voice deepened to a growl '—your behaviour was incredibly foolhardy.'

Not that she took the slightest notice of him, turning to wash her hands with water from a bottle then kneeling beside a woman who'd been pulled from the rubble.

Alex checked and re-checked the injured, one by one, doing what she could for each of them in these appalling circumstances, aware, all the time, of the presence of Azzam, not because the local people were treating him with such deference but because some kind of awareness— definitely unwanted and totally bizarre—was tweaking at her body.

Had it started in the rose garden, this attraction? Had she been drawn to him when he'd revealed just a little of his grief for the brother he'd so obviously loved?

Surely it couldn't be the bare chest. His lower half was decently garbed in what looked like a once-white sarong-type thing, though in the ingenious way of these people it was now fashioned into, yes, Sinbad-type trousers.

But it *was* the bare chest, olive skin, streaked with ash and dust, over heavy slabs of muscle, the chest of an athlete, not a doctor or a prince, that was causing her uneasiness. Not that she knew what princes' chests *should* look like but not many doctors she knew had time to work out sufficiently to keep such well-defined muscles.

What was she doing?

How could her mind be wandering like this—
she who prided herself on her focus and professional
competence?

She moved to the next patient, focussing all her attention
on the injured.

Until she heard the cry.

'That's a baby.'

She looked over towards where the school had been,
sure of what she'd heard.

'It was a bird,' Azzam told her, but already the little girl
who had sat beneath the table beside her injured brother
was stumbling across the wrecked buildings towards the
hole.

'There couldn't have been a baby in the school,' Azzam
said, patient common sense accentuating the denial. But
already Alex was following the child.

'Ask her,' she called back to Azzam. 'Ask her why she
knows the cry.'

Alex caught the child and passed her back to Azzam,
who, although she struggled and objected loudly, held her
gently and easily in his arms, calming her with his voice.

'She says her mother always came to meet them after
school. She brought the baby. She says her father is away—
he is gone, she says, although I don't know what she means
by that.'

'They could have been outside the school—the mother
and the baby. I'm going back down,' Alex told him, then
saw the fury in his face as he thrust the child into someone
else's arms and stepped towards her.

'I will *not* leave an infant down there!' Alex told him,
hoping the defiance in her voice was visible in her face for
there was no time to be arguing with this man.

'You know you won't fit and neither will any of the men
I've seen here,' she added, before he had time to open his

mouth for his objection. 'If you want to be useful, you can hold the rope.'

Alex eased herself feet first into the tunnel, dreading a return to the hole beneath, but hearing the baby's cries more clearly now. She'd pocketed the torch and when she dropped onto the table, she shone it around, shuddering as the light passed over the body of the school teacher and the child, wishing, as she had earlier, that she didn't have to leave them down here in the darkness.

The indignant shrieks of the infant, no doubt hungry and wondering why its demands were not being met, seemed to come from the opposite corner. Alex played the light around the area, seeing a twisted frame of what might once have been a door, still with sufficient strength to shore up the debris above it, making a kind of cave.

Approaching cautiously, Alex shone the torch into the depths, but although she knew she was closer to the baby because the cries were louder, she could see nothing.

'Come up, we'll widen the hole,' Azzam commanded from above.

'And bring the whole lot down?' Alex retorted, pulling carefully on a piece of broken masonry, praying the doorframe would still hold. The masonry came away, another rock, a piece of wall—slowly she widened the gap behind the doorframe until eventually she felt the softness of a person. Not the baby, the hand she grasped was too big for a baby's, and the wrist she held had no pulse.

Tears of grief and fear spilled down Alex's cheeks and deep inside her anger stirred as well. She didn't know this woman, but two children up above, and the baby if she got it out, would now be motherless. How did fate choose whom to harm? Was it just on a whim that the earth threw open a great chasm and caused this devastation?

Aware she was raging against the fates to stop herself

thinking about the possibility of not being able to rescue the infant, she set to work again, pulling out small stones, always checking, no matter how tiny her target, that moving it wouldn't cause a collapse.

The infant's cries ceased, and Alex moved more swiftly now, still careful but aware that time might make the difference between life and death, and suddenly, what she wanted most of all, was for this child to live.

She felt a small hand—even better, felt the tiny fingers move and grip her thumb. More tears flowed, but now Alex cursed them. This was no time for emotion. She had to concentrate—she had to somehow ease the baby out from beneath its mother.

Edging closer, she slid her hand along the ground, easing it beneath where she now knew the infant lay. It whimpered at the movement—was it injured? Had she hurt it?

But she *had* to get it out!

Her hand had met resistance. The baby was somehow tied to the mother. Alex closed her eyes and tried to picture the different types of slings a mother might be wearing to hold her baby close to her body.

All she could think of were the kind of things sold in baby shops at home, and this would surely be a less complicated arrangement. But whatever it was, she needed some way to cut the baby free.

Backing out of the space, she hurried to the table beneath the hole and called up to Azzam.

'I need some scissors or a sharp knife. The baby is in some kind of sling, tied to the mother, who is dead.'

Azzam heard the waver in her voice as she said the last word and wondered at Alex's strength of character that she'd even gone back down the hole in the first place, let alone be determined enough to remain and cut the baby free. He found a sheathed knife and knelt beside the hole, frustrated by again playing a secondary role in this rescue but wanting to help however he could.

'Mostly, our women tie their babies in a criss-cross fashion, their scarves dangling from their necks then crossing in front and tied at the back. Can you picture that?'

'Clearly,' came the reply, 'and thanks for that. I can cut at the back of the neck and not risk stabbing the baby.'

Azzam shook his head. He'd teasingly called her wonder-woman earlier, but that's what she was proving to be. And he'd had doubts about her? He felt ashamed, not only about those doubts but about the poison he'd allowed to spread through his heart and soul, infecting his whole body not only with pain but with suspicion.

'I have the baby, I've wrapped it well—can you pull really gently?'

The woman he no longer doubted sounded exhausted and he worried that *she'd* be able to get out.

He *had* to get her out!

'Azzam?'

Once again, her voice reminded him of the immediate task.

'I'll be gentle,' he assured her. 'Tug when you're ready.'

He felt the tug and hauled slowly and steadily, the weight so slight he had to force himself not to hurry lest he injure the baby in his haste. Then suddenly it was there and he pulled the wrapping from the little face and saw wide brown eyes staring up at him and the tiny mouth open in a wail of protest.

'It's all right, little one,' he murmured, then realised he was speaking English and translated, although he was reasonably sure it was his tone of voice, not the words, that had hushed the baby.

But with the baby held against his chest he again felt

that rush of longing he'd experienced earlier. Children were the future—Alex had been right. The baby *had* to be rescued.

But for now, perhaps he should be concentrating on the baby's saviour.

'Alex? Can you climb up?'

'I guess I'll have to,' she said, injecting a laugh into her voice, although he suspected she was using it to cover if not fear then definitely apprehension.

'I'm going to squirm down as far as I can so reach up and grasp my hands and I'll haul you out,' he said.

Quite how he'd manage it he wasn't sure, but he feared she might not make it on her own. He'd sent everyone off the rubble to make the situation safer so now he set the baby down and wriggled as far as he could into the hole, forcing his shoulders between the boulders and building fragments, praying everything would hold. Two small hands grasped his, and a jolt of lightning seemed to pass right through him. He could not fail her now.

Fear for her lent him strength as he drew his knees up under his body to get some leverage. With one almighty heave he pulled her out, collapsing back onto the ground, the woman held securely in his arms, the warmth of her transferring itself to his body, his mind in turmoil as he tried to make sense of myriad reactions—relief, some anger still that she had risked so much, and—surely not—but, yes, definitely sexual attraction.

His arms tightened, and for an instant he imagined she'd snuggled into his embrace, but before he could process the thought she moved, almost abruptly, picking up the baby, and though Azzam kept a hand on her shoulder, he knew he shouldn't be holding her. Already people might be wondering why he'd held her at all, but she'd been so close to collapse, he'd had to.

'I *had* to get her out!' she whispered as she held the baby against her body. 'The mother is dead but for those two to lose a sibling as well, I couldn't bear that.'

If she was aware of Azzam's hand on her shoulder she gave no sign of it, simply rocking the baby against her chest.

'Family!' she whispered. 'Family ties are strongest, for good or ill. I *couldn't* let the baby die.'

And he wanted to hold her again. The words, he was sure, were spilling from her subconscious, but she was uttering the thoughts he'd had himself—thoughts that were ingrained in him through breeding and upbringing.

But now, looking down at her filthy, straggling hair— had she used her scarf as wrapping for the baby?—and watching as she dripped water on her little finger and held it to the infant's mouth, he wondered if it had been pain he'd heard when she'd talked of family, and what had happened to her in the past that she'd risked her life a second time to reunite the children with their sibling.

CHAPTER FIVE

REACTION to what she'd been through. That was all it was that compelled Alex to sit very still on the rubble and drip water into the baby's mouth. She was aware of Azzam squatting beside her, making her feel extremely uncomfortable about giving way to emotion against his bare chest a little earlier.

She tried to tell herself it was his fault, because the gentleness with which he'd held her after he'd hauled her out of that dark hole had broken through her reluctance to show any weakness.

Any weakness!

But the stoicism of the trapped children, the way the little girl had stayed beside her brother—these things had already cracked the protective shell she'd built around her heart and soul to prevent further damage. The man's arms had just widened the cracks and let feelings in...

'You must move from here. You are able to stand, to walk?'

Azzam would have liked to lift her in his arms and carry her and the baby to safety but she'd shied away from him earlier, thrusting her body apart from his as if being held in his arms was an affront of some kind.

Not that he'd wanted to keep holding her—well, not that he *should* have wanted to keep holding her...

She stood up and he reached out to grasp her elbow as she stumbled. She didn't pull away, allowing him to guide her to a safe area of the *wadi*, where the little girl remained, a silent sentinel beside her brother.

Azzam watched as the woman knelt beside the girl, holding the baby for her to see. He saw the questions in the child's eyes—the big question—and knelt on the other side of her.

'We will keep looking for your mother,' he said gently as the child took the baby, tucking the infant against her chest as if she was accustomed to looking after it.

Did the baby recognise its sister that a little hand reached out and grasped the girl's finger?

Azzam found he had to swallow hard and turned to find Alex had also looked away, her fingertips brushing at tears that were leaking from her silvery eyes.

She recovered first, standing up and looking around her.

'Where can I start?'

'Prioritise,' he replied. 'These high mountains mean up-draughts that would make night-flying in a helicopter very dangerous. So, we won't be airlifting patients out tonight, and need to consider shelter.'

She looked bemused.

'Shelter? Is it likely to rain? Do you have heavy dew? Will it be cold?'

'No to the rain, but yes to the dew. The village headman is organising the survivors. Those able enough will continue to move rubble from the areas where it's most likely people are still trapped, particularly around the market. The children? With the teacher gone, I have arranged for some of the mothers to take them to a safe area until night-fall. There's a date palm grove a little way along the *wadi*.

They will be sheltered there, away from the rubble should aftershocks occur.'

He paused, unreasonably pleased when she nodded agreement to his suggestions.

'You and I—if you feel strong enough to continue to be involved—will stay with the injured. We have some emergency packs of fluid and I've already started IV drips in five people, but I haven't examined any of the children closely. If you could examine them again, and work out what we need to keep them comfortable, I would be grateful. The headman has a generator and he is setting up lights for us to work by.'

He wondered if he should mention the leopards and for a moment regretted that he and Bahir had nagged their father into setting up the protected national park area for them and instigating a breeding programme.

No! He wouldn't mention the leopards—not yet.

Alex began with the unconscious child, again feeling all around her head for some displacement in his skull and finding, this time, a small swelling behind her ear, as if something had struck her there.

She looked up to find a man who'd been squatting a little distance away had moved closer.

'You are her father? Daddy? Papa?'

The man nodded, anxious eyes asking questions Alex couldn't understand, let alone answer. Although she could guess at their content—would she live, his daughter? Was she in pain? Why did she lie so still?

The girl had been awake earlier, she remembered, just unresponsive, but feeling the lump she realised that whatever had struck her had hit her hard enough to cause external swelling, which meant that internally her brain would have been jolted against her skull and the likelihood was that her intracranial pressure was raised. Alex thought with longing of all the tools she'd have at her disposal in a hospital to assist in a diagnosis, but this was emergency medicine at its most basic.

Azzam was setting up a children's hospital! Did it follow he was a paediatrician?

She called his name and he was beside her within seconds, kneeling to examine the little girl, feeling as Alex had felt, around the skull.

'We need to handle her carefully,' he said, and she knew he was talking to himself as much as to her, running through the protocols for head injury. 'I'll lift the head a little and we need to keep it straight to decrease pressure on the jugular veins.'

Although it was some time since she'd worked with children, Alex knew what he was thinking—the sticks she'd used to make a neck brace could be adding pressure to the blood vessels, so she unwrapped them, making a pillow out of Azzam's now-filthy gown instead.

'Slip it under her head when I lift it, then pad some of the material against her temples so she can't turn her head,' Alex told her.

The father, seeming to understand what she was doing, put his hands beside the little girl's head, holding it steady.

Azzam spoke quietly to the man, no doubt explaining the injury and what they would have to do.

'Should we intubate her to keep her airway clear?' Alex asked, her mind moving through the stages of what was little more than first aid—all that could be offered here.

'She's breathing well herself but if you can find a small face mask, we'll deliver oxygen through that.'

How could he be so calm when her fingers were shaking as she delved into the medical supplies, seeking the smallest mask she could find? She'd been in situations like this before and surely her hands hadn't shaken?

Now, consciously steadying them—thinking only of the task in hand—she fitted the mask over their patient's face, relieved to find it sealed well. Azzam had already adjusted the flow on the oxygen tank's small dial and now he secured the outflow tube to the mask, the father watching every move they made, the anxiety he was feeling evident in his anguished eyes and the tension of his body.

Thinking medically to block out all other thoughts, Alex's mind raced through different scenarios. But she wasn't alone here—she had Azzam!

'Swelling in the brain—should we restrict fluids?'

'The child needs *some* fluid,' he responded. 'Let's try thirty per cent of a maintenance dose for a start. She'd weigh, what? She's so slight. Twenty-five kilos?'

Alex understood he was asking her as a colleague, a fellow professional, and the idea steadied her, although why she'd imagined he wouldn't she had no idea.

'I'd say twenty-five kilos,' she responded, doing the sums in her head. 'You've started five drips—how much fluid do we have?'

'Enough,' he told her. 'We have to give her diuretic drugs to relieve the pressure on her brain and we can't do that without giving her some fluid. I think you'll find another bag of fluid in the kit by that tree. I'll find some mannitol in this bag and we can titrate it into the fluid.'

He paused, then said quietly, 'She'll need to be watched through the night. If the pressure builds, we might have to release it manually.'

Manually?

Alex shuddered as she stood up to fetch the fluid. Manually meant boring a hole into the child's skull, not exactly the kind of operation you wanted to carry out in the dark on a bare patch of earth that was likely to tremble any time.

Had the father understood some of the conversation that he was looking more anxious now?

This was a child—a loved child. She deserved a chance at life, so of course if they had to operate they would do it.

Alex watched as Azzam, with infinite gentleness, swabbed the little hand, found a vein, and eased a cannula into it, attached a tube, fitted the other end to the bag of fluid, calibrated it to drip in slowly and added the mannitol to filter slowly into the girl's blood.

He passed the bag to the father, picked up a hunk of masonry and spoke to the man, obviously indicating he should build a small stand for the bag, but the father shook his head and held it high, understanding what was needed but determined to do this small thing for his daughter.

'In a hospital we'd be measuring fluid output as well,' Azzam said quietly, the rest of the sentence, *but we're not in a hospital*, left unspoken.

Alex moved on to the next child, one she hadn't found an injury on earlier, although the child had been huddled by the teacher. He'd been totally unresponsive, this little boy, and he was still limp, now held across his mother's lap, her fingers moving restlessly against his skin, smoothing his face and hair, her dark eyes filled with despair.

Alex touched the woman gently on the arm before beginning her examination, and the woman nodded to her.

The boy's stomach was distended, his pulse racing now, his breath coming in shallow gasps.

Internal bleeding?

Alex moved his mother closer to the light so she could see the child more clearly but could find no sign of bruising on his skin. She was pressing gently on his ribs when

the little body went into a violent spasm and she knew
he'd died, drowned in his own blood perhaps, or his heart
compressed by the fluid inside him to the stage where it
stopped beating.

Azzam was by her side in an instant, no doubt having
heard the woman's wail of despair. He took the little boy
and laid him on the ground, his finger checking the mouth
was clear of obstruction, listening for breathing, blowing
two quick breaths into the child's open mouth, before his
hands moved to the small chest, delivering thirty quick
compressions before breathing for the boy again.

'Let me do the breathing,' Alex told him, shifting to the
child's head, vaguely ashamed she hadn't acted faster, but
she'd been so struck by Azzam's immediate reaction that
she'd watched instead of moving.

They worked together, Alex counting the compressions
out loud now, willing the little boy to live, but eventually
the mother moved, taking Azzam's hand, speaking urgently
to him, all but pushing him away from her son.

'She says it is the will of God,' he whispered to Alex,
and she heard the despair of defeat in his voice.

Standing up, she took his hand, squeezing it as she
helped him to his feet, keeping hold of it as the woman
lifted her son into her arms, rocking him against her body
as she swayed back and forth, moving to her harsh cries
of grief.

Azzam removed his hand and walked away, and Alex
could only watch him go, aware of the burden he was carrying but not knowing what to say or do to ease it.

'You did try,' was all she could offer. 'And even if we'd
got him breathing again, with no facilities to operate and
fix whatever was injured inside him, he would surely have
died before reaching hospital.'

Azzam ignored her words, walking on to where most of

the injured adults had been assembled, close by a gnarled old tree.

Alex watched him for a moment then moved on to the next child—the boy with the broken humerus. Beside him sat his sister, the baby in her arms. The baby was asleep but would surely wake hungry. How to tell the girl to take it to where the uninjured villagers were gathered so they could both get some food?

Using sign language, bringing her hands to her mouth to indicate eating, then pointing towards the palm grove, she urged the girl away, but the child had no intention of deserting her post. Alex bent and kissed her head, thinking of her own brother—Rob—whom she had loved just as devotedly, and whom she couldn't hate no matter how much he'd hurt their mother, or how much chaos he'd left behind him.

But it was *this* child she had to treat—*this* boy she had to consider! He was in shock, trembling all over, and she found the scarf she'd discarded after coming out of the hole with the baby and wrapped it around him, carefully avoiding his arm, which she'd bound against his body earlier.

'I've thirteen serious injuries, patients who, if they survive the night, will have to be airlifted out.'

Azzam had returned and his words sent shivers down her spine. Two, maybe three, people could be lifted out at a time, the helicopter flying back and forth, maybe two helicopters, but would they have the support staff, paramedics, necessary to staff two?

'So I should splint and bandage the boy's arm to hold the bone aligned until he can be taken in an ambulance?' She looked up at Azzam as she spoke.

His face was shadowed, the light behind him, but she'd heard the horror of what they were experiencing—and the death of the child—in his voice and knew that, as these were his people, he would be feeling the pain of the disaster even more deeply than she was.

'We'll only airlift out the most severely injured,' he agreed, then knelt beside her, her response to his presence gratitude that he'd returned to share the decisions that had to be made, nothing else.

Or so she told herself!

'I will help you with the boy,' he said. 'It's easier with two, and there is nothing I can do until more survivors are brought out of the rubble.'

The little girl scuttled sideways to make room for him, but now watched both adults, her gaze switching from one to the other, a pint-sized guard ready to defend her brother should they attempt to do him any harm.

'Can you tell her where to go to get some food, and if possible some milk for the baby?' Alex asked him, nodding at the child. 'Maybe do your prince thing,' she added, smiling at him, although there was little to smile about in this place of devastation.

Azzam saw the smile and felt his heart lift, the hopelessness that had been creeping on him dissolving like desert mist before the sun.

He didn't question what the woman had that could make him feel this way, just accepted the gift of optimism she'd handed him.

'Prince thing?' he queried.

'My helper by the school was most impressed by your standing, repeating your name and saying "He is the prince" in tones of absolute awe.'

'I would rather be a doctor,' he muttered at her, but he did speak to the little girl, telling her to take the baby to the date grove.

The child left, reluctantly.

'You can't be both?' Alex asked as she unwrapped the

cloth—her scarf, he noticed—from around the boy's fractured arm.

'I doubt it,' he answered, although a simple 'No' would have been more truthful. 'Maybe, later on, when I know the duties expected of me and can see a path forward—maybe then I can give some time to the project of my heart.'

Project of his heart? Was it the circumstances in which they found themselves that he was telling this stranger—this female stranger—something he'd never said aloud, not even to Bahir? Oh, Bahir had known his brother was obsessive about the new hospital, but hadn't understood it was for people like these mountain folk, who feared the city and its ways, that he'd wanted to build the special hospital for children—a place where the whole family could stay beside their sick child—a place where they would not feel intimidated by machinery and uniforms and strangers tending their child.

Fortunately Alex didn't hear the phrase, or, if she did, she forbore to question it. She'd found some morphine in the kit, worked out a dose and administered it to the child while Azzam's mind had drifted far from the job in hand.

Concentrating now, he took the boy's arm, aligning the bone as best he could by feel, Alex holding the splints in place while he bound it.

She looked up at him and smiled again.

Alex—a woman he'd met less than, what, forty-eight hours ago? Yet her smile—several smiles now—had shifted his world…

The exhaustion still dogging him had caused the shift, not the smile! He had trained himself to not respond to female smiles, the hurt inside still too raw to want to trust his feelings.

Although was the hurt still there?

He tried to think when he'd last felt that stab of pain.

Maybe his lack of interest in seeking out female company lately had been more because of his immersion in his work than the fear of new heartbreak.

Heartbreak?

Did he really believe that?

Hadn't his pain been hurt pride more than anything else?

Azzam shut off the stupid thoughts racing through his head, concentrating instead on the job in hand. He finished binding the boy's arm and fashioned a sling to hold it against his chest, his mind still muddling over motives and reactions—in all honesty, it would be easier to be considering the leopards.

'We should keep watch tonight.'

The words brought him out of his thoughts and he looked up to see the headman of the village had approached them. Welcoming the distraction, Azzam stood up to talk to him and to listen to tales of recent leopard sightings near the village and how the villagers now kept their animals inside at night to prevent attacks.

'I've been thinking about the leopards,' Azzam told him, unconsciously using not the local word, *nimr* but the English word so that Alex looked up, repeating it.

'Leopards? Leopards out here? You can't be serious? Don't leopards live in Africa? Don't they sprawl on the limbs of trees ready to drop on unsuspecting passing animals? Where are trees here?'

She sounded so indignant he had to smile.

'Arabian leopards live in the mountains—they climb rocks and cliffs to drop on their unsuspecting prey. They were close to extinction twenty years ago, but a good breeding programme means the mountain areas have been restocked with them.'

'Great!' she muttered. 'Here I was thinking that the worst thing that could happen was another earth tremor and the mountain would fall on us, but now you tell me a very large and probably hungry cat could cart me off into the night!'

Azzam found himself chuckling now, then he translated her words to the headman who also laughed, though he quickly added, 'But she is right, they'll smell blood and could prove a danger.'

'We'll set a watch. Keep everyone together, light fires if we can find fuel, and do whatever is necessary to keep the people safe. I don't want to move the injured, so perhaps we should set up camp close by where they are, although the date grove would provide better shelter.'

'We can make shelters,' the headman told him. 'We have tents for the goat and camel herders who move the animals to different pastures. We have not lost our traditional ways, not all of us.'

The man departed and before long the uninjured began to gather on the grassy area, close to where the injured lay but not too close.

Alex watched the survivors drift like shadows through the night, heard the quiet chatter as they settled around the area where she sat with the children. Some men, and possibly some women, were still removing debris and she could hear their voices, warnings sounded and sometimes cries that told of joy—another person rescued.

'Who will protect the workers on the rubble from the leopards?' she asked Azzam when he returned with the headman and began to organise the erection of temporary shelter over the area where the wounded lay.

'I will call them in shortly,' he told her. 'It is too dangerous both for them and for anyone who might still be buried underneath for people to work at night, and the generator only has so much fuel, so it's best to conserve it for emergencies.'

'And these three children—the boy and his sister and the baby? Isn't it strange no adults have come looking for them? In a village, wouldn't someone be related to them?'

Azzam frowned down at the little boy.

'Of course there should be someone who would care for them. I will ask.'

You didn't have to be a prince to be efficient, Alex thought to herself as he walked away. But did the aura of the ruler add weight to his suggestions and advice? Did him being here bring solace and comfort to people who had lost everything, including, in some cases, a loved one?

Men and women seemed to share the chores, erecting tents, finding food, lighting fires, and now the scent of the frankincense she'd first found in the shampoo perfumed the night. Was it special, as Hafa had said, because it protected the people? Or because it was from some plant native to this country?

The little girl returned, the baby in her arms and a baby's bottle, miraculously found somewhere, full of watery-looking milk. She settled beside her brother, and once again Alex's heart ached for the three children—the little that remained of the family. The child lay down beside her brother, obviously exhausted for her eyes closed and the baby slipped from her grasp.

Alex picked up the infant, awake but uncomplaining, and used her now-filthy scarf to tie it to her chest. She could work among the injured knowing the baby was secure, but she didn't want to move too far from the children either— not until someone had claimed them.

Azzam, too, returned.

'You should sleep, but first you must eat. I have brought

some bread. It isn't much, but with water it will make your stomach think it's been fed.'

Once again Azzam had appeared beside her as if tele-ported there, for she'd heard nothing of his approach, but how he'd reached her paled into insignificance against the effect the man's presence had on her. Was it the sight of the light from the fire dancing on his bare chest that sent shivers up her spine? Or was it nothing more than the male-ness of him, she who hadn't known a man intimately, who hadn't even kissed a man since David's defection? The man smell—sweat and dust and something deeper. She probably smelt pretty bad herself, but this smell was—

Idiot! Of course it wasn't intoxicating! She was tired, that was all, and in a strange country with leopards stalk-ing the night it was only natural her instincts would tell her subconscious to seek out a protector.

She took the bread from him and bit into it, finding it so tough she had to tug at it to free a bite. He passed the water bottle, his fingers brushing against hers, an acciden-tal touch that caused much the same reaction as the smell of him had only minutes earlier.

'I think the little girl's ICP has decreased slightly,' she said, reminding herself she was a competent medical practitioner, not a weak and needy—and possibly slightly hysterical—female.

Azzam heard the words, but they seemed so strange, out here in the mountain pass with tumbled houses all around them and coming from a dirty, dishevelled woman standing there, a baby strapped roughly to her chest, and shapely ankles showing beneath the hem of her trousers.

'That's good,' he said, because something was obviously expected of him, but beneath the words he sensed another conversation going on. Was she afraid? Was it fear he could feel in the air between them?

She *should* be afraid! Alone in an isolated place, in a country she didn't know, surrounded by strangers, she certainly had cause to be a little fearful if not downright terrified. Yet he didn't want to diminish the courage she'd shown earlier by saying something—by asking her if she'd like him to stay close to her, to protect her through the night.

No matter how much he'd like to do it!

'The children? Did you find out anything about them, find anyone who would take care of them now they are apparently orphaned?'

He shook off the strange thoughts he'd been having, thoughts related to being close to this woman through the night.

'It seems they are incomers, a family who arrived here a few days before the baby was born. They have been living in an abandoned cottage. The father took off within weeks of their arrival, leaving the mother and the three children.'

'And no one has befriended her?'

Even as Alex asked the question she thought of country towns back home where newcomers might be treated with suspicion but surely not totally ignored.

'Our connections are tribal,' Azzam explained, 'and although the link might be generations in the past, the people of the tribe are all related. Some tribes naturally affiliate with others, but maybe these people were...'

He paused and Alex guessed he was wondering how to explain.

'Not enemies, exactly, but from a tribe that didn't inter-marry with the locals.'

'But surely children don't carry any stigma from their breeding? Wouldn't someone want to take care of them?'

'I am guessing here and will continue to ask,' Azzam

told her, 'and maybe we will find someone, but you must realise these people have lost everything. To take on three extra children when you have nothing...'

He didn't need to finish. Alex nodded, thinking the villagers had probably been poor before the earthquake had struck, taking away what little they'd had. But she held the baby more tightly against her chest as her heart ached for the children no one wanted.

Azzam was talking again and she stopped thinking ridiculous thoughts of taking the children home with her and listened.

'I must go,' Azzam said, though he didn't want to leave the woman, who looked so vulnerable as she held the baby against her chest. 'I will take a shift with the men who are patrolling. Someone has found a rifle so don't be alarmed if you hear a shot. It will probably be someone firing at shadows, but if a leopard should approach, a shot will frighten it away.'

She sank down onto the ground, one arm still held protectively against the baby.

'I'll be all right,' she assured him, but he heard the quiver of alarm in her voice and remembered the tears that had slid down her cheeks earlier.

He knelt beside her and put his arm around her shoulders, drawing her close against his body.

'You have been incredibly brave, you have done more than should be asked of any human for people you do not even know. It is all right to be afraid, even to cry, now the worst of it is over. It is also right to grieve for the ones we couldn't save.'

'The mother of the children is dead, and the school teacher and two of the other children, too—one that I rescued and the one I left behind,' she whispered.

'But many are alive because of you,' he reminded her,

feeling the softness of her in his arms, the fragility of her small bones—feeling her as a woman so once again his body stirred.

She shook her head as if denying herself the praise and the comfort of his words then shifted so they were no longer touching.

'You must go—there are things you should be doing.' Her voice was husky—tears or just exhaustion? He couldn't tell and didn't want to think about it as either would strengthen his desire to stay close to her. 'I'll be all right on my own.'

'I *must* go,' he agreed, knowing his duty lay outside this shelter, organising, making arrangements to see them all safely through the night. Yet his body was reluctant to move—the softness of the woman a temptation he hadn't felt for a long time.

Not *this* woman, his common sense warned.

He rose and left the shelter, not looking back.

Although he would have to return—he knew that. It would be unacceptable to leave Alex and the children on their own throughout the night.

'You still intend to sleep here with the children?' Azzam asked, finding Alex much as he had left her two hours earlier, sitting by the children in the makeshift shelter.

'Of course,' she said. 'The boy is still unwell and the baby will need feeding during the night. I can't abandon them.'

Neither could he abandon her, Azzam realised. Apart from anything else, she was a guest in his country, his mother's friend. And he'd heard not fear but distinct uncertainty in her voice as she'd told him of her plans. She wasn't stupid and would realise that this tent, on the outskirts of the little tent village now set up, would be the first visited by a leopard should one come prowling, yet she'd asked nothing of him.

On the other hand…

How to explain?

'While it is understood that all people will sleep close to each other for warmth and safety, they will do so in family groups, as that is our way,' he began, aware he sounded far too tentative but unable to explain the customs that dictated this. 'The families are already settling into tents but if we share a tent, you and I, it would be…'

'Remarked on? Unseemly? Not done? There's been an earthquake, for heaven's sake. We have to do the best we can.'

He had to smile at the incredulity in her voice, especially when she added, 'Anyway, if people want to get picky, we can point out we have the children with us as chaperones.'

There was a pause, taut and expectant, before she added, 'Not that I need you to share the shelter with me. You said people will patrol the camp. I'll be quite safe.'

If she'd sounded a little less defiant—defiance hiding uncertainty—he might have let it go, but duty to this woman who was helping his countrymen insisted she be protected.

'The children would not count, neither can I leave you unprotected. I am sorry, but my position—it must seem ridiculous in your eyes, I can see that, but in this village it would be seen as…'

He turned away, battling to find the words he needed, English words that would convey the extent of dishonour him sharing a tent with her would bring, not only to his name but even more so to this woman who was innocent of anything other than a desire to help.

But there were no words—well, none he knew—in English to cover such a situation.

'It would be impossible!' He settled for simply dismissing the idea, before bringing up a solution. 'However, there *is* a way that we can do this. If you would sleep easier with my company—and I would certainly feel happier about your safety if I was with you—then we can make a marriage.'

'A marriage?' Incredulity didn't cover it—this was stark disbelief! 'We get married so you can share a tent with me? In an earthquake-stricken village where the choice of shelter is non-existent?'

'It is an old arrangement, usually made for the convenience of both parties but without the obligations of a real marriage. It is legal to do this, to make a *misyar* marriage for both our convenience so the people do not think that I am shaming you, or that are you a shameless…'

'Hussy is the word we'd use,' she said, actually chuckling as she said it. 'I can't believe this. It is just too weird. I know other cultures have their boundaries and it's the difference between people that makes the world the fascinating place it is, but…'

Laughter swallowed up the words and now instead of fanciful smiles in the night air, Azzam felt the stir of anger.

'Is marrying me so ridiculous?' he demanded. 'Many women would be gratified to—'

'Be proposed to by a prince?' The words were accompanied by a further gurgle of laughter. 'Oh, dear, I have to stop laughing but you must admit it's funny. Here I am, given a choice of facing a stray leopard on my own or marrying a prince, and I'm dithering over it. And on top of that there's the fact that you have this convenient kind of pseudo-marriage, which sounds to me as if it's there to cover men who might want to cheat on their wives.'

'It was not intended for that.' He sounded far too stiff and formal, but that was because he knew it *was* used in that way from time to time. Though not to cheat, for the wife would surely know of it. 'It is also convenient for older women, widows even, who might be happy on their own but sometimes desire male company.'

He completed his explanation, his voice so cold Alex realised she'd have to stop joking about the situation, although the only way she'd been able to handle the uneasiness inside her that had followed his strange proposal had been with humour. She was wondering if she should apologise when he spoke again.

'It was intended too, for times like this, for when a woman might need the protection of a man but is without a brother or a father. If it has been made a convenience of by some people, that is by the way. For tonight and however many nights we need to remain here, would you be willing to go through with it?'

'Marriage or the leopard—it's really not a choice,' Alex said, deciding this was just one more bizarre memory she would have to take home with her. 'What do we have to do?'

'Agree, have two witnesses and the headman, who will be the local marriage official. I'll go and see him now.'

Within thirty minutes they were married, it seemed, although her husband had departed with the headman as soon as the ceremony, if it could be called that, was over. He was checking the arrangements for keeping watch, he'd said, and would talk to people about the possibility of someone taking the children into their own family.

Married so they could share a tent?

Forget that—it was nothing more than a formality. She must concentrate on what needed to be done.

Alex fed the baby, cleaned him as best she could, wrapped a bit of cloth around his nether regions then set him down, asleep, beside his sister. She wished she had something to cover them with, but all the available materials had been used.

With the siblings asleep, she moved across to the next tent where the unconscious girl lay, her father still holding the bag of fluid. The girl's pupils were still unresponsive to light and her limbs failed to react to stimuli. Despair crept into Alex's heart as she began to think this child, too, might die, but when she felt the child's fontanelle, nearly but not entirely closed, she found the small gap between the bones at the top of the skull was no longer bulging. It meant the pressure in the child's brain had decreased, and she smiled at the girl's father, hope lightening her heart.

She returned to the children—her children, as she was beginning to think of them. Azzam had left a bottle of water in the tent, and, using her bra as a washer, she wet it with a little of the precious fluid to give herself a quick wash, thankful she'd had the forethought to bring her emergency pack with the spare pair of undies in it, although she hadn't thought ahead enough to bring nappies for a baby!

The baby—he'd stir, probably wake during the night. Best he sleep next to her. But as she'd retrieved him, she'd felt the little girl's skin, had felt how cold she was, although the night was still young. She *had* to find some cover for them.

Her clothes, of course, were filthy, but the tunic top she wore came to just below her knees. She could slip off the long cotton trousers and still be as decent as a woman in a dress at home. There was enough material in the wide trousers to cover the children for the night, and in the morning, before anyone was around, she could pull them back on.

She settled down beside the children—not hers at all but three who needed someone to show care and perhaps a little love towards them. With the baby wrapped against her chest, she curled her body protectively around the siblings, resting her arm across them so they were all snuggled up together.

Azzam stood his shift on watch then walked back to where the children were, looking down at the woman in the light shed by the fire outside the tent. While he'd been gone, she'd lost her trousers, the sleeves of her tunic had fallen back and the hem of it had ruffled up, so shadows of dark and light played across her pale, slim limbs, highlighting scratches that made him angry for some reason.

Angry that she'd been hurt...

He blocked the image and the thought from his mind, seeing the way she had placed herself between the edge of the shelter and the children. She may have been afraid of leopards but that fear hadn't blotted out her protective instincts.

He lay beside her now, adding another layer of protection for the children, but it was the warmth of *her* body that stirred him, thoughts of *her*, not the children, drifting through his mind until sleep claimed him.

CHAPTER SIX

THE baby stirred against her chest and gave a feeble whimper. Not wanting it to cry and wake Azzam or the other children, Alex slid out from between them. She unwound the scraps of material with which she'd bound the baby to her chest, found the bottle of milk, and held the teat to the infant's lips. She tried not to think where the milk—or the bottle—might have come from, and dismissed all thought of sterility from her mind.

Which wasn't that hard, as thoughts of the man who'd slept beside her were clamouring for attention.

She'd woken to the feel of his warmth and the solidity of his body, and had felt her own warmth build in response to his closeness. Not sexual warmth—or she didn't think it was—more just a feeling of security, a sense of shared responsibilities.

He was her husband...

Nonsense, he wasn't a real husband—not in any sense. It was convenience, nothing more.

Definitely not sexual warmth!

The baby sucked avidly, reminding her of where her attention should be. Holding the bottle and baby with one hand, Alex searched through the medical supplies until she found another sling, and, padding it with cotton wool, fashioned a nappy for the infant.

'There,' she said to him as he finished the milk and snuggled against her chest, 'now you'll be more comfortable.'

She checked his sleeping siblings then tucked the baby in between them, so she wouldn't be hampered, and he wouldn't be disturbed, if she had to move to tend another patient during the night. In fact, now she was awake she should check on all the patients.

Or was she looking for an excuse to escape the man who lay, sleeping so soundly, right beside her?

An excuse to escape her thoughts?

She smiled to herself as she realised that to someone who'd battled on alone as she had recently, the warmth of shared responsibilities might be more alluring than sexual warmth.

Well, almost...

Although it had been such a long time since she'd felt any stirrings of a sensual nature, she couldn't really judge. She'd stopped feeling them long before David had opted out her of life so precipitously. When first they'd met, his insistence they not make love until they married had seemed so quaint and old-fashioned she'd admired him for it—even felt special in some way. But why had it never occurred to her to wonder why the decision didn't irk her?

Because being with David hadn't stirred her body and her senses the way this man's presence did?

Because she'd never felt much physical frustration over his decree? Maybe a quiver or two when they'd kissed, but even that had stopped long before they'd parted. In fact, in retrospect, she had to wonder if David had remained engaged to her to protect himself—to avoid a permanent commitment to another woman. Any woman!

So, if she was to feel strange stirrings now, would it be so surprising? Even in the dim light of the dying fire, the man who lay beside her was clearly something special. His face had struck her earlier, outlined against the bright whiteness of his headdress, then his body—his naked chest—so well developed.

Now the heat of him, so close…

She sat and looked at him, aware this wasn't quite right, to be studying a stranger while he slept.

Except he was her husband—didn't that excuse her?— even if he had only married her to save her name. Although he *had* made out it was equally to protect his own good standing that he'd taken the step of marrying her.

His own good standing as prince, or as a man?

She had no answer to that or to any of the questions that taunted her.

What would it be like to be truly married to such a man? To feel his body held against hers? To know him intimately?

Now the warmth she felt had nothing whatsoever to do with security. It burned along her nerves, awakening responses between her thighs, reminding her she *was* a woman and this was what all her friends would consider a very beddable man.

A beddable man? Was she becoming addle-brained? How could she think such a thing?

She stood up and slipped away from the sleeping children—and Azzam—moving to the next temporary shelter where the man who had stayed beside his daughter had attached the fluid sac to a stout stick he'd stuck in the ground, and he now lay sleeping, one hand on the little girl.

Alex moved quietly on, into the shelter where the generator hummed, providing dim light for the people caring for the wounded adults. It was the first time Alex had seen them all lined up together, and she wondered how some of them had survived, so severe were their injuries. A woman moved between them, moistening lips with water, answering cries of pain.

'I am nurse,' she said to Alex. 'I have a little English from school and university. I am doing the work of doctor in the village. Our new Highness, before he was the prince, organised health centres in all villages and I run the centre here.'

Alex nodded her understanding and was impressed by the caring way the woman worked among her patients. They were in good hands and she could return to her children, for dawn was lightening the sky and she didn't want them waking and not finding her there beside them.

Her children?

The unresponsive little girl had her father, the mother of the boy who'd died had carried her son away, and all the other children she'd rescued must be with their families. Leaving her with the three motherless ones.

Her children...

Azzam woke to the roar of an engine and the clatter of rotor blades, sounds that told him the sun was up and the helicopter had returned. He stirred and groaned as his muscles told him it was too long since he'd slept on bare earth.

He looked around, aware of an emptiness he didn't understand.

Inner emptiness?

No, that was surely hunger.

But Alex *was* gone, the baby also, although the little girl remained steadfastly by her brother's side.

'I've been foraging for food.'

Alex returned as he sat up, shaking his head to clear it of the fog that sleep had given it. Part of the fog was an image that had lingered, of this woman's slim, pale limbs, but thankfully she was now fully covered again, except for her hair, which was so dirty she was no longer recognisable as a blonde.

She had a slab of flat bread in one hand and a flask of what looked like milk. The baby, he noticed, was once again strapped against her chest. Was it instinct that she carried the baby as the local women carried their infants? Or practicality?

Probably the latter, to keep her hands free, he was deciding when she spoke again.

'I need most of this for the baby, but you need to drink something and I couldn't find any water.'

Couldn't find any water? Last night, in all the confusion, he'd heard men talking about water—about the oasis in the *wadi*—but he'd taken little notice, intent on doing what had to be done.

'There should be water,' he told her. 'It might be dirty from the debris but this is an oasis.'

She shrugged.

'Well, this is all I could find.'

He took the bread, his mind fully focussed now. Had the debris from the earthquake completely filled the oasis, or had the earthquake itself opened up the ground sufficiently for it to leak away? He'd need to set men digging further up the *wadi*—the survivors would need water, and soon.

He took a gulp of the milk—camel milk, he'd forgotten the strange taste—and ate some bread, touched the baby on the head and left the shelter before he reached out and touched Alex as well. Maybe not on the head, but on the shoulder, although every instinct told him touching her was madness.

He'd slept too soundly, that was the problem.

Now, focus on the present.

Focus on the next move.

Focus!

It sounded as if the helicopter had landed, so the most seriously wounded would have to be carried down the valley to it. So much to do, so many things to think about, but as he left Alex said his name.

'Azzam!'

He looked back at her, standing straight and tall in her dirty clothes, a baby that she didn't own strapped to her chest.

His wife, albeit a *misyar* one…

'The unconscious little girl should go on one of the helicopter trips,' she said to him, 'but can they take her father as well? I don't know for sure but it seems to me they are all that are left of their family for wouldn't the mother be here if she was alive?'

Azzam knew what she was saying and understood the father would not be separated from his daughter. Of course he would be clinging to the one remaining member of his family. Wasn't this why he, Azzam, was building the special hospital?

Yet the father would take up the space where one of the injured could be, and would add weight in an aircraft where weight had to be considered carefully.

'I will try to arrange it,' he told her.

She nodded as if understanding all the permutations of his thinking, and returned to the next shelter to examine the child once again. He watched her sign to the man before leaving the little girl and moving on to help the nurse with the adult patients, the two women tending them as best they could while they waited for their turns to be carried down the valley to the helicopter.

'That's it for today but at least all the badly injured have been airlifted out.'

Azzam appeared as night was closing in. Alex had seen

him at various times during the day, although he'd spent most of his time helping carry the injured to the helicopter, remaining there with them until they were airlifted out.

Alex had stayed at the village, helping move rubble, tending survivors who were still, miraculously, being found, and keeping an eye on the three children. As better tents, flown in by helicopter, were erected, to be used as housing until the village could be rebuilt, the local nurse tried to fit the children into other families. One woman offered to take the baby, another family was willing to care for the boy and girl, but the little girl stubbornly refused to have the family split up, remaining where she was, caring for the baby when Alex was busy elsewhere.

'There are still injured people being found beneath the rubble,' Alex reminded him, using the bottom of her tunic to wipe her face.

'The helicopter will return tomorrow and keep returning as long as it is needed,' Azzam replied. He slumped onto the ground beside where she was sitting, outside the small shelter that she thought of as 'hers'.

Theirs?

'This village is at the border of my country,' Azzam continued, tiredness making his words sound gruff and strained. 'Our neighbours in the big town further down this old trade route have been affected as well. The town is not as badly damaged but because it had a bigger population there have been more injuries. Their rescue services are at full stretch so we couldn't ask them for help, but by tomorrow evening our road to the village should be clear and we can bring in heavy machinery not only to clear the rubble but to dig a new well for the village.'

'The rescue people who've already flown in have made a difference,' Alex told him. 'They've given all the villagers a break from the digging and rubble shifting, and brought optimism as well as their strength.'

'Not to mention food and water,' Azzam said, swinging the backpack he'd been carrying onto the ground and delving into it. 'Abracadabra—isn't that what your magicians say?'

'Your magicians too, surely? Or was it "Open sesame"?'

She was more disturbed by his presence at the moment than she'd been since she'd first met him, finding herself uneasy and a little at a loss because she couldn't understand her uncertainty. Not that he appeared to notice for he was delving into the backpack.

'Aha! Just for you!' He produced a pack of wet tissues, handing them to Alex.

'Can you manage a bath with just these?' he asked her. 'I'd have liked to ask someone to pack clean clothes for you but necessities like food and water seemed more important.'

'These will do just fine,' she managed, then, clutching the treasures to her chest, she retreated into the tent. The little girl was sitting by her brother, apparently telling him a story, the baby asleep on her knees.

'Look,' she said to the girl. Talking to the child had become a habit, although Alex knew she couldn't understand. 'Wet wipes.'

She knelt beside the children, pulled out a wipe, and wiped the boy's face, then with a clean cloth wiped the baby, finally handing three wet tissues to the little girl, who looked at them with delight before using them to scrub her face, hands and arms.

Deciding to keep the wipes for the children, Alex retreated further into the small tent, where she used the waterless cleanser from her emergency pack to wash her hands, arms and face. Then, aware of how grubby she was, she slipped off her clothes and, once again using her bra as a washer, washed the rest of her body as best she could.

Her clothes might be filthy but at least now she was kind of clean underneath. Her hair, hanging in a dirty braid down her back, didn't bear thinking about, but, deciding this was as good as it was going to get, she dressed and went back out to find that Azzam had, miracle of miracles, produced a packet of disposable nappies for the baby.

'Are you more delighted by those than by the food I'm preparing?' he asked, and she realised he was heating something in a small pot over a tiny gas stove.

'Definitely more interested in the nappies,' she told him. 'I was running out of things to use to keep him dry. As for food, I found bread and milk for the children earlier, so they're okay, but now I can smell whatever it is you're cooking there, my stomach is more than interested in the food.'

She squatted beside him and Azzam looked at her face, pale but clean, although rimmed with dirt around her hair-line. A truly remarkable woman, he realised, uncaring of her own needs as she helped the strangers among whom she found herself.

Why?

She was a doctor, it was natural she should respond by helping, but surely going down that hole to rescue the children had been beyond the call of duty?

He switched his mind from the mystery of this woman to practical matters.

'When all the injured have been airlifted out, we will be able to leave, probably some time tomorrow,' he told her. 'A paramedic will come in on the first flight in the morning and he and the nurse should be able to cope with the less severely injured, who are staying here. Most of the personnel we'll fly in next will be people to continue digging and others to get services set up so the village can function while it's rebuilt.'

'And the children?' she asked, nodding her head towards the inside of the tent.

The children? He found himself frowning at her question.

'I thought the headman was arranging for other villagers to take them.'

'The boy is feverish, probably with an infection, and the girl won't leave him, or the baby, and no one in the village can manage all three.' She hesitated, then frowned as she asked, 'Do you know what has happened to the father? I know you said they were from a different tribe but there's something more. The nurse couldn't explain when I asked her, but it seems to me as if these children are—well, some kind of outcasts? Could that be? Does that happen? Could their father have done something bad? And if so, would that mean that if the children remain here, they might not be treated as kindly as they should be?'

'I will ask,' Azzam told her, 'but for now forget the children and eat.'

He tipped half the rations into a bowl and handed it to her, offering a plastic spoon he'd scavenged from the helicopter, thinking she'd find it easier than using flat bread to scoop up food.

'I wouldn't like to think they'd be unhappy—unhappier than they must already be with the loss of their mother. And it seems strange that they are so alone when your mother said it was a long-held tradition to welcome others to the camp. So there must be some definite reason they *weren't* welcome.'

He turned towards her.

'Are you always this persistent?'

She smiled and once again he felt something move inside him, although he knew it couldn't be attraction.

Gratitude, perhaps, that she'd done so much for his people.

'Only when it concerns the welfare of small children,' she said, 'and possibly patients who aren't very good at standing up for themselves.'

'And elderly women who are against a management plan for their asthma,' he added. 'I read the way you worded my mother's plan, making it simple for her yet emphasising the importance of prevention rather than cure. I know she is unwilling to take drugs unless it's absolutely necessary. That is why you were concerned for her?'

She glanced up from her meal but as night had fallen and he'd turned off the stove he couldn't read the expression on her face.

'I liked her,' she said, and he believed her, though it brought into his mind once again the disparity that kept niggling at him about this woman. Here he saw unselfishness of spirit as she gave generously of herself in the devastated village, so why did he still see the faint shadow of Clarice behind her, the shadow of a woman who'd come to his country to get as much as she could out of it?

He knew, instinctively, that Alex was different, so why couldn't he get Clarice out of his mind?

And suddenly it came to him—the answer so simple he could have laughed out loud. The betrayal he'd felt hadn't been heartbreak at all—pique maybe but nothing irretrievable. His pain had come from the physical side of things, from the fact that Clarice had been able, without a second's hesitation, to go from his bed to Bahir's. That, to him, who had believed in fidelity, had been the ultimate betrayal.

He was shaking his head at the fact that he'd let it poison his life for so long, all because he hadn't seen his own reaction clearly, when Alex's voice recalled him to where he was.

'That meal was delicious,' she said, setting down the empty bowl. 'Thank you.'

Then she chuckled, a warm, rich sound that seemed to fill the night with smiles.

'A meal cooked by a prince,' she teased. 'Not everyone can boast of such a thing.'

But the laughter didn't linger, her voice serious as she added, 'You haven't answered me about the children. I wouldn't like to leave here not knowing what will happen to them.'

'Arrangements will be made,' he said, speaking firmly so the subject could be dropped and he could go back to considering where such a fancy as a night filling with smiles could have come from. He was a practical man, always had been. Bahir, now, he might have thought such a thing, for at heart he'd always been a romantic dreamer. Yes, his brother was still with him—just a little…

Alex moved, standing up, thanking him again for the meal and the things he'd brought, saying good night…

More unsettled than ever by Azzam's presence, Alex escaped into the tent. He would stand a watch, surely, and she could be asleep before he came in to sleep, and if that was regret she was feeling, she needed her head read!

Proximity, that's all it was, and being alone in a strange place—of course she'd feel drawn to a man who wanted only to protect her.

Protect her body *and* her reputation, she thought, smiling to herself, although the nurse had told her of leopard sightings during the previous night and protection of her body wasn't such a joke.

Yet, remembering how it had felt the previous night, the warmth she'd drawn from his body, she felt a shiver of apprehension, admitting to herself how easy it would be for his body to seduce hers.

Not that he'd have the slightest interest in her that way, which made her reactions even more shaming.

Except that humans were designed that way for the continuation of the species. Without attraction between men and women, the race would have died out centuries ago.

Having thus excused herself for her wayward thoughts and feelings, she lay down, curled around the children, her arm across them once again.

The children!

Thinking about them would take her mind off her other wandering thoughts.

If she was married, could she adopt the children?

Though how could she work the hours she did and bring up a family?

If Azzam would agree, perhaps, to provide enough money to keep the children, she could take them home with her. No, it wouldn't work. Bad enough for them to lose their parents, but to lose their country? How could she consider bringing them up in a strange land, she who didn't even understand them when they spoke?

Her arm brushed against the lamp she'd found earlier in the rubble, a beautifully shaped brass lamp that the little girl had claimed as hers.

Now it reminded Alex once again of the fairytales that kept recurring to her throughout this whole adventure and she had to wonder whether, if she rubbed the lamp, a genie might appear. A fantasy, of course, but there was no harm in dreaming. She could ask the genie for a home for all of them. A second wish would be for money—not a lot, just enough to cover the debt—and she'd keep the third for when it might be needed. With Rob's debt paid, she could stay here, in this strange and fascinating land, and bring up the children with their friends…

She chuckled as she held the lamp, laughing at herself because she couldn't bring herself to rub it. The whole experience she was going through was so unbelievable a genie *might* just appear.

'You are laughing again? Surely not still at our marriage?'

Azzam had entered the tent as silently as he always appeared, and she rolled over and looked at the dark shadow that was him, hunkered on the floor beside her.

'No, now I'm laughing at my own silly fancies,' she said. 'Working out what three wishes I would ask for should a genie emerge when I polish my Aladdin lamp.'

She passed the little lamp to him, and Azzam ran his hands over it, wanting to ask what she would wish for but already too confused about this woman to be hearing of her wishes for the future.

The less he knew of her the better. He'd decided that while walking the perimeter of the camp with the headman. Already he knew he'd have a problem with the children who were, he'd discovered, not exactly outcasts but from a family held in disrepute by their own tribe and therefore not likely to be exactly welcome in a family here.

He'd have to take them home with him. There were plenty of staff to care for them and they would give his mother a new interest. His family had a tradition of taking in lost or orphaned children running right back through the centuries, and his mother would take a personal interest in them.

Yet as he sat down on the rock-hard earth and felt the proximity of the woman who was now his wife, he wanted more than anything to know her wishes, and to hear her talk and laugh again. Well, maybe not more than anything, because somewhere deep inside a desire to hold her was also building up within him, and if that wasn't stupidity, he didn't know what was.

He went for the easy option.

'What would you wish for?'

'You can't tell wishes,' she told him, her voice, and her face as far as he could tell in the dim light, deadly serious. 'Otherwise they don't come true.'

And now the urge to hold her had changed to an urge to give her a hug, for the words had had a wistful quality about them, and this strong woman who'd crawled into a dark crevice to rescue children, and who had worked with the men shifting rubble, sounded...vulnerable!

'Money can make most wishes come true,' he pointed out.

She shook her head.

'I've never had enough to know if you're right or wrong, but while I agree it could help—that it could make some things easier in a person's life—I wonder if it's true, generally speaking? Can it buy happiness, for instance? Can a designer handbag or a brilliant diamond bring true happiness? And can money guarantee the people you love won't die?'

As soon as the words were out of her mouth, Alex regretted them. She turned to Azzam and rested her hand on his arm.

'I'm sorry, that was a totally insensitive thing to say. You must miss your brother terribly.'

He was looking away from her, but she felt him move, and he put one hand over hers where it lay on his arm, holding it there.

'Will you sit with me outside for a short time? The stars are out and everyone should see a night sky in the desert.'

Sit under the stars with him?

Let starlight work its magic when she suspected she was already on the way to being in love with this man?

Of course she couldn't!

'Please?' he added, and she knew she would. She stood up and walked in front of him, stopping just beyond the door to their shelter and looking up at the magic of a billion bright stars in a black-velvet sky.

He took her hand and led her to a smooth rock not far from the tent, then used gentle pressure on her hand to ease her down beside him. Her hand felt safe in his.

How peculiar!

When had hands felt unsafe?

And was her mind wandering down this obscure alley so she wouldn't think about the profile she could now see clearly in the bright starlight? The clean, strong profile that would be etched forever in her mind?

'I felt such anger at first,' he said, speaking so quietly she had to strain to hear the words, but even straining it was hard to miss the pain behind them. 'It was such a use-less waste of life—and of a life that had so much to offer. Anger blotted out the grief, and now the situation—not the earthquake but being thrown into a role I wasn't trained for, and certainly never wanted—that has taken all my attention.'

Alex squeezed the fingers of the hand that still clasped hers.

'Grief will come when you are ready for it,' she said quietly. 'I know this for a fact. Some people find it there immediately, and find release in it, but others need to get through that fog of disbelief—and anger too, that's a le-gitimate reaction—that follows sudden death before they can remember the person they loved and truly grieve their loss.'

He moved the hand that had held hers imprisoned, freeing her fingers.

Was she sitting too close?

Had her words been too personal?

He didn't shift away, or remonstrate, instead using his freed hand to touch her cheek, turning her head towards him in order to drop the lightest of kisses on her lips.

'My good wife,' he whispered, as he drew his head back just a little. 'Offering comfort and wisdom to your husband.'

Alex was still coming to terms with the kiss, attempting to still the commotion in both her brain and her body, when he added the compliment—and with it added to the commotion…

'I'm not a real wife, remember,' she said lightly, hoping to relieve the tension in the air around them.

'You're very real to me,' he said, then he pointed to the stars, naming the constellations they could see, different names from the ones Alex knew, although apart from the Southern Cross she'd never been able to identify stars.

'This is Alchibah,' he said, pointing upwards where she strained to pick out one particular star from all the others. 'His name means tent, and over there, beyond that bright constellation, is Adhara, the maiden. So I am sitting here, outside the tent, with Adhara, the maiden. How fortunate can a man be?'

He slid one arm around her shoulders and held her close as they both continued to gaze in awe at the magic of the night sky, but the warmth Alex felt, being held so casually, was out of all proportion to the situation. Somehow, the words, and being pressed against his side, had raised a firestorm of reactions in her body—rapid heartbeat, heat racing along her nerves and a heaviness in her blood that made her want to let go of all her cares and, just for a while, experience nothing but feeling and emotion.

Could he feel it? Did it have to be two-sided, this intense attraction that stroked against her skin, even brushed her breasts, making her nipples tingle? But she didn't want to move, for to do so might spoil the moment, might break the web of sensation his body was spinning so effortlessly around her.

She *had* to move!

She *had* to rub her hand across her chest to stop the ache that started there and zeroed down between her thighs.

'You feel it too?' he murmured, then he was kissing her, kissing her properly. 'Is it nothing more than the magic of the night, do you think?' he continued murmuring against her lips, 'or something very special that involves just the two of us?'

She answered by initiating the next kiss, and when she drew away to catch her breath found herself admitting ignorance.

'I've no idea,' she told him honestly, revelling in the arms that held her firmly against his chest, revelling in the feel of his hard body against hers. 'It probably is the night—moon magic or starstrike, perhaps—because it's nothing I've ever felt before.'

She'd offered him a gift with that confession, Azzam realised. A gift he would hold close to his heart.

But it was a gift that prevented him from taking this attraction further—not here and now anyway. Yes, she was ripe for seduction, he could feel desire thrumming in her body, but would it not be a betrayal of her innocent admission, to take advantage of her? And what of later—back in the real world—what of the consequences of such an action?

Having finally sorted out the reasons the pain of Clarice's

defection had lingered so long, he knew he couldn't go into an affair with this woman lightly. It was something he needed to think clearly about, and his mind, right now, was beyond clear thinking.

He kissed her once again, but gently this time, and equally gently disengaged himself from her.

She looked at him, questions in her eyes, then must have read something in his face that made her offer him a rueful smile and a little nod before she rose to her feet and went inside their little shelter.

CHAPTER SEVEN

THEY flew back to the palace at about midday, Alex, Azzam and the three children the only passengers in the helicopter.

After a relatively sleepless night—he shouldn't have kissed her or mentioned the attraction, he shouldn't have seen her face by moonlight, the pale, ethereal beauty of her remaining in his head to haunt his dreams, he shouldn't have unburdened himself to her or talked about the stars or held her close—Azzam was happy to be returning home.

Until the helicopter landed and he stepped out to realise Clarice was there to meet them. For all her earlier protests that she was too distraught to handle her duties as the ruler's widow, mourning had obviously passed her by. The traditional white that was the colour of mourning had been set aside and she was dressed in the bold, vivid blue she knew set off her eyes, her skin and her hair tones, the tunic and the bottom of her loose trousers elaborately bejewelled so she dazzled in the sunlight.

The draught from the rotors had blown the head-scarf— something she'd never secured too well—back from her golden locks, so she came hurrying towards him, all bright and golden, crying out his name.

'I have been so worried for you,' she said, ignoring the staff gathered there *and* the other passengers and flinging her arms around him. 'Had anything happened to you on top of Bahir's death, I would have had to die myself.'

Her lush body pressed against him and for a moment he was a young man once again, meeting this golden beauty for the first time. She had dazzled him then in a way he'd never felt before and he'd fallen headlong into love, only to discover, once she met Bahir, that he, Azzam, was not the man for her.

The chatter of the children as they disembarked reminded him of where he was, and he turned to see Alex carrying the baby and herding the boy and girl away from the rotors of the aircraft. He eased away from Clarice, suspicious now of this unexpected welcome. Clarice, he had long since learned, always had an ulterior motive.

He reached out to Alex, took her hand, and drew her forward, aware that what he was about to do was wrong, yet unable to resist. He told himself it wasn't payback for that long-ago rebuff, and in truth it wasn't. This was instinctive, preparation for something that lay ahead, although he wasn't quite sure what.

'Clarice, this is Alex, my wife.'

Alex stared at the vision of golden beauty in front of her, frozen in place by the words Azzam had uttered. She realised this was some kind of ploy, one she didn't understand, and anger at being used this way began to grow inside her.

'I need to get the children inside, to bath and feed them and find a bedroom for them,' she said to Azzam, removing her hand from his grasp. 'Then I must get the boy to a hospital so his arm can be x-rayed.'

'I will organise it,' he said quickly, perhaps registering, even regretting, that he'd upset her. 'I will find a woman who will care for them. As for the boy, I shall take him myself. If the break is well aligned, we can put a cast straight on it.'

The woman, Clarice, made a protesting noise, but Alex's problem was with the man, not her.

'The boy is injured,' Azzam told Clarice, then he turned again to Alex.

'I will find someone also, to help you. You, too, need food.'

'Not to mention a bath!' she snapped, disturbed in ways she didn't understand by the tension she could feel in the air.

Who *was* this woman?

His girlfriend?

And if so, why aggravate her by introducing his 'wife' when she, Alex, wasn't a real wife at all?

Clarice?

Had she heard the name before?

She was far too tired to think right now, and getting the children bathed and fed was a priority. Several servants had appeared, Azzam rattled off some orders, and one young girl came forward, talking gently to the children, another stepping forward to take the baby from Alex.

'No, I'll take him. Just lead me back to my room,' Alex said, remembering this young girl as one she'd seen helping serve at dinner with Samarah about a hundred years ago. Could it only have been three days?

She followed the two young women and the children from the helicopter pad into a rear entrance to the palace, then along a familiar corridor to her room, where Hafa was waiting for her.

'We had word from the helicopter that the children were coming,' she said. 'The room next to yours is prepared for them and Ghaada, who loves all children, will be looking after them. I will help her bath and clothe and feed them, and His Highness will take the boy for X-rays, leaving you free to have a bath yourself.'

Brooking no argument, Hafa took the baby from Alex's arms and went with the children to the room next door, now talking in their language and waving her free arm, apparently assuring the little girl that Alex would be nearby.

Another young servant was waiting in Alex's bedroom, and to Alex's delight she, too, spoke English.

'I will help you,' she said simply, then she moved forward and as Alex raised her arms, the woman drew the filthy tunic over her head. Then she released the band around the plait and teased out Alex's hair, murmuring at the state of it.

'I have run a bath for you,' she said, ushering Alex into the bathroom, where there was a foaming tub with the scent she now knew so well rising from the bubbles with the steam.

Stripping off the rest of her clothes, Alex stepped into it, lying back in the warm water and feeling fatigue, as well as grime, ease from her body.

The young woman had followed her, and now she proceeded to wash Alex's hair, ignoring Alex's feeble protest that she could manage. Instead, she gave herself up to the luxury of it, and lay there, relishing the woman's fingers massaging her scalp—relishing the simple pleasure of being clean.

She eventually emerged from the bath and had a quick shower as well, washing off the grime she was sure would have lingered in the bath water. As she stepped out, the young woman wrapped her in a thick, warm towel, patting her dry.

'Enough!' Alex finally told her. 'I can look after myself now, but thank you anyway.'

'No, I am to see you eat and rest,' she said, polite but

stubborn. She held out a white towelling robe for Alex to put on then led her to a table by the window in the huge bedroom. An array of food was laid out there, with jugs of fruit juices and pots of coffee as well. Suddenly aware of her hunger, Alex sat down at the table and began to pick at what was on offer—sliced fruit, flat bread, meat and cheeses of different kinds, all things chosen to tempt a very tired woman's appetite.

Once fed, she realised sleep had become a priority, and she explained to the girl that she really needed a short rest. The short rest became three hours, and she woke with a start, unable to believe she could have slept so long and so deeply.

'Where are the children? Are they all right? The boy, how is his arm?'

Hafa had returned and must have been watching over Alex as she slept, for she came forward, assuring her all was well and that the older children had been playing in the garden once the boy's arm had been set.

Now she waved her hand towards the dressing room.

'When you are dressed, I will fix your hair,' she said. 'His Highness wishes you to bring the children to his mother in half an hour. We do not have much time.'

Alex found herself smiling for the first time since her return to the palace.

'I'm a doctor,' she said. 'I can be dressed and ready to move in two minutes. Half an hour is a luxury.'

Hafa returned her smile.

'But today you need not hurry like that,' she said, leading Alex, still clad in the cotton robe, across the dressing room and opening the doors to reveal that Alex's meagre wardrobe had been supplemented by at least another dozen outfits, far more exotic looking than the plain tunics and trousers that had been there originally.

Before Alex could protest the children returned, the boy and girl now dressed in pristine white clothing, the baby swaddled in a soft white muslin cloth. The little girl, Tasnim, Alex remembered, stared in awe at the clothes in the closet then pointed to a pale, silvery tunic and trouser set, pointing next at Alex.

Laughing at the child's delight, Alex stooped and hugged her, then turned to Hafa.

'I know she is Tasnim, but could you find out the other children's names, and tell her mine is Alex? I have tried with sign language but we both get muddled.'

Excited conversation followed and in the end Alex knew the boy was Zahid, the baby Masun.

Ghaada removed the children, promising to wait in the colonnade just outside the door until Alex was ready to take them to meet Samarah. Alex dressed in the outfit Tasnim had chosen, although she felt self-conscious about donning such beautiful clothes. The material was the finest silk, the palest blue-green colour shot through with silver. She had no make-up, but Hafa produced a box of lipsticks and a beauty case of unused cosmetics.

Shaking her head at such unimaginable luxury—that a guest room should come complete with new, expensive cosmetics—Alex chose a pale pink lipstick and used that on her lips before brushing her hair, tugging at the tangles, then covering it with a scarf that matched her outfit.

'I'm done,' she said to Hafa, who looked concerned that anyone could pay so little attention to her toilet, but Alex waved away the protest she began to make, saying, 'Samarah wishes to meet the children. She already knows me, although she might not recognise me in these beautiful clothes.'

She came towards them like a silvery ghost, carrying the baby and herding the two little ones in front of her.

Azzam knew he was staring, but he couldn't stop himself. He, who'd always thought golden beauty unsurpassable, was now struck dumb by this delicate, silver wraith.

'You have brought me children to love,' his mother cried, holding out her arms and speaking now to the two little ones in their own language. They came to her, as children always did, and she held them close then looked up at Alex, standing there with the baby.

'You will let me hold him too?' she asked, and Alex passed the white bundle to Samarah then knelt to put her arms around the children as well, so all three of the orphans were enclosed in the loving embrace of the two women.

The scene was burning into Azzam's eyes, like a painting seen and never forgotten, when he realised Clarice was speaking to him—Clarice, who had never been far from his side since his return, objecting when he turned her away from his own quarters so he could wash and dress.

'I have been thinking about Bahir,' she was saying, and Azzam had just restrained himself from demanding to know what else she should be thinking about so soon after his death, when she continued.

'And what he might wish for me.'

Ah, that was more like the Clarice he'd come to know. She was concerned about herself, not about her dead husband—concerned about her place in things now.

'He would not wish for me to be sad and lonely,' Clarice continued. 'You, his brother, must know that's true.'

Unfortunately, Azzam did. Bahir had been so besotted he'd have given Clarice the world, had it been at his disposal. He'd certainly lavished her with riches—palatial homes back in the U.S., which she visited regularly, a ski lodge in Switzerland, an apartment in London, not to mention jewellery worth more than the GDP of many small countries. She was hardly going to be cast out into the world as a poverty-stricken widow.

Yet she was after something more. He knew her well enough for that to be more than a suspicion.

'*Are* you sad and lonely?' he asked.

'Of course I am,' she snapped. 'That's why we're talking. I think we should be married. It is within the bounds of propriety in your country for a man to marry his brother's widow, I've read about it.'

A rage he'd never felt before rose up in Azzam.

'How can you be thinking of marriage to another man when my brother has been dead little more than a week? How does your mind work that you are putting this pressure on me? Have you no feelings? No propriety? No sense of right or wrong?'

She turned to face him, the beautiful golden hair lit from behind by the sun so she seemed to gleam with light, her perfect features beautifully made up, her blue eyes shining at him. And as he watched she slid the tip of her tongue along her lower lip, wetting it so it, too, shone.

It was a gesture she'd used on him many years ago and now he wanted to turn away from her—to never see that face again.

'You would have married me all those years ago had Bahir not come along,' she reminded him, making him feel ashamed at the truth she spoke.

'I cannot think of this now, let alone talk of it. It is beyond anything anyone could imagine, that you would talk of marriage now. Bahir is barely dead. At least respect the rules of mourning if you're throwing rules at me.'

'Three months and eleven days?' She all but shrieked the words at him. 'You expect me to be without a man for all that time?'

The crudity of it, on top of the lack of respect she was

showing his brother, angered Azzam so much he had to turn away from her lest he say something he would later regret.

'We will talk again,' he managed to say, through teeth clenched tight to keep in words that would do more harm than good.

'Soon!' she retorted, and he heard a threat in the words.

He spun towards his own quarters, knowing she wouldn't follow him there, then remembered he'd left Alex with his mother, and in a kind of limbo, for she'd be uncertain what her role was now, and would no doubt be thinking of returning to her home.

A stab of something he hoped was only regret slashed through him, but what would hold her here?

The children?

For a while—until they were settled in the palace. He thought he knew her well enough now to understand she wouldn't just walk away because they had shelter, food and clothing. She was the adult they'd clung to after losing their mother—she would understand that.

He returned to the open part of the wide colonnade where it was the habit of the women to gather every afternoon. Alex was seated on carpets by his mother's knee, the little boy this time on her lap, while the little girl, Tasnim, chatted to his mother, who still held the baby in her arms.

The thought of marrying Clarice had made him feel nauseous, while the sight of Alex by his mother's knee had him feeling very different—and unlikely—things.

Bahir, I need you!

The inner cry went up, so heartfelt he could feel it rip right out of his chest, but Bahir was gone and he had

to solve the riddles on his own. It was his job to make decisions, not only for the country but for this family...

Alex listened as Samarah and one of her aides, Afifa, translated snippets of Tasnim's conversation. She felt strangely
at ease—peaceful—here at Samarah's knee, Zahid dozing
on her lap, listening to the chatter of the women and the
wondering questions of Tasnim.

It was nothing more than a reaction to the last few days,
she understood that. The tension she'd kept hidden beneath
the surface as she'd helped the earthquake survivors was
now gone, and in its place not emptiness, just a feeling of
contentment.

Which would, she knew as she watched Azzam return
from his assignation with the beautiful Clarice in the
garden, soon be over, for once the children were settled,
she would return to Australia and this little interlude would
be as much a fairy story as Aladdin and his magic lamp.

'You will stay while they become used to life here?'

Alex smiled up at Samarah.

'I was thinking that just now. I shouldn't stay. There are
reasons why I should return to work at home but, yes, I
won't leave the children until I know they feel comfortable
in their new surroundings.'

Samarah reached out and Alex felt her light touch, like
a blessing, on her head.

'You work too hard. I knew that when I met you, though
you always pretended it was nothing to be visiting me outside your working hours. You were too tired, too thin, too
worn down by work. There is a reason?'

Alex looked at the woman she had grown to admire,
and knew she couldn't lie.

'There was—is, in fact—a reason, but it's personal,
Samarah. Just something I must do.'

It sounded feeble so she added something she knew Samarah would understand.

'A family thing.'

Samarah studied her for a moment then nodded, as if accepting that to question Alex further would be rude.

'But while you are here,' Samarah continued, 'you must see more of my country than a few rooms in the palace and a destroyed village. A car shall pick you up in the morning. Take the older children with you, for they, too, will enjoy the sights. Hafa will accompany you, and Ghaada will mind the baby.'

'It is I who should be showing you around.'

Alex looked up at the sound of Azzam's voice, and realised that, as ever, he'd rejoined the group in that silent manner he had, so quietly she hadn't heard him come.

'Of course you can't take time to do that.' Clarice must have been right behind him, for the words, cold and dismissive, spun through the air. 'You've already been neglecting your duties, Azzam. Some things can't stop because Bahir is dead. Trade delegations, important politicians visiting from overseas, your own business people—your days will be too full to be taking children and their nanny on a guided tour.'

Alex looked from one to the other. Clarice was probably right, but from what she, Alex, knew of Azzam, he wasn't a man to take orders from anyone.

She knew she'd guessed right when he came to sit beside her.

'Their nanny, as you call her, is my wife,' he said, the coldness in his voice cracking in the air like ice crystals. 'And after what she has done for my country and my people—*my* people, Clarice—I should be spending my life trying to repay her.'

This was entirely too creepy to be true, Alex decided, processing the words but guessing they were being said for a reason beyond the charming compliment embedded in them. The problem was that it was hard for her to work out what was going on when the bits of her that were touching Azzam, so close she couldn't avoid contact, were feeling drawn towards him, as if wanting to cuddle into him, for heaven's sake!

Why was he talking this way? As if he owed her— worse, as if he cared...

Clarice had thrown one look of fury in Alex's direction then stalked away, and suddenly Alex understood. It was a little play for Clarice's benefit.

To make her jealous?

Though why would she be jealous of any woman in her brother-in-law's life? What was Azzam to her apart from her husband's brother?

And worst of all, did Azzam think so little of her, Alex, that he would use her as a weapon against this woman?

The thought killed the treacherous warmth as suspicion wormed its way into her heart.

'She has different ways of showing grief so we must forgive her,' Samarah was saying, and Alex knew she was trying to ease a situation that had grown suddenly tense, for all the women were now looking from the departing Clarice to Azzam, as if asking themselves the same questions Alex had pondered.

'Grief is no excuse for rudeness, Mama,' Azzam said, though he softened the words by adding, 'although I think you would excuse the devil himself, you are so soft-hearted.'

Silence fell on them, not an uncomfortable silence now but one in which Alex's awareness of Azzam had time to grow again, so, in spite of the reservations she was now feeling about this man, her nerves twitched and twittered at each other and sent wayward messages to her brain.

'Unfortunately she is right.' Azzam broke the quiet. 'I do have duties that will prevent me showing you my country, but tonight I'm free. No one has expectations of me tonight. Will you trust the children to Ghaada and Hafa and have dinner with me?'

What could she say? Samarah and the other women were all urging her to agree, and the wild chatter that followed their English words made her think they were suggesting places he should take her.

'Let Azzam plan his own adventure—he's a grown man,' Samarah said calmly. 'But you, child—' she touched Alex on the head again '—wear the silvery gown you will find in your dressing room. I was right in thinking the pale colours would look much better on you than the dark ones you chose for practicality rather than beauty.'

'*You* chose those clothes for me?' Alex asked her. 'Thank you, but there are far too many, and they are way too fancy.'

'Hush,' Samarah said. 'After what you have done for our people, we should be giving you a palace, not just a few articles of clothing. As for the gown, you can wear a cloak over it if you feel it too bare to wear in public, but somehow I think Azzam has a private tour in mind.'

Azzam stirred beside her, while Alex puzzled over the words. She turned to him, but his face revealed nothing, the strong lines giving no hint of what might lie ahead.

Until he smiled and said, very quietly so only she could hear, 'If the silver gown makes you look more beautiful than the outfit you are wearing, it might be best you wear the cloak over it and we go to *very* public places.'

Was it really a compliment? Did he mean it? Alex looked

around, thinking Clarice might have returned to within earshot, but Bahir's widow was nowhere in sight.

Which didn't stop Alex feeling distinctly uncomfortable. How long had it been since anyone had paid her a compliment? Well, sometimes someone at work might remark on a job well done, but a compliment on her looks? And coming from a man who was surrounded by beautiful women?

Suspicion returned, but excitement had sneaked in as well. She hugged Zahid and set him on his feet, watching as he went into the garden to explore with Tasnim, his wounded arm held securely in a sling.

Tonight, she, Alex, would forget all the confusing questions her brain kept throwing at her, and behave as if she'd rubbed her lamp and wished for just one magical night. She'd wear the silver gown, and the high-heeled silver sandals she'd spotted in the wardrobe.

She'd dance with the prince and have the wondrous memory of it all to take home, tucked into her heart. And when work and the life she'd chosen got too much for her, she could take it out and marvel at it, remembering...

'You are rubbing your lamp and wishing again,' Azzam said softly. 'I can tell from your smile.'

Now she smiled directly at him.

'Actually, I'd shifted from the magic lamp to one of our European fairy tales. I was thinking I'd be like Cinderella going to the ball. Do you know the story?'

He grinned at her.

'Can you imagine a father in my culture allowing his boys to be brought up on fairy stories? Oh, my mother told Bahir and I the stories of our land, but fairy stories from another land? I have heard of this Cinderella but I don't know the story. Perhaps later you will tell me.'

Alex needed only an instant to realise that it wasn't a

story she would wish to tell this man—particularly not the bit about Cinderella getting to marry the prince.

'Or we can talk of real life perhaps,' she said, and heard a faint whispering sigh as if a dream had just floated out of reach.

CHAPTER EIGHT

HAFA helped her dress, as excited as if it was she, not Alex, going out to dinner with the prince. She brushed Alex's fine hair until it shone, then plaited two strands of it, one from each side of her parting, linking them behind her head with a silver ribbon.

'Not only will they keep your hair from trailing in your dinner,' she joked when she pushed Alex in front of the mirror to admire her work, 'but they make you look like a princess.'

'Which I'm not,' Alex told her, but Hafa shook her head.

'Of course you are. It is all over the palace that His Highness introduced you as his wife.'

Alex smiled at Hafa's innocent acceptance of what had played out in the colonnade.

'Our *marriage* was to protect both my and his reputation. It wasn't real.'

She didn't add that he'd brought it up—made it public—for some reason of his own, neither did she add her suspicions of this reason. She couldn't work out why, but she was certain it had something to do with his sister-in-law, because if looks could kill, Alex would be dead and buried by now.

She was still thinking about this, while Hafa fussed

over the dress, when a young girl came to tell her Azzam was waiting. The girl led Alex out the back way—the way she'd gone to find the helicopter, and to her surprise it was a helicopter awaiting her. Not the big one, which was probably based at the hospital now, still involved in missions to the ruined village, but a small one, like a monster dragon fly, painted in what she now recognised as the royal colours of black, white and silver.

Apprehension shafted through Alex's body—this was too much, she couldn't do it, she couldn't go flying off into the night in a glamorous silver dress with this man she barely knew. This *wasn't* a fairy story and this kind of thing didn't happen to ordinary, everyday Alexandra Conroy.

Something very like panic built in her head, swirling there, while something that definitely wasn't apprehension slithered along her nerves, and the feelings she'd been beginning to suspect she had for this man made her body tingle with awareness.

'Not a carriage made from a pumpkin, my lady, but the best I could do,' Azzam said, although he'd had to force the words out through a very dry throat, so beautiful did Alex look.

The silvery eyes flashed suspicion. This was not a woman you could win with sweet words or easy compliments.

'I thought you didn't know about Cinderella,' she said, obviously not as impressed by him in his best gown with the silver braid down the front as he'd been by her in the silver gown.

He offered a smile that he hoped looked genuine, although from the inside it felt strained and tight. He, who was normally relaxed with women, was suddenly tense and uneasy in ways he didn't understand.

'I looked her up on the internet,' he said. 'As you seem to know of our Aladdin, I thought I should know of her.'

At least that had her smiling! He took her hand to lead her to the aircraft, helping her into the passenger seat, touching her with hands that felt hot and clumsy.

'We are not going far and this little beauty is not very noisy so you won't need the communication helmet.'

Even more dry mouthed now, he tucked the silver dress around her legs so it wouldn't get caught in the door, and felt the warmth of her flesh beneath the fine material. He should stop right now. This was madness. He could invent an urgent phone call, pretend a text message had come into his cellphone as he walked around the helicopter to take his seat...

Except he'd deliberately not brought his cellphone with him, wanting to give this woman one special night to remember of Al Janeen before she disappeared out of his life.

Or was he hoping for something more?

Hoping she might fall in love with his country and maybe not disappear?

Fall in love with *him*?

He was aware this was the height of stupidity because she hadn't given the slightest indication that she was interested in him, so he had to believe that the attraction, if that's what it was, growing inside his body was totally one-sided.

Although last night attraction definitely had been there—the way she'd responded to the kiss...

That was *physical* attraction, probably heightened by the danger they'd shared...

As for his country, she'd seen the inside of the palace—or a small part of it—and a ruined village, so how could she fall in love with it?

And hadn't he decided, back when he'd still had some working synapses in his brain, that what he needed in the way of a real wife was someone from his own country and background and culture?

'You haven't seen the city so I will fly you over it, but I thought for dinner we would go somewhere special. You have seen flamingos?'

'Flamingos?' she echoed in such delight he had to smile, and the tension that had captured his body began to ease. 'Big birds, long legs, pink?'

'That's them,' he told her.

'You have flamingos here? In a desert country? The leopards haven't eaten them?'

Now he laughed at her disbelief and the little joke, and his laughter dispelled the last of his tension.

'The leopards live in the mountains, the flamingos by the lagoons that are not far inland from the sea. Their habitat, too, is protected.'

He lifted off, and headed for the lights of the city, flying low above it so she could see the mix of old and new that made the capital of Al Janeen unique.

Alex peered down, fascinated by the square and rectangular buildings beneath her, the lights on the roofs showing people preparing to sleep beneath the stars, then, beyond the older area, clustered like jewels in a crown, a clutter of high-rise buildings, brilliantly lit, the new part of the city.

She turned to see this glittery grouping from another angle, then realised they were flying over nothingness again, although now she looked ahead she could see what looked like a huge, shining mirror.

'It is called Shahlah because the birds, when they are there in numbers, turn it pink, and *shahlah* means a blush.'

'A blushing lagoon? None of our fairy stories can compare with that,' Alex told him, as he set the little aircraft down far enough away from the lagoon to not disturb the birds she could now see clustered on its shore.

Were they sightseeing here?

Or had this magic land more surprises to offer her? A fancy restaurant hidden behind the dunes? She'd slipped the fine-spun cloak that went with the gown into the handbag that matched her silver sandals, just in case she needed it, but now she peered around her, she wondered if she should have brought her sneakers instead. Just how practical would silver sandals be, for walking in the sand?

Well, she could always slip them off...

Azzam opened the door and, looking at him as he stood just slightly beneath her, she felt her heart turn over. He was a good-looking man at the best of times, but out here, with the darkening dunes behind him, he *looked* like a prince—the prince of all he surveyed! Was that phrase from a fairy story as well?

He held her hand to help her from the little aircraft, easing her down, not onto the sand she had expected but— she should have guessed—onto a carpet. This one wasn't red but it was patterned and long, like a beautiful path leading her into the night. It was only as they drew near that she saw a darkened area ahead, then lights came on, revealing a long, low tent, as dark as the night itself but lit by filigree lamps, their fractured light, patterns of gold and emerald and crimson, beckoning the visitors closer.

Outside the tent, beneath one raised side of it, more carpets had been spread, with huge soft pillows like the ones in the colonnade plumped down on them.

'Madame!' Azzam said, leading her to the pillows, offering her the choice of where to sit with a sweep of his white-clad arm.

Alex sank down into the largest part of the pile, and realised they were stacked in such a way she could sit, or recline just a little. She chose to sit, bemused by the surroundings—an Ali Baba tent, flamingos turning a lake blush-pink—but not wanting to miss anything.

Which was just as well, for now soft light lit up the lagoon so she could see the pink shapes of the sleeping flamingos clearly now.

'This is a night light for viewing them in the evening, but you must come in daylight to see them picking their way through the shallow water to fully appreciate their beauty and see the mud mounds they build to lay their eggs on.'

Now Azzam had mentioned them, Alex could see the strange-looking mounds clustered together at one end of the lagoon, but although she wanted to learn more about the habits of these beautiful birds, Azzam was explaining something else—explaining the delicacies a silent servant had set down before them on a huge silver platter.

'What you might call appetisers,' he said, 'so don't eat too much or you won't want your dinner.'

Alex felt herself relaxing, although she'd been extremely nervous about this outing with Azzam, about being alone with the man who was occupying so much of her thoughts *and* disturbing her body.

'Try a date—not an ordinary date like you might buy in your supermarket but a date from the family grove. Most of our traditional food traces back to our Bedouin ancestry, when our people roamed the deserts so food had to be easily transportable.'

He was sorting through a bowl of shiny, red-brown dates as he spoke and finally selected one.

'The seed has been removed, so you can bite into it.'

He held it to her lips, and their eyes met, messages that could never be put into words passing between them—provocative messages that sent heat coursing through Alex's body.

She bit into the date, her lips just grazing the fingers that held it, so, before he took the remainder of it to his own lips, his little finger flicked her lip, making the heat spiral downwards.

You're sharing a piece of fruit, for heaven's sake, her head was yelling at her, but her body was way beyond the control of her head, whatever common sense it might be preaching at her.

A small ball of cheese came next, milky and tart, a perfect contrast to the date.

'*Labneh*,' Azzam explained. 'A cheese made from fermented goat's milk.'

He was telling her the tastes of his country, yet the words came into Alex's ears not as words of love but definitely words of seduction.

Or was she imagining it?

She had just decided she must be when he wiped the water dripping from the *labneh* off her chin then once again brushed her lips, this time with his thumb.

Her body was zinging now, so alert she felt he must be able to hear it, the way you could hear the wind through electricity wires in a storm.

And *was* she in a storm!

She should draw back, choose food for herself—the little meatball kind of things looked tasty, but now Azzam's eyes were meeting hers again and she was pinned within this sensual bubble he had woven around them, powerless to resist.

Could she feel it? Was she as aware of him as he was of her? Azzam knew he should stop feeding her, for it was also feeding his need, his hunger for this woman. Nothing could come of it, for all she was his wife. She was a visitor, heading home to her own life as soon as the children were settled.

Heading home considerably richer, he'd make sure of that, for she'd served his country well, and even *misyar* marriages demanded a dowry, although he hadn't mentioned that to her.

Because thoughts of money made him doubt her?

Not anymore!

Whatever suspicions he'd harboured about her when he'd heard of her arrival in his country had been dismissed when he'd seen her in action. He'd come to know she was giving and unselfish, not grasping and avaricious. His doubts had been destroyed by her behaviour...

He offered her the plate of *sfiha*, tiny pies, being careful not to touch her in any way now, for the conjunction of his thoughts—of wanting her and payment—had shamed him so much the fires inside him had...not died, but certainly ebbed.

He began to explain the food, pointing out how each piece was made.

'The dates, grains and legumes, along with dried fruit and nuts, were carried by the tribes, who also had their animals for milk and meat. Because the Bedu acted as guards for the caravans from India and China, they could barter for spices, although saffron was a local spice, and salt a local commodity.'

Had she stiffened when he'd touched her lips?

Alex felt the shift in the atmosphere between them, and felt a sense of loss out of all proportion to the situation, but she hid it behind questions and became fascinated by the answers as he talked of the history of his people.

They ate mysterious meat dishes, drank juices of fruits

she didn't know, and finished with a type of sweet, made from yoghurt and honey, so delicious she didn't deny herself a second helping. Then the shadowy serving people were gone, vanishing as mysteriously as they had appeared, leaving another silver platter behind them, this one laden with the finest fruit. She and Azzam were alone on the carpet with moonlight touching the dunes and turning the lagoon to a shimmering silver, weaving a spell of enchantment about them.

Azzam broke the silence.

'Do you know how beautiful you are? As silver as the lagoon, as beautiful as the moon.'

He half reclined on the cushions beside her, and held a bunch of grapes above her, close to her lips.

'There is an illustration in one of our fairytales of a man feeding a woman grapes in this manner.'

Alex, bemused by the compliment he'd paid her, and still caught in the moonlight's spell, bit a grape off the bottom of the bunch and felt it explode with juice and sweetness in her mouth.

'Looking at the picture,' he said, holding the bunch above his own lips and taking one, pausing while he swallowed it, 'one imagines they are lovers.'

It's the spell, the situation, the magic of it all, Alex told herself, but her body rebelled and, aware in some instinctive way that the first move would have to come from her, she took another grape in her lips, then leant over the man beside her, transferring it to his mouth.

'Ahh...'

The soft sigh seemed to go on forever, floating above them like steam from a boiling cauldron, then Azzam's arms drew her against his body, and his lips, still tasting of grape, brushed against hers.

'I wondered if you felt it,' he whispered between kisses

so light they were like the touch of the moonlight. 'For me, the attraction was so strong I thought surely you must, but you hide your feelings well, Alexandra Conroy.'

She knew no words for this situation, so she answered with a kiss, a proper kiss, capturing the lips that had been teasing hers, pressing hers against them, hard and demanding, greedy now for more, although she wasn't entirely certain what more was.

More was a response like nothing she'd ever felt or imagined, for Azzam took control of the kisses, deepening the contact by sliding his tongue along her lips, delving into her mouth, darting flickers at first, then thrusting in mimicry of what she knew was sex, although she was discovering that knowing something, even viewing it on screen, was very different to the actual thing.

His hands slid along her arms, touching her so lightly the nerve-endings shivered beneath her skin, then his hands moved to her back and explored the contours—her shoulders, sliding to her waist, finishing up on her buttocks, cupping them and pressing her against him so she felt the hardness of his erection.

Should she tell him?

Would it matter?

But how to explain the weird vows she and David had taken, as high-school kids on a youth camp, deciding marriage lay in their future so they would wait…?

David hadn't waited…

She hadn't known it at the time, hadn't even considered he might not be faithful to her, not that it worried her because once he had decamped she'd been so busy there'd been little time to think of him or his betrayal.

Now, here in the present, in the moonlight, one of Azzam's hands still held her close, while the other was moving higher, lifting her hair so he could press kisses on her neck, shifting the strap of the dress so he could kiss the skin on her shoulder.

So far, apart from that first kiss, she'd been the receiver of sensation, but now she wanted to join him in exploration. But could one remove a headdress from a prince to feel his hair? Could one slide a hand beneath the sleeve of his gown to feel his skin, and the muscles beneath it?

Sensing hesitation in the woman in his arms, Azzam drew back, turned her so she lay against the coloured cushions. With unsteady fingers, he spread the silver hair around her head.

'We are at a point, Alexandra Conroy, beyond which there will be no turning back. You must know I want nothing more than to make love to you, here in this beautiful place, in this peaceful setting. You are my wife but that does not bind you to me, neither does it mean you must consent. I would never take a woman against her wishes, but your body tells me you want this as much as I do. Am I right?'

She frowned at him, and Azzam wondered what she was thinking. Had he put it badly? Should he have asked first if she would stay here in Al Janeen and be a real wife? For he felt that things could work well between them for all his misgivings about marrying a foreigner. But telling her that might put extra pressure on her, and this woman had already done so much for his country.

Still frowning, she reached out and touched his head scarf.

'Will you take this off?' she asked, and the smile she gave him told him her answer.

'One piece of clothing each,' he challenged, and though he thought a look of shock had crossed her face, he dismissed the idea. She was a grown woman, no doubt experienced with men.

'Why not?'

She had answered his challenge but now sat up, slipping the ribbon from her hair.

He removed his headdress, then his gown, casting it down on the carpet near their feet.

'Your turn,' he said, as desire burned so fiercely inside him it was a wonder he could speak at all.

She shifted, shuffled, lifted the hem of the beautiful silver dress, then slid out lacy white undies, throwing them on top of his gown.

'That might be cheating,' he whispered, his voice husky with the hunger he felt for her. 'But I will let you get away with it and do shoe for shoe.'

He took off his sandals, setting them aside, then slid off one of hers, his hands drifting up her leg, feeling the swell of her calf, the hardness of knee bones, the soft back of her thigh.

She was shivering, her skin covered with goose-bumps, and that excited him even more, so with the removal of the second sandal he ventured further, sliding his hand high beneath the dress to touch her between her legs, feeling the soft, silken hair there, imagining it, burning to see it—

But she had stiffened, and he knew he'd gone too far, too fast. Slow down, he told himself, standing up in his *wuzar*, the white cloth his people wore as underwear, moving to be close to her again, to kiss her and touch her and feed the fires he knew burned as brightly inside her as they did within him.

She returned his kisses with a fierce need that raged through his blood, and her hands pressed against his naked back, fingers digging into his muscles, fingernails scratching against his skin, so desperate was her touch.

'The dress,' he whispered, when he knew she was riding the excitement once again.

'You do it,' she murmured back, softly acquiescent now, tremulous beneath his questing hands.

He wondered if his hands should be shaking this way as he eased the shoulder straps away, found a zip, then slowly pulled the dress down along her body so bit by bit her pearly skin, luminous in the moonlight, was revealed, and the shape of her body, of small, pert breasts, a tiny waist and swelling hips, was laid out before his gaze.

'You are beautiful.'

He breathed the words then followed them with kisses, not hard and hot but worshipful, kissing the hollow of her neck, her chest, her stomach, leaving the breasts for last then running his tongue across first one and then the other.

She moved now, abruptly at first, as if the caress had startled her, but then she lay back and reached out to pull him closer, kissing his chest as he'd kissed hers, while his hands now found a peaking nipple, and his fingers played with it, her little whimpers of delight exciting him beyond endurance.

Lost in wonder at the delight of Azzam's touch, at the magic of his kisses, at the response of her body to his exploring fingers, Alex drank it in with the thirst of someone who'd been lost too long in the desert. Her body was responding in ways she'd never imagined it could, and a tension beyond anything she'd ever felt was building up inside her.

Now his mouth had taken over the teasing of her breasts, sending fiery pulses down to the place between her legs where his hand worked a subtle new magic. He was touching her so lightly, so gently, yet the heat that had been building inside her had seemed to plateau, and she hung, suspended, in some other world.

Now his fingers probed, but gently, and she knew she

must feel hot and wet for all sensation in her body was now concentrated in that one small area. His thumb moved, touched a part of her she would never have considered sensitive, yet her body jolted beneath him, like someone who'd been hit with an electric charge.

Now he calmed and soothed her again in some way—with kisses on her lips—while she wanted to scream at him to keep going, to show her exactly what she'd been missing out on all these years.

'Soon,' he whispered, as if he sensed her impatience. 'Lovemaking is too special to hurry.'

And once again he took her to that other place, but this time, as she hung there, her body taut with wanting, though what she wasn't sure, his fingers continued touching her, moving into her, his thumb again brushing her clitoris, then one more touch and the world went black, stars exploded in this inky darkness, and her body dissolved into a puddle of sensation too unbelievable for there to be words to describe it.

'Ah,' he said, nothing more, but his hand remained cupped around her and, as more tremors rent her apart, he held her safe.

But this wasn't all—she knew that—and now she'd experienced one part of this sex business she wanted all of it. Boldly she felt for him, found the iron-hard penis that had taunted her earlier, and ran exploratory fingers of her own over it. Of course she'd felt David's excitement, back when they'd been courting and sex had been a fumble in the back seat of his car, but touching David had never made her hot and anxious, never made her move restlessly against him, her body begging to be taken.

Azzam shifted until he was lying above her, his body supported on his strong arms, his undergarment gone.

He was so magnificent in the moonlight she could barely breathe for the wonder of it.

'Guide me in,' he ordered, and she hurried to obey, gasping at first as her body opened to accommodate him, gasping again as a fierce thrust caused a jolt of pain, then she found the rhythm of his movements and moved with him, aware of something primal, something elemental, in this mating dance beneath the stars and moon.

But thoughts became entangled and disappeared altogether as she realised that once again she'd reached that strange plateau, but this time she knew the wonder of the experience that lay beyond it, and she moved beneath him, searching for the connection that would repeat it, moving faster, with him, rising higher, wanting the nearly unbearable tension to break again, to shatter her so she could be new again.

It came, and with it a shout of exultation from Azzam, then his movements slowed and he collapsed on top of her, his body hard and hot, slick with sweat, his lips by her ear, murmuring words she didn't understand.

She held him tightly, aware this might be the only time they could lie this way, and knew she loved him—probably would always love him. She looked up at the moon, silently telling it of her love, and knew, too, that the magic of this memory would light her life just as the moon had added magic to their lovemaking.

Azzam rolled away from her, remaining close, raising his upper body on his elbow, his head on his hand, looking down at her, his free hand running across her skin.

'You are a ghost, an apparition, a thing of wonder and delight. That is what I said to you in my language.'

Now he touched her face.

'You are happy? No regrets?'

Still lost in a place beyond words, she smiled and

shook her head, then, as if remembering something, he frowned.

'Alex?'

Her name was more tentative on his lips than she had ever heard it, then, still frowning he ran his hand down her body, sliding it between her legs, touching the wetness lingering there.

Now he frowned, as if remembering something, studying her, the frown deepening.

'You were a virgin?'

It was more an accusation than a question and it cut into her hazy, drifting thoughts, bringing her back to earth with such a jolt she sat up and stared at him.

'Is that a sin?' she demanded, so annoyed at being shaken out of her little bubble of happiness she could have slapped him.

'Not a sin, no,' he said quietly, touching her on the shoulder. 'But you should have said— I could have hurt you— I wouldn't—'

'If you say you wouldn't have had sex with me if you'd known, I *might* just hit you,' she warned. 'And if you mention it again—as if I had some kind of rare sexually transmitted disease—I will walk home from this place if it takes me all night.'

Angry and feeling somehow humiliated, as if her virginity had been an affront to him, she reached out and grabbed the first thing that came to hand, which happened to be his gown. Clutching it in front of her, she moved away from him.

'Alex!'

Azzam said her name but had no words with which to follow it. Somehow, on top of what had happened, he'd made it worse—offended her in some way he didn't understand.

'Well?' she demanded, his gown wrapped around her body, tucked in above her breasts so she wore it like a sarong while she searched among the tumbled cushions, presumably for her gown and underwear.

'I don't know what to say,' he admitted. 'I don't know what to tell you. I want to say I'm sorry, but I'm not, for what we shared was, to me, truly amazing—something very special and something I will always remember.'

'Then that makes two of us,' she snapped, finding her gown. Discarding his robe, she pulled the silver sheath over her head. But she wasn't done. Grabbing the small silver bag she'd brought with her, she pulled out a cloak. In the haze of what was happening, Azzam still registered the fact that it must have been silk for it to have folded so small. Now she'd donned it over the silver dress and stood, a slender, muted figure all in black, the milky white skin no longer tantalising him, although the shining hair still shamed the moon with its beauty.

'You are still you beneath the gown and cloak,' he reminded her, but she didn't speak and he knew he'd broken the bond between them—a bond he'd been beginning to believe might form a solid foundation for something special.

CHAPTER NINE

THEY flew back to the palace in silence, Azzam wondering if he'd ever understand women. From the helipad behind the palace he could walk her as far as the door to the women's house where she was staying, or to his own quarters—equidistant.

He wanted to do the latter, not because he had any intention of making love to her again this evening but so they could talk and maybe sort this out. But how to ask? The woman was a puzzle to him, an enigma! She must be, what, late twenties? And undoubtedly there were plenty of women of her age who were still virgins, but a woman as beautiful and desirable as she was?

He shook his head, further thought beyond him.

'I don't like to part like this,' he said, when they were on the ground, the engine off and the blades slowing. 'Would you come with me to somewhere we can talk—only talk? I realise you are upset, and with me, but whatever I said it was inadvertent. The experience we shared was very special to me, more special than I can put into words.'

The black-garbed figure shrugged her shoulders.

'I don't think there's anything to talk about,' she finally said. 'After all, I'll be gone before long. As soon as the children are settled I'll be leaving.'

The cool, offhand statement thudded into Azzam's

belly like a punch from an assailant and desperation grew
within him.

'We could talk about that—about your plans,' he said.
'Must you go so soon? Might you not stay a while, see my
country, learn a little of its ways—maybe stay—'

He'd been about to say 'forever' but had pulled back
the word at the last moment, thinking it might frighten
her. Women needed to be wooed, not hit with marriage
proposals out of the blue. And though they were technically
married, he was beginning to realise that what he wanted
with this woman was a real marriage…

What had he been about to say? Maybe stay—what?
Alex found herself pondering this to stop herself thinking
of other things. Like the pathetic way she'd reacted to the
virgin thing out there in the desert! Like the way her body
was behaving as if the coldness between them didn't exist.
Beyond all reason, it was yearning for his touch, and the
excitement of his lovemaking…

'I don't think talking will help,' she finally replied,
knowing the more she was in this man's presence the
less likely she'd be to get over this yearning business.
Discovering she was in love with him had been one thing,
but discovering what his body could do to hers, that was
entirely different. She could hide her love, but was she
strong enough to control these new urges of her body, and
if she gave in to them, wouldn't he guess the other part?

'Perhaps tomorrow,' he said, his voice sounding
strange—hoarse? Strained?

'Perhaps,' she agreed, lying through her teeth, knowing
she would do everything in her power to avoid him and,
if it was impossible, to see him only in the company of
others.

He climbed out of the helicopter and walked around

to help her out. She held the cloak around her as if it was armour that might somehow protect her, but he put his hands on her waist and lifted her easily from her seat, and the heat of his hands burned through the layers of cloth so she felt as if he'd branded her, the outline of his fingers burned into her skin.

He walked with her to the rear door she now knew led to her quarters, and spoke quietly to a man who sat nearby. The man slid off into the shadows, and Azzam stood with her, this time resting his hands on her shoulders and peering into her face.

'You won't change your mind? Won't sit with me a while and talk?'

'No, thank you!'

She knew she sounded tetchy but she was feeling that way too, for the man's hands on her had reawakened the barely diminished fires of earlier and her body clamoured to lean into his, to feel his contours—to know him…

'Then there is only one thing left to say,' he said, with the smile she'd seen so rarely, but which had the power to light up her heart.

'And that's goodnight,' he murmured, and before she could retreat he bent his head and kissed her lips, the softness of his skin accentuating the hard demand behind that simple kiss. Her heart rate soared and imps danced in her head, distracting her from the common sense she knew she needed—desperately.

Now her body was leaning into his, the kiss was deepening, and the longing to be with him, naked, feeling all of him, was all but overwhelming her. Then one small thread of common sense came through for her. If this was how she felt after making love one time, how much worse would it be after two—or four—or fifteen…?

She broke away. What was the point? She didn't want an affair with this man. She didn't want it to be *more* difficult to leave this country. Already it would be bad enough, leaving Samarah and the children, whom she was coming to love.

He released her, and it was only in her foolish heart she felt reluctance in the release.

'We *will* talk,' he said, opening the door for her, waiting until a young woman appeared then speaking to her, no doubt asking her to see Alex to her room.

'Goodnight,' she said, though with sadness. But what else was there to say?

'Goodnight,' he echoed, then he walked away.

Alex followed the young woman to her room, then shooed her away, assuring her she could undress herself. She stripped off the cloak, then the silver dress, casting it into a heap on the floor, wanting to bundle it up and drop it into a rubbish bin then wanting to see it cleaned so she might take it home as a reminder of a magical, if thoroughly disturbing night.

Seeing herself in the mirror made her grimace, faint red marks that would turn to bruises on her limbs and body. But remembering how they'd got there, remembering the pleasure the man had generated in her body, she couldn't regret anything that had happened. The only regret she had for was the way it had ended. But how else could it have ended? There could be no affair—she was going home—and that was quite apart from the fact that for some reason he hadn't liked her being a virgin.

Well, bother him!

She went to bed, wondering if sleep would come, her body more alert, more wired than it had ever been.

Sleep came.

* * *

She woke to sunshine making patterns on the silk coverlet again, and she stretched, lazily, a little sore, but with no regrets.

Sitting up in bed, she realised she had company. Tasnim was sitting by the door, the child as silent as she usually was. Alex opened her arms and the girl ran into them, hugging her tightly, then she slipped off the bed and went away, returning with Zahid and the baby, Masun.

'All my family,' Alex joked, as she hugged them all, then waggled the baby in the air so he crowed with laughter. If only they *could* be her family—*her* laughing, happy children.

Impossible!

A selfish dream...

But one that bit in deep, probably because her own family was all but gone, leaving behind such pain and hardship...

Ghaada was by the door now, and she translated as Tasnim and Zahid rattled on, telling Alex the car was waiting, they were going in a car, please could she come.

Now!

Alex laughed. Typical family! The children had been waiting, not to see her but to go for a ride in a car, obviously something new for them. Ghaada took them out of the room so Alex could dress, reminding the children Alex also had to have her breakfast.

'I will keep the baby here,' she said to Alex, 'for the car would be too tiring for him and you do not need the distraction.'

'But I thought you could accompany us and tell me what I am seeing,' Alex said, and Ghaada shook her head.

'As well as a driver, His Highness has arranged a—is it tour guide you say? He has planned the tour for you and told this young woman where she is to take you. Hafa will bring your breakfast, and the car is waiting when you are ready.'

Soon after Ghaada and the children departed, Hafa entered, carrying a tray with a coffee pot, a cup, sugar and sweet pastries on it.

'I select an outfit for you?' she asked, as Alex sat down to breakfast, surprised at how hungry she was feeling.

'I think for sightseeing my own jeans and shirt,' Alex told her, determined to get her mind off the children and dreams of a new family, and into 'going home' mode.

Hafa seemed about to argue, but in the end she disappeared into the dressing room, returning with the clothes Alex had been wearing when she'd left Australia what seemed like a lifetime ago.

Their tour guide spoke perfect English, acquired, she explained, because she'd grown up in England where her father had run the European end of one of the royal family's businesses. They went first to the markets in the old part of town, where Alex was dazzled by the multitude of aromas—herbs, spices, strange fruit and the ever-present frankincense. But a riot of colour also assaulted her senses, for the vivid yellow of open bags of turmeric powder and the deeper gold of saffron, the bright sheens of bolts of colourful silk, draped across stalls piled high with goods.

The children oohed and aahed as any children would, seeing such an array of goods spread out on either side of narrow alleys. They reached the area where metal objects—pots and pans, urns, vases and lamps—were sold, and Alex stopped to look more carefully. Surely she was entitled to take home one small memento, and if she could discover a small, shapely lamp like the one Tasnim had found, it would be the ideal souvenir.

And she could dream of wishes…

The children poked around among the treasures and it was Zahid who found a tiny lamp, holding it up to show Tasnim, no doubt commenting on how like hers it was. He held it out to Alex, who turned to the guide.

'Can you ask how much—?'

She stopped, an unbelievable awareness striking her. She had no money! Not even Australian money, for her wallet was back at the palace, the last thing she'd thought she'd need.

'It is very cheap,' their guide told her, mentioning a sum in Al Janeen money that meant nothing to Alex.

'No, it doesn't matter,' Alex told her, and she hustled the children on to the next stall, and the next, through the markets and back to the car, her mind in a whirl as she came to terms with just how isolated she was and how totally dependent on Azzam's goodwill to get back home.

Although Samarah would surely help if Azzam's promise to arrange her flight home didn't eventuate—

No way! The thought of borrowing from her kind friend was too much. Bad enough she'd had to ask Azzam for wages.

They drove through the city, visited a museum that had reminders of the past, beautifully bejewelled camel saddles, magnificent gowns and exotic headdresses. Pictures of a distant past were arrayed along the walls, showing nomad camps, and herds of goats summering in the mountains— maybe not far from the children's village. Also on the walls, photographic portraits of memorable faces, ordinary people going about their lives but with the strong, proud profiles of their race, the same profile Alex so admired in Azzam.

Eventually, when the children tired, Alex suggested they return home.

'One more stop,' their tour guide said, and now the big black limo left the city streets, heading out on a bitumen road across the desert. They drove for maybe an hour, then crested a dune and there beneath them spread the shining lagoon, pink around the edges with the daintily stepping flamingos.

'The blushing lake,' the guide said, as the children gazed in wonder at the birds. Alex was less interested in them, orienting herself by the nest mounds but seeing no sign of the tent in which she'd spent such a memorable evening. Wasn't there a saying about desert people folding their tents and disappearing into the night?

Yet her memories couldn't be folded away so easily, and a physical ache started up inside her as she longed to be back at the beginning of the magical night and maybe handling it all differently.

Better—oh, certainly better—for didn't everyone make things better in their dreams?

Both children fell asleep as they drove back to the palace, and Ghaada appeared when the vehicle pulled up, so she carried Zahid while Alex, after thanking their guide, carried Tasnim, feeling the girl's slight body against her breast, feeling the love that had crept into her heart where these children were concerned.

It was a different love from the other love in there—the one that had slammed in without warning over what was a matter of days.

Could love happen like that?

So quickly?

Maybe it wasn't love. Maybe it was nothing more than a strong physical attraction.

But as Alex left the sleeping Tasnim on her bed and returned to her own quarters, she knew that was wrong. Yes, she was physically attracted to the man—even more so after last night—but what she felt was more than that. It was a mix of admiration and respect and something that she couldn't explain—some inner connection to the man—as if they were linked in the way speakers on phones in distant places were linked—brought together by some unseen, and to most people mysterious, power.

Hafa was waiting for her, with a message that Samarah would see her and the children in the colonnade at the usual time.

Alex thanked her and sent her away, assuring the kind young woman she could bath and dress herself, wanting to be alone for a while with her straying thoughts. But being alone didn't help make sense of the chaos in her head, neither did it soothe the agitation of her body, although maybe Azzam wouldn't be in the group at the colonnade this evening.

She lay on her bed, studying the marble fretwork of the window, marvelling as always at the talent of the master craftsman who must have carved it, thinking about shifting patterns to distract her mind and body. The knock on the door was louder than Ghaada's or Hafa's usual light tap, but without stirring much Alex called, 'Come in.'

To her surprise it was Clarice who swept into her room, cast a knowing eye around it, and sniffed in a way that suggested the sumptuous suite was only a small step up from servant's quarters.

'I thought as we're both strangers in this land—although I've been here long enough to be accepted and adored by the locals—we should get to know each other.'

Alex sat up on the edge of the bed, but before she could offer Clarice a chair, the woman had sat down by the window, where the play of light made patterns on her skin, illuminating her golden beauty.

'I'm going home any day now,' Alex told her, then realised it might have sounded rude, so she quickly added, 'not that I wouldn't want to be friends with you, but as I say...'

She left the sentence hanging.

'Really?' Clarice said, and it seemed to Alex that there was relief in the word, although it was a mystery why Alex's departure should please Clarice.

'Once the children are settled here,' Alex expanded, 'I'll be free to go. It just seemed wrong to take them from their village and dump them somewhere strange without a little bit of time for them to adjust.'

Clarice looked perplexed, or as perplexed as someone who had very little in the way of facial expressions could look. Her eyebrows had moved as if to come together in a frown, but no lines marred her smooth forehead.

'But why would you care?' she asked. 'You didn't know the children and they barely know you and they must be so delighted to get out of their squalid little village and come to live in a palace, they wouldn't care who looked after them.'

The local people adored someone who spoke of 'squalid little villages'?

Alex pushed the thought away and concentrated on the main issue.

'These children have lost their mother. No matter where they came from or how magnificent their current circumstances might be, they are grieving and need time to adjust to the worst loss a child can suffer. They need to feel secure in their surroundings, and to know they can trust the adults around them. They need to feel wanted and loved and to know that their little family won't be split up.'

Clarice stretched and ran a hand through her glorious mane of hair.

'Sounds like a load of psychological claptrap to me,' she said. 'Kids are kids, they adapt.'

Swallowing the growl that rose in her throat, Alex rose from the bed.

'I really need to shower. Was there something else you wanted?'

Clarice seemed put out.

'I only came to chat,' she said. 'With Bahir gone, there's no one in this place I can talk to. I should just get out of here—go home to the States, I've houses there—but there's this mourning thing they do and I don't want to upset everyone in case I want to come back some day.'

Alex sat down again. The words sounded false, somehow, but the woman *was* recently bereaved.

'I am sorry for your loss.' It was a trite statement, but Alex meant it.

Clarice waved it away.

'I gather you made a *misyar* marriage with Azzam while you were out there at the earthquake place,' she said, and Alex wondered if that was what her visitor had come to discuss.

'Apparently it was the only thing to do,' she answered, hoping she sounded calmer than she felt because whatever had happened between Azzam and herself was not only private but also precious in a way she didn't fully understand.

'Oh, yes,' her visitor agreed, rather too readily. 'He couldn't have had his reputation tarnished by sharing a tent with a foreigner. Of course, no marriage in these parts, even a *misyar* marriage, is legal until it's consummated.'

Alex's breathing stopped, and her heart stood still, then picked up and raced, while small, shallow breaths saved her from passing out completely.

Had Clarice seen her reaction?

Alex sincerely hoped not, but the statement had raised so many questions in Alex's head that she needed to get rid of the woman so she could at least *try* to sort through them.

Realising some kind of reply was needed, she shrugged her shoulders.

'I wouldn't know about any of that,' she said, hoping she sounded a lot more casual than she felt. 'Now, I really must shower and dress. Samarah wants to see the children.'

Now Clarice stood up.

'Oh, well, whatever Samarah wants Samarah must have,' she said, not even attempting to hide the bitchiness in the words. And on that note she swept out of the room.

Alex lay back on the bed.

Azzam would have known this thing about marriage and consummation.

She'd sensed the previous afternoon in the colonnade that he was using her against Clarice in some way.

Introducing her as his wife.

When, apparently, she wasn't his wife.

Was that why he'd taken her to that magical place last night?

Was that why he'd seduced her?

Be honest, she told herself, it had hardly been a seduction—she'd wanted it as much as he had.

Maybe more?

She sighed and rolled over on her stomach, pressing her hot face into the pillows, aware of how little she knew of male-female relationships, aware of how lost she was...

She'd go home. The children would adapt. They were already at ease with Ghaada, for Alex had seen them laughing and playing with her in the courtyard gardens, and Samarah would give them love. They would be all right.

She heaved herself off the bed, showered hurriedly, then stood in front of the wardrobe. Much as she'd have loved to put on her jeans and a clean shirt, she didn't want to hurt Samarah's feelings by not wearing one of her gifts.

Sorting through them, she found a pale pink tunic and trousers, less fancy than the other sets, although once she was dressed she realised the pink material took on a life of its own, deepening in colour in the folds, paling almost to white where it crossed her breasts and hips.

It was beautiful and a tiny little bit of her was glad because *she* looked beautiful in it—or as beautiful as someone as nondescript as she was ever could look. She hooked her hair up using two of the jewelled combs from the bathroom, wrapped a scarf around her head and once again put pale pink lipstick on her lips.

The children came bounding in just as she finished and she knew from their excited chatter that they were complimenting her. Ghaada translated their exuberant comments so Alex was blushing as she made her way with them, Ghaada carrying Masun today, along the colonnade to where Samarah held her daily court.

In Alex's mind, as she approached the gathering, she had it sorted that she didn't want Azzam to be there, but when she saw him, seated beside his mother, her heart gave a treacherous little leap, and warmth flooded recently excited parts of her body. Breathing deeply so she appeared calm and focussed, she greeted Samarah, nodded hello to Azzam as if he hadn't ignited her body in ways she still couldn't believe possible the night before, then urged the children forward to greet both adults.

Zahid greeted Azzam like an old friend and showed him a treasure he had found—a small white stone from the lagoon—while Tasnim drew close to Samarah, who lifted the child onto her lap and gave her a hug.

'I am blessed to have these children in my life,' Samarah

said. 'Last night I read to them before they went to sleep. I had forgotten what a simple joy that was.'

Hearing Samarah's sincerity in the simple words, Alex could only smile, certain that the children had found a secure home here at the palace and a very special guardian in Samarah.

'I, too, have something special,' Azzam said, and, thinking he was speaking to Zahid, Alex barely glanced his way, but he was handing a little lamp to Zahid, speaking to him in his own language, although when the little boy came and shyly presented the lamp to her, Alex could only stare—first at it, and then at Azzam.

'The guide told me you admired one,' he said, as she turned it around in her hands, looking at it from all angles, aware that it was very different from the market lamp, yet not understanding how.

'It's beautiful,' she said, 'but it looks expensive. I can't accept expensive gifts from you.'

Samarah waved away her protest.

'You are his wife so he can give you anything—far better things than an old lamp—although I suspect objects, possessions aren't as important to you as people, isn't that so?'

'Not important at all,' Alex assured her, remembering how it had been the need for possessions—a fine house for his wife, good art works, the best furniture—that had started Rob's gambling.

Azzam had watched her approach, drinking in the sight of her. She'd tied a pale pink scarf across her head, the material so fine he could see, beneath it, the combs she'd used to hold her hair back from her face.

She'd looked so serenely beautiful his mouth had gone dry and he'd wondered if he'd be able to speak to her at all, let alone say the things he wanted to say.

Now he watched her turning the lamp in her hands, answering his mother, rejecting any wish to have possessions. Something in her past has made her this way—not only about possessions, but had made her remote, untrusting, Azzam decided.

If he managed to speak, how could he bridge the gap between them—a gap he very definitely wanted to bridge?

He accepted that they barely knew each other, but he believed the bond between them, forged in the chaos of the disaster, was rare and special, something that should be nurtured so it could grow and flourish into a deeply loving marriage.

But he'd upset her, and she'd drawn away, and he had no idea how to bring her close again. He watched her, still studying the little lamp—a trinket, nothing more—and wondered what she'd think if he told her he'd, foolishly he knew, already wished on it—wished for her to stay here in Al Janeen, to stay as his wife and consort.

Ask her, his mother had said when he'd sought her advice, but how to ask? When?

She held the lamp, showing it to the children, then smiled at him, a smile that seemed to rip his heart apart, so much did it hurt him.

'Thank you. It will be a wonderful reminder of Al Janeen for me to take home with me.'

'Must you go?'

Really smooth move, brother, the ghost of Bahir teased, but desperation had prompted the words.

Now she smiled again, a sad smile this time that tore a bit more of his heart.

'You know I must. Originally I came to tend Samarah on the flight—I've already stayed longer than I should.'

'There is family back at home? You miss them? Is that why you are so determined to leave us?'

He was saying this all wrong, but he badly needed to know she had pressing reasons to go—apart, of course, from putting a vast distance between herself and him.

'Family obligations,' she replied, not meeting his eyes but with enough emotion in her face for him to know it hurt her to say it. Because she didn't want to leave?

Or maybe it was the obligation that hurt her?

How could that be?

He wanted to know more.

Put bluntly, he wanted to know everything about her, but for him to learn about her, and she about him, she had to stay.

Could he order it? Wasn't he the ruler—couldn't he command it?

Command this woman?

Of course he couldn't. Not her or any other woman, realistically…

'But now you have obligations here, too,' he said, speaking quietly, although his mother's women friends had withdrawn, taking the children into the garden so only he, Alex and his mother remained on the carpets. 'There are the children, and as my…'

He hesitated before saying the word 'wife', knowing it wasn't right for he'd told her there'd be no strings attached to their *misyar* marriage but desperate to get her to change her mind about leaving. Fortunately, before the word came out, Clarice had appeared, coming to stand beside him, taking his arm, urging him a little apart.

'This conversation isn't finished,' he said to Alex, then he followed Clarice a little way along the colonnade.

'Your mother is finding happiness in the children,' she began, and Azzam wondered where the conversation was leading for Clarice rarely gave a thought to other people's happiness.

'She is,' he replied. 'I think it takes her mind off her loss.'

Clarice smiled at him—more a smirk than a smile for it sent coolness through his blood.

'Then perhaps soon I will give her more pleasure—the greatest pleasure of all. I'll give her a child with real meaning for her.'

He heard the words but they made little sense, but as he turned to look at her he saw she was patting her stomach and looking unbearably pleased with herself.

'You're pregnant?'

He spoke quietly, not wanting to raise false hope in his mother, should she hear the quiet conversation.

'It would seem so,' Clarice said, but now the smile he'd once let light his world seemed smug and even devious.

'That would be good news indeed,' he said, wondering why he was feeling so doubtful.

'The child, if it's a boy, will be the true heir, of course.'

She was looking at him now, as if the words might hold some hidden meaning.

Did she think it would hurt him? That he might resent his brother's child? How could he, he who'd loved Bahir better than himself?

Of course Bahir's son would be the heir. Perhaps, even, should the child be a girl, his country would have grown enough to accept *her* as the ruler. Such a time, he was sure, wasn't that far away.

But Clarice was still talking to him, standing a little behind him and speaking quietly so no one else would hear the conversation.

'That's the real reason I thought we should marry, you and I. That way the succession is protected. Bahir's child grows up as yours, and becomes the prince in due time.'

The conversation that had begun, he felt, at the worst possible time, had now taken such a truly outlandish turn that it took him a moment to get his head around it.

'We do not have to be married for the child to grow up to be the ruler,' he told her. 'Bahir's child would be the heir, my place that of a regent until he was of age.'

'And if I were to marry someone else? Take my child back to my homeland of America so he grows up there? How would that suit your ideas of national identity?'

Cold fear gripped him as he realised what the woman was doing. She was bartering with the life of her unborn child, for how could a child raised in another country understand the people and the land he was born to rule?

And how could he allow Bahir's child to be raised by another man—particularly the kind of man Clarice, now she had more than enough money than she would need to keep her in style for life, might choose?

He took her arm and led her down into the garden courtyard, staying away from the children and in the shade of trees for the sun was still hot. But for all the heat, his body shivered as the dreams he'd spun of a real marriage between himself and Alex vanished into the ether, dreams of love crumbling to dust beneath his feet, lost forever because of the obligation of family.

The obligation he felt towards his beloved brother, his twin, his other half…

CHAPTER TEN

This conversation isn't finished. Wasn't that what he'd said? Yet he'd walked away with Clarice. Alex excused herself to Samarah and went to play with the children in the garden, chasing the two older ones around the beautifully crafted hedges and topiary shaped as balls. Tired at last, she sat on the edge of the fountain and took Masun from Ghaada, dabbling his feet in the water, making him laugh, his innocent chuckles bruising her heart because she would never see him grow up.

'It is time for the children's dinner,' Ghaada said, taking the now sleepy baby from Alex and leading the children back to their rooms.

Alex remained by the fountain. Trailing her fingers in the water, drinking in the peace of the tranquil setting, seeing the fierce red sun dropping below the high walls of the palace. Darkness fell swiftly and she saw the women moving back towards the building that housed them, next to what she now knew was the visitors' building, where she and the children had rooms. Looking around, she realised it was more a series of houses than one large palace, for there were other buildings she didn't know, but all were linked by the colonnade.

One would be Azzam's, of course, and presumably Clarice still lived in what had been Bahir's building, and from what Samarah had said, there were receiving areas where people came to meet their prince, and places where dignitaries were entertained. There were areas also for servants and old family retainers, and for cousins and aunts and the women who were friends. Alex was considering how reassuring it must be, this self-enclosed community, how safe people must feel within it, when she felt, rather than saw, Azzam approach.

'I thought you would be eating with my mother,' he said quietly, sitting beside her but not touching her. Not that touch was needed, for awareness was flaring between them with a galvanic power that singed the skin and burned along the nerves.

On her side, anyway...

'I wanted to see the sun set,' Alex told him, unwilling to admit she'd been lost in thoughts of safeness and community.

'And I need to talk to you, but I find I have no words for what I want to say, or, now, the right to say them,' he said quietly. He took one of her hands in both of his, and held it, warm and—yes, safe!

'I would have asked you to stay,' he said then he gave a short, abrupt laugh. 'Asked? How stupid! I probably would have begged you to stay.'

He turned her hand over and dropped a kiss into the palm, then folded her fingers over it to keep the kiss, the hand again held between his.

'But circumstances have changed and I cannot tell you things I would have said. For that, I am truly sorry. But know that when you go, and it can be tomorrow if you wish, you will take a piece of me with you.'

A feeling akin to panic flashed along Alex's nerves and she stood up, moving slightly away, then turning back towards him because she was puzzled as well, and aching with her love for him.

'Is this to do with my overreaction last night? Is it because of that you cannot talk?'

He stood up, put his hands lightly on her shoulders, and looked down into her face.

'It is not to do with you, but with a—a constraint I suppose you would call it, put on me by family obligations.'

For a moment Alex thought he might kiss her, then he muttered what sounded like an oath of some kind and walked away, heading for a shadowy part of the garden she hadn't yet explored.

Drawn by the pain she'd heard in the words, she followed, finding him beside an ancient, black-trunked, gnarled old tree.

'This tree was here before the palace—here before my ancestors first camped in this place. It symbolises continuation, shows us that life goes on no matter what. It is frankincense—you know it?'

Alex came forward and touched the rough trunk.

'I know the scent of it now,' she said. 'It's everywhere.'

'It made our fortune in the early days—not just this tree but many like it. They grow in only a few places. Here, feel the trunk.'

He took her hand and held it against the rough bark, pressing her fingers into what seemed like a cut in it.

'The frankincense gatherers cut through the rough bark to the living tree beneath and it bleeds. Can you feel the small lump there? We call it a tear, as if the tree cries with pain yet its pain gives us life in the same way as a mother's pain gives life to her child.'

He took his hand away and Alex looked up at the night sky through the fine silvery leaves of the ancient tree, wondering exactly what Azzam had been telling her, knowing it was important to him.

Now, as she watched, he pulled a small pen-knife from his pocket and again ran his hands across the bark of the tree, feeling for a cut perhaps, because when he turned back to her he had two small, clear, tear-shaped lumps of frankincense which he pressed into her hands.

'You take my tears with you when you go,' he said quietly, 'and also my heart.'

Alex closed her fingers tightly around the little buds, and was trying to make sense of his words when he bent and kissed her lightly on the lips, before disappearing as quietly as he had come.

Alex stayed beneath the tree, the tears of frankincense biting into her palm, until the sky was dark enough to see the stars. She tried to find the constellations Azzam had pointed out to her, but their brightness was blurred by the tears that had filled her eyes.

Eventually she made her way back to her room, where Hafa scolded her for sitting outside when the cool night air was descending. Waving away the young woman's concern and fending off offers of dinner—food was the last thing her churning stomach would accept—she went into the dressing room and found the jeans and shirt she'd put on one morning that seemed an aeon ago.

'You can go home tomorrow if you wish.' Wasn't that what Azzam had said?

She didn't wish to but she had to go sometime and the way she was feeling, the sooner she made the break, not only from him but from the children and Samarah, the easier it would be.

She *would* go tomorrow...

She put out the jeans and shirt, telling herself she'd leave in her own clothes, set her socks and sneakers beside them, aware how pathetic they looked on the chair in the sumptuous dressing room. She was contemplating a shower when a knock on the bedroom door sent her back in that direction.

Clarice!

'Hi!' she said, breezing in as if they were best of friends. 'Azzam said you're leaving soon so I thought I'd say good-bye and offer a suggestion. I was going to fly home to the States to see my folks tomorrow, but things have changed so the plane is free. I know the pilot well. Shall I let him know you'll go tomorrow? The plane's all fuelled up and the staff on standby so it's a shame not to use it.'

Had Azzam sent her?

Was this what he'd wanted to say but couldn't?

Pain filled Alex's body but there was no way she was going to show it.

'If that suits Azzam and the rest of the family, tomorrow would suit me too,' she said, enunciating each word carefully in case a careless syllable might open the floodgates of her pain.

'I'll arrange it all and send someone to let you know when the car will pick you up,' Clarice told her, smiling brightly as if she'd just accomplished some difficult mission.

Hafa returned as Clarice departed, bringing a tray with juice and fruit on it.

'You must eat something,' she told Alex, and to please her Alex took a piece of melon, but she knew she'd never get it down past the wedge of sadness in her throat.

'I am leaving tomorrow,' she told Hafa, who cried out and waved her hands, chattering half in her native language and half in English, obviously not happy about it.

'I would like to see Samarah before I go. Would it be best now or in the morning, early?'

Hafa frowned then shook her head, finally going across to the phone and phoning someone, talking volubly with much hand-waving.

'Samarah's woman said to come now. They have finished dinner and are having fruit and sweets. You will join them?'

How could she not? Alex thought. Samarah had become a friend.

'I don't think I like goodbyes,' she said to Hafa as the young woman led her to Samarah's rooms. 'I'm not used to them.'

'But you will return,' Hafa said. 'You will want to see the children, and maybe the village when it is rebuilt.'

And risk seeing Azzam?

Risk renewed pain when just maybe some of the wounds she could feel now in her heart were healing over?

'I don't think so,' she said, but so quietly perhaps Hafa didn't hear her.

'There are visitors,' Hafa explained as they entered the big room. 'They came late but will take sweetmeats with us, as will you.'

Hafa led her to what Alex now realised was a privileged position by Samarah's side. Alex sank down onto a cushion, and smiled at the older woman, who was looking so much better since she'd returned home. Except her dark eyes were concerned and worry creased her forehead.

She touched Alex's hand.

'I am sorry you are leaving,' she said quietly. 'Sorry in too many ways to tell you. My son, I think, is making a mistake, but a mother cannot do more than guide her children, she cannot bend them to her will.'

'I am sorry to hear that,' Alex said, giving Samarah's fingers a little squeeze, wondering what Azzam had done to make his mother looked so worried. 'But he is a good son, you know that,' she added, hoping to reassure the woman.

'Yes, perhaps too good,' Samarah said, then to Alex's surprise she leaned forward and pressed a kiss on Alex's cheek. 'We will meet again, my dear,' she said. 'The genie in the lamp has promised me this.'

And reaching into the folds of her tunic, she pulled out the little lamp and handed it to Alex.

'You left it in the colonnade when you played with the children, but I kept it safe for you, as I will keep the children safe. You may be sure of that.'

Tears were brimming in Alex's eyes again, and the lump in her throat now made speech impossible. She gave Samarah's hand one last squeeze, then stood up and moved towards the door, Hafa behind her, chattering about the children, but Alex's head was too full of sadness to hear the words.

After six weeks back at work it seemed to Alex as if she'd never been away. One day slid into the next. She worked night shifts at the hospital, day shifts at the clinic, slowly but steadily reducing Rob's debt.

She hadn't heard from the money-lender so she'd assumed Azzam had been as good as his word and transferred a week's wages into her account to cover the payment that would have been taken out while she was away. One day she'd have to check the figures, so she'd know how much she had in reserve for an emergency, but right now doing anything apart from going to work, doing her job and coming home was beyond her.

She picked up the little lamp and rattled the tears of frankincense she kept inside it, the only tangible reminders of that magical time. She touched the lamp gently, wanting to rub it, to find a genie, to make a wish…

But what wish?

Not money, that was for sure. She'd pay off Rob's debts in time. No, what she'd wish for was impossible, for how could Azzam suddenly appear in her tiny bed-sit?

Yet her hands still held the lamp, feeling its warmth, wondering if wishes might come—

The sharp knock on the door made her drop the precious object, but she caught it before it hit the floor and she put it down safely on the small table before going to see who was there. Working the hours she did, she rarely socialised, and never had visitors, not ashamed of her tiny home but aware that even two people made it feel crowded.

Azzam barged through the door then stared around him in amazement, before turning to stare at her in what looked very like disbelief.

'Why are you living like this?' he demanded, anger she didn't understand written clearly on his usually inscrutable features.

Not that she was understanding much of anything. What was he doing there? How had he found her? What did he want?

Of course she hadn't rubbed the lamp!

'It's my home,' she managed, eventually, but apparently that didn't satisfy him, for he took a turn, three strides, around the small space and faced her again.

'Your home? What are you? Some kind of stoic? Are you doing penance for some unnameable sin? You have a million dollars in the bank and you live like this? Ah, it's that you won't touch my money! That's it, isn't it? Do you feel I did you such wrong you won't accept it from me? Well, let me tell you, *misyar* marriage or not, you were entitled to a dowry! It is *your* money, Alex, not a gift but an official dowry such as is required by law.'

Alex had slumped onto the end of her divan when

he'd mentioned the money in the bank, and her mind had stopped working about then. However, he was looming over her, still angry, but looking down now as if he expected some kind of answer.

There was only one thing she *could* say.

'*What* million dollars?'

Maybe two things.

'*What* bank?'

All that did was make him angrier, for this time he whirled faster in his pacing around the room while she battled the silly delight dancing in her heart at the sight of him.

'You don't know?' he growled as he came past her again. 'Do you never check your account?'

'My bank account?' Alex queried, but faintly, as it was hard to get her brain working on this subject when it was busy trying to stop her heart misbehaving. 'My pay goes into it and my expenses come out of it by automatic transfer. I usually know, maybe not to the cent, about how much I have in there. A couple of hundred dollars for emergencies—I always try to keep that.'

Azzam shook his head. He'd come to ask Alex to marry him—to be his wife forever—but first he'd had to practically force the woman at the clinic where she worked to give him Alex's address, and now he'd walked into a room smaller than his dressing room, to find it was her home. Now she was telling him she tried to keep a couple of hundred dollars in the bank for emergencies. This was poverty…

'You're a doctor, you earn good money, yet you try to keep a couple of hundred dollars in the bank for emergencies. Where does your money go, Alex? What is this obligation you spoke of that forces you to live like this?'

Wrong question and big mistake! Fire flashed in her

pale eyes and she stood up, tall and proud in front of him, confronting him just as she had in the rose garden so long ago.

'That is none of your business,' she said, her small, determined chin tilted towards him, eminently kissable lips right there.

Which was when his anger died away!

'Oh, but it is,' he whispered, and he leaned forward and brushed the lightest of kisses on those irresistible lips. Then, as she'd neither slapped his face, nor moved away, he put his arms around her and tucked her slight body up against his, holding the precious woman he'd so nearly lost close to his heart.

'You see, I love you,' he said, because there didn't seem any other way to say it. 'Love you so much that to walk in here and see you living like this, I was shocked and hurt and angry. And if you want the truth, because I was so uncertain coming here, so afraid I wouldn't find you, or worse, find that you didn't love me, anger took over.'

She squirmed against him and he realised he was holding her far too tightly. He eased his grasp and she looked up at him again.

'Say that last bit again,' she suggested, frowning at him now.

'Which last bit?'

'The bit about being afraid you wouldn't find me, or worse—the bit after "or worse".'

He tried to think what he'd said but the words had come out in such a rush they'd disappeared beyond recall.

'I can't remember.' He was probably frowning right back at her, but over not remembering, nothing to do with her, with Alex, with the woman he loved.

'You said you were afraid I might not love you,' she

reminded him, speaking sternly and adding, 'what makes you think you no longer need to be afraid of that?'

He had to smile.

'Because you're still in my arms? Because I know that when I kiss you properly in a couple of seconds, you're going to kiss me back? Because the love I feel for you is so strong it cannot possibly be one-sided? We are one, Alex, you and I, destined, some would say, to be together.'

Enough of words, his hunger was for her lips.

He bent and kissed her, *properly* this time.

Alex had told herself she wouldn't respond. But only seconds earlier she'd told herself she'd escape from his hold and that hadn't worked either. Now she tried, really tried, to hold the emotions welling up inside her in check, but as his lips moved against hers, questing and exploring, her good intentions vanished and she kissed him back.

Her lips took on a life of their own, demanding and voracious, as all the pent-up love and disappointment, the heartbreak of parting and the joy of seeing him again melded into an inferno of need, transmitting itself to him through something too volcanic and elemental to be called a kiss.

Yet that was all it was. She realised that as they broke apart, silent, breathing deeply, staring at each other. Alex's legs gave way and she sank back down onto the divan, looking up at the man who'd reappeared, like a genie, in her life.

She shook her head but the image didn't go away so she knew he was real. Actually, the taste of him on her tongue and the slight soreness of her lips told her he was real. He crossed the room, two strides, and took her only chair from beside the table, bringing it across to sit in front of her.

'If I sit on that thing you obviously use as a bed, we

won't talk and we need to talk, Alex, both of us. I will start
for I have wronged you in too many ways to count.'

He reached out and took her hand, holding it, as he had
once before, in both of his.

Touched her palm.

'Did you keep my kiss?'

She held out her other hand, fingers curled as if holding
something.

'It's safe in here,' she said, and the smile he gave her,
so full of love, flooded her body with happiness.

'That is good,' he said, serious again, 'for with that kiss
I gave you my heart.'

She could only stare at him, words beyond her. Did he
mean it? Had he loved her back then but not asked her to
stay? What—?

He held up one hand as if he sensed her questions.

'That night, in the colonnade, I came with the intention of asking you to marry me, to stay on in Al Janeen
as my wife—a real wife, not just a *misyar* one. In some
ways I was confused and uncertain about that because the
time had been so short, yet I knew, deep inside me, I had
found a very special love, a love that would not only last
forever but would grow and flourish into something beyond
imagining.'

Alex shook her head. Just so had she begun to feel, although she'd had no idea Azzam had shared those feelings.
Should she tell him? Was it her turn to talk? This was so
unbelievable, sitting here in her tiny bed-sit with a prince
telling her of his love. How had Cinderella managed it?

He touched her lips, telling her he wasn't finished, and
she guessed she wasn't going to enjoy whatever was coming
next.

'Before I could speak to you, Clarice came to me,
she told me she was carrying Bahir's child, and unless I

married her, she would return to America and bring him or her up there. Later, when my mind was less confused, I realised she wanted nothing more than to stay on in Al Janeen, but as the queen she'd always believed she was, not just as Bahir's widow. If you understand families, you will understand I could not let her take Bahir's child to America, to grow up not knowing his or her heritage and people; to grow up perhaps with a stepfather with different values and beliefs, who saw no need to instil the right principles in the child.'

Alex imagined the scenario only too clearly. Hadn't Clarice told her the plane was booked to fly her, Clarice, home to the U.S., taking Bahir's unborn child with her?

'She blackmailed you?'

Azzam shook his head.

'It's an ugly word, Alex, one I doubt you even understand, but in effect that's what it was. She…required, I suppose is the word, that I marry her, even wanted it to be immediately, but I could not marry my brother's widow before the mourning period was over—the very idea was beyond consideration. But I knew I had to save the child—my brother's child—and so I agreed.'

'And now?' Alex prompted. 'What's happened now?'

'She isn't pregnant, never was,' Azzam said bitterly. 'She lied when she first told me, even showed proof with a test stick one of her women friends gave her. Later, when she was still insisting on an immediate marriage, I began to wonder and arranged for her to see an obstetrician and that's when it all came out. But in deceiving me that way, she made me hurt you. That is what angers me most, that she made me cause you pain.'

'Oh, Azzam,' Alex said softly, and she slid off the couch to kneel beside him so she could put her arms around his waist and rest her head against him, knowing words alone wouldn't heal the hurt he was feeling. 'You did what you had to do. Believe me, I know about family.'

He didn't answer for a moment then he tilted her chin so he could look into her face.

'Tell me,' he commanded, and she found herself obeying, telling him of Rob, of his job in the bank, of his need for 'stuff', as she'd always thought of it, and the embezzlement, then his stupidity in thinking he could borrow more to pay it back, her mother's shame and drawn-out death from cancer, and her—Alex's—determination to protect her brother's wife and child from the money-lender and to clear the family name.

'I'm getting there,' she said, 'and I didn't thank you for paying me those wages. I know you must have put the money into my account because the money-lender's bully hasn't been to see me.'

'Wages? You thought all I'd paid you were some piddling wages?'

He seemed angry again.

'Why would you have paid me more? Why would I have expected there to be more?'

Azzam found himself groaning again. How stupid had he been to have even thought of judging this woman by his experience with Clarice?

He stood up, lifted the woman he loved with ease then sat down on the divan with her in his lap.

'Later, you will tell me how we can repay these debts, and maybe make life easier for your sister-in-law and niece, but now I need to apologise to you because right from the beginning I let the past and my experience with Clarice when she first came to Al Janeen influence my judgement of you. Yet that first time I saw you in the rose garden I felt something for you, and afterwards, when I watched the way you helped the children at the earthquake village and held the orphans in your arms, I understood you had that rarest of gifts, a love that reached out to all humanity.'

He kissed her neck, lifting her hair and pressing his lips to the pale skin.

'That's when I fell in love, although maybe I fell a little bit in love in the rose garden when you turned on me with such fierce anger. This is a woman with iron in her soul, I thought, and was intrigued.'

'Iron in my soul?' Alex echoed, but she'd turned her head and was kissing his ear as she spoke, teeth nipping at it. 'I'm not at all sure that's a compliment.'

He moved so their lips met.

'Believe me, it is. My country needs women with iron in their souls as leaders of the community, and I—' he kissed her more firmly '—I need a woman with iron in her soul as my consort, and in my bed as well, and as mother of my children, and grandmother of my grandchildren—'

She broke away.

'The children? I didn't think! I was so surprised to see you my mind went blank. The children are all right? Did anyone find out anything about their father? Is the new oasis dug? Is the village being rebuilt?'

Azzam smiled at her.

'The children are well and happy. The baby is starting to walk around furniture, Zahid's arm is out of the cast, and Tasnim asks me every day when you are coming back. She tells me she is learning English words from Ghaada so she can talk to you. As to the rest, you must come and see for yourself. We cannot marry yet, you and I, because of the mourning period, but you will return with me and we will be together as *misyar* man and wife, then in time we will have a more formal marriage, maybe out beside the lagoon, just you and me, Samarah and Hafa as witnesses, and the children, for they, too, are special to us both.'

Had she rubbed the lamp unintentionally? Or was this real? Alex returned the kisses Azzam was pressing on her lips, but her mind was not on kisses. It was whirling, doing sums—if the million dollars was really hers, she could pay off the debt then buy a house for her sister-in-law and niece, and have plenty left over to invest for her niece's future, enough to pay for any equipment or treatment she might need. And surely she, Alex, could fly them over for a visit, take them to the blushing lagoon and out to the village, show them the desert...

'I've lost you,' Azzam said, straightening up and looking at her with a slightly wary expression on his face.

'It's okay,' she assured him. 'I was just tying off some loose ends in my head. I'm with you now.'

And she kissed him to show that she was.

SIX-WEEK
MARRIAGE
MIRACLE

BY
JESSICA MATTHEWS

MILLS &
BOON®

First published in Great Britain 2011
Harlequin Mills & Boon Limited,
Eton House, 18-24 Paradise Road, Richmond, Surrey TW9 1SR

© Jessica Matthews 2011

ISBN: 978 0 263 88572 9

Harlequin Mills & Boon policy is to use papers that are natural, renewable and recyclable products and made from wood grown in sustainable forests. The logging and manufacturing process conform to the legal environmental regulations of the country of origin.

Printed and bound in Spain
by Litografia Rosés, S.A., Barcelona

"I want us to reverse course. To go back to the way we were. Before everything happened."

"As great as the idea sounds, I don't know if we can," she said honestly. "We aren't the same starry-eyed people we once were, and no amount of magical fairy dust will change us back."

He tugged her arm until she didn't have a choice but to perch on the edge of his bed. "Maybe we aren't the young, naive kids we once were. Maybe the hopes and dreams we once had have died. But that doesn't mean we can't create new ones. Together."

Darn it, but his grip was comforting, and once again his voice was so sincere—so full of faith—that the wall she'd created in her heart to hold back her hurts and disappointments began to crumble. Quickly she struggled to shore up those widening cracks, before emotions overwhelmed her.

Jessica Matthews's interest in medicine began at a young age, and she nourished it with medical stories and hospital-based television programmes. After a stint as a teenage candy-striper, she pursued a career as a clinical laboratory scientist. When not writing or on duty, she fills her day with countless family and school-related activities. Jessica lives in the central United States, with her husband, daughter and son.

Recent titles by the same author:

EMERGENCY: PARENTS NEEDED
THE ROYAL DOCTOR'S BRIDE

Dedication

To Judi Fennell for her Spanish language expertise.
Any errors are my own.

To adoptive and foster parents across the world.
Your generous spirit is truly an inspiration to all of us.

CHAPTER ONE

"ANOTHER ambulance is coming."

Leah Montgomery didn't spare her nursing colleague a glance as she stripped the used hospital sheets from the bed. "Tell me something I don't already know," she said wryly. "The moon was full when we came to work this morning."

Although it wasn't a scientific fact, hospital staff the world over recognized and accepted that full-moon shifts were the proverbial shifts from hell. So far, this was shaping up to be one of them. Everything from car wrecks, heart attacks, lawn mower accidents, and simple sore throats had flooded the Spring Valley ER on this hot August day.

While many of her staff bemoaned the extra workload, she didn't mind the increased pace at all. Being busy kept her mind off things she didn't want to think about—things like her husband's plane crashing in the Mexican jungle a month ago today. Or the report stating that there were no survivors, which meant Gabe was dead.

Dead!

After four painfully long weeks, it still seemed surreal, as if she might wake up some morning and discover she'd simply had a horrible nightmare. To her disappointment, each day was like the one before—the facts hadn't changed overnight. Neither did they change when she worked until she was too exhausted to reflect on the losses in her life.

If her boss would allow it, she'd cover more shifts than her PRN status allowed in order to keep her demons at bay. She was willing to do *anything* to stay busy until time took away the anguish over her last conversation with Gabe—the one where she'd asked to make their separation permanent with a divorce.

Some might call her crazy, others might say she was being silly and sentimental, but the truth was, she was mourning for Gabe on so many levels. Grieving that his vibrant life had been cut short at age thirty-eight; grieving that their marriage had reached an impasse; grieving for the loss of their dreams and missed opportunities. Was it any wonder she needed the fast pace of the hospital, the steady stream of new patients and drama as a life raft she could climb aboard?

"I hear Maternity is swamped," Jane rattled on, blithely unaware of Leah's inattention. "They're so packed with new moms, they're overflowing into the med-surg unit." She unfolded a fresh sheet and began tucking the corners under the mattress.

Leah pictured a nursery filled with bassinets of sleeping babies wearing pink or blue stocking hats, the hallway crowded with beaming fathers and proud grandparents while new mothers, some having already forgotten the pain of childbirth, looked on benevolently. She didn't begrudge the new families their happiness, but a familiar pang of disappointment shot through her chest.

At one time, she'd imagined herself in similar circumstances, with her parents waiting for their first peek at her child while Gabe passed out the bubblegum cigars and strutted as only a new father could. She'd fallen pregnant almost immediately after they'd decided it was time to start their family, making that dream seem like a sure thing and easily within her grasp. In her mind, and Gabe's, the future couldn't have been brighter.

Life, however, had rewritten her beautifully scripted scene.

Instead of joining the ranks of other new mothers, she'd become one of a small percentage of women who became a gynecological emergency. Shortly after entering her last trimester of an unremarkable pregnancy, her placenta had separated without warning. She'd lost the baby as well as her hopes for future children when profuse and unstoppable bleeding had necessitated a hysterectomy. Afterwards, she'd been whisked away to the surgical floor where babies weren't seen or heard.

Her parents had been there for her, of course, but pity, not pride, had shown on their faces. As for Gabe…he'd been on one of his occasional trips for the Montgomery family's medical foundation. He'd come as soon as her parents had called him, but time zones and flight schedules had prevented his return until the day she was ready to be released.

"I just love to stop and peek at the newborns," Jane gushed. "They have such cute little wrinkled faces." Suddenly, she stopped short. "Oh, Leah. Here I am, babbling on so insensitively about babies after everything you've been through. First a miscarriage, then the adoption fiasco—"

Leah cut off her friend's reminder of their failed foray into the world of adoption. After her surgery, still hazy from the grief of her loss, Gabe had convinced her to think about adoption and then so many things had fallen into place with amazing speed—Gabe's lawyer had known a young woman who'd wanted to relinquish her baby. They'd hurriedly filled out the necessary paperwork and completed the required governmental home studies and background checks. The entire time the birth mother had been adamant about her choice—she was making the right decision for both her and her unborn child. Yet when the hour arrived for Leah and Gabe to pick up the baby from the hospital, the young woman had changed her mind and Leah had once again driven home empty-handed.

Leah couldn't fault the girl for her change of heart—it had to be difficult to relinquish one's child, especially after seeing that tiny person for the first time—but understanding didn't take away her gut-wrenching disappointment.

"It's okay," she lied. "I don't fall apart just because someone talks about babies or mentions how cute they are."

Admittedly, they were, but seeing those adorable little faces was tough, which was why she never, *ever*, entered the secured area to stare at them through the plate-glass window. Why add insult to injury? she'd rationalized.

"I know, but—"

"It's okay," Leah repeated, as much for her own benefit as Jane's. "Honestly."

Jane nodded, but the worried wrinkle between her eyes suggested her good-mood bubble had burst. Determined to regain their easy footing, Leah thought it best to gently steer the conversation in another direction, for both their sakes.

"OB isn't the only busy department in this place," she commented as she tucked a fitted sheet around a corner of the mattress. "Our daily patient census is above average across the entire hospital and we both know our ED visit numbers are up, too. The extra business should make the bean counters happy."

"Maybe this year we'll get a Christmas bonus for a job well done," Jane responded hopefully.

Word from the last supervisors' meeting was that the

possibility was remote, but Leah wasn't going to rain on Jane's picnic. "Maybe, but, bonus or not, more patients means more nursing staff are necessary, which means I work more often."

Jane paused from working on her own two bed corners. "Look, hon," she said kindly. "I know you're probably feeling guilty because you'd never resolved your differences with Gabe, but killing yourself now that he's gone, working sixty-plus hours a week, isn't the way to cope."

"I'm not killing myself," Leah protested mildly, pointedly ignoring Jane's opinion about her reasons for the pace she'd set for herself. "I'm merely keeping busy. Just like I have for the past year."

"Keeping busy is one thing. Doubling your hours is another."

"Okay, so I am working a few more hours," Leah conceded reluctantly, "but I was off duty yesterday and I spent the day puttering around the house. And then I treated myself to dinner and a movie."

"Dinner *and* a movie?" Jane's eyes brimmed with curiosity. "Did you *finally* put Jeff out of his misery and go on a *date*?"

About six months ago, Dr. Jeff Warren, one of Spring Valley's ED physicians, had invited her to a concert, then a community theater play. Both times she'd declined, not because she didn't enjoy his company or didn't want to attend those particular events. No, she'd gently refused his invitation because in spite of being separated from her husband of ten years, going out with another man while she was still officially married made her feel as if she was cheating.

Which was why she'd wanted Gabe's signature on those divorce papers. It was past time to stop expecting a miracle and start thinking about the future—*her* future—instead of the past. As it had turned out, she didn't need his signature after all.

Leah shot her friend a spare-me look. "Are you kidding?" she asked. "I haven't even buried Gabe and you're asking if I'm seeing Jeff?"

"Buried or not, you've been separated for over a year," Jane reminded her. "It's time to move on."

"I will," Leah promised. "But I can't until I've dotted all my 'i's and crossed all the 't's."

Jane rolled her eyes. "What's left to dot and cross? From what you've said, his body may never come home."

How well she knew that. The Mexican authorities had reported the discovery of the airplane's charred remains in a ravine. They lacked the resources to recover the bodies and in their bureaucratic minds the burned-out shell of the aircraft made it pointless to do so. Undaunted, and after greasing palms for several weeks, Gabe's second-in-command Sheldon Redfern had received permission to send in a private recovery team. As of yesterday, they hadn't reported any more encouraging news than what the authorities had already shared.

Their success, however, wasn't the reason she was dragging her feet…

"The annual foundation fund-raiser is coming up in a few months," she pointed out. "It seems tacky to plan a tribute to my deceased husband while I'm dating someone else." Their relationship may have been rocky the last two years and she might be finally ready to look for male companionship and find romance again, but in honor of the good times and the love they'd once shared, she owed it to Gabe to wait.

"Did you tell that to Jeff?"

She nodded, remembering their conversation. He'd been so understanding, which not only came as a relief but also endeared him to her all the more. "He's agreed to give me time," she said, deciding not to mention that she'd set their first official date for the Saturday night after the fundraiser. If Jane knew that, she'd be bouncing off the walls with excitement and Leah didn't want to see her sly smiles and winks in the meantime.

Jane stared at her thoughtfully. "Personally, I think you're worried too much about what other people think, but another month or two won't make much difference. Just be sure your decision to stay out of the dating game is based on the right reasons."

"What other reason could I have?"

Jane shrugged. "Oh, I don't know. Maybe that you still love Gabe and are waiting for the ultimate proof that he won't be coming back."

"Don't be ridiculous." She avoided her friend's gaze because she didn't want Jane to recognize what she herself refused to dwell on or admit. "If I loved him, why would I have moved out?"

"You tell me. I just don't want you to be stuck on hold for the rest of your life."

"I'm not," Leah insisted. "I'm merely being cautious. There's no sense rushing into something I might come to regret." She grabbed a fresh cotton blanket and shook it out of its folds with a decisive snap, effectively signaling an end to their conversation. "Do you know what's coming in next?"

Jane shook her head. "All I heard was that they were bringing in three from the airport."

"*The airport?*" She considered for a moment. "Bigwigs, no doubt."

"What makes you say that?"

"It's probably food related and the only folks who get

food on a plane are seated in first class. And who usually can afford to sit in first class?"

"Ah." Jane's eyes gleamed. "Bigwigs."

"Exactly."

"You're stereotyping, you know. Regular people buy first-class tickets, too."

Leah flashed her a wide smile. "Okay, so I'm generalizing but, mark my words, it won't be three average Joes who roll into our ambulance bay. They'll be fellows wearing suits and ties, carrying briefcases and BlackBerrys, and wanting a magic pill to fix whatever ails them. Oh, and can we hurry because they're already late for a meeting."

Jane laughed, probably because Leah's scenario had actually taken place often enough to become a legend in the ER. "We'll find out if you're right in about three minutes. Marge wants us to be on the dock, ready to go."

As the emergency department's nurse manager, Marge Pennington was a person who believed in keeping busy every minute, so it seemed odd she would ask them to waste time waiting. Her request only seemed to substantiate Leah's prediction of several Very Important People arriving on this transport.

"Far be it from me to argue," she said, although it bothered her to think Marge was willing to discard her normal habits in order to impress people with money. Having married into a family with the Midas touch, Leah had always been leery of people who didn't treat her as they would anyone else.

"According to her, the person radioing in specifically asked for you."

Leah's eyes widened. "Me? Why me?"

Jane shrugged. "Maybe it's someone you know from Gabe's trust organization."

Leah mentally ran through her list of regularly

generous contributors to the Montgomery Medical Charitable Foundation. As chairwoman of the annual fund-raising ball, which would take place in six weeks, she was acquainted with nearly all of the supporters, but none knew she worked in the Spring Valley Hospital Emergency Department.

"Impossible," she said.

Jane shrugged. "Who knows? In any case, I'm only following Marge's orders and if you know what's good for you, you will, too."

Marge wasn't the easiest charge nurse to work for, but she was a model of efficiency and a brilliant nurse. No one, not even the hospital's CEO, crossed her when she was in battle mode.

Leah gave the bed a final pat, pleased with their results. "Okay, then. Let's go. I can use a few minutes of fresh air while we're waiting." She grinned. "Just think, we might even get to sit and rest our weary feet."

Outside, Leah did exactly as she'd hoped to. Ignoring Jane and the two extra staff who'd joined them with wheelchairs and an extra stretcher, she sat on the concrete loading dock and dangled her legs over the edge as she breathed in the fresh air and soaked up the heat.

If only the summer sun would chase away the coldness inside her—the same coldness that had settled into every cell, the same coldness that had taken hold ever since she'd realized Gabe's plane had gone down with her request for a divorce ringing in his ears.

She'd agonized for weeks over taking their separation to its logical conclusion before she'd contacted a lawyer, but they'd lived apart for nearly a year. After the adoption had fallen through, they'd simply shut down. It was understandable, she supposed. They'd been obsessed with the baby when she'd been pregnant, and then they'd focused exclusively on adopting a child. Their marriage had been so driven toward that end goal that their sudden failure had simply sidelined their relationship.

Consequently they'd drifted apart until the only solution had been to ask for a change of scenery. She'd wanted time and space to redefine what she wanted out of life and, more importantly, she wanted Gabe to have the same.

A year later, she'd finally faced the facts. Remaining in their legal limbo wasn't doing either of them any favors. They both needed the freedom to pursue their dreams—she wanted companionship and Gabe wanted a family. Although she hated the idea of Gabe finding a woman who could give him what she couldn't, it had seemed silly, selfish and almost spiteful to keep him from his heart's desire. With the stroke of a judge's pen, they would end their estranged state and could move on with their lives. To start over, as it were.

In the end, her altruistic decision had been wasted. Fate had stepped in and had the last laugh at their expense before he could sign the papers dissolving their marriage. Before he'd created the family he'd always wanted.

Since then, she'd told herself on a daily basis to stop beating herself over everything from procrastinating to her bad timing. After all, divorced or widowed, she was still alone.

Alone or not, though, it pained her to imagine what final thoughts had run through Gabe's head. No doubt his last one of her had involved the unpleasant scene when she'd asked for a divorce. Some would say she was being too hard on herself. Others would say she was worrying over nothing. After all, if she wanted to completely sever their matrimonial ties, why did she care what his last thoughts of her had been?

In one corner of her heart, she'd wanted Gabe to realize their marriage needed as much attention as he gave his family's charitable foundation, but if he'd entertained any regrets during his final moments, she'd never know. Chances were, she repeated to herself for the millionth time, he hadn't thought of her at all…

Jane straightened, her gaze riveted in the distance. "Looks like they're about two blocks away." She glanced at her watch. "Right on time, too."

Leah slowly got to her feet then brushed the seat of her scrub pants. "I wish we knew what we were getting," she fretted.

"We'll find out soon enough."

A black Lexus squealed to an abrupt stop in the aisle of the parking lot. Apparently the driver didn't care about the traffic snarl he'd created.

"Security is going to eat him alive," Leah commented.

"Maybe you should tell him."

The ambulance pulled in and began backing up to the dock, its warning beeps intermingling with the other city noises. "He'll have to take his chances," Leah said. "We have things to do and people to see."

As the ambulance inched backwards, Leah heard someone call her name. A familiar figure, Sheldon Redfern had jumped out of the Lexus and was running toward her.

"Leah," he panted. "Wait!"

"Sheldon, what are you doing here?" she asked, amazed to see him.

"I have to tell you—"

The ambulance braked. "Save it for later," she ordered. "I'm busy right now."

"This can't wait."

He grabbed her arm at the same time she saw Jane twisting the handle to open the back door. "Sheldon," she protested. "I have work to do."

"Leah," he urged. "It's about Gabe and the search team we sent."

Instinctively, her heart sank. Sheldon's eagerness to contact her only meant one thing.

"They finally located his remains," she said dully, feeling her chest tighten and a painful knot clog her throat as her eyes dimmed with sudden tears. For all the problems they'd had, she hadn't wanted anything so drastic and so *final* to happen to him. Yes, a divorce was like a death—the death of a marriage—but part of her consolation had been that they each would carry on and eventually find the happiness they couldn't find with each other.

Unfortunately, Sheldon's announcement had irrevocably destroyed that thin hope. Why had he felt compelled to deliver the news now, *at this very moment*, with patients breathing down her neck, when she wasn't mentally prepared to deal with the finality of the situation?

"No," Sheldon corrected in her ear.

"No?" She stared at him in surprise.

"What he's trying to say unsuccessfully is that they found *us*." Sheldon's voice suddenly sounded closer…and deeper…and more like…Gabe's.

And it was coming from inside the ambulance.

She focused in that direction, ignoring the paramedic to glance at the human cargo—two men and a woman. They looked tired and dirty in clothing that was tattered and torn, but broad smiles shone on their faces. An uncanny sense of familiarity struck her.

In spite of their gaunt and disreputable appearance, she *knew* all three. Yet her brain couldn't reconcile what she was seeing with what she'd been told.

She homed in on the man who'd spoken. He was just as dirty as the other two and equally as disheveled. His right pants leg had been cut open at some point but in spite of being tied closed with strips of gauze, she glimpsed a white bandage circling his shin. A splint encased his left forearm and another bandage was visible above the open neck of his torn shirt. But there was no denying that this man was Gabe.

"I tried calling you all morning," Sheldon babbled in the background as the identities of Gabe's colleagues—Jack Kasold and Theresa Hernandez—registered before they stepped onto the concrete. "You never answered my messages."

The pink scraps of paper tucked in her tunic pocket suddenly weighed like the proverbial ton of bricks. She'd ignored them when she'd seen who'd phoned because she'd assumed he simply wanted to hash out more details for the foundation's upcoming charity ball. Apparently, she'd been wrong.

"I was going to call you during my break," she said numbly as she looked past all the people to study her husband once again.

Tape bisected his forehead, his beard was scruffy, his hair shaggy, and lines of apparent pain bracketed his full mouth, but his midnight-black eyes were so familiar.

Could it be true? Really *true*? Her heart skipped a beat as she feared she might be hallucinating and hoped she was not.

"Gabe?" she finally asked, aware of how thin and reedy her voice sounded.

He stepped out of the ambulance, balancing himself on one crutch. His reassuring smile was one she'd seen before—the same one that belonged to the man she'd married when their future had been bright and it had seemed as if nothing could stop them from living their dreams.

"Hi, honey. I'm home."

CHAPTER TWO

UNCERTAIN of the reception he'd receive when he finally saw Leah again, Gabriel's tension had escalated with each mile closer to his destination. Considering how Sheldon hadn't been able to reach her all morning, Gabe had expected her to be surprised and shocked by his astonishing return and she didn't disappoint him.

"Gabe?" she whispered in that soft voice he remembered so vividly. "Is it really *you*?"

He met her gaze and offered a rueful smile. "A little the worse for wear but, yes, it is."

"Oh, my." She covered her mouth with both hands. Suddenly, she turned pale and a dazed look came to her eyes.

She was going to faint. Cursing because he wasn't in a position to catch her himself, he roared, "Sheldon!"

Fortunately, his second-in-command was beside her and grabbed her arm. At the same time the paramedic did the same. For an instant she sagged, then straightened and shrugged off the two men's hold.

"I'm okay," she insisted, losing a bit of her deer-caught-in-the-headlights look.

"Are you sure?" The paramedic didn't sound convinced as he eyed her closely.

"I'm fine. Really."

Of course she was, Gabe thought wryly. Leah thrived on her ability to handle anything and everything by herself, without help from anyone. In fact, at times he'd felt rather superfluous in their marriage, but he intended to change all that.

"Truly," she insisted, tentatively reaching toward him.

Eager to touch her and prove just how wrong the reports of his death had been, as well as to reassure himself that he was truly home, Gabe grabbed her hand.

Her skin was soft and warm and soothingly familiar. Oh, how he'd missed her!

Before he could say a word, before he could do anything but entwine his fingers with hers, she flung herself against him and buried her face in his shoulder.

His crutch clattered to the concrete and his ribs protested, but having her in his arms where she belonged was worth the pain. When his plane had landed and Leah hadn't been standing with Jack's and Theresa's elated families on the tarmac, he'd been so afraid…but this was the response he'd dreamed of and hoped for every night they'd been lost in the jungle.

The coldness of despair, the survivor's guilt, and the soul-racking regret that he'd labored under for weeks now began to diminish until he slowly felt warm from the inside out.

His wife's fresh, clean scent filled his nostrils and reminded him of how desperately he needed soap and water. If he'd been thinking properly, he might have asked Sheldon to detour to his corporate offices where he could have made use of the executive washroom, but he'd been too eager to see Leah to consider it. Quite frankly, though, with his stiff shoulder and the slow-healing gash on his leg, he wasn't sure he could manage the feat on his own, anyway.

He gripped her with his good arm, feeling her slight

frame shake beneath his hand. As her tears soaked his shirt, his throat tightened and his eyes burned with more emotion than he could begin to describe.

"Oh, honey. Don't cry," he said hoarsely, relieved by her reception and grateful the paramedics and ER staff were giving them a few minutes before they whisked him away.

"I'm not," she sniffed, swiping at the moisture on her cheeks as she stared at him. "Oh, Gabe. I can't believe it."

As he gazed at her, one thought ran through his mind. She was beautiful—more beautiful than the picture he'd slipped out of his wallet and stuck in his shirt pocket shortly after they'd crashed. The photo was now dog-eared and a little dirty, but her image had given him the incentive to keep going when he'd sworn he couldn't hobble another step.

"I can't quite believe it, either," he said ruefully. As far as he was concerned, this was a dream come true. A bona fide miracle.

More importantly, it was a miracle he wasn't going to let slip through his fingers.

"What happened?" she asked.

"It's a long story." Rather than dwell on that fateful day and the events leading up to it, he drank in everything about her, from her acorn-colored hair and eyes that reminded him of the Grand Canyon's various shades of brown to her retroussé nose and sensual mouth. She'd lost weight, too, if his hands hadn't deceived him.

The paramedic stepped close to interrupt. "I don't mean to cut short your reunion, Dr. Montgomery, but let's get you inside before you fall."

Whether she suddenly realized how heavily he was lean-ing against her or the paramedic's statement had reminded her of his injuries, his prim and proper wife—and she still *was* his wife, even if they'd lived apart for the last twelve months—unwrapped herself from him and took his good arm. Although he missed her embrace, he was glad she hadn't completely turned him loose. Granted, she'd fallen back into nurse mode, but he wanted to believe she needed the contact as much as he did to reassure herself that he was, indeed, alive and well.

Maybe not "well", he corrected as he lowered himself into a hastily provided wheelchair, but his aches and pains now seemed inconsequential. For the past month he'd fought his fears of failure—fears that the feelings she'd once had for him were gone—but he took heart that she hadn't rejected him. In the nightmares that had often startled him awake, he'd dreamt she'd take one look at him and walk away. Thankfully, none of those painfully vivid dreams had come true.

They still had issues to resolve but he was cautiously optimistic about success. If he played his cards right—and he intended to because he'd had a month to plan a strategy— there wouldn't be any more talk of a divorce. Fate had given him a second chance to correct his mistakes and undo the past. He would not fail.

Leah wanted to ask a hundred questions, but Gabe's slumped shoulders as she walked beside his wheelchair told her how exhausted he was. In all the years she'd known him, she'd never seen him so drained, even during his residency when forty-eight-hour shifts had been the norm. There would be plenty of time to hear his story after his medical needs were addressed—starting with how he'd survived a supposedly fatal accident.

It wasn't until he'd gingerly moved from his wheelchair to the bed with her help and that of a paramedic that she realized the awkwardness of the situation. As a nurse she belonged in the room, but as his estranged wife she certainly didn't. Unfortunately, by the time she'd come to that conclusion, the other nurses had already disappeared into their respective patients' rooms, leaving her no choice but to continue. Asking for a reassignment now would only draw unwanted and unnecessary attention. As soon as word leaked of Gabe's return, speculation would run rampant anyway.

In spite of resigning herself to her temporary fate, her awkwardness grew exponentially as Jeff Warren took that moment to walk into the room. The normally implacable blond physician stopped abruptly in his tracks, as if he hadn't realized the identity of his patient until now. Immediately, he glanced back at Leah and she shrugged helplessly, realizing that this moment was as uncomfortable for him as it was for her. The only difference was Jeff seemed to recover more quickly from his surprise than she had.

"Gabe," he said, reaching out to shake his hand. "Welcome back."

"Thanks. It's great to be home."

"I'll do my best to get you there," Jeff promised. "Let's have a look at what you've done to yourself, shall we?"

Leah had planned to act as usual, giving Gabe the same objective care she'd give any other patient. However, that was easier said than done. The minute he shrugged off his tattered shirt, she saw the physical evidence of what he'd endured. His bones stood out in stark relief to the scabbed-over scrapes and large, brilliantly colored patches of purple, yellow and green that dotted his skin, while other areas were rubbed raw.

"Oh, Gabe," she breathed.

"It looks worse than it is," he assured her.

Objectively speaking, he was probably right, but through the eyes of someone who'd once carefully and lovingly mapped every inch of his six-foot body, she wasn't as certain. It became far too easy to imagine how he'd earned each scrape and each bruise and then marvel at how he'd endured the trauma and still returned home. His obvious weight loss made her wonder what he'd eaten, if anything, which was another facet of his ordeal she hadn't considered until now.

Part of her wanted to hug him again, to erase those physical hurts with a soft and gentle touch. The other part of her wanted to rail at him, ask if his injuries had been worth those extra duties he'd assumed and the additional trips he'd taken on behalf of his family's charitable organization.

More importantly, though, she wanted to lock herself in the restroom so she could cry because, however illogical it seemed, she somehow felt responsible—not for the crash itself, or even for this particularly fateful international jaunt, but for sending him into the ever-eager arms of the Montgomery Medical Foundation. Had she not rejected his comfort after their adoption had fallen through, he wouldn't have found his purpose in his work. With the schedule he'd set for himself, both before their separation and after, it was almost amazing that disaster hadn't struck before now.

Regardless of where she laid blame or how she took responsibility, what mattered most for now was the state of Gabe's health, not rehashing the mistakes or hurts of the past.

"Leah?"

Hearing her name, she pulled her thoughts together and met Jeff's questioning gaze. He was obviously reading more into her inattentiveness than she wanted.

"Maybe you should take a break," he suggested softly.

She was tempted to take his advice, but she'd never

deserted a patient before and she wouldn't start now. She shook her head and squared her shoulders. "I'm fine. Really."

Jeff simply shrugged, then listened to Gabe's chest sounds as he spoke. "You still have some nasty injuries. What did you do? Hit every tree in the jungle?"

"It seemed like it," Gabe mentioned ruefully. "I picked up about half of my bruises and bumps during the crash. Splitting my leg open came later."

"What happened?"

"In regard to my leg or the crash itself?"

"Both."

Curious about the details surrounding his experience, Leah listened closely.

"Minutes before we crashed, there was a thump, then an engine sputtered, and Ramon yelled something about birds. The next thing I knew, we were going down." He paused. "When it was all over, I had a dislocated shoulder and a bad wrist. Jack relocated the bone and immobilized my arm with the supplies out of our first-aid kit. Then we went to find help."

Leah tried not to imagine the pain he must have endured while Jack had worked on his shoulder without any anesthetic. As an internist, Jack's basic orthopedic skills were no doubt rusty, but he would have had to proceed because the potential complications like a lack of blood supply and damaged nerves were too serious to ignore. As she surreptitiously studied Gabe's fingers, the pink skin color and lack of swelling were reassuring signs of his success.

"Needless to say, it took us a while to find another human being," he added wryly, "although, technically, a few locals found us when they stumbled across our path. We stayed in their village overnight but before they took us to the next town, the search team had tracked us there. And here we are."

"You're lucky they found you at all," Leah interjected. "We were told you were dead." Thank goodness Sheldon had persisted with cutting through the red tape to send in their own team. If they'd accepted the official verdict and let matters lie… the idea of Gabe and his colleagues still wandering through the jungle sent a chill down her spine.

"I'm not surprised the authorities assumed the worst," Gabe said, his voice pained. "We'd stopped inches away from a ravine and thought we were on safe ground. Not long afterwards, the ground gave way and the plane slid over the edge. On its way down, the fuel tanks blew."

Mentally picturing the scene, Leah shuddered as her grip tightened on the blood-pressure cuff she was still holding.

"You three are celebrities now," Jeff remarked. "Not many people walk away from an experience like that."

Gabe's face became stoic, his expression shuttered. "Two of my group didn't."

"Who?" she asked, hating it that not everyone associated with Montgomery Medical would have a happy ending.

"Will. Will Henderson, and Ramon."

Will was an information technology guru Gabe had hired about eighteen months ago to facilitate the internet connections between remote medical clinics and hospitals to specialists at centers like Spring Valley. Leah had met him a few times but had never had any dealings with him.

Ramon Diaz, however, was a man she knew quite well. As the first pilot Gabe had ever hired and the organization's most senior pilot, Ramon had usually taken charge of Gabe's flights. He'd also begun dating Theresa, one of the foundation's nurses, right before Leah and Gabe had split up, and had recently proposed to her. No doubt they'd both been thrilled to go on this trip together. How sad it had ended so horribly.

"Oh, Gabe," she breathed, knowing how the loss of two people who had been more friends than employees must weigh heavily on him. She dropped the cuff and clutched his hand in sympathy. "Did they…suffer?"

"Will didn't. He died in the crash. Ramon…died later."

Gabe's tight-lipped expression suggested there was a lot more to his story, but she didn't press for details. "I'm sorry, both for you and the company. Theresa must be devastated."

"She's having a tough time," Gabe agreed.

Making a mental note to visit with Theresa as soon as she was able, Leah watched as Jeff unwrapped the bandage around Gabe's leg. The gash was red and swollen, but didn't look nearly as bad as Leah had anticipated.

"I've seen worse," the doctor remarked, apparently agreeing with her opinion. "How long ago did this happen?"

"About ten days. I slid down a hill and bumped into a few rocks along the way. One of them sliced my skin."

"Then it definitely isn't healing as fast as I'd like."

"We cleaned it as best we could but, as you can see, our topical ointment couldn't quite do the job." Gabe winced as his colleague probed the area and his grip on her hand tightened. "Sutures might have helped, but those weren't available, either."

Leah wasn't fooled by his innocent tone or his condensed version of events. He could probably talk for hours about their struggle for the things she took for granted—food, water, protection from the elements and safety from predators. And he'd definitely had a difficult time because his clothing appeared as if he'd walked through a shredder.

As for his injuries, he'd made them sound as if they were nothing more than minor inconveniences when they were visible proof of his harrowing ordeal. Cracked ribs and a dislocated shoulder were painful under ideal conditions and to "slide down a hill and bump into a few rocks" before they'd healed would have been agony. If the truth were known, it wouldn't surprise her to learn that his so-called "hill" could probably compete with Pikes Peak and his "few rocks" had probably been boulders.

She wanted to throttle him for acting as if his stint in the jungle had been as easy and effortless as a Sunday stroll through the city park. Making a big deal out of bumps and bruises, gashes and cracked bones went against his macho grain, even if he was speaking to a physician who recognized what it took to create this degree of damage. There were two females in the room, too, and it wouldn't do to appear weak in front of them. In essence, it was a guy thing—part of that caveman, show-the-woman-who's-strongest mentality.

It was also a Gabe thing. He'd always tried his best to insulate her from the harsh realities of life instead of treating her as a partner in the challenges they faced—and they'd had a number of personal difficulties and tragedies to contend with. Obviously, he still pictured her as being too weak to face the truth. While some women might appreciate being treated like a Fabergé egg, she wasn't one of them. After ten years of marriage, Gabe should have learned that, but he hadn't.

As soon as she recognized the familiar resentment building inside her, she wondered why her former frustrations were rearing their heads again. She should be elated Gabe was home safe and more or less sound and not dredging up old complaints. Her only excuse was that she could finally give herself permission to be angry about his decision to take this flight in the first place.

Yet, however one might psychoanalyze her reaction, Gabe's return didn't wipe their slate of problems clean. They still had to be addressed in some manner and the easiest and most expedient method was to get his signature on those divorce documents, wherever they currently were.

Realizing her fingers were still entwined with his, she pulled her hand free.

Jeff's gaze was speculative as he glanced at her. He'd clearly noticed how her touch had lingered longer than was actually necessary, but he didn't comment. Instead, he finished his exam and tucked his stethoscope back into his pocket with deliberate movements.

"All things considered," he said, "you're not in too bad a shape." He paused ever so slightly as his gaze slid sideways to Leah and then back to Gabe. "You're a lucky fellow in more ways than one."

"You don't have to remind me," Gabe answered fervently.

A meaningful note in his tone made Leah question if the two men were discussing Gabe's health or if this was some sort of private male discussion, but before she could wade into the conversation, Jeff fell back into his professional mode.

"You've probably diagnosed yourself, but I want X-rays to check your ribs and your arm as well as basic bloodwork and cultures. To be honest, I'm not happy with the way your leg is healing, so prepare yourself for a few rounds of IV antibiotics." He glanced at Leah. "I want those started immediately."

Considering the state of Gabe's leg, Jeff's treatment plan was not only sound, it was necessary to stop the infection from turning septic. Without a word, she began pulling the appropriate IV supplies from the cabinet.

Gabe sighed audibly, as if he also knew the IV was necessary but wasn't particularly happy about it. "I'd expected as much."

"I'm glad we agree. After I see the films and lab results, we'll talk again."

"Any chance I can shower in the doctors' lounge before you run me through the testing mill?" Gabe's expression was hopeful. He might be the full-time CEO of the Montgomery Medical Foundation but he was also a member of the surgical staff at Spring Valley Memorial and, as such, he filled in a few nights a month and the occasional weekend when the regular surgeons took time off.

"Of course," Jeff agreed, "but if we delay your tests, we also delay your treatment. So let's do the cultures, blood samples and X-rays first, then by the time you finish your shower, we'll have answers and can decide what comes next."

Knowing how Gabe hated to compromise, Leah expected him to argue, but to her surprise, he didn't. "Okay. If it means I'll get out of here sooner, we'll do it your way."

Jeff grinned. "I'm glad to hear it. While you're stuck in Radiology, I'll see about arranging for first-class bathroom accommodations." He turned to Leah. "He's all yours for now."

It was a throw-away statement, a figure of speech, but she wondered if his qualifier referred to tending Gabe's injuries or if it had more personal overtones. Because it was far easier to fall back on the comforting routine of following a doctor's orders, she did so, determined to leave the soul-searching for later when her mind had stopped reeling.

Thank goodness experience allowed her to perform her tasks without thinking as she still considered Gabe's return as nothing short of miraculous. Thankfully, and perhaps Jeff had alerted Marge to the situation, Jane came in to help.

"Stay," Gabe said when Leah tried to escape, and so she did, but by the time he'd finished the lab draws and X-rays, his face was white and pinched with pain. Clearly, he was in desperate need of rest.

"I think the shower should wait," she began.

His jaw squared. "No way."

"Not even until you've napped a few hours?"

"Not even then."

Seeing how unsteady he was on his feet, she offered, "How about a sponge bath instead?"

His eyes lit with an unholy gleam before it faded. "As intriguing as that sounds, I want a shower that lasts until I empty the hot water tanks. I *need* a shower because I'm tired of smelling myself."

"You smell fresher than some patients who've walked through our doors," she replied.

"Too bad. I know what I want and I want water. Gallons and gallons of it."

"But you can hardly—"

His gaze was determined. "Trust me. I can and *will* do whatever I have to."

She wanted him to be reasonable and take her advice, but if he'd found the fortitude to survive the jungle, he'd find the energy reserves to shower. However, as both his nurse and his wife, she'd watch to ensure he didn't over-extend himself.

"You always were stubborn," she remarked.

He nodded. "I'll take that as a compliment."

"Well, hang tight while I see what I can arrange."

After a short consultation in the hallway where she couldn't speak privately to Jeff because Jane was part of their group, Leah wheeled Gabe to the nearby med-surg wing and into a patient room. She expected him to protest at the obvious implication, but he was too intent on his prize and didn't.

While he brushed his teeth with the spare toiletry kit she'd commandeered from their supply cabinet, she located towels and soap so he could finally indulge in his much-wanted and much-needed shower in the wheelchair-accessible bathroom.

After removing his splint—the X-ray had shown the bones in his arm and shoulder weren't broken—she covered his IV site with plastic so it wouldn't get wet.

"I'll be out here if you need me," she told him. "Be careful with your leg and when you're finished, I'll dress it."

While he hobbled into the shower, she turned down his bed and double-checked the medications that Jane had delivered. When she had everything in place except for her patient, she returned to the bathroom and stood in the doorway.

"How are you doing in there?" She raised her voice over the rushing water, noting he'd had at least a seven-minute shower.

"Fine." A groan came from behind the curtain.

That didn't sound good. Instantly worried, she straightened, ready to invade his privacy. "Are you okay?"

"Yeah. God, this feels so good."

The awe in his voice reminded her of other times when he'd said the same, under more intimate circumstances. She quickly stuffed those thoughts inside her mental box labeled "to be opened at a later date". "I'm sure it does, but Jeff wants those antibiotics started ASAP."

"Just a few more minutes."

"The shower will still be here, waiting for you, tomorrow," she coaxed.

"I know, but five more minutes. Please."

It seemed cruel to deny him this simple pleasure when those extra minutes probably wouldn't affect his treatment outcome. "Okay, but I'm timing you."

"You're the boss."

If that were only true.

"I'd get done faster if you scrubbed my back for me," he added.

He sounded so hopeful and so like the old Gabe—the Gabe before their lives had drifted apart—that she flashed back to those happier times when they *had* shared a shower. The memory of the subsequent lovemaking burst into her head, but it was more than simple recall. She replayed how it had *felt*—from the sensation of his rough skin against hers, the tickle of his breath and his lips on sensitive areas, his clean, sandalwood scent teasing her nose.

His suggestion was so very tempting…especially when she reflected on their stolen moments during the early days of their relationship. In his position as a surgical resident and hers as a newly minted ED nurse, as long as a deadbolt guarded their privacy, they'd been happy.

Unfortunately, they didn't have a locked door and Gabe had become a celebrity, which meant privacy was impossible. Although those details didn't present an insurmountable problem, making love at this point implied that their personal life was fine and dandy.

And it wasn't.

"Not a good idea," she pointed out.

"Why not?"

"You mean, other than that you're barely able to stand?"

"Yeah."

"This place will be like Grand Central Station before

long," she reminded him. "Everyone wants to drop by and give you a personal welcome."

"They can wait. Besides, people will understand if we have a quiet, intimate reunion. They're probably expecting it, which means no one will interrupt us unless there's a fire."

The sad fact was he was probably right. Most people knew they were separated, but no one, other than Jane, knew the D-word had been floated between them. Everyone loved a happy ending, which meant everyone would speculate—if not hope—that Gabe's return would be the turning point in their relationship. Perhaps under other circumstances, it would have been, but their differences were more deep-seated than a conversation or a few promises could fix.

"They can expect all they want, but it isn't going to happen."

His sigh was audible. "I suppose not, but I really would like you to wash my back. I can't reach."

Instantly, she felt ashamed for not realizing how his bruised ribs and stiff shoulder made his request completely valid. Irritated at herself for jumping to the wrong con-clusion, she shoved the curtain aside to see her dripping husband struggling to touch those hard-to-reach places.

"Turn around," she ordered, determined to handle her task with clinical detachment. Yet, as she ignored the spray of water on her scrub suit to run a soapy washcloth down his spine and over the lean muscles of his back before moving around to his front, her concern over what he'd endured grew. This wasn't the body of the man she'd last seen a month ago. Oh, the birthmark in the small of his back was the same, as was the general shape of his torso, but while he'd once reminded her of a lean mountain lion with rock-hard muscles and sinew, now he resembled a starving wolf.

"If you keep that up," he said dryly, "our private reunion will be extremely one-sided."

Realizing she'd come dangerously close to an area of his body where she hadn't intended to go, she froze.

"Although," he added softly, "there's always later."

The promise in his voice sent an unexpected tingle through her body but, then, a mere glance, a simple touch, or a softly spoken word from Gabe had always carried enough power to melt her into a puddle. What truly surprised her was how she could respond so easily in spite of the issues that had driven them apart. Was she so starved for attention and affection that when he showered her with both, she would greedily accept it?

Disliking what her response suggested, she dropped the washcloth over the handrail. "Rinse off. I'll be waiting." Suddenly realizing what she'd said, she clarified. "Outside. I'll be waiting *outside*."

As he laughed, she flung the curtain closed and counted to twenty so Gabe could finish and she could recover her composure.

"Time's up," she called.

He didn't respond.

"Gabe?" she repeated. "Your time is up."

Still no answer.

"Gabe?" Although she hadn't heard a thump or other worrisome noise, his silence raised her concern. She flung back the curtain once again to find him leaning against the tiled wall, his eyes closed, his dark hair dripping.

"I knew it," she scolded as she cranked the taps until the water stopped. "You've stayed in here too long. You're about to fall on your face."

"Maybe, but being clean would be worth it."

CHAPTER THREE

GABE hated feeling weak. For a man whose body had never failed him before, it was a humbling experience to be at less than peak condition. However, if his injuries convinced Leah to give him another chance, he wouldn't complain too loudly.

Although, in spite of his aches and pains, he'd been relieved to discover one part of his body still worked quite well. If he hadn't stopped her from toweling him off like a child, he would have needed a second shower—an ice-cold one.

"I don't suppose I can wear a scrub suit instead of that," he said, eyeing the hospital gown she held out.

"We'd never be able to take care of your leg if you were wearing trousers."

"I could wear a pair of athletic shorts."

"You could," she agreed, "but a pair isn't available at the moment. You're stuck with this for now."

"You could cut off the legs and turn the pants into shorts," he coaxed.

"If you were going to stay a few days, I would, but I suspect you're not, so I won't. Now, stop arguing." She tied the string at the back of his neck then guided him to the nearby bed.

He sank gratefully onto the mattress before he rubbed his face. "Did you bring a razor?"

"Not this trip. Count your blessings for the toothbrush I found. Would you like to sit or lie down?"

"Sit."

She immediately adjusted the bed to accommodate his wishes then pulled the sheet over his good leg, leaving his injured extremity uncovered while she fluffed his pillows. "We'll tackle the beard later. You've done enough for the moment."

He hated to admit she was right, but although his spirit was willing, his flesh was weak. He'd been functioning on adrenalin for too long. Now that he'd enjoyed a hot shower, although a much shorter one than he would have liked, he'd crash soon. With any luck, after a rejuvenating nap, his IV would have run its course and he could convince Leah to drive him home, where he'd deal with the proverbial elephant in the room.

"Maybe," he conceded, fighting to keep his eyes open. "But the beard has to go. It itches."

"We'll get to it," she promised, "but first things first." She reattached his IV tubing to the port just above his wrist before he recognized his surroundings.

Suspicion flared. Patients weren't shown to a regular room if they were leaving the hospital in a few hours. "What am I doing here?"

"Jeff ordered IV fluids and antibiotics. Remember?"

"I know that," he snapped. "Why am I *here*, instead of back in Emergency?"

Jeff strolled in at that moment, carrying films and a fistful of paper. "You're here, Gabe, because I'm admitting you for observation."

"I don't need observing. I'm fi—"

Jeff held up his hands. "Yes, you're fine," he said in a

placating tone, "but you could be better and that's what we're going to do—make you better. I showed your X-rays to Smithson in Orthopedics and he agrees with me. You suffered a severe sprain to your wrist when you dislocated your shoulder. According to him, your shoulder is okay but he recommends a wrist brace for a few weeks." He peered over his reading glass with a warning glare, "However, he still wants you to take things easy, so don't lift anything heavier than a pen for a while."

Gabe took the films to see for himself. "Fair enough."

"As for your ribs," Jeff continued, "they'll get better on their own, provided you slow down and rest. But you already know that."

Jeff's advice fell in line with Gabe's plans, as he'd hoped it would.

"My main concern," Jeff continued, "is infection and I want to hit those bugs hard." He glanced at the IV pole. "I see your antibiotics are running."

"Thanks to my ever-efficient nurses," Gabe quipped.

"I'm glad you agree because you're going to be at their tender mercy for a few days."

His jaw squared as he shook his head. "No can do. I'm going home."

Jeff shook his head. "Not a good idea, buddy."

"Good idea or not, I'm sleeping in my own bed tonight. I can either do it with your permission or I'll check myself out AMA." Gabe hated to play the against-medical-advice card against a colleague, but he was *home*, dammit, and he wasn't going to postpone his heart-to-heart with Leah another day. He had too much to say and he couldn't say any of it here where walls were paper-thin and interruptions were commonplace.

"I can't give you my blessing to leave in a few hours."

Jeff emphasized his statement with a brisk shake of his head. "I honestly can't."

"Are you keeping Theresa and Jack?" Gabe demanded.

"No, but, unlike a certain person, they only need good food and rest to recover from their experience," Jeff said wryly, "not high-powered antibiotics."

"If the IV is stopping you, I can handle it. Or Leah can do the honors. Just give her the supplies and we'll take it from there." Gabe heard her muffled gasp, but ignored it to fix his gaze on his doctor.

Jeff pursed his mouth as his eyes darted between Leah and Gabe. "She could," he finally agreed, "but you know the dangers of septicemia as well as I do. You belong here where we can monitor you." He held up his hands to forestall his objections. "At least until the lab gives me preliminary culture results."

"Sorry. I'll stay a few hours to finish this IV, but I'm going home tonight."

After muttering something about physicians being terrible patients, Jeff turned to Leah. "Talk some sense into him, will you?"

She shrugged. "Sorry, but you're on your own. If he won't listen to you, he certainly won't listen to me."

Her matter-of-fact tone surprised Gabe. Did she really believe that he didn't value her opinion? And yet, in hindsight, he could understand how she might feel that way. After they'd lost their son and their dreams of having a child of their own, he'd wanted to do *something* to make things right again. When the opportunity to adopt a baby had literally fallen into his lap, he'd gone full-steam ahead over her halfhearted objections when he should have allowed Leah—and himself—more time to deal with their first loss. In the end, they'd had *two* losses to cope with and clearly hadn't done well with either.

Regardless, he'd had weeks to reflect on their relationship and if he wanted to prove to her that he was giving his marriage and her opinions top priority, then this was his opportunity.

"I'm listening now," he pointed out, avoiding references to the past in order to avoid a potential argument. "What do *you* suggest I do?"

"Follow your doctor's instructions," she said bluntly. "Jeff isn't being unreasonable."

No, Jeff wasn't, but Gabe hated being tethered to a hospital bed when Leah was free to go about her business. If his mental radar was working correctly, her "business" probably involved his own physician.

"You also," she continued, "aren't in a position to fend for yourself. Taking a shower completely wore you out. How will you function on your own?"

"I'll manage," he said, unwilling to spring his plan on her just yet.

Now she looked exasperated. "Fine. Do whatever you want, regardless of what your doctor or anyone else suggests. Frankly, with your attitude, I'm surprised you bothered coming to the hospital at all for medical attention."

Her comment struck home as he realized she was right. He *had* gotten to the point where he assessed a situation and made a decision without asking for advice or input, and if any was given contrary to his opinion, he didn't follow it.

The question was, had he always been that way? He truly didn't think so. At one time he hadn't been able to wait to share everything in his day with her and he hadn't made any plans without consulting her first, but now that he thought about it, that aspect of their life had changed after they'd lost both babies. Granted, the second child hadn't died, but when the birth mother had taken her daughter home instead of putting her in their care, it had felt the same.

Conversation had dwindled when she'd been grieving and although he'd tried to get his feelings out in the open, he'd soon given up. Leah's sorrow had been so overwhelming he hadn't wanted to burden her with his own pain, so he'd bottled his emotions and carried on.

Instead of coping together, they'd coped separately. He'd focused on his job and expanding the foundation's services while she'd flung herself first into a remodeling project and then into her job at the hospital. Eventually, their diverging interests had allowed them to drift apart until their marriage had reached breaking point.

He should have done things differently but he hadn't. Fate, however, had given him another chance and he was determined to make the most of it. The first step, however, was to prove that he *was* listening and valuing her opinion, even if her opinion conflicted with his own wishes.

"If you want me to stay, then I'll stay, but only on an outpatient basis until tomorrow morning," he qualified.

"I can live with that," Jeff immediately agreed, as if he realized this compromise wouldn't remain on the table for long.

Gabe continued, "And only if Leah is my nurse. My private nurse."

Leah's jaw dropped, plainly surprised he'd included her as part of his conditional surrender. A moment later, her expression cleared. "I cover the ED, not this ward," she pointed out, somewhat smugly.

He steadily met his colleague's gaze. "Jeff?"

The other physician pressed his lips together, then nodded. "If she's what it will take to keep you in that bed, I'll work it out," he promised.

Leah's jaw immediately closed with a decided snap, her eyes flashing fire. It was a small victory and one that she clearly didn't support, so Gabe forced himself not to smile. As compromises went, he'd gained more than he'd expected, although it was less than he'd wanted. What really felt good, though, was finally seeing Leah with her normal spark instead of appearing as if all the life had been sucked out of her.

"Fine," she said a trifle waspishly, "but I'm adding a condition, too. You'll stay until he releases you."

"Okay, but he *will* release me tomorrow morning." He glanced at his colleague. "Won't you, Jeff?"

Jeff appeared more interested in the tug-of-war between Leah and Gabe than in Gabe's capitulation. "If nothing horrible shows up on your cultures and you don't spike any fevers, then you have my word you'll be out of here in twenty-four hours."

Gabe leaned his head against the pillows, too exhausted to complain about how their final agreement had as many exemptions as a bill before Congress. He'd face those scenarios when and if he had to. "I want to know everything the minute you do."

"I wouldn't expect otherwise." Jeff addressed Leah. "In the meantime, good luck with your patient."

Gabe tried not to be jealous of how easily she smiled at his colleague—his divorced, *single* colleague—the same divorced colleague who'd probably been more than happy to comfort Leah during the past year, especially during the month after he'd been presumed dead. However, jealousy was a good thing, he decided, because it gave him added incentive to win her back again.

"Not to worry," she said airily. "If he misbehaves, I have a sedative with his name on it."

* * *

"I'd rather eat a steak, medium-well, with baked potato," Gabe said as he eyed the tray of food Leah had organized from the unit's kitchenette.

A steaming bowl of chicken broth with assorted crackers, strawberry and lime gelatin squares, and chocolate pudding were the result of her raid.

"Maybe you'll get those for dinner tonight," Leah said lightly, knowing he wouldn't. As much as she'd like to reverse his weight loss as quickly as possible, his digestive system needed to acclimate first. "This is just a snack until then."

"There's nothing here for a man to sink his teeth into."

She ignored his grumbling as she studied his skin tone with clinical detachment. Now that he'd scraped off his beard with the disposable razor she'd provided, he was paler than she'd like. His face, although still handsome with his straight nose and strong chin, was thinner and his cheekbones more pronounced than the last time she'd seen him.

"For good reason," she answered. "You hardly have the strength to chew."

"I can find the energy if it's worth my while," he said. "A cheeseburger, fries and a milkshake would—"

"Come up as fast as they went down. Would you rather hug the toilet for a few hours? Now, just try this," she wheedled. "If your system can handle this without any problems, I'll personally deliver a greasy cheeseburger from your favorite fast-food restaurant later on."

His sigh was loud enough to be heard in the hallway, but he picked up a package of crackers. After struggling unsuccessfully to tear the Cellophane, he finally gave up and tossed the packet of crumbs onto the tray in disgust.

"Would you like me to open it?" she asked, reaching for the mangled package.

Hating to admit his weakness, he grimaced. "I changed my mind. A fellow can do that, can't he?"

"Of course you can," she soothed, aware of the hit the tiny packet had leveled against his dignity. It was also clear that her time in the kitchen would be wasted if she didn't take matters into her own hands, so she picked up the spoon and began feeding him soup.

"I can do this myself," he protested between swallows.

She doubted it. He was clearly exhausted from the poking and prodding, the round of X-rays and his stint in the shower, but for some reason he refused to sleep. Maybe a full stomach would work for him as well as it did for babies.

"I know," she agreed, "but I'm trying to earn my pay. I am your nurse, remember?"

It still rankled how Jeff had marched into the nursing vice president's office and when he'd come out again, it was official. Leah was assigned to one patient and one patient only—Gabriel Montgomery.

"This is all so pointless," she had railed at the emergency physician. "Gabe doesn't need nursing care. He only needs someone to fetch and carry and help him in and out of bed, and anyone can do that. He doesn't need me and I can't believe you agreed to this. We have a date coming up!"

"I did it *because* of our date," Jeff had told her kindly. "You've been riding an emotional roller coaster for the past few weeks. Now that he's back, you need to rethink exactly what you want—"

"I *know* what I want," she'd interrupted.

"You *think* you know what you want," he'd corrected, "but having Gabe return from the dead changes everything."

"It doesn't," she'd insisted, trying to convince herself as much as him.

Jeff had smiled benevolently at her. "It may not, but

you owe it to yourself, and to me, to be absolutely certain of what you're looking for in a relationship. But I'll be honest," he'd said as he'd squeezed her shoulder. "As much as I respect Gabe, I won't be rooting for him."

And so she'd accepted the inevitable, even though she believed her skills were being wasted and that she knew her own mind when it came to her broken marriage.

Yet, after it had taken all of her concentration to reel her thoughts in far enough to figure out the microwave controls to heat his broth, she had to admit that perhaps she *shouldn't* be working in the ED right now. While she felt guilty over leaving her department short-handed, she shuddered to think of how ineffective she'd be in handling a trauma victim when a life hung in the balance. To her utter disgust, feeding Gabe seemed to be the only task her jumbled mind could handle.

"Are you ready to try the gelatin?" she asked, spooning a red cube into his mouth before he could refuse.

He swallowed. "Do you work with Jeff often?"

"Usually. Like I said, I normally work in Emergency."

His brow furrowed. "Don't PRN nurses work everywhere in the hospital?"

She spooned another bite into his mouth. "Some do, some don't. I haven't since I completed my advanced trauma nursing coursework six months ago."

His brow furrowed. "I didn't know that."

"You didn't notice the nursing textbooks on the coffee table before I moved out?"

"I did, but I thought you were boning up because you'd accepted this relief position."

"I was. Then I decided to take the next step." She hesitated, realizing that while he could have asked, she also should have volunteered the information. Now she wondered if the reason she hadn't said anything had been because she'd wanted *him* to notice and express an interest in what she was doing. And when he hadn't, she'd counted it as a strike against him.

"I should have told you," she said.

He shrugged. "We both had problems with communication, didn't we?"

At least he wasn't putting the burden all on her and if he could be magnanimous, so could she. "To be fair," she began slowly, "some of your staff had quit and you were trying to take up the slack. You had larger problems than wondering why textbooks had appeared on the table. More gelatin?"

He shook his head, his gaze intent. "Are you working full time?"

"Officially, no. Unofficially, yes, but I'm not reaping the benefits," she said ruefully. "However, the director of nursing told me yesterday that the next available position will be mine." She shoved another gelatin cube in his mouth.

He chewed, swallowed, then surprised her with his next question. "How was your cousin's wedding?"

She froze. "You knew about Angela's wedding?"

"She sent me an invitation. I would have gone, but I didn't want to make the day awkward for you. Things will be different, though, for your next family function."

Different? "Excuse me?"

"I want us to save our marriage, Leah. To fix what went wrong with our relationship."

At one time those were words she'd dreamt he would say, but too much time had passed. He was asking for the impossible.

"I know you went through a traumatic experience," she said slowly, "and as a result you want to right the perceived wrongs in your life as part of whatever foxhole conversion you experienced, but what happened to us—to me—can't be fixed."

"It can," he insisted.

"Not if our relationship is tied to my medical history."

"It isn't."

She raised an eyebrow because, to her, it was. "Oh?"

"It never was."

She eyed him carefully. "Maybe I should have Jeff order a CT scan because I think you suffered a concussion. In case you've forgotten, our relationship began its downhill slope when I lost Andrew and any chance for more children."

"It may have, but we can turn our life around. Children or not, we can make our marriage into whatever we want it to be."

His fierce determination was almost contagious, but his rhetoric didn't change one important fact. This man, who should have gone into pediatrics because he loved little people, was destined to remain childless because she refused to risk another adoptive mother changing her mind in the final hour. And he'd made it quite plain over the years that his biggest wish was to fill his house with children—children she couldn't give him, whether they were his or someone else's.

Neither did his sincerity change the fact that his work at the foundation was probably far more rewarding than simply coming home to her each night. And, yes, she could join him on his trips as she had when they were first married and she'd rearranged her hospital schedule, but deep down she was a homebody while he was a traveler. Eventually, the difference would become an issue again.

"For what it's worth, I *am* glad you're back," she said simply, "but now isn't the time to discuss what went wrong in our life." She rose to push his bedside table away. "Your only concern should be to give yourself time to heal."

He frowned, clearly not liking her response. "I can't believe you're giving up on us so easily."

"To you, I'm giving up, but to me, I'm finally putting the past behind me. Which is what you should be doing, too."

He paused. "How long have you been seeing Jeff?"

She froze, startled by his question. "Jeff? I'm not… We haven't… We're just friends," she finished lamely, wondering how Gabe had drawn that particular conclusion when she'd been so careful to hide her burgeoning interest in the other man.

"But you'd like it to be more."

"You're guessing," she countered, hating it that he could read her so well.

He shrugged. "I saw the way he looked at you. I only want to know what I'm up against."

She didn't know why she felt compelled to explain, but she did. "We went for a beer a few times with the rest of the ED crowd on a Friday night, but nothing more than that. You and I may have lived apart, but I still took my wedding vows seriously, which was why I was waiting to pursue a relationship with Jeff until after…"

"After I signed the divorce papers?" he finished.

"Yes."

"But once you heard my plane had crashed, you didn't need them. Why didn't you two take things to the next level right away?"

He sounded more curious than argumentative, so she answered as honestly as she could.

"If you must know, I wanted to wait until after the foundation's annual fund-raiser. I'd already decided it would be my last one—and it seemed appropriate for our chapter to end there. Now that you're back, there isn't any point in waiting, is there?"

He paused. "Is that what you want? For me to sign your papers?"

Was that what she wanted? Perhaps if their differences weren't irreconcilable, perhaps if they hadn't grown apart, perhaps if Gabe treated their marriage as a partnership rather than a boss-employee relationship, she could risk giving him another chance, but she couldn't.

"While I'm thrilled you aren't dead," she said softly, "you have to admit we're better off apart than we are together."

"I disagree."

"How can you say that?"

"Because we've *been* apart and it hasn't worked for me. I've missed you, Leah. More than you can imagine."

"How is that possible?" she asked, more curious than cynical. "You were busy with your work. We rarely talked or saw each other."

"That doesn't mean I didn't miss the days when we *did* talk and I spent more time at home than any place else. I want us to reverse course. To go back to the way we were. Before everything happened."

Before everything happened—such a polite way of saying *before her world went to hell in a handbasket.*

Her mind's eye flashed to the nursery they'd prepared on two separate occasions. The same room that remained closed to everyone except the housekeeper who periodically dusted and vacuumed. The sore spot in her heart had lessened from the day she'd given up and finally locked the door, but it hadn't completely disappeared. Her plans to avoid the OB and nursery wing were proof of that.

"As great as the idea sounds, I don't know if we can," she said honestly. "We aren't the same starry-eyed people we once were and no amount of magical fairy dust will change us back."

He tugged her arm until she didn't have a choice but to

perch on the edge of his bed. "Maybe we aren't the young, naive kids we once were. Maybe the hopes and dreams we once had died, but that doesn't mean we can't create new ones. Together."

Darn it, but his grip was comforting and once again his voice was so sincere—so full of faith—that the wall she'd created in her heart to hold back her hurts and disappointments began to crumble. Quickly, she struggled to shore up those widening cracks before those emotions overwhelmed her.

"Life has seasoned us," he continued softly, "but deep down, we're the same two people who fell in love. Getting ourselves back on track won't be easy and won't happen overnight, but anything worth having is worth fighting for. I've had weeks to do nothing *but* think and I'm asking you to not give up on me or on us." He paused to caress her hand. "Please."

Once again, he'd surprised her. He could have so easily *demanded* this of her, but instead he'd spoken in a humble manner. Maybe Gabe *had* experienced a change of heart…. However, as he'd said, he'd had the luxury of time to think about their life while she had not.

"I love you, Leah," he added hoarsely. "I want another chance."

As his words soaked in, tears sprang into her eyes and the wall inside her completely gave way. Instead of being happy, she felt angry.

She jerked her hand out of his and rose as she clenched her fists and stuffed them into her pockets.

"What's wrong?" he asked, his gaze puzzled as he followed her retreat to the opposite end of the room. "I thought you'd be thrilled—"

"Do you know…?" She fought the tears clogging her

throat. "Do you know how long…it's been…since you told me that?"

"Judging from your response, longer than I thought," he said wryly.

"I'll say. And I had to wait to hear it until after you were nearly killed in a plane crash! You can't spring that on me, out of the blue." She watched him struggle to swing his legs off the edge of the bed. "What are you doing?"

"I'm getting up," he said as he put action to his words.

"You can't. Your IV—"

"To hell with my IV," he said fiercely as his first step toward her pulled the tubing taut.

Fearing he'd rip out the needle and undo her hard work, she hurried close to survey his hand for signs of damage. She'd taped everything down to avoid accidental dislodging, but tape wasn't a deterrent to a man determined to escape his tether. "What are you trying to do?"

"I'm trying to get to my wife."

Before she could move, she found herself pulled into his embrace. She resisted at first, but the moment his arms surrounded her, she realized this was where she wanted to be. Oh, how she'd missed times like this, when they'd simply been happy to hold each other for no reason, other than "just because".

He kissed her forehead before pressing his cheek against hers. "I'm sorry," he murmured, "but everything is going to be okay."

She didn't answer because she didn't believe it to be true. How could it? So much had happened, so much had been lost, and they couldn't regain any of it. Then, after she'd reflected on the bittersweet moment, she pulled away and cleared her throat.

"You'd better get back into bed," she fussed, falling into her nurse persona as she avoided his gaze.

He didn't quibble but simply allowed her to help him sink onto the mattress, which spoke of how much his gesture had cost him. "I liked where I was," he said instead as she covered his legs with the blanket.

How could she answer? She had enjoyed his embrace, too, but she shouldn't. She'd wanted a divorce, for heaven's sake! Ending their marriage was the only solution because she could no longer define their relationship. Were they friends or enemies, or just two hurting people who'd lived together until she'd realized the status quo wasn't enough? Did she still have feelings for him or was she just falling into old habits because she was relieved that he hadn't died? Did she respond because of those feelings, or because it had been so very long since someone had comforted her or held her in his arms?

"Didn't you?" he pressed.

She hadn't followed his conversation because she'd been so caught up in trying to answer her own questions. "Didn't I what?"

"Like where you were?"

Knowing his tendency toward persistence—he wouldn't stop asking until she answered—she intended to deny her feelings until she met his gaze. To her surprise, she didn't see a smirk or satisfaction in those dark depths. Instead, she saw hesitation and uncertainty.

Her strong, silent, take-charge husband suffered from the same doubts and insecurities she did, and she'd never noticed until now.

"Come on, Leah," he coaxed. "Talk to me."

"If I tell you the truth, will you hush and rest?"

He nodded.

"Yes, I enjoyed where I was, but—" she injected a firm note into her voice "—that doesn't mean anything. It can't."

"Because you still want a divorce."

She didn't necessarily *want* one; she simply didn't have any other option. "It's for the best," she prevaricated.

He fell silent. "Okay, then," he said. "I'll sign your papers."

CHAPTER FOUR

GABE looked on as Leah stared at him in mute surprise. Clearly, she hadn't expected him to give in so readily. "You will?" she finally asked.

"Yes, but I have some conditions."

One corner of her kissable mouth turned up in disgust. "Naturally. And they are?"

"We move back in together first and see if we can make our marriage work."

"No."

"It's the only way I'll sign."

She opened her mouth then snapped it closed before she glared at him. "This is blackmail."

"It's negotiation," he countered.

"Your idea is pointless."

"We'll never know if we don't try. Whatever we do, don't you want to be sure, absolutely *certain*, that we're doing the right thing?"

"I'm already certain," she told him. "I was certain weeks ago, when I came by and delivered that folder of documents."

"Well, I'm not." He softened his tone. "Come on, Leah. If you're so certain, think of this as your opportunity to convince me it's the right thing to do."

"We don't need to live together for me to convince you."

"Maybe not, but it's one of my conditions."

"*But*—"

"Next," he interrupted her to add, "we have to really *try* to heal our marriage. Not simply live together like we did before, as married singles with each of us going our own way. We'll spend time together and we'll talk. No more overworking, no more avoiding our emotions or minimizing our feelings. We say what we mean and we mean what we say. And if we can't open up to each other, we'll go to a professional counselor."

She fell silent and Gabe hardly breathed as he waited for her answer. "Is that a condition, too?"

He nodded. "We'll definitely fail if the effort is one-sided or if we focus on the negatives instead of the positives. Surely you can invest a few weeks to salvage a ten-year marriage?"

"And who's to say one of us isn't working 'hard enough'." She made quotation marks in the air.

"If you think I'm not holding up my part of the bargain, you have to say so. I'll do the same."

Once again, she hesitated. "How long do you want this ridic—this exercise to last?"

He had a feeling she'd intended to call his trial run "ridiculous" but the fact that she'd corrected her negative remark suggested she was warming ever so slightly to the idea. "Until the foundation ball."

"Six weeks?" she sputtered. "No. Impossible."

"Are you afraid?"

"Absolutely not. I'm objecting because six weeks is a long time to prolong the inevitable."

"Six weeks will pass by in a flash. As for the outcome being inevitable, maybe it is and maybe it isn't, but if you quit one day short of our agreement, I won't sign the papers," he warned. "We'll end up with the messiest divorce in state history."

Dividing their property wouldn't be the problem. Leah hadn't been interested in his family money and hadn't touched a dime in the account he'd created for her after she'd moved out. Her Achilles' heel was the notoriety and publicity associated with divorcing the heir to the Montgomery fortune. And from the resignation in her eyes, she realized he could turn their divorce into a headline or a simple record on the district court blotter.

"You aren't playing fair," she complained. "A month should be more than enough."

"Oh, I don't know. Six weeks doesn't seem like very long when you'll have the rest of your life to spend with Jeff, or anyone else for that matter."

Her shoulders slumped in obvious capitulation. "I suppose not."

"There's also one more thing."

She rolled her eyes. "Why am I not surprised?"

"I want you to go with me when I head to Ciuflores, Mexico, in three days."

"What?" she screeched. "You're going back to Mexico, and you want me to go with you?"

"Yes."

"That settles it," she said firmly. "You definitely need a CT scan. Heck, probably a neurologist."

"My head is fine."

"Fine or not," she snapped, "my answer is no. Absolutely *no*."

He shrugged, as if unfazed by her outburst or her objection. "Then no signature."

"Why in the world would you want to go on another trip?" she asked, clearly ignoring his comment. "You barely came back alive from the last one. You should be giving yourself time to recover, not rushing to jet around the world again."

"In three days, I'll have recovered."

"No one heals from cracked ribs that quickly. You'll be sore and bruised. And you'll still need antibiotics for your leg, too."

"I'll take the antibiotics with me. And with you there to make sure I take them I'll be fine."

"Fine or not, why you, Gabe? You can't be the only member of the Montgomery Foundation who can travel."

"No, I'm not, but Sheldon told me just before you came in with my lunch that Father David had called and asked for supplies. They're in the middle of a flu epidemic and the situation is dire. I can't refuse his request—he's my friend."

Father David Odell was Gabe's old schoolfriend and although they'd taken different paths in life, they'd kept in contact. For the past few years David had served as the spiritual advisor to a poor community and had been instrumental in introducing Gabe to the two physicians who were the sole medical providers in the remote area. It hadn't taken long for the local doctors to recognize the advantages being handed to them through the generosity of the Montgomery Medical Foundation. Eventually, Gabe had arranged for the tele-medicine link for which his organization was famous, and two months ago he'd delivered the equipment and trained the staff on its use.

"Fine. If you want to go, then go. But I'm—"

"I need you, Leah," he said simply. "The people of Ciuflores need you. An extra pair of medically trained hands is in as much demand as anything I can supply."

She rubbed the back of her neck in obvious indecision and he pressed on. "There was a time when you couldn't wait to go on one of my trips," he reminded her. "And if I recall, you loved the experience."

"Yes, but I have responsibilities of my own here," she argued.

"I've checked out your work commitments and I know that as of today you're officially off the work schedule for the next ten days," he said. "Plenty of time to go on a three-day mission of mercy."

"And what comes after that? There's always another deserving community waiting in the wings."

"Not for me," he said firmly. "Oh, I may go places once or twice a year, but for the most part my traveling days will be over."

"Oh, please," she scoffed.

"I don't mind if you're skeptical. I would be too if I were in your shoes, but it's true. Saving our marriage requires time and proximity." He paused. "Is it a deal?"

"When does this unholy pact start?"

"Tomorrow. As soon as we get home."

"And in six weeks, when you finally accept that we're incompatible, you'll sign the papers, no arguments?"

There was no way they were incompatible—they'd had too many good years together—but if she wanted to think their time together would prove it, then she could. He, on the other hand, intended to show her just how *compatible* they really were.

"No arguments," he said, "but this is an all-out effort on both our parts. No halfhearted attempts at reconciliation. We give it our best shot." He knew he was repeating himself, but he wanted the terms perfectly clear. She wouldn't be able to cry foul down the road.

She let out an exasperated sigh. "Fine. Then you'd better get some rest tonight. Tomorrow will be an extremely busy day for both of us."

Physically he was exhausted, but emotionally he felt as if he could move mountains. He'd gotten Leah to agree to one last-ditch effort to save their marriage and with far less effort and cajolery than he'd expected. He wanted to believe that she'd given in because she wasn't quite as convinced about her plan as she'd originally let on but, whatever the reason, he was getting his second chance and he intended to make the most of it.

He'd handled things poorly before and now, after replaying those scenes and imagining ways he should have acted differently, he could straighten out those kinks. He'd start with sharing his own fears and feelings instead of hiding them behind his work. Hopefully, time had faded enough of Leah's hurts so he wouldn't feel guilty for dumping his own pain on top of hers. His father had taught him to be tough at all costs, but in this case the lessons he'd learned had come at the expense of his marriage.

"Okay, but—"

She held a hand in the air. "We've talked enough for now. Get some sleep."

He'd pushed all he dared, but he'd gotten more than he'd expected on his first try. Even so, he was curious…

"Why are you so eager for me to doze off?" he asked as she adjusted his bedding once more. Her actions were completely unnecessary because there wasn't a wrinkle in sight.

"Gabe," she chided. "People sleep while they're in the hospital. Rest is part of every patient's treatment plan."

"What will you do?"

"I'll think of something."

"You won't leave?" He hated the plaintive note in his voice, but he'd awakened far too often to the disappointing discovery that Leah's presence had only been a dream.

"I'll be here when you wake up."

"Promise?" he asked, hiding his worry behind a light-hearted tone.

She nodded, offering him a slight smile. "I promise."

"Ramon! Hold on!"

Gabe's rising voice and restless movements brought Leah out of her catnap. As she had done so many times during the last twelve hours, she padded across the dark room to pull him out of his nightmare.

"It's okay," she repeated as she sat in the chair next to his bed and held his free hand. "It's only a dream."

"I'm sorry," he murmured, still in the grip of his memories. "'Sall my fault." Then, "Not Will, too!"

His anguish was almost palpable and all Leah could do was watch him relive those moments of horror with tears in her own eyes.

"So sorry, guys," he murmured as tears slipped out from behind his closed eyes and his shoulders shook. "So sorry. My fault. All my fault."

Slowly, he settled back into his uneasy slumber, although she didn't know if her voice or her touch had caused that particular scene to fade.

Oh, Gabe. You went through hell, didn't you?

As she lightly blotted the moisture from his face with a damp washcloth, stroked the hard lines of his cheekbones and brushed aside the lock of hair on his sweaty forehead, she murmured what had become her litany. Idly, she wondered if Jack and Theresa were reliving their horrible memories, too. No doubt they were. Poor Theresa.

With his face freshened, she continued to hold his hand and stroke his fingers, thinking about how he'd glossed over his experience to her, to Jeff, and probably to everyone else he'd spoken to since he'd returned. Now, though, in the dark of night and without his full awareness, he'd given her a glimpse of the tragedy and trauma he'd endured.

She'd been so caught up in having him home again and worrying over what his return meant to her personally that she hadn't considered the emotional aftermath of his experience. For the past two years she'd thought him cold, unfeeling and insensitive, but he'd obviously been more adept at hiding his emotions, compartmentalizing his feelings and carrying on in the face of adversity and disappointment than she was.

Worse, though, was how, as a nurse, she should have *known* he would feel survivor's guilt, not only because he'd lived through his ordeal and his friends had not but also because *his* organization had been responsible for sending them on this trip in the first place.

No wonder he felt as if he were to blame.

He should have told her all this, she thought self-righteously, but almost immediately she understood why he hadn't. He couldn't blurt out the whole traumatic tale the moment he saw her, could he, especially when they'd lived separate lives for a year? Ever since they'd been reunited, they'd been surrounded by people and hadn't had the time or the privacy to delve into the details.

Had that been the problem with their own losses? Had they been surrounded by so many well-meaning friends and family that they'd never had the opportunity to deal with their pain as a couple? And when they'd tried, had they both buried it so far underground that they hadn't been able to reach it?

As she gazed at his face and smoothed away the agony etched there, his vulnerability tugged on her heartstrings. No, she decided, she felt more than compassion for a traumatized patient. She felt the pain of seeing a loved one suffer.

A *former* loved one, she amended. She didn't love Gabe in the same eye-sparkling, heart-racing way she once had because there were too many hurts and philosophical differences between them, but underneath all the bad stuff, the stuff that had gone wrong, the affection they'd once shared was there.

Unfortunately, affection didn't make a marriage. Love did, and hers had faded. Gabe might think they could rekindle those feelings but even if that were possible, he'd still want the family she couldn't give him. And as she'd told her mother when she'd phoned her earlier in the evening to share the news of Gabe's miraculous return, eventually they'd wind up in the same untenable situation.

Her mother hadn't been as certain about the outcome as she was but with Gabe's parents having died years earlier— one in a car accident and the other of a heart attack—her mom had always carried a soft spot in her heart for her son-in-law. While she was willing to support Leah's decision, whatever it might be, she'd also thought Gabe's suggestion made sense.

Clearly, everyone was hoping she and Gabe would have a happy ending, although Leah had given up believing in them.

But happy ending or not, she'd made a deal in order to win the prize she wanted—his name scrawled across the bottom of legal papers. In the meantime, she'd follow the letter of their verbal contract. "Say what you mean and mean what you say," he'd said, and she intended to live by that rule.

Perhaps the best place to begin was with the deaths of his friends. Their loss obviously weighed heavily on him and if he would express his feelings openly on that subject, perhaps they could work their way into dealing with their personal issues.

Relieved he was finally resting easier, she stifled a yawn. She should go back to her recliner, but decided she didn't have the strength or the desire to let go of his hand. Perhaps it was wishful thinking on her part, but it seemed as if this small contact was enough to hold his nightmares at bay.

She'd never felt as if Gabe had needed her, but in this, at least, he apparently did. For now, it was enough.

Gabe drifted awake to find the sun shining through the half-opened mini-blinds covering his window. Leah stood in the sunlight, gazing into the courtyard, arms crossed, her brow furrowed as if contemplating a serious subject.

For a moment, he simply lay there, looking his fill. They'd lost so much these past few years and, if not for his accident, they might have continued down their separate paths to an irreparable end. In fact, during the first few days of his trip, he'd seriously considered agreeing to her suggestion of a divorce, not because he wanted one but because he'd felt like such a failure. After being unable to give Leah her heart's desire—a baby—in this, at least, he could give her something she wanted.

The plane crash, however, had changed everything.

As he stared at his wife, who was more beautiful now than she had been when they'd married, he knew he would do everything in his power to make her happy again.

Suddenly, she faced him and smiled, looking more relaxed than she had a minute ago. "You're awake," she said.

"Hello to you, too," he said, his voice rusty from disuse.

She approached his bed, clearly intent on his IV pump, but he reached out and snagged her hand. Her hand was soft, her bone structure fine and her eyes uncertain.

Gabe, however, had no doubts, no reservations about

what he wanted. He tugged her just hard enough to shift her center of gravity in his direction.

"Gabe," she protested.

Before she could utter another word, he tipped his chin to meet her mouth. Gradually, her lips softened under his and a small noise escaped her mouth—the same small sound that came out as a satisfied sigh.

He wished he could give her the sort of kiss he wanted to, but he didn't want fuzzy-teeth breath when he did. "Good morning," he whispered.

"Same to you," she answered, her voice as husky as he remembered from their more lighthearted days. Then, as if she recalled where she was, she straightened and began fiddling with his tubing. "How do you feel?"

The nurse was back and the bride he remembered had vanished. No matter. There would be time to find her again—just as soon as he sprang himself from this joint.

He took stock of his aches and pains. They were still there, and a few new ones had cropped up, but his bone-weary exhaustion was gone. "Pretty good. How about you?"

"Me?" She seemed startled by his question. "I'm fine."

"I wondered. From your expression as you were staring out the window, I'd guess you were solving the world's problems," he said offhandedly.

She disconnected the tubing from the cannula in his wrist and draped it over the IV stand. "Not the world's, just the foundation banquet's."

"What's wrong?" he asked.

"Sheldon and I had planned a memorial ceremony, but with your return we should turn it into a celebration."

"Keep the memorial idea," he advised. "It doesn't seem right to celebrate when two of my group didn't come home."

"Okay, but your friends, associates and donors will want to hear about your experiences. You intend to speak as usual, don't you?"

"Only briefly," he said. "I'd rather review the year in pictures."

"Then we will." She flicked his blankets off his feet. "Are you ready for a stroll to the bathroom?"

"I thought you'd never ask," he said fervently as he levered himself up with his good arm and swung his legs off the edge of the bed.

"Take it slow," she advised. "You're probably stiff and sore."

Every muscle ached and his ribs protested his movements but he ignored the pain as he hobbled across the room to his destination, aware of his wife hovering beside him in case he should fall en route. "No kidding, I can manage from here."

He closed the door for privacy to take care of his most pressing needs. Then he studied his face in the mirror and rubbed at the stubble before proceeding to remove it.

Fifteen minutes later, he left the bathroom and found a meal tray waiting on his bedside table. "I'd rather eat at home," he said.

"Good luck with that," she said. "I emptied your refrigerator and pantry a few weeks ago when we thought you weren't coming...back. By the time we shop for necessities, it will be well past lunchtime. Besides, if you don't eat this, this delicious hospital cafeteria cuisine will only go to waste."

"Is that what you're calling it these days to make it taste good? *Cuisine*?"

"How did you guess?"

"You can have it," he offered.

"Sorry. You need the nutrition more than I do."

"Then I'll share. Remember when we shared a piece of pie?"

She smiled. "That was only so I could appease my sweet tooth at a fraction of the calories. This, however, is a *healthy* meal and you need to eat every bite. You should be starved."

"I am a little hungry."

"I would think so. You haven't eaten since the soup and crackers I'd fixed for you yesterday afternoon, so dig in before your eggs get cold."

"Okay, okay," he groused as he headed for the chair, "but I'll sit in the recliner. Lolling in bed makes me feel like I'm sick and I'm not."

"No, you're not," she said. "How did you sleep?"

He vaguely remembered her unhooking his IV before stumbling to the bathroom at some point, but other than the occasional murmur of Leah's voice, there was nothing he could focus on.

"Fine, I guess," he said slowly, watching as she whipped the stainless-steel dome off his plate to reveal several strips of bacon, two generous scoops of scrambled eggs and four pieces of buttered toast. "I can't believe I missed dinner, though. Eating is something we all looked forward to. Jack kept talking about his famous grilled chicken and Theresa wanted anything covered in chocolate."

"And what did you want?"

"Your Irish stew. Any chance we can have that one night?" he asked as he dug into the eggs and decided they didn't taste like hospital cooking. However, if she expected him to polish off the double portion, she'd be sorely disappointed.

"I'll see what I can do. Maybe I'll work on it while you're napping this afternoon."

He shook his head as he chewed. "If I nap, I won't be able to sleep tonight."

"You might surprise yourself. Being at home, in your own bed can make a big difference with how well you sleep."

Something in her tone put him on alert. Worry over what he might have said knotted his stomach. "I had a nightmare, didn't I?"

"It was pretty intense. Do you have bad dreams every night?"

He carefully placed his fork on his plate, his appetite gone. "At first, yes. The last week or so, not as often. I'd hoped they'd disappear once I got home."

"Would you like to talk about it?"

He let out a deep breath. "No," he said honestly. Then, because he noticed her stiffen, he finished his sentence. "But I should."

"You said we have to be more open and express our thoughts and feelings," she reminded him. "It's part of our contract."

"I know, and I will. The problem is, I don't know where to begin." He pushed his plate back. "Here. I'm not hungry anymore."

She bit her lower lip, clearly not happy with his answer or his sudden loss of appetite, but she simply nodded. "Too much too soon?"

He wondered if she was asking about the food or the conversation, but he didn't press for clarification. "Yes," he admitted.

"Small meals more often is probably best."

She'd been talking about food, which was a relief. "Probably," he said.

"The same holds true for our conversation. Even if you

can't share everything all at once, a little bit here and there is better than holding it all inside."

She'd caught him off guard, but her analogy was sound. He let out a deep breath. "I know."

"Good, because I'll let you slide this time, but once we're home, the kid gloves come off," she told him.

Relieved by his reprieve, he nodded. "I wouldn't have it any other way. By the way, when can I leave?"

"As soon as you have another blood test," she said. "In fact, someone from the lab should be here shortly."

As if on cue, there came a knock at the door and it was, as Leah had predicted, a phlebotomist. A few minutes later, the woman left with her vials and Gabe opted to enjoy the shower once again.

This time, when he came out of the bathroom, he felt like a new man and said so.

"You certainly look better than you did when you first arrived," she responded.

"I had nowhere to go but up," he quipped.

"On the contrary, you could have gotten worse," she said sternly, as if he needed the reminder. "Thanks to your overnight stay and the miracle of antibiotics, the redness on your leg has faded a lot already. I'm sure your ribs benefitted from the rest, too."

"Maybe so, but—"

"Jeff was right and you know it," she insisted. "In fact, if your roles had been reversed, you would have done the same."

"Okay, okay. I'll cry uncle. But I know Jeff has designs on you so don't expect me to praise him as if he's the next Albert Schweitzer."

The sound of her laughter caught him by surprise. It had seemed like forever since he'd heard it. "What's so funny?" he asked.

"You." She smiled. "You're jealous."

"Of course," he said smoothly. "I'm not embarrassed to admit it, either, especially when the prettiest woman in the hospital is my wife."

At first, she appeared taken aback, then a pink hue colored her skin, which suggested that he was long overdue when it came to paying compliments and giving attention to his spouse. He'd fallen down in that area, too, but that was another mistake he planned to correct.

Although, as he studied her, he noticed a few other details, too. Details like wrinkled scrubs, dark smudges under her eyes and an occasional stifled yawn.

"Did you stay here all night?" he asked, guessing her answer.

"I said I would."

"I can't believe you didn't go home."

"I didn't know when you'd wake up," she said simply, "and I promised I'd be here when you did."

The fact that she'd put her own comfort aside and gone to such lengths for him when he didn't deserve it was humbling.

"While I appreciate your gesture, you should have left at some point to get some rest," he chided.

"I should have," she agreed. "If I'd known your nap would stretch into eighteen hours, I would have."

"Why didn't you?"

"Glutton for punishment," she said lightly. "By the way, you had a steady stream of visitors, so I made a list because I didn't want to forget anyone." She grabbed the yellow steno pad lying on the table and held it out. "Would you like to…?"

He waved her offer aside. "I'll read it later."

"Sheldon came by several times. He insisted you call him the minute you're awake."

"He can wait."

"He won't be happy," she warned.

"I'll see him soon enough." He glanced at the wall clock. "Any chance you can call the lab and get my report?"

"Impatient as usual."

"If I have to sit and do nothing, I'd rather—"

"Sit and do nothing at home," she finished for him.

He grinned sheepishly. "I've said that before, haven't I?"

"Yeah, but you'll have to hold tight for a few minutes while I pester the lab for the results."

"Okay, but don't forget I want to see the report, too."

"As if you'd let me forget," she answered wryly, before she slipped out of the room.

CHAPTER FIVE

GABE found a pair of loose-fitting chinos and a button-down shirt in the tiny closet and decided to beat the proverbial rush and change now rather than later. He unhooked his IV, leaving the cannula in his arm for Leah to deal with, then slowly dressed. The process wasn't pain free by any means, but his struggles only gave him another good reason for needing Leah at home with him.

He was sitting on the edge of his bed, waiting for the sharp pain in his ribs to fade, when Dr. Taylor Ewing strolled in.

"How are you, Gabe?" the chief of surgery asked in his booming voice.

"Doing better now that I'm home," Gabe answered.

"Good, good. Getting dismissed soon, I take it?"

"As soon as my latest blood test is done."

"In that case, before you go, would you mind reviewing a case? It came via email through your medical organization and as it's my first official foray into your world of tele-medicine, I'd like you watching over my shoulder. I'd hate to delete a crucial file by accident."

Gabe had signed Taylor as a consultant in exchange for filling in as a surgeon when the department was short-staffed. The arrangement had been in both of their best interests. It gave Gabe a break from his organization's administrative duties and kept his surgical skills from growing rusty. Not that becoming rusty was a problem... when he and his staff were invited into an area with their supplies and equipment, they often assisted the local medical community.

"Who's asking for a consult?" he asked.

"A Dr. Hector Aznar."

Hector was one of the two Ciuflores physicians Gabe had come to know quite well. He and his partner, Miguel Diego, were dedicated young doctors who'd returned to their village after completing medical school. Both were intelligent men who could have established their practices anywhere in the country, but they'd chosen to take care of hometown folks.

"I'd be happy to, but I'm waiting for Leah to get back."

"No problem. We'll stop at the nurses' station and tell her where you are. Do you want a wheelchair or can you walk?"

Just that easily, it was settled. Within minutes, Taylor had left a message for Leah with the ward clerk and Gabe was heading to the man's office.

"Let's see what you have," Gabe said as he pulled a chair close enough to Taylor's desk to view the monitor.

"A formerly healthy fifty-two-year-old woman with nausea, diarrhea, vomiting, jaundice and sudden weight loss."

Gabe's instincts went on full alert. The last time he'd been in Ciuflores and helped with a clinic, he'd run into a case very similar, if not identical. At the time, he'd had limited diagnostic capabilities and had urged Hector to send the woman to a more advanced facility. "Any palpable masses?" he asked, because at the time he'd seen this particular patient he hadn't found any.

"Yes," Taylor mentioned. "In her belly."

Gabe hoped this patient wasn't the one he knew...
"Labs?"

"I have the basics. There are more abnormals than not."
Taylor handed Gabe a sheet of paper. "Her conjugated bili-
rubin is elevated, along with the liver enzymes, including
alkaline phosphatase. From what I can tell, there's a lot of
organ involvement."

According to the numbers, it was clear the woman had
cholestasis—a blockage in her bile duct—as well as issues
with her liver. Her amylase was also off the charts and her
glucose was abnormal, indicating pancreatic problems, too.
As Taylor had stated, very few of her results fell within the
reference range.

"They also sent a few ultrasound pictures." The older
surgeon clicked a few times with his mouse and the images
appeared on screen.

In spite of the grainy quality, the mass in the region of
the pancreas was unmistakable and the diagnosis grim.
Eighty-five percent of pancreatic masses were aggressive
cancers and of those sixty to eighty percent had tumors that
had spread into surrounding tissue.

"I hate to make a definitive diagnosis with so little to
go on," Taylor said. "According to Dr. Aznar's email, a CT
scan and MRI are out of the question."

"Hector and his colleague operate a small clinic and their
resources are extremely limited. They didn't even have an
ultrasound until I gave them one two months ago."

"How well do you know this Aznar fellow?"

"He's a smart fellow. Cares deeply about his patients
because he grew up in the area."

"Can he handle a biopsy?"

"If he doesn't have a choice then yes, but he doesn't have
any pathology capabilities. He'll have to ship the specimen
to another hospital, which will take time, depending on how

far it has to go." Gabe tried to remember where the nearest pathologist might be other than Mexico City, but came up blank.

"I assume they can't send their patients to a larger facility?"

"They can, but the nearest one is a half day's drive away and is only a step above their own clinic. The problem is, most of the natives either won't travel the distance or can't afford the trip, which is why internet access to specialists is so important."

Gabe leaned back in his chair. "The question is, do you think the tumor is operable?"

"It's difficult to say for sure," the nearly sixty-year-old physician said soberly. "Considering the size, one would have to guess that the cancer has already spread. The lab results seem to support that theory. If so, surgery won't help." He paused. "I assume chemotherapy isn't readily available."

"It isn't."

"Then Dr. Aznar doesn't have a choice. His patient has to go where she can receive proper testing and an accurate diagnosis. We can't discount the possibility of a benign tumor, which can be a curable condition."

"No," Gabe answered, "but even if it *is* benign, we can't guarantee a positive outcome."

He glanced at the patient ID and the name immediately jumped off the screen. Carlotta J. Salazar. His gut churned as he pictured the woman who'd come to his clinic. The same woman who lived at the local orphanage with her three precious grandchildren as the facility's main cook. From what David had told him, the poor woman hadn't had an easy life, and now a serious illness had added to her troubles. It was a good thing he would be going to Ciuflores in a couple of days. While he was there, maybe there would be something he could do for the woman who'd always fussed over his team like a grandmother.

Immediately, her three grandchildren came to mind. If he couldn't do anything for Carlotta, maybe he could do something for her family.

Taylor looked thoughtful as he stared at the images. "I like to play the odds and until we have a biopsy report, we have to. I'll email Aznar and talk him through a biopsy procedure if necessary. Meanwhile, I'll send the case on to a pancreatic specialist I know, unless you already have one in your network." He raised an eyebrow.

Gabe thought a moment. "We do. Let me call Sheldon for his contact information."

A phone call and a few clicks of a mouse later—along with several muttered curses as Taylor clicked the wrong buttons—Taylor had an address and phone number in his inbox.

Gabe watched as Taylor painstakingly typed a short message to Hector, then another to Dr. Stephen Wilkerson, before asking Gabe's help in attaching the digital files for the specialist's review.

Finally, Taylor leaned back and grinned. "Done. Medicine has certainly changed since I first became a doctor," he said ruefully. "Who would have thought we would send images and reports around the world and back in less time than it takes to dial a phone number?"

"Who would have thought?" Gabe echoed.

"Knock, knock," Leah's voice came from the doorway. "I hear you've stolen my patient, Dr. Ewing."

Taylor rose with a hearty smile. "You heard correctly, my dear. Come in, come in. How have you been?"

"I'm great. Thanks for asking. Did you two finish your business?"

"Just now," the surgeon informed her. "I imagine you're in a hurry to get our boy home."

In Gabe's opinion, her smile seemed a bit forced, but it was a smile, nevertheless. "He is rather impatient, as you can imagine," she said.

"Then I won't keep you." He shook Gabe's hand. "Stay in touch, okay?"

"I will," Gabe promised.

In the hallway, he tried to read Leah's reaction, but couldn't. "I'll bet you were surprised to get Taylor's message," he said, to test the waters.

"Surprised to learn that you were wandering around the hospital with Taylor? A little, but, knowing how eager you were to leave, I assumed you had a good reason."

"I did. He got his first tele-medicine consult and wanted me to walk him through it."

"How did it go?"

"From a technology standpoint, great. Not so good for the patient, though. What's really unfortunate is that I know the woman."

"Someone you've worked with?" she asked.

"Not really. Whenever my team and I visited Ciuflores, she took care of us. Cooked, did our laundry, that sort of thing."

"I'm sorry to hear she's not well. Will she recover?"

"The odds aren't in her favor." He shifted gears. "Did you get my lab results?"

"I did. Your white count is down and Jeff says you can go."

"Hot damn!" he exclaimed, pumping his fist in the air.

She grinned. "I thought you'd be pleased. As soon as we get back to the room, I'll take out your cannula and we'll be on our way."

"Fa-a-a-ntastic!"

But as they meandered through the hospital corridors to return to his starting point, he realized Leah had taken the long route. He knew she wasn't trying to give him more exercise or to delay his departure. She'd done it purely to avoid passing by the OB unit and the nursery. He'd hoped she'd gotten past her aversion, but apparently she had not.

One day, soon, they would have to clear the air about that, but not today. Today, he was finally going home.

Leah drew a bracing breath before she stepped through the garage door into the house she and Gabe had built. As she clutched the two grocery bags in her arms, a hundred memories bombarded her—memories of feeding each other strawberries during a late-night refrigerator raid to the day when she'd plunked the packet of divorce documents on the counter. She'd half expected the pages to still be there, but they were gone. Either Gabe, or Carrie Erickson, their housekeeper for the past four years, had moved them.

Asking about the folder would subtly remind him of why she'd agreed to his unholy pact, but she couldn't do it. Not only had she vowed to herself that sniping and innuendo wouldn't make the next few weeks any more bearable, but the look of sheer delight on his face as he slowly turned a three-sixty wouldn't allow her to say anything that would mar his homecoming. Cruel, she was not.

"I was afraid I'd never see this place again," he said simply. "It's good to be home."

"I'm sure it is," she answered, still trying to decide if she felt the same way. She wasn't particularly happy about being here because of all the memories, both good and bad, but Gabe had insisted she move in with him instead of vice versa. It was infuriating to realize he'd stacked the deck in his favor but, as she'd told herself many times during the last eighteen hours, this wasn't any different than enduring a mammogram. According to her mother and others who'd had one, the aggravation—and the pain—didn't last long. In the grand scheme of things, six weeks wasn't long, either.

Although perhaps once Gabe recognized and accepted that they both had fundamental differences about what they wanted in their futures, he'd sign those papers much sooner. She could only hope.

"Yeah," he said with satisfaction as he glanced through the doorway into the living room before smiling at her like a kid on Christmas morning. "Just like I remembered."

She took stock of the gleaming black granite countertops, the shiny stainless-steel appliances and the glistening cream-colored ceramic tile floor that she and Gabe had selected during what seemed a lifetime ago. A simple jar candle of her favorite Fresh Rain fragrance rested on the round table in the breakfast nook.

Nothing had changed and yet everything had.

He sniffed the air. "It even smells fresh."

"Carrie came by yesterday to air out the house and get it ready for you. For us," she corrected.

"Did you call her?" he asked.

"After our little talk. From the way the kitchen looks, she must have worked through the night dusting and polishing. She always did take good care of things."

"I'll have to call and thank her." He leaned against the counter to gaze around the room again. "If you only knew how many times I pictured this. Your fresh flowers on the table, the dishes stacked in the sink, the shoes by the door, the smell of your banana bread."

The flowers on the table had disappeared two years ago. Several months later her desire to bake had vanished and the dishes in the sink had eventually dwindled down to a coffee cup, saucer and a spoon because they'd eaten out more often than not. The only shoes by the door were the ones she'd deposited there a minute ago.

And yet could she blame him for thinking back on happier times in order to survive the most stressful period of his life?

A wrinkle appeared on his forehead, as if he realized real life wasn't comparing to his memories. "It's been a while since those days, hasn't it?"

"Yeah." Then, because she felt awkward and didn't want to say anything that might sound petty, she changed the subject. "Would you like a cup of coffee?"

"That would be great."

"Why don't you relax in the living room and I'll bring it when it's ready?"

"I'd rather sit here." He pulled a chair away from the breakfast table and sat down, wincing as he did so.

She'd noticed. "Ribs still sore?"

"Afraid so. They're better than they were, though."

"After another week or two of rest, you'll be back at the gym as usual."

"Probably," he said. "Do you still go?"

She shook her head as she poured water into the reservoir and spooned several tablespoons of Gabe's special dark roast they'd bought on their way home from the hospital. "I prefer walking or jogging outdoors." Truthfully, she'd started that so she wouldn't risk running into Gabe because he didn't work out on a set schedule.

"When I'm able to, I'd like to join you."

Surprised by his suggestion, she blurted, "But you hate to run. You always lifted weights, or swam laps."

"Nothing says I can't try something new. And I'd like to jog with you. We used to go to the park together."

"To walk," she corrected, "and it was when we were first married. That was a long time ago."

"So? Going back will be like old times. Remember when I flagged down the ice-cream truck in the middle of traffic because you wanted a vanilla cone?"

"Yes, and you almost got run over by a vehicle for it."

"True, but my quick reflexes saved the day."

"Quick reflexes?" she scoffed. "I saw that car hit your leg."

"It was a tap, not a hit," he insisted. "I didn't even get a bruise, which, if you recall, we spent hours looking for."

She remembered the evening in question quite vividly. It had been the same evening that had ended in a midnight kitchen raid for strawberries, peanut butter and chocolate ice-cream topping. The next day she'd sent their comforter to the dry cleaners to deal with the sticky stains.

"I know what you're doing," she said suddenly.

"What?"

"You're hoping to get what you want by going through the back door when you normally tear down the front."

"Is it working?" he asked hopefully.

"Not so far."

"Too bad. But for the record, I know how difficult it is for you to move into our house when you weren't mentally prepared."

His insight caught her by surprise and she simply gaped at him.

"But we have to learn to talk to each other again and dusting off the good memories seems a good place to start."

Her eyes narrowed. "Did you read a do-it-yourself marriage counseling book somewhere?"

"No. I just spent a lot of time thinking," he said simply. "So, how does my theory sound? Shall we begin there?"

She didn't want to because she sensed what would follow. She'd drop her defenses and be vulnerable, but they couldn't spend the next six weeks limiting their conversation to the weather or medicine. To be honest, she'd like to know what had been going on in Gabe's mind during those days when life had become so dark and bleak because he'd appeared so…unmoved by it all.

Or, as she'd already considered briefly, had he simply been better at hiding his reactions? Or worse yet, had she pushed him away so completely that he'd felt as if he *couldn't* talk? The latter question was one that she hadn't considered before, and the potential answer didn't sit well on her chest now. But, as he'd said, they had to start somewhere…

"Sure, why not?" she said. "We can stroll down memory lane, but I never have denied that we had some great years together. However, all good things come to an end."

"That's debatable, but for now we need to deal with a few housekeeping issues first. Moving your things comes to mind."

"I thought after you were settled, I'd run home and—"

"I'm coming with you."

She raised an eyebrow. "Afraid I won't come back?"

"No," he said solemnly. "You gave your word and I trust you. I want to come along so I can help."

"You want to *help*? You're limping worse than a Saturday night drunk, your ribs hurt if you breathe too deeply or move suddenly, and you aren't supposed to lift anything heavier than a pen."

"It's not that bad," he defended.

She cast him a you've-got-to-be-kidding look. "No offense, but let's be realistic. How much help do you think you'll be?"

"Maybe not much, but I want to go with you."

"What for? To supervise?"

"No. To keep you company."

He wanted to keep her *company*? Once again, he'd surprised her. "Oh."

"Do you mind?"

Of course she did. The little house she was renting was her childhood home—her sanctuary. She didn't want Gabe's overwhelming presence to ruin that for her.

Yet, once again, it seemed cruel to make a fuss over something so trivial, especially when they wouldn't be on the property any longer than it took to empty out her refrigerator and throw a few clothes into a travel bag.

Letting out a soft sigh, she surrendered. "Suit yourself, but if I catch you overdoing things, I'll convince Jeff to re-admit you."

"Understood. Is the coffee ready?"

She found the cups in the same cupboard where she'd always stored them and filled two. As she carried them to the table where Gabe was sitting, a brisk knock at the back door caught her off guard.

"Are you expecting someone?" she asked.

"No."

There were few people who qualified as back-door guests and she already guessed their visitor's identity. She wasn't wrong.

"Sheldon." She greeted him halfheartedly, not entirely shocked by his appearance given his eagerness to talk to Gabe while he'd been in the hospital.

Gabe's second-in-command stood on the threshold, his face somewhat apologetic. "Sorry to bother you because I know this isn't the best time, but I'd like to talk to Gabe. I promise I'll be gone before you realize I've been here."

Heaving a sigh, she stepped aside wordlessly and tried not to read anything into the way Gabe's eyes brightened at the sight of the familiar face.

"What's up, Shel?" he asked.

"The memorial service for Will and Ramon is set for day after tomorrow," he said.

"You worked fast."

"The families wanted it this way," he said simply.

Gabe simply nodded. "Of course."

"And," Sheldon continued, "we've been trying to make head or tail out of your notes for our Ecuador project and haven't had any luck. We're scheduled to go there in two weeks, and to make matters worse the health ministry is dragging its feet over the permits again. Would you mind setting me on the right track?"

"Not a problem," Gabe answered.

"Wait a minute," she protested. "You just got home from the hospital. You're supposed to *rest*, not work."

"This isn't physical labor," Gabe pointed out. "I'm only answering a few questions."

"That's right," Sheldon chimed in. "As soon as Gabe brings me up to speed and we sort through the problems, I'll be out of here. Ten minutes, tops."

"Do *any* of your projects run smoothly?" she countered.

"Lots do, but not this one. While you're waiting, why don't you relax? Shoot, lie down for a few minutes. I know you didn't sleep much last night."

He wanted her to *lie down*? When she had so much to do, the least of which was changing her address? Wasn't it enough that he'd blackmailed her into spending the coming weeks together, simply because it was what *he* wanted? Disbelief instantly filled her.

"It's only for a few minutes," Gabe coaxed. "Sheldon wouldn't be here unless it was important."

And therein lay the rub. His work *was* important. She knew so many people who wouldn't have gotten the medical help they'd needed now did, and it was all because of Gabe.

The problem was with her. She simply wasn't as philanthropic of his time as he was. Perhaps she needed to live in a third world country to get her husband's attention.

Deciding she was being petty, she sighed. "You're right. Everything else can wait."

His gaze searched hers and, apparently satisfied by the acceptance he saw, he cupped the side of her face. "I know this isn't working out the way we'd planned."

"It isn't the first time."

"I promise we'll hurry."

"Yeah," Sheldon interjected. "I only need a few minutes."

Leah had learned long ago that "a few minutes" was code for "a few hours", if not longer. So much for things being different...

On the other hand, Sheldon probably did have a lot of questions. Gabe was involved in every aspect of the foundation and unless he'd left copious notes—which he wasn't known to do because he carried so much of his information in his head—Sheldon had been left to unravel the mess left behind.

Resigned to the inevitable, she simply nodded before she addressed Sheldon. "Would you like a cup of coffee while you're working?"

"I'd love one," he said fervently.

As soon as she handed a fresh mug to Sheldon, Gabe stepped forward to brush a kiss on her cheek. Instant awareness shot through her as she felt his lips touch her skin and she inhaled the scent that was only Gabe. *Stop that*, she mentally chided her traitorous body.

"Thanks," he murmured. "Would you like to join us?"

Another first. Well, not really a first. At one time he'd included her when he'd discussed foundation business at home, but that had ended after their adoption had fallen through. Then he'd stopped asking, as if he couldn't bear to be around her any more than necessary.

"Maybe next time," she answered. "While I'm waiting, I'll make my lists."

"Good idea." He turned away, then stopped short. "Is my computer still here?"

"It should be. I haven't taken anything," Leah replied. In fact, she'd been postponing the task of cleaning out the house to list it with a real estate agent. Now, she was grateful she'd dragged her feet. It would have been awful for Gabe to suddenly find himself homeless. "Sheldon?"

He shrugged. "I haven't taken anything, either."

Gabe seemed relieved by the news, which was understandable. "I presume you didn't cut off my network access or delete my files?"

Sheldon grinned. "Do I look stupid, boss? Of course not."

As the two men headed toward Gabe's home office, Leah was certain they'd both lose track of time once they began discussing work.

She found a pencil and notepad in the drawer near the telephone and sat down to begin her list. Unfortunately, her mind couldn't get past the fact that they hadn't been in the house for five minutes and she was already competing with his job. Her temper simmered.

She wanted to march in and yell at him, to remind him of his "things will be different" speech, but doing so with Sheldon in the room would only make the situation uncomfortable for everyone. But if Gabe wanted complete and total honesty, she intended to give it to him. No more holding things inside, no more being the sweet, forgiving, *pushover* wife.

Yet as she stared blindly through the window into the garden she'd once loved, her irritation faded. She hated the way she'd overreacted, even though no one knew it except her. Sheldon wasn't purposely sabotaging their life. Deadlines had to be met and questions had to be answered so the job could go forward, but what would he have done if Gabe hadn't been here? He would have muddled through on his own and probably done a wonderful job.

On the other hand, did Gabe have to run every time Sheldon, or anyone else at his office, called? She had so many questions and so few answers, which, according to Gabe, was what the next few weeks was all about.

Six weeks suddenly seemed to stretch into forever.

Gabe had tried to watch the time—he really had. However, one thing had led to another and by the time he'd checked the clock, two hours had passed.

So much for his "few minutes" promise, he thought glumly. "Sorry, Shel, but that's it for today."

Sheldon glanced at his watch and cursed under his breath. "Hey, man, I'm so sorry. It's just been such a relief having you back that the questions just kept coming."

"I understand."

"Tell Leah I'm sorry, too, and that I'll make it up to her."

"I'll tell her," he said, before Sheldon let himself out. Unfortunately, he had more to tell her than Sheldon's promise of restitution. A sincere apology was in order. He'd vowed things would be different but so far he'd failed his first challenge. Now he had to hope she'd give him another chance, although he would wager his old Beamer that she'd simply been waiting for him to screw up so she could say "I told you so" before she walked out the door. She'd given him one pass already in the hospital when she'd questioned him about his nightmares. He didn't think she'd do it again.

Yet he wasn't willing to surrender so soon. If that was

her plan, then he'd argue they were both bound to make mistakes on their way to getting things right.

Practicing his apology, he slowly made his way past the living room to the kitchen, but she wasn't there. Thinking she'd gone upstairs and taken a nap, as he'd suggested, he ignored the pain in his leg and grimly climbed the stairs, hoping to find her in their bedroom, tucked under the covers, fast asleep.

At least, he hoped she was there because *he* wanted to wake her and he knew exactly how he wanted to do it. He'd first run a light finger along the side of her face before moving down her neck to take a detour along her collarbone. From there, he'd meander through a most luscious valley until she finally reached for him.

Anticipation, coupled with his months of celibacy, created a physical response so strong he could hardly turn the doorknob. When he did, he saw the master bedroom's king-size bed covered in the familiar green-and-gold comforter she'd bought when she'd decorated the room. A variety of matching pillows were artfully arranged near the headboard, but the bed itself was empty.

Leah wasn't there.

He checked every room upstairs—the guest room and even the nursery—but she wasn't in any of them.

He went downstairs, through the house and into the backyard where she'd once loved to sit and enjoy the butterfly garden.

No Leah.

Where had she gone? More importantly, was she coming back? His gut churned at the possibility.

No, he decided logically, she would be back. She wanted his signature too much to give up so quickly. She was probably running an errand or, having grown tired of waiting for him, she'd left for her place without him. No doubt she was on her way back this very moment.

Reassured by that thought, he returned to his office—his favorite room of the house. They'd spent many comfortable hours within these four walls, he realized as he sat behind the oak desk Leah had given him one Christmas. Leah would often curl up in the overstuffed chair with one of her fiction books while he'd read through his stack of medical publications or taken care of business paperwork. Music or the television would play in the background and when they had both tired of whatever it was they'd been doing, they'd put the smooth desk surface to good use.

Now, though, instead of being cluttered with medical and cooking magazines or her latest knitting pattern, the highly polished wood only held his pen and pencil set, a framed photo of the two of them, which had been taken shortly after she'd learned she was pregnant, and a desk calendar with its top page showing the day he'd left on his last trip.

He didn't need to open the top left-hand drawer to know what it contained. A phone book, the *Yellow Pages*, and the divorce papers she'd delivered. With any luck at all, those documents would soon be shredded and residing in the trash.

He glanced at the wall clock and saw another hour had passed. Telling himself not to worry about things like car accidents, ambulances or the county morgue, he broke down and dialed her cell phone number from memory, but his call went straight to her voice mail.

He told himself to wait. Traffic could have snarled, checkout lines could have been horrific, or she'd simply got caught up browsing and had forgotten to watch the time. He hoped the latter was the case because then he wouldn't feel so badly about doing the same.

After another fifteen minutes he simply couldn't wait any longer. He had to do *something*, even if he had to drive from one end of the city to the other, but he'd find her.

One way or another, he *would*.

CHAPTER SIX

LEAH watched the play of Gabe's muscles underneath his cotton shirt as he soaped her little blue Mustang. It was still almost hard to believe he'd married her when he could have had his pick of all the beautiful women in the world, but the shiny new ring on her finger said it was true. So did their marriage license and the wedding picture proofs she'd picked up from the photographer that morning.

Suddenly, a blast of cold water struck her chest.

"Gabe," she protested. "Look what you've done. I'm all wet."

His appreciative glance suddenly wiped away her irritation.

"So am I," he reminded her.

"But I wanted to wear this to my parents' house," she protested without heat. "Now I'll have to change."

"Can I help?" he asked hopefully.

"You can't." She pretended to pout as she struck up a sultry pose. "You're busy."

"Not anymore," he said, immediately shutting off the tap.

In a flash, she was in their bedroom, entwined in the sheets as his mouth and hands roamed over her body. "Oh, Gabe," she murmured as he caressed her breast and nipped at her neck. "That feels…"

"Wonderful?"

"Yes."

"How about this?" *His fingers skittered a path down her body to a secret spot only he had found.*

She arched in his arms. "Oh, my…"

Suddenly, the pleasant, swirling sensation disappeared as she felt something solid underneath her.

That wasn't right. How had the mattress become that hard…and bony?

She wiggled, wanting Gabe to fly her back to the clouds before she'd been so strangely and rudely interrupted, but she couldn't get comfortable. She and Gabe had fit so well together, but now there was this thing between them.

She elbowed the object, but it wouldn't budge. Irritated now, she pushed harder, but it only moved a fraction. Determined to remove this strange obstacle, she raised herself on one elbow and opened her eyes to see just what had dared to ruin her romantic interlude—

Leah gasped as she realized Gabe was lying beside her. Lying in *her* bed, in *her* house, on top of *her* quilt. And right now he was watching her with his intensely dark eyes.

This is certainly awkward. "What…?" She swallowed. "What are you doing here?" she asked faintly.

"Looking for you."

Oh, dear. "Is everything all right?"

His gaze didn't waver. "You tell me."

Instinctively, she understood his unspoken question. "I'm not upset because Sheldon came by," she assured him. "Well, I was at first, but I got over it once I put myself in his shoes."

The intensity in his eyes faded and he visibly relaxed. "I'm glad."

"By the way, what time is it?"

"Quarter before five."

She sank onto her back and flung her arm over her eyes. If he was right, then she'd been here for over four hours, and had been sleeping for most of them.

"How...how did you get in?" she asked.

"I recognized your fake rock in the flower bed near the front door. You really should find out a better place to hide your house key," he said.

"Apparently so, if all sorts of riff-raff can find it," she said meaningfully.

He laughed at her veiled barb. "Let this be a lesson to you."

"How long have you been here?" she asked.

"About an hour."

An hour? "You should have woken me."

"I could have, but you were tired."

She had been. She'd slept very little the previous night, watching over Gabe and helping him through his nightmares. Tired or not, though, she hadn't planned her afternoon to turn out this way, and she told him so.

"Oh?" he asked, more curious than skeptical.

"After you didn't show any signs of wrapping up your conversation with Sheldon, I decided to run here, pack my things and get back before you noticed I was gone." She offered a weak grin. "Obviously, my plans didn't turn out the way I'd hoped."

"I'll admit we took longer than I'd intended," he admitted, "but when Sheldon went home and you weren't in the house, I started to wonder..."

"I should have left a note," she said, "but, honestly, this was supposed to be a simple, thirty-minute errand. When I walked into the house, though, a shower sounded good, and then the bed looked so comfortable. I decided to lie down for a few minutes and, well, the next thing I know, you're here in bed with me."

She narrowed her eyes, but before she could question him he put on a complete air of innocence. "You told me I should rest, so I did."

"I didn't mean you should do it in *my* bed."

"It isn't as if we made love while you were dead to the world," he calmly pointed out. "Furthermore, we aren't breaking any moral or legal laws if we share the same mattress. If it makes you feel better, notice how I'm on top of the blanket and you're not."

She clutched the sheet to her chest, aware that only a flimsy piece of fabric was between them. Granted, he wouldn't see anything he hadn't seen before, but it was the principle of the matter. They were a hairbreadth away from a divorce, for heaven's sake!

"Just so you know—we may be sharing a house, but that's *all* we're sharing. I'm taking the guest bedroom."

"We're trying to make our marriage work, Leah," he reminded her. "As I recall, our bedroom was the one place we didn't have any problems."

"I don't deny how wonderful our sex life was, but making love now only clouds our issues."

He looked somewhat disgruntled, although not surprised. "I was afraid you'd say that," he said ruefully.

"Because you know I'm right."

"Okay," he agreed. "I'll accept your decision. "For now."

Which meant he would address this subject again, but at this moment he was backing off. She would be satisfied with that, although if Gabe ever got a glimmer of her dream, he'd do his best to change her mind. Quickly.

"Did I...?" She paused. "Say or do...anything?"

He grinned. "You mean, like crawl all over me and whisper sweet nothings in my ear?"

Oh, dear. "Did I?" she asked, bracing herself for the worst.

"All I can say is that your elbow should be registered as a lethal weapon." He rubbed his side.

She was too horrified by the possibility of having caused him serious damage to be embarrassed, and she began pulling at his shirt to look for evidence. "Did I hurt you? Oh, my, your *ribs*!" she wailed.

He caught her hand. "They're fine," he said. "You didn't hurt me. Well, maybe a little, but hearing you say my name was worth the pain."

She was mortified. She'd never convince him she wanted him out of her life if he'd heard her moan his name or if he knew he'd starred in her erotic dream.

"So," he said matter-of-factly, "do we want to stay in bed or get up and gather your things?"

"Get up," she said promptly.

"Okay. Ladies first."

She raised her eyebrow. "Not a chance, buster. As you well know, I'm only wearing this sheet and I'm not dropping it. I'll see you downstairs."

"Spoilsport."

He gingerly swung one leg over the edge and rolled upright with a small grunt, reminding Leah of his injuries. "I assume you haven't packed anything yet?"

She was embarrassed to answer. "No."

"Then I'll put on a pot of coffee." With that, he limped from the room.

For a minute Leah simply lay there, realizing how her best-laid plan had gone awry. Gabe's presence had already tainted her safe haven, much as the spirits of the two children she'd considered hers had tainted the house she and Gabe had built. There, she'd done her best to confine the atmosphere by locking the door to the nursery, but the gloom had invaded the rest of the house like a noxious fume and nothing she did could dispel it. The only way she could break free had been to move where she didn't see memories everywhere she turned.

Now, thanks to not setting an alarm, to not returning before he'd realized she'd left, she wouldn't ever banish the image of him in this specific bedroom and in this specific bed.

Damage control was in order, which meant she had to get him out of there as quickly as she could. She dashed to the bathroom and shimmied into a fresh pair of jeans and a clean T-shirt.

Next, she pulled her suitcases out of the closet and began tossing in clothes haphazardly. A quick sweep of the bathroom's counter and medicine cabinet took care of her personal items and within minutes she was packed. Neatness, in this instance, didn't count.

Downstairs, she set her cases by the door. Through the window, she caught a glimpse of Gabe's SUV parked at the curb.

"Your vehicle's outside," she said inanely as she accepted the mug Gabe handed her.

"How else was I supposed to get here?" he asked.

"Sheldon didn't give you a ride?" she asked.

"No."

"You *drove*? Are you *crazy*?"

He snagged a butterscotch out of the candy bowl on the nearby end table and nonchalantly unwrapped it. "I may have been out of the country for a few weeks, but I still have my driver's license."

"This isn't about the legality. It's about your health," she scolded. "You shouldn't be behind the wheel with your bum leg and sore ribs. Your reflexes are compromised and what if you're in an accident? You could be seriously injured, even killed! Not to mention the damage an air bag could do."

"Those scenarios are possible," he said, clearly unconcerned at the prospect, "but after surviving a plane crash, a car wreck seems mild in comparison."

"For heaven's sake, Gabe. You were lucky once, but you aren't invincible."

He folded the wrapper in half then in half again, as if he had nothing else to concern him, but she knew his casual air belied his sharp-eyed gaze and keen powers of observation. "You seem worried over something that didn't and probably wouldn't happen."

She couldn't believe he was asking her that question. "Why wouldn't I worry when you do something foolish?"

He shrugged. "It's nice to know you care."

"Of course I care," she snapped. "You're my—" She stopped short, unable to supply the word he was obviously waiting to hear and feeling as if he'd led her down this path.

"Husband?" he supplied helpfully.

She raised her chin. "Yes. For now."

"Then, as your husband, don't you think I'd worry about you, too?"

"I already explained and apologized for not leaving a note," she pointed out. "If I'd known I was so tired, I would have taken a nap when you suggested it."

"But you thought you could get by without one."

She nodded as she sipped her coffee, pleasantly surprised he'd remembered her preference for peppermint creamer and two packets of non-calorie sweetener. "That and…." She debated explaining the rest, but he wanted honesty, so she'd give it to him. "It just seemed as if once again you were telling me what to do."

"I'm sorry you thought so because I was only offering a suggestion," he said slowly. "It seemed kinder to suggest a nap than to mention the bags under your eyes or your haggard appearance."

No doubt she *had* looked like death warmed over—a twenty-four-hour stint in the hospital tended to do that to a person. "You're right, it was," she admitted. "I was cranky and finding fault. I'll try not to be so sensitive next time."

"And I'll keep Sheldon's interruptions to a minimum."

"Do you really think it's possible?"

He grinned. "You bet, especially if I don't answer the phone or the door."

"So you'll let the phone screen your calls and I get to weed out your visitors."

"Precisely."

"The next question is, will *you* be able to stay away from the office?" she asked, thinking of the hours he'd devoted to his foundation. Twelve- to sixteen-hour days hadn't been uncommon during their last year together. "I know how difficult it is for you to relinquish the driver's seat of your organization."

"I can, and I will," he said. "During our time in the jungle, Jack and I speculated on what might be happening here at home without me, and neither of us saw a pretty picture. My father wouldn't have agreed with me, but it isn't good for the entire workings of the foundation to hinge on one person. Until I implement more permanent changes, Sheldon is in charge. After I take hold of the reins again, I plan to delegate more."

"I'm sure you'd like to implement your ideas, but I'm not convinced life will be any different than it was before."

"I haven't convinced you *yet*," he corrected. "But I will. In fact, I'm willing to dissolve the trust fund and turn the foundation over to someone else if time becomes an issue."

His news clearly caught her off guard because she stared at him with the same incredulity he'd seen on her face when the ambulance doors had opened. "You're kidding."

"I'm not."

"I can't believe you're offering to relinquish your family's legacy. You've helped so many people—"

"I learned what's important in life," he said simply. "Yes, the foundation fills a need for a lot of people, but in the end my wife has to come first."

"Why?" she blurted out. "I know you cut back on your hours when we thought we were starting our family, but our situation is different now."

"Not really," he mentioned. "We're still a couple and I want to spend time with you."

He made it sound as if their future was settled, but in her eyes it still wasn't. And yet, if they were to have any *hope* of a future, they certainly had to do more than see each other in passing.

However, being around each other twenty-four seven meant that certain subjects were bound to come up. Certain subjects on which she'd already made her stand. Certain subjects that had brought them to the brink of a divorce...

She studied him through narrowed eyes. "And what happens if, by some miracle, we restore our relationship? What then? What's next on your agenda?"

He frowned. "I don't have an agenda, other than avoiding the divorce court."

"It isn't in the back of your mind to convince me to try the adoption route again? If that's your end game, then we may as well visit my attorney now rather than later."

"That isn't my plan," he insisted. "Whether we have

children or not, we can still have a wonderful marriage. Just the two of us."

He sounded sincere and nothing in his eyes hinted at subterfuge, but she knew how badly he'd wanted children and she said so.

"Yes, I wanted to raise a couple of kids and still do if the opportunity arises," he admitted, "but our relationship comes first. If that isn't healthy, there's nothing left."

His quick response and his calm gaze caught her off guard. She hadn't expected him to give up his heart's desire so easily and it startled her to the point where she couldn't find the words to reply.

"Is that why you've been digging in your heels about this divorce business?" he asked, clearly amazed. "You're trying to save me from myself, aren't you?"

"It isn't fair to ask you to give up something you've desperately wanted and dreamed of," she defended. "You'll wake up one morning and realize you've wasted all those years and then we'll be back in the same boat, sailing down the same river to nowhere. I can't go through that again—"

"Will you let me be the judge of what I want?"

"Children are all you've ever talked about. As an only child, you wanted a houseful, you said."

"I did, because I believe siblings teach life lessons that an only child doesn't learn. Things like sharing everything from toys to parental attention and getting along with others, even when they irritate the heck out of us. But, Leah, we have to play the cards we're dealt and if we don't have children, then so be it."

"Then why…?" She bit her lip in indecision.

"Why what?"

"Why did you push so hard for us to adopt right after

we lost Andrew? You'd lost your chance to be a father and you grabbed at the first opportunity that came along."

"Is that what you think?" he asked, incredulous. "That I rushed into the adoption only because I wanted to be a *father*?"

"Didn't you?"

"No," he exploded. "Absolutely, not! I did it for *you*."

"How was your decision for me, Gabe? I was still grieving for my baby and any future children, and the next thing I knew we're trying to complete home studies and prepare for another baby."

He raked his hair with his fingers. "Hindsight says we should have waited, but at the time the opportunity seemed heaven sent. It would have been, too, but no one anticipated Whitney changing her mind in the final hour."

Leah let out a sigh. No, no one had known or even guessed the outcome would turn out completely different than everyone had planned. Whitney Ellis, the birth mother, had been so sure of her decision—until the time came for her to live with it.

"I had to do *something*, Leah, because I was losing you. You wouldn't talk. You wouldn't tell me how you felt. Later, after we began discussing adoption and you met Whitney, you came around. You were happy again."

After she'd recovered from her initial surprise and the situation had felt real and not just a dream, she had been. Deliriously happy.

"Then," he continued, "as soon as she decided to keep her baby, everything fell apart again. And then, before I knew it, you were moving out."

Gabe had struggled with so many conflicting emotions during those long months, but the day she'd packed her bags had been the bleakest day of his life. The day she'd asked for a divorce hadn't been a high point of his thirty-eight years, either. However, this was the first time he realized she had attributed selfish motives to him.

Then again, how could he have guessed? They'd never expressed themselves this openly before.

He should have pushed her harder to unburden herself in the weeks and months after their adoption had fallen through. He'd waited for her to broach the subject, thinking she'd talk when she was ready, but she never had. On the other hand, he'd *wanted* to talk, to pour out his disappointment and his pain, but he hadn't known how or where to begin. Consequently, they'd never discussed what had obviously lain so heavily on their hearts until eventually they'd found solace in other ways. He'd taken refuge in his work and she'd accepted a relief position at the hospital.

In the end, they'd drifted apart. Now he was trying to steer them back together, unable to believe he might be too late.

"Regardless of what you were trying to do, I don't want to live through the same experience," she said in a flat tone. "Putting our lives on display to birth parents in the hope they'll choose us, being interviewed and trying not to sound over-eager, not to mention the waiting, the *interminable* waiting. Then, after all that, our hopes and plans can fall through at a moment's notice."

"I understand how you feel."

"Do you, Gabe?"

"I went through the same disappointments you did," he pointed out. "It wasn't easy for me, either."

She frowned and cocked her head to study him. "You didn't act upset."

"I was. I wouldn't let myself show it because I felt like I had to be strong for you."

"I see." She paused. "Now that you know how I feel, if

we reconcile—and that's a big *if*—would you be satisfied with my decision?"

"Absolutely," he said firmly, "As long as you don't let fear influence your choice. But whatever we do, whichever route we take, we have to move forward. Doing what we've done before—avoiding the issue, locking off a room of our house—didn't work then and it won't work now.

"That said," he continued, "at this particular point in time we have to concentrate on *us*. When we're on track again, the rest of our concerns about families and homes and jobs will fall into place."

Her expression suggested that she was skeptical, but if she truly thought he'd only been trying to fill *his* emotional needs, then he simply had to prove to her how wrong she'd been. Their future wouldn't be secure until she trusted him to mean what he'd just said.

"You can say those other things don't matter, but they've influenced our marriage."

"Then we'll deal with those things as they come up. What do you say, Leah? I know you aren't a quitter."

She sighed. "I don't have a choice. I have to play your game."

Obviously, she still felt as if she was being blackmailed— that she simply had to endure all this unpleasantness so she could get what she wanted. And yet, after lying beside her on the bed, hearing her whisper his name in her sleep, he suspected she still harbored feelings for him. He simply needed to tap into those.

"Yes," he said bluntly. "For the next six weeks, anyway."

She nodded, plainly resigned to their agreement.

Then, because he didn't know what else to say, he gestured around the room. "How much of this shall we take with us?"

"Just the afghan and my knitting bag." She pointed to a corner where yarn spilled out of a canvas tote. "If I need anything else, I can always get it later. Meanwhile, the refrigerator comes next."

He followed her into the kitchen, noticing Leah's touch wherever he looked. Silk sunflowers and wheat stalks sprouted out of several slender vases and lined the top of the kitchen cabinets. The ceramic bowl they'd bought at a flea market held fruit in the middle of the table. Her purse lay on the counter, her billfold and keys spilling out of the open flap. And several pairs of shoes stood in a neat row by the back door.

This was how a house should be, he thought. It should look lived in, not sterile and lifeless, like his. In a few short hours their house would look like he remembered, filled with color and flowers and the organized clutter that had always seemed to follow Leah. He could hardly wait.

"What made you decide to move into your parents' house?" he asked. "I thought they were going to sell it when they moved to Oklahoma to be near your sister."

To spoil their grandchildren, Tricia Jordan, Leah's mother, had told him. Although Leah hadn't seemed to begrudge them their decision, it had to be difficult for her to know that her sister was as fertile as a bunny while Leah's branch of the family tree had withered.

"They'd intended to," she admitted, "but the Realtor suggested they'd get a much better price if they updated it. So, when I wanted a place of my own, I moved in with the understanding I'd redecorate and modernize."

He glanced around the room. "You did a wonderful job. You always did have a good eye for detail."

"Thanks."

"Can you show me the rest?"

He saw her hesitation—as if she didn't want to share this with him—before she finally shrugged. "Sure, why not?"

Gabe followed her through the dining room, back to the living room, then upstairs to the three bedrooms and a bathroom. The walls had all been freshly painted in neutral colors and airy curtains covered the windows.

"Quite an ambitious undertaking to work on by yourself," he remarked as they returned to the kitchen.

"I didn't mind. I needed to keep busy."

"I suppose." He noticed a collage of photos on the refrigerator and strolled over for a closer look. The pictures were all scenes he remembered, but one in particular stood out.

"I'd forgotten all about this," he said offhandedly as he pointed to the snapshot of the two of them at a summer carnival, posing in front of the duck-shoot booth. "I spent a small fortune trying to win this giraffe."

She came close to peer around his shoulder and smiled. "You were determined to win that prize. I think it cost you more than the animal was worth, though."

"Yeah, but we wouldn't have had nearly as much fun."

"Probably not," she agreed. "You were bound and determined to hit the grand prize duck."

The concept had been simple—to shoot the toy ducks floating past with a suction-cup dart gun. Knocking over specially marked ducks earned special prizes and he'd decided early on which one he'd wanted.

He grinned. "It took me, what—an hour? As I recall, you named it Gemma. Because of the purple jewel around her neck."

The jewel was actually a piece of colored plastic, but it was pretty and sure to catch a baby's eye, which was why Leah had insisted the giraffe would be the perfect addition to their nursery. Now the toy stood behind a closed door, gathering dust instead of occupying a child's attention.

An image of the nursery they'd designed flashed his mind's eye, accompanied by the scent of baby powder and the tinkling music of a crib mobile.

"Would it be easier if we started over in a new house?" he asked. "A clean slate, so to speak?"

"You're getting ahead of yourself again," she pointed out. "We don't even know if we can make a go of our relationship and you're already talking about new homes?"

She clearly still hadn't bought into the notion they could make their marriage work, but he refused to consider otherwise.

"I know everything between us is unsettled, but we have to approach our relationship as if it can and will succeed. If you recall, we both agreed we'd give this our full commitment, and that means we can't entertain thoughts of failure.

"Besides," he continued, "I'm not suggesting we sell our house and buy a new one next week. My idea is simply something to think about, especially when we both know there's one room you can't bear to enter."

"Going into the nursery isn't easy," she admitted, "but even if our life together was settled, I'm not certain a new house is the answer, especially if you spend the majority of your time either at the office or jetting around the world. Any marriage where one party is thousands of miles and three time zones away three weeks out of every four is going to suffer under the strain. Call me selfish, but I don't want to be philanthropic with your time."

"Like I said, Jack and Sheldon will be taking a more active role in the foundation," he assured her.

Wearing a puzzled wrinkle on her forehead, she met his

gaze. "This sounds crazy, but I feel as if an imposter has replaced my real husband."

He smiled. "No imposter. I'm the real guy."

She paced a few steps before she faced him. "I appreciate your offer of a different house," she finally said, "but let's follow your advice to focus on us and deal with permanent living arrangements later."

"Fair enough," he said, satisfied with his first real sign of progress.

CHAPTER SEVEN

AFTER dinner that evening, Gabe pushed his empty plate aside and leaned back in his chair. "That was delicious, Leah. You always were a wonderful cook."

His praise brought a heated blush to Leah's face. "It was only scrambled eggs and toast," she chided. "Hardly an impressive meal."

"Maybe not to you, but it was to me. 'Impressive' is a matter of perspective."

"I suppose," she said, unconvinced by his assurance but grateful for his appreciation, "but I should have fixed something more substantial, like the chicken breast or the sirloin steak we bought this afternoon."

"Or we could have gone out for dinner, as I suggested," he said.

After hurriedly packing her necessities and driving them across town in their vehicles, she'd wanted to organize the kitchen and her closet before calling an end to the day. Visiting a restaurant would have taken far more of her evening than she'd wanted to spare.

Plus, she'd have been Gabe's captive audience while their meal was being prepared. She wasn't ready for that, yet. It was one thing to have a civil conversation in the privacy of their home. It was another to hold a conversation where they would be under public scrutiny.

"It would have taken longer to get ready than it did to scramble a few eggs," she remarked, "and chances were we would have run into someone we knew who would have wanted to visit. I still have a lot I'd like to accomplish tonight."

The real problem, in her eyes, had been the possibility of well-meaning friends congratulating them on being a couple again. She certainly didn't want to navigate that particular minefield.

"Whatever the reason, I appreciate the trouble you went to. Simple meal or not, what I had was perfect," he declared. "After all, just this morning you said I needed to go easy on my stomach."

"It seems like we had that conversation ages ago."

"Considering how hard you worked this afternoon, I'm not surprised," he said. "Where you found the energy to accomplish what we did, I'll never know."

"I didn't do that much," she said.

Gabe had wanted to empty her house, lock, stock and barrel, but she hadn't been ready to go that far. Fortunately, she'd been able to use the excuse of minimal storage and Gabe's sore ribs to dissuade him. However, she sensed he would have ignored his sore ribs to haul whatever she wanted, regardless of how big, bulky or heavy it was.

"We could have accomplished more if you'd let me," he complained good-naturedly.

"You heard the doctor's orders. No lifting."

"And I obeyed," he answered.

"Then why did I end up scolding you for carrying boxes you shouldn't?"

Remembering how she'd huffed whenever she'd caught him, then pull the load out of his arms, brought a smile to Gabe's face. At first, he'd been affronted by how little she'd allowed him to carry. Then it had become a game to see how much he could get away with. Best of all, being caught and hearing her scold only meant that she cared, even if she wasn't ready to admit it…

To his great relief, though, most of her things were back at home where they belonged, the refrigerator and pantry had been restocked, and the house that had previously looked like a model home now had a lived-in appearance.

He couldn't be happier.

Well, he could be, he amended, if Leah had moved into the master suite instead of the guest room, but being under the same roof was better than the alternative and with luck the hall would only separate them for a short time. Meanwhile, his vision of Leah tucking her finger under his collar and leading him upstairs would give him something to dream about and work toward…

"More coffee?" she asked as she rose to grab his mug.

"I've had enough caffeine for one day. I won't sleep tonight as it is." At her questioning glance, he added, "Too excited about being home, I guess."

"It doesn't quite seem real yet, does it?" she asked softly.

"No. I'm half-afraid I'll wake up and find myself still in the jungle," he confessed.

"I've been thinking along the same lines—that I'll discover your return was nothing more than wishful thinking."

He nodded, grateful she understood his fears so clearly. He only hoped she didn't press for details about the crash or the events afterwards. Yes, he'd answer because being open and honest was part of their agreement, but he'd really rather not revisit such a traumatic episode when he wanted to revel in her company on their first night together.

"I'm sure the truth will soak in soon enough," he said casually. "I certainly wouldn't be able to ignore the facts if you warmed your cold toes against my leg. How your feet can be such icicles, I'll never know."

Her answering chuckle was a melody he hadn't heard for a long while. He wasn't particularly surprised by how rusty it sounded—she'd had little to laugh about during the past few years. As for the smile she gave him…it was the sort that brightened a man's day no matter how difficult or ugly it had been, and reminded him of the girl in the carnival photo. The joyful woman with whom he'd fallen in love hadn't disappeared—she'd only been hiding behind a dark cloud.

Restoring their formerly close relationship suddenly seemed elementary. The key to rekindling their marriage was to rekindle Leah's spark, he decided, and he was just the man to do it.

"It's a gift," she said virtuously. "Although I recall offering to wear socks."

"My way of warming up your feet was more fun." He wriggled his eyebrows.

Once again, her face turned a familiar rosy hue. "It was," she agreed. "Good thing it's summer and cold feet aren't a problem. Shall we clear the dishes? I'm ready to relax for a while."

As she jumped up, he also rose. "Relaxing on the deck sounds good," he said, carrying his own place setting to the sink. "But do you know the best part about dinner tonight?"

"So few dishes?"

"Hardly. It reminded me of old times."

Her hands froze over the faucet and she stared at him as if he'd sprouted an extra nose. "Old times?"

"Yeah. Remember when we were first married? I'd come home from the hospital, starving to death but too exhausted to stay awake, and you'd fix this very meal for me so I could eat before I fell asleep on my feet."

She smiled, her tentative expression disappearing again. "And sometimes you did. I always said I should publish a cookbook—*101 Scrambled Egg Recipes.*"

"Or created your own show on the Food Network."

This time she laughed, a full-bodied laugh that sounded like the carefree Leah she'd once been. The same Leah who'd found happiness in small things like sunsets, the neighbor girl's kitten, and the wildflower he'd pilfered from Mrs. O'Shea's garden near their garage before he'd walked in the door. The same Leah who hadn't been able to wait for their love to grow into a family.

"It wouldn't have been on the air long," she said lightly as she shut off the faucet and slid their plates into the soapy water. "Frankly, I was getting to the point where I thought I'd sprout feathers if I swallowed another egg, scrambled or otherwise. I shudder to think what our cholesterol levels were."

"Ah, but back then I didn't care. I was more interested in sleep, food, and…" he snaked an arm around her waist, pulled her close and planted a swift kiss against her mouth "…my wife, although not necessarily in that order."

Her small intake of breath proved that she definitely wasn't immune to his touch. "What are you doing?" she asked.

"What I should have done a long time ago," he told her. "I'm focusing on us."

Leah knew that for the next six weeks to be bearable, they had to find their footing when dealing with each other. Over the next two days they talked and they laughed, but controversial subjects were avoided, although she didn't know if that was by chance or design. Oddly enough, she found herself feeling…content.

She told herself it was only because she was within weeks of settling her life once and for all. She'd obtain Gabe's signature and that would be that. Her feelings had nothing to do with discovering how she could enjoy his company.

However well their temporary truce was holding, the door at the top of the stairs remained locked. She would have to venture inside to face her ghosts before long because her grace period would eventually run out, but in the meantime she'd lump that ugly bit of their past in with what he'd called "the rest of the stuff".

The only tense moments came when Leah followed Gabe into their house after the memorial service for his colleagues. Although he seemed to be bearing up well, she recognized the strain he'd been hiding underneath the smiles he'd shown to everyone.

"Would you like some coffee?"

He jerked at his Windsor knot as he headed into his office. "I've had enough caffeine, thanks."

She trailed after him. "A glass of wine?"

"No."

"Something to eat? I noticed you didn't sample any of the snacks after the ceremony."

"I don't want anything."

His clipped tone spoke volumes about his mood, but Leah knew how destructive brooding was. How ironic to find herself in circumstances where their former roles were reversed. This time *he* was the one hurting and *she* was the one who wanted to banish the pain but couldn't find the key to doing so.

"Okay," she said with equanimity as he sank into his executive chair. "When you are, let me know." She perched on the desk's edge. "You delivered a beautiful eulogy today. I know how difficult it was to share your personal stories and anecdotes."

"Their families deserved to hear them."

"You did an excellent job. I didn't know Will and Ramon as well as you did, but from the few times I'd been around them, I could tell you'd described their personalities and characters perfectly."

"They were good men."

"Theresa was especially grateful for your kind words. She said she has more wonderful things to tell her baby when he grows up." She paused. "I didn't know she was pregnant."

"She just found out. Ramon never knew."

"I'm sure he does now," she said softly.

He made a noise that could have meant anything from agreement to skepticism. "What did you feel when she told you?" he asked.

She thought for a moment. "Surprise. Sadness that she'd have to raise the baby alone and that Ramon would never enjoy being a father. Happiness that she'd have someone to remember him by, not that she'll need a child to help her remember the man she loved.

"And…" she drew a bracing breath, hoping Gabe would share his confidences if she shared hers "…I was a little angry. Angry at life for being so unfair."

He nodded slowly. "Me, too. I felt all of that, and then some."

"You did? I couldn't tell."

"I did," he assured her. "Just like before."

She finally faced a hard truth. "I was so wrapped up in my own pain that I didn't see yours, did I?"

He sighed. "Neither of us handled our losses well. Let's hope we've learned from our mistakes."

"I also felt something else," she added tentatively. "Disappointment."

"Because you can't get pregnant?"

"No," she said slowly. "I've accepted that. I was disappointed because my husband knew about Theresa's condition and didn't tell me. You don't have to protect me, Gabe. I can handle it."

He met her gaze. "Handle it, how? Like the way you still won't walk past the OB unit after nearly two years?"

Ouch. "Okay, maybe I don't deal with the excitement and joy as well as I should, but it would have been easier for me if I'd been prepared to hear her talk about the baby."

"You're right. I should have mentioned her news."

"You're forgiven," she said lightly. "Frankly, I'm overwhelmed just thinking of what she'll face as she raises this child on her own—dealing with hormones, teenage angst and hi-jinks. It won't be easy."

"She won't be alone," he said. "She'll have plenty of support from her family, Ramon's family, Jack, and all of us who worked with him."

Leah suspected he considered himself a large part of that support, especially when she thought about what he'd done for the single mother-to-be so far. He could say what he wanted, but guilt probably fueled a huge part of his motivation.

"You shouldn't blame yourself, you know."

"I don't. Not about the plane crash, anyway," he corrected. "Who could have known we'd fly into a flock of blasted birds?"

"But you still feel responsible."

He fell silent. "Yes."

At least he'd finally admitted it. "Because you survived and he didn't?"

He fell silent for several long seconds. "He was alive

when Jack and I found him, you know. We did everything we could, but he didn't hang on like I begged him to. He just...slipped away."

"I gathered as much from your nightmares, but you're doing a nice thing, Gabe. You established a college fund for his child and paid off his mortgage so his son or daughter would always have a place to live."

"It would have been nicer if I could have saved him."

That, her intuition told her, was really why he was struggling with the tragedy. "You were in the jungle," she reminded him. "Not in a fully equipped emergency department or surgical suite."

"He had so much to live for. Why him? Why Will? Why them and not the rest of us?"

"That's one of the mysteries of life. The thing is, there were three medical professionals at the scene, and one of them was the woman he loved. If he couldn't hang on for her then he physically wasn't able to, and you shouldn't feel as if you failed."

He smiled at her. "For an amateur psychologist, you're a pretty smart gal."

"It's nice of you to notice."

"By the way, we're leaving tomorrow at seven a.m."

She sighed. She'd been hoping he'd had second thoughts about his latest trip. "Then we're still going?"

"Why wouldn't we?"

"Oh, I don't know. I guess because you haven't mentioned a word about it. I thought maybe you'd changed your mind."

"I haven't. Sheldon arranged for the cargo to be loaded today so we'll be ready for takeoff as soon as we arrive at the airport." He studied her a moment. "You really aren't happy about this, are you?"

"No," she said bluntly.

"Why not?"

"One, you seem awfully eager to go. Like you did before." A cold, foreboding chill ran down her arms. This was the way the distance between them had first started, and how it had grown with each subsequent trip. She'd stayed at home with nothing to occupy herself but her thoughts while he'd jetted around the world, seemingly without a care.

"Eager isn't the right word. This isn't a holiday."

Her fears churning like Grand Canyon rapids, she began to pace. "Exactly. You're working and you said you wouldn't."

"Leah—" he began.

She held up her hands to forestall his arguments. "I know. This is only for three days."

"And it's strictly a mission of mercy," he told her. "Or are you implying I can't ever respond to a critical need anywhere ever again?"

"No, but I don't like the way you took away my choice, Gabe. You reduced this Mexico trip to an obligation, a condition, when it should have been, at the very least, a mutual decision."

He looked thoughtful, as if he realized his mistake. "Okay, so I handled that poorly, but I was desperate. I wanted you with me because I was afraid if I left, even for a few days, I'd lose my advantage and, ultimately, I'd lose you, too."

"Gabe," she said softly, "we'd already negotiated to spend the next six weeks together. Did you think so little of me that I'd renege on our agreement?"

"I couldn't take that chance. Regardless of the way I forced your cooperation, I really do need you there."

"You need a nurse," she corrected. "Not necessarily me."

"The nurse I need is you." He leaned forward. "I'm not

looking forward to flying for obvious reasons and I'd travel another way, if I could. Unfortunately, my other choices aren't practical or timely. With you beside me, though, I can get on that plane." He paused. "If I hadn't been coming home—to you—I doubt if anyone could have forced me to board the last one."

She'd never considered how difficult his return must have been. No doubt every noise had had him thinking the worst. "Oh, Gabe."

"The point is, we have both seen how working with a common purpose builds a team, which is what I want for us. I'm hoping we can accomplish it, but…" He hesitated. "If you truly refuse to join me, I won't stop you."

His offer startled her. "You'd let me stay behind?"

"Yes. According to what I heard this morning, they have a tremendous amount of critically ill children, especially infants. It won't be easy on you."

She didn't know if she should be grateful for his understanding or affronted by the implication that she would be too affected to do her job. More importantly, though, knowing they had so many sick young patients and a shortage of nurses, how could she refuse and still be able to sleep at night? Besides, he had apologized and explained his motivations, misguided though they'd been.

If he'd been so desperate to fix their marriage that he'd resorted to blackmail, then he wasn't simply giving lip service to the idea.

"All right, I'll go." Seeing his suddenly broad smile, she added, "Someone has to make sure you don't overdo it."

"Thanks. You won't regret it."

She already did, not because she didn't want to help those people but because Gabe was obviously expecting more from her than she could give. "I'd better start packing."

He caught up to her before she reached the bottom step. "This could be the thing our relationship needs."

She stared at him with a sad smile. "It might also be the thing that breaks us."

CHAPTER EIGHT

LEAH accompanied Gabe onto the tarmac with mixed emotions. From a medical standpoint she wanted to be a member of his team, but from a personal standpoint she was afraid. He believed working together would foster teamwork and co-operation, and it could. However, it could promote dissension just as easily. This would be a stressful three days for both of them and stress didn't usually bring out the best in people.

Maybe this trip would be a game-changer for their relationship, but if it changed for the worse, it was better they learned it now, rather than later.

However, her thoughts of what might or might not happen faded as soon as she saw how Gabe struggled to climb on board the plane. He drew a deep breath, braced his shoulders and squared his jaw before he finally ducked through the doorway. His hands shook as he buckled his seat belt and on the strength of his reaction she wondered how he'd been able to fly home immediately after his accident.

Helping him cope became her top priority. Throughout the entire flight she held his hand and chatted about everything and anything, asking question after question about Ciuflores. If he noticed she repeated herself, he didn't comment.

Sheldon and Ben, their other team member, obviously

anticipated Gabe's reaction, too, because when she was at a loss for words, they took up the slack. The two men kept up a steady stream of chatter through their headsets in a not-so-subtle effort to divert his attention from their position high above ground.

"Try to get some sleep," she advised.

He shot her an are-you-crazy look, but dutifully closed his eyes.

Luckily, the trip went without incident. As soon as the wheels touched down on the level patch of ground that constituted the small airstrip outside Ciuflores, the look of relief sweeping over Gabe's face told how agonizing this trip had been to him. She had to admit to a grudging respect for a man who faced his fears in order to help a friend...

"Thanks for being here," he said simply.

"I'm glad I could help." And she was, she realized. He'd needed her, which thrilled her to the point where she was almost glad she hadn't stayed at home.

Hating the slight tremor in his hands, she kissed his cheek. "Enough lollygagging," she said cheerfully. "It's time to go to work."

As she'd suspected, facing his mission and fulfilling his purpose for being there did wonders for his composure. He squared his shoulders and began issuing orders to Sheldon, Ben and Corey Walsh, their pilot, as he opened the door and exited the plane.

Leah stepped outside the new twin-engined Cessna and was immediately struck by the humidity and the earthy aroma. Flowering trees lined the eastern edge of the clearing, which probably accounted for the floral scent she detected. A hint of something more unpleasant—like the community dump—drifted in from the north, but the thick foliage hid it from view.

A man wearing jeans, a casual shirt and a clerical collar rushed to greet them.

"David!" Gabe exclaimed as he hugged the tall fellow, confirming the priest's identity as Father Odell, Gabe's old classmate who'd established this mission church some seven years earlier. "It's good to see you."

In his late thirties, David had light brown hair and crow's-feet around his eyes, and his skin was tanned from the Mexican sun. He also looked tired but, as Gabe had explained on the plane, David not only ministered to the spiritual needs of the area but also was the director of the only orphanage in the vicinity.

The idea of running across so many parentless children had troubled her, especially as this was the first mention of a local orphans' home, but if Gabe could face his fear of flying, she could deal with the children if it became necessary. She had to because by then she couldn't walk out with the plane at ten thousand feet.

"The feeling is mutual," he answered. "When we heard about your plane crash, I said a lot of masses on your behalf. Then, when you phoned, I could hardly believe our prayers had been answered."

"That makes two of us, David, but with a man of your spiritual pull on my side, how could it have turned out any other way?" he joked.

"All things considered, I didn't expect you to fly here yourself," David chided gently.

"I wouldn't have for anyone except you," Gabe said.

"I'm glad you decided to get back on the horse that threw you, although I wish you'd come under better circumstances."

"Me, too. By the way, this is my wife, Leah."

It was obvious the two were close friends. "Father," she

said as she shook his hand. "Gabe has told me so much about you."

"Now, that's a scary thought," the priest teased. "But, please, call me David. What are titles among friends?" He turned back to Gabe. "I assume you brought the supplies Hector requested?"

"And then some," Gabe told him. "If you have a few strong backs, we can start unloading."

David waved forward a group of men standing near the edge of the field. In no time at all the cargo had been moved from the plane to the waiting trucks and they were bouncing their way into town.

Leah clung to Gabe and hoped she'd still have teeth and eardrums when they finally reached their destination.

"Still no shocks on this beast?" Gabe yelled over the noisy muffler.

David grinned. "Why bother with shock absorbers? They'd just wear out. Honestly, though, think of this as nothing more than a free carnival ride."

Because it was futile to talk, the rest of their short trip passed without conversation. Ten minutes later, they reached Ciuflores.

The village's poverty was painfully evident by the dirt-packed streets and ramshackle houses. Grass had long since given up its struggle to survive, although a small patch appeared every now and then. Chickens and dogs roamed freely through the town and goats remained tethered to their owners' yards. What surprised her most was seeing only one person and he had tied a handkerchief over his nose and mouth, bank-robber style.

"Where is everybody?" Gabe asked the same question Leah had on her mind.

"They're staying at home," David explained. "Normally, this is a bustling time of day but with the flu hitting so hard, most aren't venturing out for anything except basic necessities. We're following all precautions but the situation has gotten worse since I called you."

"And your kids?"

Concern spread across David's face. "They fall into three groups. Those who are recovering, those who are currently sick, and those who will probably show symptoms before long. We've also lost four to pneumonia. Because an illness like this spreads through group homes like wildfire, we've sent the sick ones to the hospital to try and contain the illness. Unfortunately, we don't have enough resources to care for everyone, which was why I called you."

He pointed ahead. "This is our clinic, Leah, which we only have because of your husband's generosity."

"And your arm-twisting," Gabe added.

David chuckled. "That, too."

The whitewashed building was unassuming and box-like, in contrast to the graceful Spanish architecture of the neighboring church. Yet even if she hadn't noticed the simple sign in front that read "*Clínica*", it was obvious this was an important building in the community because of the satellite dish perched on the flat roof like an oversize bird.

Inside, four patient wards, which had been designed to hold five patients each, held double that number. Of those, nearly every bed contained a child. One of the rooms was filled with cribs and padded boxes to accommodate the littlest. A few had IV poles standing beside their beds. Some were coughing, some crying, and some were too ill to do either.

In the last room, Dr. Hector Aznar was sitting on a young boy's bed, listening to his lungs. As soon as the nurse beside him murmured in his ear, he looked in their direction and a relieved smile suddenly grew on his face.

"Gabriel, welcome," he said as he approached and shook his hand effusively. "You are a sight to see." He launched into Spanish, which Leah couldn't follow.

Hector seemed to be at least ten years younger than Gabe, but his eyes reflected wisdom and experience that went beyond his years.

As the two men talked, presumably touching on Gabe's accident because Leah understood a few words, she studied her surroundings. One woman in uniform who was obviously a nurse from the way she checked IV bags and listened to lung sounds cared for the twelve toddlers and infants. A few other adults—probably parents—sponged little bodies, held cups and cuddled those who needed cuddling.

"Gabriel says you are a nurse, no?" Hector asked her in his thick accent.

"I am," Leah answered, anticipating his request.

"Good. Any assistance you can give us will be appreciated. Our girls are, shall we say, exhausted."

"I'll do what I can," she said simply. "What strain of influenza are you dealing with?"

He shrugged. "We have not tested anyone, but the ministry of health tells us it is most likely H1N1 Influenza A. Regardless of what name we use, we are fighting an uphill battle. Now that you are here, we can hope to turn the tide, yes?"

"Yes," she said. "Are you the only physician on duty?"

"My partner, Miguel Diego, is here, too, but now that you have arrived, he hopes to travel to the towns we normally visit once a month. Those people are probably in the same dire straits we are but sadly there are more of them than of us."

"Then you have a large caseload," she remarked.

Hector nodded briskly. "Larger than we can adequately

care for, but we do our best. Your husband has been what you would call our guardian angel."

Leah stole a glance at her husband. The local physician's praise had brought a tinge of pink to Gabe's face as he grinned sheepishly at her.

Suddenly, all those hours when she'd begrudged his work made her feel extremely small and petty. It was one thing to know her husband's charity made a difference in the lives of so many people and quite another to actually *see* the difference with her own eyes.

Hector spoke rapid-fire Spanish and eventually Gabe nodded before he translated.

"Here's the deal," he began. "Ben, because you're a pediatrician, he would like you to evaluate every child here, starting with the most ill. According to Hector, pneumonia is a real problem so we have to start the IV antibiotics ASAP. The nurses speak English fairly well so you should be okay on your own, but if you run into problems, let me know."

"Okay, but don't wander away too far," Ben said as he shrugged on a gown that Hector provided. "My Spanish is so rusty I could ask for a blood-pressure cuff and get an enema."

Gabe grinned. "Yeah, well, do your best."

As Ben strode off to begin, Leah asked, "Did we bring the IV supplies for—?"

"Pediatric infusion sets are being unpacked as we speak. As soon as we get a handle on the hospitalized, you and I are going on house calls while Hector covers the walk-in cases."

She raised an eyebrow. "Do you really think we're going to accomplish all that today?"

He grinned boyishly, looking far more energized than she'd expected, considering his emotionally and physically stressful journey. She was feeling overwhelmed and she'd slept on the plane for a few hours, whereas Gabe had hardly closed his eyes. "Welcome to my world."

After one of the nurses shyly identified herself as Elena, she steered Leah to her first patient—a three-year-old girl who cried fitfully but sucked greedily on the bottle Elena handed her.

"It is electrolyte drink. She is not as sick as others but now you are here, she will have IV, too. If you would sponge her down, please?"

Leah saw how the little girl lacked the strength to hold her own bottle. Immediately, she sat in the nearby chair, cradled the child in her arms and held the bottle. As the child relaxed against her, she brushed away the sweat-dampened dark curls from her forehead.

"Where are her parents?" she asked Elena, who was wringing out a wet rag in a nearby basin of iced water.

"At home with their other children," she answered, handing the cloth to Leah. "They are sick, too, but not as sick as Sofita." She stared down at Leah and smiled. "She rests. Good. When bottle *está vacío*, go to next."

At the rate Sofita was guzzling the fluid, it wouldn't take long for her to finish. In the meantime, Leah propped the drink against her chest and held it in place with the same arm she'd crooked around the child's head. With her right hand, she ran the cool cloth over her face and arms.

The small sigh of obvious pleasure and the twitch of a smile were all the thanks Leah needed.

A short time later, she gently laid the toddler in her crib. After washing her hands, she moved to the next patient, as Elena had instructed. The Spanish nurse had placed IV sets in or near every bed, and with her help they began inserting the lines into tiny veins. Most of the children were too ill to give more than a token protest, which threatened Leah's composure more than once. As soon as they had the fluids and antibiotics running, she gave each one a bottle, a cuddle and a cooling sponge bath.

Time didn't matter. Caring for these kids did.

Finally, she reached a five-year-old boy who was so severely dehydrated she couldn't raise a vein. When he hardly flinched at her failed attempts, she knew she was in trouble.

"How's it going?" Gabe asked. His timing couldn't have been more perfect.

"Thank goodness you're here," she said, frustrated. "He's so dehydrated I can't start his IV. I've tried twice and I can't poke him again. I was hoping you'd try."

"Okay." Gabe took her place on the bed and began his search for a suitable site. When he'd succeeded and the IV fluid dripped at a steady pace, Leah wanted to cheer.

"Are you ready for a break?" he asked.

She stared at him, horrified by his suggestion. "I'm not finished. I still have IVs to start and—"

"This is the last one," he told her gently. "See?"

She finally glanced around the room and, sure enough, an IV bag hung near every bed.

"But I haven't cuddled this one yet," she said. "Or bathed him, or—"

"I will do that, Señora Montgomery," Elena came up to say. "We have done well. Go with your husband."

"But you've worked longer than I have."

"Go." Elena tugged her away from the bed. "I will sit as I watch Felipe."

"Come on, Leah," Gabe coaxed. "You won't be much of use if you wear yourself out on the first day."

Reluctantly, she followed him. "Where are we going?"

"To eat," he said, leading her past the patient areas to an average-sized room that served as Hector's office and staff lounge. There, two covered plates of food were waiting, along with a pot of rich black coffee.

"Hmm," Gabe said, sniffing the air and whipping the napkins off the plates. "This smells like Carlotta's cooking. She makes the best tamales, beans and rice." His hand froze and a thoughtful expression crossed his face.

"Carlotta? Is this the woman you suspect has pancreatic cancer? The one who cares for her three grandchildren?"

"Yes."

"If she's in the kitchen, maybe she isn't as ill as you thought."

"Maybe. When I have a minute, I'll find out."

At first, Leah thought she was too keyed up to eat, but the delightful aroma convinced her otherwise. She tasted the beans while Gabe poured two mugs of coffee.

"Has everyone else eaten?" she asked as he rejoined her at the table for four.

"I assume so. We took the last two places."

"Is it always like this when you visit a place?" she asked.

"The experience is never quite the same," he said. "We've conducted clinics before and treated a lot more people, but never this many seriously ill cases at once."

"I almost feel as if I'm in the middle of a disaster drill, except this isn't a practice. These children are really sick. I haven't stopped until now and I haven't stepped out of the one ward."

"What's sad is how the patients in the other three are just as ill, if not more so."

"You realize that three days isn't nearly enough time to make a dent in treating these people?"

"Believe me, no one is more aware of that than I. What's more disconcerting is when you realize Ciuflores isn't the only village experiencing this scenario. What we're seeing is taking place across the country. A lot of those communities aren't as lucky as this one."

The picture he'd painted wasn't pretty.

"Because they don't have a Father David who has a personal connection to the CEO of a charitable organization?" she asked.

His mouth curved into a gentle smile. "Exactly."

Gabe polished off the food on his plate then leaned back. "Are you hinting you'd like to stay longer?"

Was she? "I'm only making an observation," she said. "But isn't it difficult to leave when you know your work isn't finished?"

"Definitely," he agreed, "but staying until the crisis ends isn't feasible. Hector and his staff know that, and they're grateful for every bit of help we provide because it's more than they had before. When you stop to think about it, Ben and I have literally doubled the number of medical professionals in a sixty-mile radius, so we can treat twice as many patients. We may be a mere stitch in a wound that needs ten, but sometimes one, if properly placed, is better than nothing."

He stared at her now empty plate. "Are you ready to tackle our next assignment, Nurse Montgomery?"

She was starting to get her second wind. "Sure."

"Good, because, house calls, here we come."

Armed with David and his knowledge of his parishioners, Gabe began his round of house calls. He found everything from a household with only one or two sick individuals to homes where the entire family was symptomatic. Fortunately, none required hospitalization, which was good because he didn't know where Hector and his staff would squeeze in another patient.

Leah, however, was a star in his eyes. She performed

basic nursing care from taking temperatures to giving sponge baths. She taught children and parents to sneeze into the crooks of their arms and, with David's helpful translation skills, encouraged them to wash their hands with soap and water for the same length of time it took to sing the happy birthday song.

As soon as it was too dark to see more than a few feet in front of them, Leah was lagging behind and even David appeared a little frayed around the edges. Gabe wasn't functioning on much more than adrenalin, either.

"We're calling it a night," he told his crew as they returned to David's truck.

"We can see a few more people," Leah protested.

"We could," he agreed, "but we won't. We're all exhausted and tomorrow is another day."

Leah dutifully climbed into the cab of the truck, allowing the two men relative privacy.

"Your wife doesn't know when to quit, does she?" David asked.

"Afraid not."

"Have you told her where you two are bunking down?"

Gabe should have, but the opportunity hadn't presented itself until now. "Not yet. I'm hoping she'll be too tired to care."

"Good luck with that. If we weren't having an epidemic, I could make other arrangements, but—"

"We'll be fine at the orphanage," Gabe said firmly, hoping he was right. "Leah will understand our choices are limited. Did you find places for Sheldon, Ben and Corey, our pilot?"

"They're bunking together down the hall. I'm sorry I only had two rooms to spare, one for you and your wife and one for the others."

"We won't spend that much time in them anyway," Gabe answered practically.

"True. By the way, in the morning, before you're torn in a hundred different directions, save a few minutes for me, okay?"

"A problem?"

David sighed. "Yes and no. It's too late to go into detail."

"I'll find you first thing," Gabe promised.

As it happened, Leah was too exhausted to notice her surroundings, or, if she did, the fact simply didn't register. Gabe gratefully ushered her into the room they'd been given, although he knew his moment of reckoning would come in the morning.

As soon as she saw the bed, she sighed gratefully and began stripping off her clothes. By the time Gabe had opened his duffle bag, Leah was curled beneath the covers.

"Sweet dreams," he said softly, but she was already fast asleep.

He undressed down to boxers and a T-shirt and slipped under the sheet beside her. Immediately, she snuggled against him and he tucked her under his arm, pleased she'd turned to him without being aware of it. Which only proved that subconsciously she knew she belonged at his side.

Holding her against him, Gabe reflected on their day. She'd been such a godsend. Not only had she kept him sane on their long flight, she'd been a great partner when they'd finally started to work. She'd anticipated his requests, offered suggestions, and both her smile and calm manner had soothed the most anxious parents and fretful kids. He'd accomplished a lot today and he owed it all to her.

As he began drifting off, he realized her presence had given him another benefit. Normally, on trips such as these, he had a hard time going to sleep. Between pushing himself to the point where he was simply too tired to doze off and thinking of everything he had to accomplish the next day, he had trouble shutting off his brain so his body could follow suit.

Now, though, having her in his arms, listening to her gentle breathing and feeling her steady heartbeat brought him peace. Tomorrow would start early and end late, but one good thing had happened already as a result of their trip.

After so many months apart, Leah was finally sharing his bed.

CHAPTER NINE

A THUMP and a giggle teased Leah as she dreamed of a summertime picnic with three children. Another giggle, a loud whisper, a foot digging into her side and a happy-sounding "Shhh" jarred the pleasant scene in her head, and she slowly opened her eyes. The two little girls straddling Gabe's chest in their nightgowns startled her completely awake.

"What in the world—?"

"She is awake?" the oldest asked, and immediately a boy, who looked to be about four years old and was wearing cowboy-print pajamas, climbed aboard, too.

The youngsters all chattered a mile a minute at Gabe, who simply laughed and answered in Spanish. Although she couldn't follow the conversation, she recognized a few words—*desayuno*, breakfast, and *señora*, lady.

"Gabe?" she asked as the smallest girl suddenly leaned over Leah and smiled at her around the thumb in her mouth. "What's going on?"

"This is Anna, Rosa and José. They are Carlotta's grand-children," he explained as he sat up, holding on to Rosa so she didn't tumble off the mattress. "Anna is the oldest. She's five. Rosa is almost two and José is four."

"Carlotta the cook?"

"Yeah. They all live here with the rest of the kids."

"The *rest* of the kids?" she echoed. "Where *are* we?"

"David gave us a room in the staff quarters at the orphanage."

"We're staying in the *orphanage*?" she asked, horrified.

"I know what you're thinking, but this is where we usually bunk down. Besides, David couldn't ask a family who's sick to take us in."

She exhaled, knowing she couldn't refute his logic. She could do this. She *would*.

"Fine, but do we have to stay in the same room?"

"David only had two available. We have one and the rest of our group is sharing the other."

"I don't suppose we can ask for another bed or a cot?"

"All extra beds and cots are being used by patients. Unless you'd like to kick one of them off their mattress so you can have one to yourself?"

She cast him a disgusted look. "Of course not," she grumbled. "Maybe one of us should sleep on the floor."

"Feel free," he said. "I'm the one with the sore ribs, remember? Besides, nothing will happen in here that you don't want to happen."

His comment wasn't completely consoling. Given the opportunity—and her own weakness where he was concerned—they'd do far more than sleep. The good news was that they'd probably both be too exhausted when they finally fell into bed to have the energy to make love.

Just then the children bounced on Gabe again as each one chattered louder than the other in an obvious attempt to get his attention.

So much for his sore ribs, she thought uncharitably, eying the youngsters. Yet their excitement was contagious. After seeing the seriously ill children yesterday, it was refreshing to see such happy, healthy ones.

"I'm sorry about the early wake-up call." He tugged on the oldest girl's pigtail. "The kids aren't supposed to barge in, but they'd heard I'd arrived and, well…" he shrugged helplessly "…they couldn't wait to see us."

He tickled José and the dark-haired imp laughed with delight.

"You have an exuberant fan club," she remarked.

Gabe's grin made him look like the man in their wedding photos. The shadow she'd seen in his eyes yesterday had lifted and joy shone in its place as he tugged on José's hair. "I'm a novelty," he said.

Leah watched as Anna leaned over and planted a sloppy kiss on Gabe's cheek. "For being a novelty, they're very comfortable around you." In fact, she thought they were more than comfortable—they all looked at Gabe as if he was their personal fairy godfather.

"They remember me from my previous trips and haven't forgotten that I usually bring candy."

Rosa's eyes sparkled with interest. *"¿Tienes chocolate?"*

"Later," Gabe promised, as he threw back the sheet and swung his feet onto the floor. "After breakfast."

Immediately the children screeched with delight. His next words sent the children scampering off the bed with several more enthusiastic bounces before they disappeared through the open door.

"What did you tell them?" she asked.

"Candy is for children who eat their oatmeal first. I also reminded them that Father David won't be happy if their grandmother reported them missing."

"Well, I guess this means we should get up and start the day, though I still feel like I need another few hours in bed!"

"Did you sleep well?"

"I must have. I don't remember a thing after I stumbled in here last night."

"I'm not surprised. You worked hard yesterday. Unfortunately, today won't be easier."

"I didn't expect a vacation when I left home," she told him. "So don't apologize."

"Okay." He rose and stretched. "Come on, lazybones. Breakfast and our adoring public are waiting."

The morning meal was a noisy affair. The trestle tables were full of youngsters of varying ages, all waiting for their food. Yet when David rose to say the blessing, the littlest to the oldest became so quiet Leah could have heard a mouse scamper across the floor.

While Sheldon and Gabe discussed their plans for the day—Ben apparently had spent the night at the clinic to monitor several patients who'd needed ventilator support— Leah sensed she was being watched. At first, she disregarded her suspicion because so many of the children kept glancing in their direction, but the feeling persisted. When she saw the trio of children who'd provided their early-morning wake-up call, she knew she hadn't been imagining things.

Rosa was studying her with a thoughtful expression and José watched Gabe with adoration. Anna's gaze drifted from Gabe to her, then back to Gabe again, and it held such longing that it nearly undid her.

There was no doubt about it. For whatever reason, these children loved Gabe. And seeing the sparkle in their eyes when they captured his attention made her realize how she, too, had once looked at him through those same eyes of love.

Curious about the children's story, she waited to ask until the meal was over and Gabe had left the table to deliver the promised treat. While he was swarmed over by the youngsters, she pressed David for answers.

"Their grandmother has been our cook ever since her husband died several years ago," David began. "After her son and daughter-in-law were killed when his fishing boat capsized about a year ago, the children came to live with Carlotta. She needed to keep her job to support herself, so we worked out an arrangement where she continued to cook at a slightly reduced salary in exchange for day care and a place for the three of them to live."

He sighed. "The really unfortunate thing is that Carlotta has recently been diagnosed with pancreatic cancer."

"Gabe suspected as much but I didn't realize her diagnosis was official."

"Unfortunately—her condition being what it is—we don't know how much longer she'll be with us."

Leah's heart went out to the three children. To lose their parents and, soon, their grandmother... Life would be tough for them. "I'm so sorry to hear that. Do they have any other family?"

"Carlotta has another son. The children's uncle. We're trying to locate him, but no one seems to know where he is, what he's doing, or if he's even alive. I've been told he was quite a hellion in his younger days and went to Mexico City, where he fell in with the wrong crowd. Carlotta hasn't heard from him in years."

"What happens to them, then, after...?"

"If we can't find their next of kin, they'll stay here. If we do find their uncle, the children will go with him, unless he doesn't want them." He sighed. "The odds aren't in favor of him accepting the responsibility, but it's hard to say what might happen."

Leah glanced at the children interspersed around the

room. "I presume all the children have a similarly sad story."

He shrugged. "More or less. Some are orphans, others have parents who simply can't provide for them."

"They're all from Ciuflores?"

"No. We're the only orphanage in the area, so kids come here from miles around. If I had the space, we could easily double our number. Life in this part of the country is difficult and the children often pay the price."

"I see." She paused, watching the three as they clung to Gabe, but it was more for his attention than the candy he provided. "Those three seem to love Gabe," she remarked.

"They all do," David said simply, "although I have to admit he has a special rapport with these kids in particular. Their faces always light up when I mention his name. I'm not sure why because he doesn't single them out but I suppose it's the same for them as it is with us. There are some people we feel more comfortable with than others.

"The thing is, he's good with children, in general," David continued. "A modern-day Pied Piper. He definitely has a gift."

"He does," she agreed, trying to ignore the sudden ache his words caused in her chest. If not for her, Gabe would have a houseful of his own children.

A sudden scuffle at the opposite end of the dining room drew the priest's attention. Either he had eyes at the back of his head or being the director of an orphanage of fifty had given him a sixth sense for trouble. "Sorry for deserting you," David apologized, "but I have to play referee."

David hurried toward the two teenagers, who were shoving each other and occasionally throwing punches. Rather than observe the drama unfolding at that end of the room, she watched Gabe as he dug in his pockets and passed pieces of wrapped hard candy to the children who swarmed him.

He looked so happy as he laughed, joked and hefted the littlest ones into the air.

She thought of the instances when they'd visited friends with children or her own family gatherings with her sister's kids. Their children had always climbed over Gabe on their arrival and she'd attributed their attraction to his freely lavished and complete attention.

His affinity for little people didn't stop there, either. Sick children responded to his smile and quiet confidence in a way that many adults did not. She'd seen that scenario more often than not in the hospital. More recently, she'd seen it during yesterday's house calls.

David's description of Pied Piper seemed apt.

Her insecurities suddenly flooded over her. It was far too easy to wonder if Gabe regretted marrying her or if he wished he'd cooperated when she'd offered a divorce. A legal piece of paper would have given him the freedom to find someone who could fill the need for a child in his life.

Although she rapidly dismissed those ideas as foolishness because he'd said he would love her regardless, one hard truth stared at her.

She was the one holding up the adoption process. *She* was the roadblock to their dreams of a family. Gabe had given control over those dreams to her, and *she* now carried the deciding vote.

Don't let fear influence your choice.

Deep in her thoughts, she didn't notice Rosa had toddled over to her until she felt a small hand on her knee.

Leah stiffened, an instinctive reaction born from her reluctance to let herself grow too close to a child...*any* child...but the trust shining in those dark brown eyes and the featherlight touch that was both comforting and tentative made her smile come easily.

"Shouldn't you be with your grandmother?" Leah asked. Then, because the little girl didn't seem to understand, she fished for the right phrases in her limited vocabulary. *"¿Dónde está tu abuelita?"* Where is your grandmother? *"Debes estar con ella."* You should be with her.

Rosa simply popped a thumb into her mouth and grinned.

Unable to stop herself, Leah stroked the tousled jet-black curls. "Don't you want to play with your friends?"

Rosa didn't answer. Instead, she simply waited, as if she had faith in Leah's ability to eventually figure out what she wanted.

Oh, please, let something else grab her attention, Leah thought. It was one thing to share her love with nieces and nephews and quite another to give it to a child she'd never see again. And yet she couldn't send Rosa away, not when she was waiting so patiently for acknowledgment. This toddler had already known more rejection than any child at her age should. She wouldn't add to it.

"Do you want me to hold you?" Leah asked. She searched her limited vocabulary for the proper phrase and came up missing. She simply patted her lap and held out her hands.

As if Rosa had been waiting for the invitation, she immediately popped her thumb out of her mouth, climbed up and made herself comfortable.

With an awkwardness that came more out of emotional uncertainty rather than a lack of the mechanics involved, Leah shifted positions to tuck Rosa under her arm.

With her thumb back in her mouth, Rosa melted against her, as if there wasn't another place she'd rather be.

Certain one of the staff would soon retrieve the toddler,

Leah allowed herself to enjoy the weight of the little body in her lap and the special scent so common to babies. Slowly, tentatively, she began to rub her shoulder.

"I wonder what you're thinking," Leah said, aware that even if Rosa understood her, she couldn't answer. "You are definitely a snuggler, aren't you?"

Rosa smiled around her thumb as if she understood or was simply happy to have Leah all to herself.

"I'll bet you've wrapped Father David and everyone else around your little finger," she murmured.

It wouldn't have been difficult to do, she decided. She'd been holding the tyke for less than five minutes and already felt the gossamer ties ensnaring her.

Somewhat amazed by Rosa's decision to seek her out, Leah simply continued to hold her and savor the moments when suddenly Anna and José appeared beside her. He held out a small battered toy truck while Anna showed off her own precious possession, a doll that showed it had obviously been well loved by the threadbare dress, broken nose and missing index finger. Immediately, Rosa squirmed off Leah's lap and disappeared as fast as her short legs would take her.

Wondering what had sent Rosa away, Leah admired the other children's toys. "Does your truck make a noise?" she asked José, then made a few questioning engine sounds. The boy beamed and he knelt down to run the truck beside her feet to demonstrate.

While he was occupied, Leah touched the doll's face. "Does your doll have a name?" she asked. *"¿Nombre?"*

Anna's smile stretched from ear to ear. "Sarita," she answered, before launching into a conversation that Leah couldn't begin to follow. It obviously revolved around Sarita because Anna stroked what was left of her doll's pigtails.

Suddenly, a new lovey was thrust into her lap—a light

brown teddy bear with matted fur, a frayed red neck ribbon and one eye. Apparently Rosa wasn't to be outdone because she waited for Leah to acknowledge her toy, too.

Conflicting emotions filled Leah's chest—pain that these children were so happy with so little, and awe that they wanted to share what obviously meant so much to them. Plus, they wanted to share it with *her*.

For an instant she couldn't breathe and her vision blurred. She was desperate to escape and began frantically looking around the dining hall for Gabe to rescue her, but Anna spoke and Leah knew she couldn't obey her instinct to run away. Leaving the three so abruptly would be a rejection they couldn't understand and didn't deserve.

So she forced herself to breathe slowly and deeply until the overwhelming feeling passed, leaving bittersweet longing in its wake.

If not for David's intervention, Gabe would never have been able to untangle himself from the children clamoring for his attention. Fortunately, after David had dealt with the two boys who'd clearly experienced a difference of opinion, he clapped his hands and ordered the children to their daily chores. Less than thirty seconds later, the noise level had dropped considerably and he saw Carlotta slowly approach, leaning heavily on the girl beside her.

"Shouldn't you be in bed?" He fussed over the woman, who didn't appear anything like she had when he'd last seen her. She'd lost weight and her skin color reflected the toll her cancer was taking on her. Perhaps if he'd been able to convince her to go to a major facility for tests when he'd first examined her, they might have been able to halt the disease and give her a bit more time, but now it was too late. According to David, Taylor had talked Hector through a biopsy procedure and a preliminary result had confirmed the aggressive nature of her disease. While surgery and subsequent chemotherapy were options, those treatments would only prolong the inevitable.

"I will go there soon enough," Carlotta told him with a smile as she accepted the chair he'd pulled out for her then tiredly waved away her helper. "I must do what I can now. Your breakfast was good?"

According to David, Carlotta had been teaching two girls to take her place in the kitchen. From the food Gabe had eaten so far, Carlotta's replacements were learning their lessons well.

"It was delicious, as was yesterday's meal," he answered.

"Good. I want to see my grandchildren. They seem happy, yes?"

Gabe turned to find his wife and saw her surrounded by the three familiar faces. For a moment he waited and watched the childless woman with three motherless children…and wished.

"Your wife has a mother's touch."

"She does."

"Yet, the padre says you do not have children."

He ignored the familiar twinge of disappointment. "We had a little boy, but he was too small when he was born. Then we tried to adopt, but things didn't work out. So, no, we don't have children of our own."

"I see. That explains why your wife isn't, what is the word, *comfortable* with my babies? She has too much pain inside."

"Probably."

"And yet she has a good heart."

"She does." Gabe watched as Leah planted a kiss against José's temple. As he squirmed, she laughed as if she found his reaction humorous.

"You carry your own sorrow, do you not, Dr. Gabriel?"

He hesitated. "A part of me always will," he said simply. Then, because he wasn't comfortable under the older woman's scrutiny, he motioned toward the scene before them. "Your grandchildren are great kids."

"Even when they wake you early?"

He chuckled. "You knew they'd paid us a visit?"

"Grandmothers have eyes everywhere."

"With those three, you need them," he said.

"Oh, yes." Her gaze drifted in Leah's direction and she smiled at José's demonstration of his truck. "He is my busy one," she said. "Always moving, even in his sleep. Anna is my noisy one because she talks, talks, talks. And Rosa…" Her face was a mixture of love and sorrow as Rosa rested in Leah's lap. "Rosa is my cuddly one. It is good they are familiar with everyone here."

"No one will ever take your place," he said kindly, "regardless of who cares for them."

"Thank you for that, Dr. Gabriel," she whispered. "You, too, have a good heart. Perhaps Father David will find someone like you and your wife to take my place."

Gabe froze. Was Carlotta hinting that she wanted Gabe to adopt her grandchildren? If so, would Leah be open to the idea, especially after she'd adamantly refused to adopt? As he glanced at the children, he admitted that in spite of telling Leah he'd abide by her decision he'd love nothing more than to take these children into their home. He truly wanted to make it happen—to barge in, full steam ahead, just as she'd accused him of doing—but he couldn't. He'd told her the choice was hers, and he'd stick by that, even if it killed him.

"Do not fret," Carlotta told him. "What will be, will be." She struggled to her feet. "Come. Those three will play all day with your wife if we let them. Shall we rescue her?"

CHAPTER TEN

LEAH knew they were pushing hard to see as many patients as possible because they were scheduled to fly home in the morning. She hated leaving when the residents of this community obviously needed her help and she consoled herself with the reminder that the assistance she'd provided had eased the regular staff's burden to a small degree.

She also had to admit that the Salazar children had captured her heart, and in such a short time, too. How could they not, especially when Rosa smiled hugely whenever she saw her, then toddled over and wanted to be held?

These aren't your children, Leah told herself as she played with Anna and José. *You're just—what did Gabe call it? A novelty. Yes. That's it.*

In one small corner of her mind she was glad they were leaving so soon. She didn't want them to become so entrenched in her affections that her departure would be traumatic. They'd have enough to deal with when their grandmother died because they were old enough to remember her—at least for a while—but too young to understand why the one constant in their lives had disappeared forever.

During her odd moments she wished she could take all three home with her, but it was impossible. Their uncle would assume responsibility, which was as it should be.

By mid-afternoon, she had lost track of the number of

homes they had visited. Most had at least one parent healthy enough to care for the sick members of their household, but the very last family they visited—the Ortiz family—was in dire straits. Every member was ill and the mother, pregnant with her third child, had an advanced case of pneumonia. The father had left several weeks earlier to find work and no one knew when he would return.

Leah, David and Gabe stood off in one corner to discuss their options.

"We can't leave her here," Leah warned. "She has diminished lung capacity with the baby pressing on her diaphragm. She needs to be in the hospital with round-the-clock nursing care, not to mention ventilator support."

"The hospital is full," Gabe pointed out.

"But if she stays at home…" Leah left her sentence unsaid. The outcome, in her opinion, was obvious.

"I know," Gabe said tiredly. "She won't make it for sure."

"Then David will increase his occupancy by two, at least in the short term."

"He still might," he warned. "Being in the hospital doesn't mean we'll provide a magical cure."

She knew as well as anyone how hard this strain of influenza was on pregnant women. "Yes, but there she has a fighting chance. Left at home, she has none."

Her argument had its desired influence because Gabe turned to David. "What will we do with the children if we can find a bed for her? Can you find someone to stay with them?"

"Ordinarily, I'd say yes, but I'm running out of healthy adults," David said ruefully. "The best I can do is bring them to the orphanage."

"But won't we expose the others?" Leah asked, hating

the thought of Rosa and the other children contracting the same disease.

"We'll quarantine them," Gabe said.

"But David doesn't have enough staff to separate these two from the rest," she protested.

He raised an eyebrow. "What do you want me to do, Leah? The hospital doesn't have room—we're going to have to squeeze her in as it is—and we can't leave them here to fend for themselves."

"We have no choice," David added. "We'll do the best we can and pray it will be enough."

She exhaled, hating their lack of options. "You're right. Just be sure your staff understands how easily the flu can spread through the orphanage if they aren't careful."

"I'm counting on you to remind them," he said.

"Then it's settled," Gabe said. "We'll move her to the hospital and the children to the orphanage."

As they turned to leave, Leah held Gabe back while David went on ahead to make arrangements. "How are you doing?"

"Fine."

"You look tired."

His smile was lopsided. "Aw, honey, I'm way past tired, but thanks for asking."

"Maybe you should take a break."

"I can't. Not now. Not with Mrs. Ortiz in her condition." He rubbed his face.

"You're worried about her," she guessed.

"I'm worried about a lot of things," he admitted. "Can we help her pull through with limited resources? Can we give her the attention she needs when so many others need it, too? Frankly, how Hector and Miguel bear up under this on a daily basis boggles my mind."

"Maybe the epidemic will play itself out soon."

"We can always hope." He dropped a quick kiss on her mouth then straightened as he gave her a rueful smile. "Gotta run."

A short time later, Leah found herself not only selecting a room for the two far away from the others but also instructing all the adults and older children on proper hygiene. Through it all, Carlotta's grandchildren became her shadows, although she refused to allow them in the same room as the sick children. A few times she was certain she'd caught a glimpse of Carlotta out of the corner of her eye, but when she looked, the woman was gone.

Leah felt guilty for enjoying Rosa and Anna's attention, especially when she knew their time with their grandmother was so short, but having three energetic children in the older woman's sickroom wouldn't be a pleasant experience for any of them. She was doing the woman a favor by looking after the three, she told herself. After tomorrow, someone else would take over, anyway. Until then she planned to store up memories of toothy smiles, sloppy kisses and gentle hugs.

Dinner was a semi-relaxed affair, eaten in the dining hall long after the children had finished and were playing outside. David had disappeared into his office and Sheldon and Ben were back at the clinic, leaving Gabe and Leah to enjoy another meal of tamales and beans.

"I can't believe we're going home tomorrow," she remarked.

"Time flies when you're having fun."

She reached across the table to cover his hand. "I wouldn't call this fun. I'd describe the trip as enlightening, challenging and overwhelming."

"But you're glad you came."

She nodded slowly. "I am."

"We make a pretty good team, don't we?"

"Is this where you say, 'I told you so'?" she asked lightly, aware that so far this trip seemed to be fulfilling Gabe's expectations. Working together had opened her eyes to many things, but most of all she'd finally been able to see Gabe's character without the vision being distorted by her own pain and resentment. In fact, she was seeing the man she'd fallen in love with and knew it wouldn't take much to push her over the edge.

"I hear the garden has a beautiful moonlit path," he said offhandedly. "Want to check it out with me tonight?"

"A moonlight stroll sounds perfect. Do you think we can disappear for a while, though?"

"I don't see why not. Everything seems to be under control."

Sheldon took that moment to approach and lean over the table. His face was solemn, his tone grave as he spoke. "You spoke too soon, boss. We have a problem."

Gabe's shoulders slumped slightly. From Leah's own experience with Gabe's second-in-command, Sheldon tended toward understatement rather than exaggeration. If he said there was a problem then the problem was usually major, not minor.

"Somehow, I'm not surprised," Gabe said wryly. "What's up?"

"Ben wants you in the hospital ASAP."

Gabe frowned. "We were just there. Did he say why?"

"Not really. Something about Hector."

Leah exchanged a glance with Gabe. "What could be wrong with him?"

Gabe rose. "Let's find out."

They found the clinic's physician lying on the small cot in his office. Ben was sitting beside him as he listened to Hector's ragged breathing while Elena sponged off his face in an obvious attempt to bring down his fever.

"What happened?" Gabe asked in a low voice.

Ben slung his stethoscope around his neck and motioned them into the hallway. "Influenza."

Gabe's heart sank. "Damn," he muttered, running his hands through his hair. "We don't need this on top of everything else."

"My sentiments exactly," Ben agreed. "I noticed he wasn't feeling well this morning, but he shrugged it off as exhaustion from too-long days and too-short nights. Then, about thirty minutes ago, he could hardly stay on his feet and wasn't making any sense when he talked. I thought maybe it was the language barrier, so I found Elena to talk to him. She was as clueless as I was."

Elena nodded, her dark eyes large with worry. "*Sí*. He was out of his head, talking crazy talk." She made circular motions near her ear.

"Elena and I convinced him to go to bed, which didn't take too much effort, I might add. Then I sent Sheldon to find you." He hesitated. "We're going to need a Plan B."

Gabe pinched the bridge of his nose, already anticipating the repercussions Hector's illness would have. From the looks on everyone's faces, they were realizing them, too.

He turned to Elena. "Do you know when Dr. Diego will return? Is there any way we can reach him before then?"

"He will be back in a week, maybe more, maybe less." She shrugged helplessly. "I can send someone to find him, but he does not always follow the same path. Sometimes he goes here first. Sometimes there first. Is no way to tell."

"What about a cell phone?"

She shook her head. "It does not work where he is going."

Damn! Gabe felt everyone's gaze as they waited for his answer. He only wished he had one to give.

"Here are our options," he said. "We leave as scheduled—"

Leah gasped. "But we can't desert these people now, when they don't have a doctor and they're in the middle of a medical crisis. Even if the patients were all doing well, the nurses can't handle Mrs. Ortiz—the pregnant woman we brought in earlier."

"Or…" he cast a meaningful glance at her for interrupting "…we stay until Miguel returns, which could be a week or more. And that will affect our other commitments." He turned to Sheldon. "The clinic in Tennessee comes to mind."

"Don't forget the trip to Alaska," Sheldon reminded him.

Sensing Leah was about to explode with frustration, he glanced at Ben. "Your anniversary is a few days away, if I remember correctly."

Ben cleared his throat and looked apologetic. "Yeah. My wife planned a big party. It's our tenth, and I promised I'd be there," he said to Leah as she was the only one who hadn't heard.

Gabe glanced at Sheldon. "How are the supplies holding out?"

"We've used about two-thirds of what we brought," Sheldon admitted. "Under normal conditions for a community this size, what's left should last a while. But…" he shrugged "…these aren't normal conditions. Everything depends on how near we are to the end of this outbreak."

"What's your opinion, Ben?" Gabe asked. "Are we on the downhill slope?"

"You've seen as many if not more patients than I have," the other physician replied. "If I had to guess, from the number and severity of the cases who've landed in the clinic, I'd say we're still in the thick of things."

Gabe agreed, although he'd hoped Ben might have drawn a different conclusion. "Then we have a third option."

"Which is?" Leah asked.

"I'll stay behind while the rest of you head back as originally planned. Sheldon, you handle the business end of sending down another shipment. Corey can help."

Sheldon nodded. "I'll get back as soon as I can." He grinned. "If not before."

"I'm staying, too," Leah declared, her chin rising defiantly. "I may not be a physician, but I can help."

She'd be a welcome addition, but he wasn't worried about her ability to hold their pace. He had three objections to her remaining behind, and they were all under the age of six. "Yes, but—"

"If you're not going home, neither am I."

Knowing she wouldn't appreciate an argument in front of everyone, he simply shot her his best we'll-talk-about-it-later look. To her credit, she didn't say a word, but her eyes promised a heated discussion.

He turned to his team. "Then it's settled. You two will fly back in the morning. Sheldon, you'll return as soon as you can arrange for another supply shipment."

"Piece of cake," Sheldon boasted.

"In that case," Ben said, "I'll take tonight's shift. This may be the only night you'll get any sleep."

It probably would be. After Ben climbed aboard their plane, Gabe would be on duty twenty-four seven.

"Okay, but call if you get more than you can handle."

Throughout the rest of their conversation, Leah didn't say a word, which didn't bode well. Still, Gabe hoped their moonlight walk through the garden would help as it could easily be the only private time he'd enjoy with her until they flew back to the U.S.

As soon as he'd finished hammering out last-minute

details with Sheldon, he grabbed Leah's arm and led her out of the clinic. Darkness had fallen and the usual night-time noises surrounded them as he walked beside her to the orphanage.

She held herself stiffly under the guiding hand he'd placed at the small of her back.

"Nice evening, isn't it?" he asked, making conversation to soften her irritation.

"Hmm."

He glanced at the building looming ahead, noticing the bank of windows in the orphanage's dormitory wing was dark. "Looks like the kids are all in bed."

"I'd say so."

She'd said a complete sentence; he was making progress.

"The garden's around the back," he said. "Watch your step. The ground is uneven." He took her hand before he led her down a small footpath and held back shrubs and branches for her to pass by unscathed. Finally, they arrived in a clearing that boasted a stone bench and a multitude of flowers. The colors were muted in the moonlight, but the white blooms seemed to glow as if nature had saved their beauty for midnight lovers. Their fragrance filled the air with a heady, sensual perfume.

"Oh, Gabe," she breathed as she turned a complete circle. "This is beautiful."

Relieved at how their surroundings had broken through her reserve, Gabe smiled. "Not as beautiful as the woman standing here."

She met his gaze. "Do you really think so?"

"I know so." He traced a line from her temple down to her jaw.

"Then why...?" She bit her lip in indecision. "Why don't you want me to stay here with you?"

The hurt in her voice was as painful to hear as it obviously was for her to say. "I want you to stay," he confessed, "because I like having you here. It simply isn't in your best interests."

"Don't yo-yo on me, Gabe," she warned. "Why isn't it in my best interests? After all the fuss you made to get me here, now you insist I go? And without you?" She shook her head. "I don't understand."

"You're growing too attached to Carlotta's grandchildren and you've only been around them for a couple of days. How hard will it be on you to leave after another week?"

"Yes, I'm fond of them. They're sweet kids." She spoke as if she weighed each word beforehand. "You're trying to protect me again but it isn't necessary. When we finally go home, I'll handle it."

"Are you sure?" Perhaps it was his job to be supportive instead of doubtful, but he wanted Leah to know exactly what she would face. "Leaving these kids won't be like leaving your nieces and nephews. Chances are you'll never see these youngsters again."

She nodded slowly, as if she'd already realized it. "They'll go with their uncle and that will be that."

Gabe didn't see any point in mentioning that no one had been able to locate Carlotta's son. Why give Leah something else to worry about, especially if knowing they had a family member who'd step in was a comfort to her?

She squared her shoulders. "Regardless, you need me and I'm not leaving until I absolutely have to."

"Leah…" he warned.

"Please, Gabe? Let me help you, and let me enjoy the extra time with them."

He hated to hear her beg, even though he knew she was only going to put herself through more anguish.

"Yes," she added as if she'd read his thoughts, "I'll

probably get teary-eyed and cry most of the way home, but I'm preparing myself for that. I'll be okay. Truly."

Her assurances were convincing, but he knew the separation, when it came, would be far more difficult than she imagined. And yet, if she understood and accepted the risks, what could he do?

"If you're certain…" He was repeating himself again.

"I am."

He hesitated, still unsettled by her choice. "You know I can just toss you on that plane," he mentioned offhandedly. "As the team's leader, I'm responsible for everyone's safety and well-being, including their emotional health."

"You are," she admitted, "but this is my decision, Gabe. I *want* to stay." Her grin widened. "And if you make me leave at first light, I'll return when Sheldon does."

He chuckled as he hugged her tight. "This is against my better judgment, but okay. You can stay."

"Gee, thanks for permission."

He grinned at her wry tone then he added a teasing note to his own to hide his own trepidation. "Are those the only reasons why you don't want to leave—because of the kids and the patients?" He held his breath, hoping to hear she'd had a change of heart about their divorce.

"Oh, I don't know," she said airily. "It could be because you're starting to grow on me, too, but I haven't made up my mind yet."

"And when do you think you might know?" he returned.

"Maybe tomorrow. Maybe next week. Maybe—"

"Right now?" He bent down to brush his lips against hers, but his light kiss soon turned heated. Perhaps it was due to the moonlight or the heady fragrance in the air. Perhaps it was because he was glad Leah wasn't leaving or that this could be their last uninterrupted night for the foreseeable future. Perhaps it was simply because Leah was the one woman who could make his blood sing, but, whatever the reason, he wanted more and he sensed she might feel the same.

"Yes," she breathed. "Maybe now…"

He hauled her against him, eager to take what she was offering and relieved that the moment he'd been waiting for was finally upon him.

"Dr. Gabriel! Dr. Gabriel?"

Leah broke off their kiss. "You're being paged."

Gabe grimaced. "So I hear."

"Maybe it's something minor."

The hopeful note in her voice and the way she'd responded in his arms made him believe that she might be coming round. That she just might have started to look forward instead of backward. That she either had or was on the brink of wanting her future to include him. Those notions were enough for him to accept this most inopportune interruption with grace, even though he really wanted to grumble and complain.

"Are you willing to wager on that?" he asked.

She grinned. "No, but it's a nice thought."

A teenage boy burst into the clearing. "Dr. Gabriel. Dr. Ben says to come."

"Sorry to cancel on you," he told her. "Duty calls."

"I understand. I'm a doctor's wife, remember?"

Leah stretched on the too-thin mattress, noticing Gabe's side was still empty. She'd waited for him to return to their room, but had given up and gone to bed two hours ago. Now her watch dial showed it was nearly midnight and the sheets were cold, which meant the emergency requiring his attention was serious.

She curled around her pillow, feeling like a contented cat

as she reflected on their evening. It had felt good to work with Gabe on a professional basis, with none of their old baggage between them. Seeing him in action was a vivid reminder of why she'd fallen in love with him ten years ago. His concern and tireless interest in the people he'd come to serve were glowing testimonies to his character. He was a man who'd move mountains if he could for the people he cared about.

He'd told her that he'd pressed for the adoption for *her*, but she'd never quite believed that, until now. After seeing him in action—seeing how quickly he responded to whatever need he found—she finally believed his motives. And, for the first time, she began to wonder if she might be wrong about other things. Maybe they *wouldn't* be better off being apart…

Although the joy on Gabe's face as he played with Carlotta's grandchildren lay heavily on her chest. Could she open herself up to the possible heartbreak if she agreed to reopen their adoption case file? And were they strong enough as a couple to weather another rejection? Was Gabe that sure that they would be okay so long as they were together? Was she?

These questions went unanswered as their bedroom door swung open and the light from the hallway spilled inside.

"You're awake," Gabe said.

"Barely." She stifled a yawn. "What's going on?"

He tugged on the blanket. "I need a scrub nurse and you're it."

"A scrub nurse? I haven't been in the operating room since I was in training."

"Which still makes you more qualified than the other nurses." He tossed a pair of jeans and a shirt at her. "Come on, sleepyhead."

Leah rolled out of bed and stepped into her jeans. "What sort of surgery?"

"Appendectomy."

"Someone we know?"

"No. Five-year-old boy with excruciating belly pain. His symptoms began two days ago and gradually got worse. I've monitored him for the last few hours because his symptoms weren't classic for appendicitis, but his temp has spiked. I don't want to wait."

"Do you think the appendix ruptured?"

"Let's hope not. Here are your shoes."

She slipped on the loafers then followed him through the silent building as she finger-combed her hair. "Are they equipped to handle surgeries at the clinic?"

"Not really, but we'll make do. I've operated under worse conditions."

"What about instruments?" Her stomach flopped like a landed fish. "Don't tell me you're going to cut on someone with only a pocket knife and a sewing kit in hand."

"I won't. Luckily, I don't leave home without my own basic tools of the trade," he said with a grin. "I've learned that I never know when they'll come in handy. One of the nurses is sterilizing them now."

What a relief! "How's Mrs. Ortiz doing?"

"Not well," he said grimly. "In fact, Ben and Sheldon would have flown her to Mexico City an hour ago, but I need Ben to handle anesthesia. In any case, they're leaving just as soon as I'm finished."

"The baby?" she asked.

"The midwife thinks the baby's showing a few signs of distress. The obstetrician Ben called said Mrs. Ortiz needs a C-section to relieve the pressure on her diaphragm, but I'm hesitant to do it because we can't take care of a preemie. The sooner we can get her to a place equipped for her problems, the better."

Fortunately, the night-shift clinic nurse had followed Gabe's instructions to the letter. His instruments were sterile and the patient was ready. Leah scrubbed beside Gabe, intent on his last-minute instructions and refresher course. Finally, between the drugs Gabe carried as part of his emergency surgical kit and what they found locked in Hector's cabinet, they were ready and their patient was unconscious.

"If we were at home, we could do this laparoscopically," he said offhandedly. "We have to do this the old-fashioned way."

"He won't care," Leah advised. "Now he'll have a scar to brag about."

Gabe's gaze met Leah's. Although she knew he couldn't see it through the mask, she offered a tremulous smile and hoped she wouldn't make a mistake because of her inexperience. As if he'd read her mind, he said, "Take a deep breath. You'll do fine." His eyes twinkled. "I won't be grading you, either."

She chuckled. "Thanks."

"Okay, then." He flexed his shoulders then held out his hand. "Scalpel."

As soon as she slapped the requested instrument into his hand, she was amazed at how quickly she fell into a rhythm. It was mainly due to Gabe, she had no doubt. His skill was obvious as he cut through skin and tissue until, finally, the offending appendix was revealed.

It was swollen and red and ready to burst.

"Looks like we got here in the nick of time," Gabe said as he clamped, snipped, then eventually sutured. "How's he doing, Ben?"

"Great," Ben said from his place near the patient's head

as he monitored vital signs. "Just the way I like surgery—in, out and no problems."

"You can say that again."

After closing his incision and bandaging the site, Gabe pronounced his work done and stripped off his gloves. Looking tired, but pleased, he said, "Let's settle him in his cot, then we'll load Mrs. Ortiz in David's truck. Are you guys ready to go?"

"Corey's at the plane, doing his pre-flight checks," Ben answered. "Sheldon's waiting outside to help us with our patient. Then it's wheels up."

Leah shouldn't have been amazed at their efficiency, but she was. If she didn't know better, she'd think Gabe's team had drilled on this exact scenario until they'd choreographed every step. This was Sheldon's first time in the field and Ben's third, but their united purpose, coupled with Gabe's experience, had pulled them into a well-functioning team.

This was what Gabe had wanted to achieve with this trip—to extrapolate the unity created by this unlikely group of individuals into their marriage—to basically give their relationship a sense of purpose.

Having a family had been part of that purpose and when that had failed, it had seemed pointless to continue the marriage. And yet before Andrew had even become a glimmer in his father's eye, her wish had been simple—to love Gabe and share their lives together. Had that most fundamental purpose changed?

It hadn't, she decided. She still loved him and wanted her life intertwined with his.

Blurting out her revelation was tempting, but it would have to wait. Not only did they have a patient to oversee, but after everything they'd gone through, they both needed to mark the occasion in a special way.

The trip to the airstrip proceeded at a tortoise's pace in deference to Mrs. Ortiz's condition, but eventually everyone and everything had been loaded. The sun was dawning as the plane took off.

Leah watched the aircraft disappear into the cloudless sky. "Strangely enough, I feel like we've been deserted."

Gabe flung an arm around her shoulders. "It does, but at least we have each other." He kissed her forehead. "So, my dear, shall we see if there's any breakfast left?"

Before she could answer, a boy about twelve years old burst into the clearing. "Dr. Gabriel," he called out, panting.

Leah paused, watching Gabe as he listened to the boy's rapid-fire Spanish. She caught a few words, *orphanage* and *hospital*, and guessed at the rest. Finally, he faced her and motioned to the truck. "The sun is barely up and we're already in high demand."

"I gathered as much."

"You're needed at the orphanage and Hector insists on seeing patients even though he can barely stand. I think breakfast is on hold."

"I'm going to predict we'll be busy today."

"So busy you may wish you'd left with the others," he said darkly.

Leah gazed at her husband's face, noticing the distinct shadow of whiskers on his jaw. They would be pushed to their limits, especially Gabe, but she would be there to watch over him and ease his burden as much as possible.

"Not a chance," she said. "I'm exactly where I belong. With you."

CHAPTER ELEVEN

WHEN Leah arrived at the orphanage a short time later, she discovered five more children were symptomatic, bringing her total of sick children to seven. After tending each one personally, it was nearly lunchtime. Anna grabbed her hand and led her to their table, so in between wolfing down her own meal she helped feed the crowd of little people by encouraging them to eat, filling cups, and wiping up the inevitable spills.

As she finished scrubbing the last face before sending them outside to play, one of David's assistants approached her, looking harried. That seemed to be a common trait among everyone she'd seen the past few days. No doubt she would look the same by the end of the week.

"Carlotta is asking for you," the young woman said. "She is in her room."

"I'll be right there."

"Oh, and she wants you to bring…" She mimicked holding something between her thumb and forefinger and made sweeping motions with her hand.

"Pencil and paper?" Leah guessed, wishing she had a better command of the language than she did.

"*Sí*. Pencil and paper."

"I'll bring them," she promised, before washing her hands thoroughly. If only she'd asked Sheldon to include a few gallons of waterless bacterial cleanser… Her skin was already chapped from the constant handwashing and harsh soap, but better to have rough hands than flu.

Inside Carlotta's room and armed with the requested paper and pencil, she was amazed at how quickly the older woman's condition had deteriorated. "Carlotta?" she whispered, lightly touching the woman's shoulder. "You wanted to see me?"

Immediately the woman opened her eyes and struggled to smile. "*Sí.*"

"How are you feeling?" Leah asked. "Do you need any pain pills or—?"

Carlotta waved aside her question. "No. Tell me, Leah, what do you think of my little ones? Do you have what you call a soft spot for them?"

"I do," she admitted, smiling. "They are special children, but you know that better than I."

The older woman's face held that soft, far-off expression, as if she were seeing into the past. "Their parents were special people, too."

"I'm sure they were."

"I want to tell you about them," she said.

Surprised by the request, and also curious, Leah nodded. "I'd love to hear your story."

"Write it down, please. So you do not forget."

Now she understood Carlotta's request, although why the woman would dictate her personal memories in English instead of in her native Spanish was a mystery. Rather than argue with the frail woman, she simply nodded and prepared to write.

"My son, Mario, was a beautiful baby and looked much as José does now," Carlotta began. "We knew his wife's family well, long before he and Jacinta took their vows. She was such a happy child and loved to sing and dance.

Anna takes after her. Rosa…my Rosa is, what do you call it…?" She paused to think. "A mixture of both."

"And because of that, all three are a comfort to you."

"Ah, *sí*. That they are. Mario was such a busy boy and as a youth, he…"

For the next hour, Leah recorded everything Carlotta shared. By the time she'd finished her fifth page, Carlotta's voice had faded. "We will continue tomorrow," she said faintly.

"Of course." Leah rose. "Rest now." Before she could move away from the bed, Carlotta grabbed Leah's arm in a surprisingly fierce grip.

"You will watch over my little ones?"

Leah didn't have the heart to explain her stay in Ciuflores wouldn't last longer than a week, and with their uncle presumably on his way it wouldn't be necessary for long. However, she also understood the dying woman's concern, so she folded Carlotta's hand in hers. "Of course. We all will."

Carlotta closed her eyes and nodded. "Come tomorrow."

Suspecting she would continue her story, Leah nodded. "I'll be here."

"Padre."

She paused. "Do you want Father David?"

At Carlotta's weak nod, Leah said, "I'll send him to you."

Rosa was waiting for her outside Carlotta's room, so Leah hoisted her on one hip as she searched out the priest. Fortunately, she found him in the chapel, on his knees. She would have tiptoed away to leave him to his prayers but Rosa began babbling and caught his attention.

"I'm sorry to interrupt," she told him as he approached. "But I spent the last hour with Carlotta. She wants to see you."

"Okay, I'll drop by for a visit. How is she?"

"Weak."

David nodded, his concern obvious in his eyes.

Leah blew a raspberry against the little girl's neck, causing her to giggle. "Would you mind taking her?" she asked, passing Rosa to him. "I want to check on the boy who had surgery and Rosa doesn't belong in the hospital."

"Ah, yes. I heard about Tomas. How is he?"

"His surgery went well and now I want to monitor his post-op care. Not that your nurses aren't doing a good job," she hastened to explain, "but…"

He grinned. "But you want to see for yourself."

Leah felt her face warm. "Yeah."

"I'll tell you what I told Gabe. Don't bite off more than you can chew. We can't afford for you and Gabe to follow in Hector's footsteps."

"I'll be careful," she promised.

Three days later, she finally admitted she had failed to keep her promise. She had tried to follow David's advice—she really had—but there was so much to do and so little time. Between sick children at the orphanage, helping at the clinic, and playing with Carlotta's grandchildren, her days didn't end until she fell into bed each night and curled around Gabe for a few hours before the routine repeated itself.

Today, though, she had the added job of using her ER skills while Gabe tended a man with severe burns on his arms and face.

"Will you keep him here?" she asked Gabe after they left the fellow to rest.

"He'll need skin grafts and surgical debridement, which is beyond what we can provide. According to Hector, there's a town about a half a day's drive away which is the equivalent of our county seat. They have a small hospital that's better equipped than our clinic. One of his friends will deliver our patient and his wife there as soon as she packs a bag."

"One thing you have to admit," she mused aloud, "everyone in this community pulls together. They don't have much, but what they do have, they're willing to share."

"You'll find that attitude in a lot of places like this."

She thought of something else he'd said. "You'd mentioned Hector. Is he feeling better?"

"Yeah, but he's still weak. I told him to concentrate on regaining his strength because when we leave, he'll need to run at peak efficiency." He rubbed his whisker-darkened face, which obviously hadn't felt a razor yet today and it was already mid-afternoon. "I don't envy him at all."

At first glance, her husband looked as perky as he always did, but she saw the tired set to his mouth and the faint smudges under his eyes. No doubt she probably looked worse.

"Why don't you take a power nap?" she suggested. "Thirty minutes and you'll feel like a new man."

"As tempting as it sounds, I'll have to take a rain check."

"Okay." She stood on tiptoe to deliver a kiss. "I'll see you at dinner in about an hour."

His face lit with curiosity, then satisfaction. "Count on it," he said.

She'd just walked through the door and into what passed as a street when a teenage girl ran up to her. "Señora Gabriel," she panted. "Come!"

Life in Ciuflores seemed to be one crisis after another. "What's wrong?"

"The midwife…she is sick and my sister needs her. We must hurry."

Surely she wasn't asking Leah to deliver a baby! She turned toward the hospital. "I'll get Dr. Ga—"

The girl tugged on her arm. "No time. We must go *now*."

After casting a longing look at the building where her husband was probably dealing with his own crisis, Leah decided to accompany the girl and assess the situation.

The bungalow at the south end of the village was like so many others in its need for repairs and paint, but inside she soon realized she was caught in the middle of a situation she'd always hoped to avoid…the young mother, a girl of about eighteen, was fully dilated and moaning in pain, while her young husband appeared as if he wanted to join in.

Sensing the man would handle a task better than he seemed to handle his laboring wife, Leah sent him to the clinic with a message for Gabe.

Obviously grateful and eager for something to do, he ran out of the house while Leah turned to the younger sister. "Do you have hot water and blankets, um, what's your name?"

"Isabella. My sister is Regina."

"Okay, Isabella. Do you have the things I asked for?"

The girl bobbed her head. "*Sí*. They are ready from the last time."

"The last time?" Leah echoed. It was comforting to know that Regina had gone through this before and wouldn't be a stranger to what was about to happen. "She has another baby?"

"No. It was born dead."

Oh, dear. No wonder both parents looked as if they were frightened out of their wits. The thought of being responsible for bringing their baby into the world with a history like that only added to Leah's pressure.

She couldn't cave in, though. She had to do this. While she wasn't a midwife, her skills were better than nothing until Gabe arrived.

Unfortunately, while Leah washed her hands and changed the sheets with Isabella's help, Regina's contractions began to run into each other without stopping. Another look showed the baby's head was crowning and there was nothing she could do to stop it. She only hoped there wouldn't be any complications before Gabe galloped to the rescue.

She glanced at the door, willing him to suddenly save the day, but he didn't. She was on her own.

"Okay, Regina," she soothed as she positioned herself between the woman's legs. "We're going to do this. You'll be fine and so will your baby. Are you hoping for a boy or a girl? I'm sure you don't care, as long as it's healthy," she chattered on, mainly to draw Regina's attention away from her pain. Although Leah had no idea if the young mother understood her or not, her soothing tone seemed to calm the stark fear in Regina's eyes.

A mighty push later, and the baby's head was free. While Leah suctioned out its nose and mouth, Gabe strode in.

"You seem to have everything under control," he commented as he gently nudged Isabella out of the way to stand beside Leah.

"Thank heavens you're here," she said, relieved she didn't have to do this alone. "You can take over."

"You're doing fine as you are," he said, making no move to usurp her place. "I'll look over your shoulder and talk you through the rest."

He spoke to Regina in Spanish and as she bore down again, one tiny shoulder slipped out, then the other, until finally the little body glided into Leah's hands, already wailing.

"Slippery little things, aren't they?" he commented.

"Yeah." It was an awesome moment, but she didn't have time to revel in it. "You can tell her she has a daughter."

The new mother leaned against the pillow, perspiring and obviously spent as she rattled on and on in Spanish.

Gabe answered calmly as he helped Leah cut the cord. "I told her the baby is fine," he said. "She was worried."

"Rightfully so. She lost her first baby. Stillbirth."

Gabe washed his hands while refreshing her memory on cutting the cord. As soon as she'd finished, and he'd wrapped the baby in the blanket Isabella had provided, he handed her the infant.

"Score her Apgar and let Mom and Dad meet their daughter. I'll finish up. You did great, by the way."

"Regina did all the work," she said. "I basically watched."

After assessing the baby at a ten on the Apgar scale which evaluated her breathing, heart rate, color, muscle tone and response to stimuli, Leah diapered and bundled her up to meet her impatient parents.

Just as she was ready to carry the baby back across the room to Regina, Gabe stopped for a look. "You have the touch," he commented. "She hasn't complained at all about leaving her little nest."

Leah grinned. "Not yet, anyway."

"And look at all that black hair," he commented. "I already see pigtails in her future."

Leah smoothed down the spiky tufts and slid an inexpertly knitted cap over her head. "Between her mom and her aunt…" she smiled at a beaming Isabella "…pigtails, braids and ponytails won't be a problem."

After staying long enough to help Regina freshen up, recite a list of do's and don'ts, and congratulate the new parents, she walked out of the two-room home with Gabe beside her.

"Are you ready to add 'midwife' to your résumé?" he teased.

"Not a chance," she said. "I'm happy with heart attacks, gunshot wounds and stabbings. Those aren't nearly as stressful. The entire time my hands were shaking and my knees wobbled."

"You didn't show it," he said.

"You weren't looking hard enough to see the signs," she responded. "All I could think about was what if this baby didn't survive, either? I didn't want them to blame me for doing something wrong."

Gabe couldn't have asked for a better opening. "Did you blame me when you lost Andrew?"

She froze in her tracks. "Blame you? Why?"

"Because I wasn't there when you started hemorrhaging."

"No." She began walking again. "You hadn't gone on a trip for months and my obstetrician said everything was fine. If she didn't anticipate a problem, why should you? Besides..." she grinned, as if remembering "...by then you were driving me crazy with all of your hovering and I didn't see why you shouldn't go."

He saw her smile fade. "The question is," she asked, "do you blame *me*?"

He frowned. "Why should I?"

"Because, ultimately, I'm responsible for what happened," she whispered, staring straight ahead as if unable to meet his gaze.

"You just said your doctor believed everything was fine. Why do you think you were at fault?"

She shrugged. "Logically, I know what everyone told me, but I can't help wondering if I'd done too much that morning. I'd wanted to prove to you that I might be pregnant but I wasn't helpless. Maybe crawling on the ladder to change a light bulb tore something loose when I reached for the fixture—"

He hated hearing her sound so defeated. He grabbed her arm and pulled her to a halt. "Stop that," he scolded. "It wasn't your fault. It could have happened if you'd been lying on the sofa all day."

Her eyes shimmered. "I know that in my head, but in here..." she tapped her chest "...it's still hard to accept. Especially when you acted as if you couldn't bear to be around me. Which was why I thought you blamed me..."

"I felt helpless because I didn't know how to break through your misery, but I never considered you at fault," he insisted. "What happened was a tragedy, but a divorce wasn't the solution."

"Maybe not, but it would have allowed you to have the things you always wanted."

"I have what I want, right here."

"That's sweet of you to say, Gabe." She began walking and he matched his pace to hers.

"It's true, not sweet," he corrected.

She fell silent, as if sorting things through in her mind, and he didn't interrupt.

"Do you think about them, Gabe?" she finally asked.

He hadn't expected that question. "Nearly every day. Especially when I see children about the same ages as they would be now."

"Really?" she sounded surprised. "You never mentioned a word or acted as if you gave them another thought."

"You weren't looking hard enough to see the signs." He repeated her earlier comment, hoping it would jar her memory.

"I suppose not," she answered ruefully.

"What about you? Do you think about them?"

"I do," she said as she tucked her hands back into her pockets. "I told myself I shouldn't, but different things would happen or be said and I'd be reminded, especially if I heard of another Andrew or an Elizabeth."

"You were going to call her Lizzie."

"Yeah," she said with a far-away expression on her face. "Of all the things we chose I had the most fun deciding on names. A name is so important to a child's self-image."

"It is," he agreed. "Andrew John and Elizabeth Anne, with an 'e'. 'A special spelling for a special baby', you said."

For a long moment they walked in silence, but it wasn't uncomfortable or oppressive. In fact, it seemed almost contemplative, as if it was finally okay to mention those names aloud.

"I didn't want the divorce because I hated you," she said without preamble. "Ending our marriage seemed like the best solution to a bad situation. You'd asked me before if I was trying to save you and, yes, I was. You'd done the same thing for me so many times and this was something I could do for you. I wanted you to be happy because subconsciously I loved you. How else could this trip have opened my eyes so quickly, unless the truth had been there all along, waiting for me to see it?"

"And now?" A combination of anticipation and dread made him unable to breathe.

"I still love you," she repeated. "I want what we had before, even though I have trouble believing it's within reach."

His pulse skipped a beat. "Our future is yours for the taking," he promised. "I'll show you."

"I want it all, Gabe. The love, the passion, the romance, the honesty, the sharing. *Everything*."

"You'll have it," he said. "And then some."

She stopped on the path leading to the orphanage's front door. "I want our future to begin now, Gabe. Not when we get home, but *now*. I'm tired of feeling empty inside."

He hesitated, not wanting to misinterpret. It would literally destroy him if they made love and she still demanded a divorce. "You said we wouldn't make love because it clouded our issues. Does this mean I can shred those papers in my desk drawer?"

"Yes, you can."

"And our marriage will begin right now," he pressed.

"Unless you're too tired." She raised an eyebrow in question.

His previous exhaustion vanished and he was positively certain he wore a goofy grin on his face. "I'm not too tired."

A tiny wrinkle marred her brow. "I'll bet you haven't eaten all day. Maybe we should—"

"The only thing I'm hungry for is you," he said.

With Gabe having earned her cooperation, he seemed as if he couldn't walk to their room fast enough. He grabbed her hand in an unbreakable grip and pulled her into the orphanage, through the common rooms and to the staff quarters without breaking his stride.

"Gabe," she warned with a smile, "if anyone sees us, they'll wonder if there's a fire."

"They'd be right," he answered with a wink and a smile.

Fortunately they didn't meet a single soul, although there had been two close calls. As soon as they shut the bedroom door, Gabe slid the deadbolt home.

"So we don't have three little interruptions," he said.

In the blink of an eye, buttons were undone, zippers

unzipped, and Gabe was following her onto the hastily turned-down bed. Impatient for him, she wriggled underneath his lanky frame.

"We have to slow down." His voice was pained.

She froze. "I'm hurting you. Is it your ribs?"

As she made a move to roll out from under him, he held her firmly in place. "You're not hurting me. I just don't want this to be over too soon," he finished hoarsely.

She studied his lean face, noticing how time had added a few wrinkles around his eyes and a few strands of silver near his temples. In spite of those small changes, he was still the guy who made every other man pale in comparison.

"If it is, then we can look forward to next time."

"I want this to be good for you…" he mumbled in her hair.

"It will be."

As she trailed her hands along his body, the evidence of his previous ordeal seemed to be fading. The ridges, hollows and bumps she'd seen in the hospital weren't as pronounced, but none of that seemed important. Loving her husband was the only thing on her mind.

With the speed of a starving man eating his first meal, he drove her to the brink until she soared over the edge and took him with her.

Too spent to move, she was only vaguely conscious of Gabe drawing the sheet over them before he tucked her under his arm.

"Are you okay?" he asked.

"Oh, yes. You?"

"Never better."

"Your ribs? I didn't hurt you, did I?"

"You didn't and even if you had, the pain would have been worth it. Now, stop worrying about my aches. You're ruining the mood," he teased.

"Can't have that," she answered with a satisfied chuckle. As she rested against him, she saw the sun still shining through white cotton curtains covering the western window. It was far too early to turn in for the night, but she was content to lie in this very spot until morning and savor his touch during every moment. "I can't move," she said, certain he'd turned her into a boneless jellyfish.

"Good, because you're where I want you," he murmured as he nuzzled her temple. "That was…fantastic."

"It was pretty amazing," she agreed.

"What's really amazing is how badly I want you again."

She met his obsidian-eyed gaze. "Really?"

"Oh, really," he said firmly as he rolled slightly toward her so she could discover the truth for herself.

"Mmm," she said, pleased by his response. "Maybe we should pace ourselves."

"Pace ourselves? I don't think I can."

"Try," she ordered, pleased because she was responsible for his lack-of-control issues. What woman wouldn't be thrilled to know she could drive her man wild?

"What if I don't want to?"

That was better yet. "We have all night," she reminded him.

"True." He kissed her collarbone before nibbling his way south. "But humor me. I'm making up for lost time."

The next morning Leah was certain everyone was wondering where she and Gabe had disappeared to the previous evening. They'd missed dinner and although Gabe had slipped out around nine to check on a patient, he'd returned shortly after and they'd spent the rest of the night enjoying each other, uninterrupted.

Although they hadn't slept very much, Leah felt energized

and was pleased to see the spring in Gabe's step as they ambled to the dining hall for breakfast.

The Salazar children immediately descended on them and halfway through their meal, Gabe suddenly announced, "I forgot. David wants to talk to us."

"Oh, Gabe. You don't suppose someone heard us raiding the kitchen before midnight, do you?"

He grinned. "I doubt if he's calling us on the carpet for something so minor. He knows doctors don't always eat on schedule."

"Then I wonder what's on his mind?"

"I don't know, but he'd asked for us to meet him yesterday."

"Yesterday?"

"I got the message right before Regina's husband came barreling into the clinic, yelling for me. After that, for some strange, inexplicable reason..." he grinned "...David's request slipped my mind."

"Ah, so if he's unhappy with us, you'll say it was my fault?" she teased.

"Would you rather I said I was with a patient? For shame," he tutted melodramatically. "I can't believe you'd ask me to lie to a priest."

She leaned closer and kissed him, uncaring that Rosa, José and Anna were watching them with unabashed interest. "Whatever. But why do I feel as if we're being summoned to the principal's office?" she joked.

"I don't know. Have you done something wrong?" he returned in the same vein.

"Not that I know of."

Her feeling rose to full strength as David welcomed them into his private office thirty minutes later. He motioned them to take a seat before he perched on the edge of his battered desk.

"You two look chipper this morning," the priest said with a knowing gleam in his eyes.

"We finally got a good night's rest," Gabe answered, squeezing Leah's hand.

"I'm glad to hear it." His expression became serious. "Now, more than ever, you need to take care of yourselves."

David's tone raised Leah's suspicions. He'd called them in for a reason. A very important reason.

Gabe must have sensed the same thing because his smile died. "Why now, more than ever?"

"Because I visited with Carlotta yesterday afternoon," David said simply. "She wants to pass guardianship of her grandchildren to you."

CHAPTER TWELVE

GABE didn't have to see the surprise on Leah's face. From her sharp gasp he knew it was there. The problem was, he didn't know how Leah would respond to such a request and he wished he'd cornered David before this meeting. As much as he would be willing to say yes, he didn't want to pressure Leah one way or the other.

"What did you say?" she asked.

"Carlotta would like you two to be her **grandchildren's** guardians. Adoptive parents, if you will."

"Oh, my," she breathed. "How? Why?"

"As Gabe knows, Carlotta and I have talked **about her** grandchildren's future from the time she first became ill," David went on. "While growing up in the orphanage is okay because she knows all of the staff, she wants her grandchildren to be placed with a family. However, she doesn't want them split up, which poses somewhat of a problem. Not many people are willing to take on three youngsters under the age of five at once."

"Of course," Leah murmured.

"In any case," he continued, "after meeting you, Leah, and watching the way you interacted with them, she thought you and Gabe were the couple she'd been praying for."

Once again, Gabe exchanged a glance with Leah. "We're honored, but—"

"But is she sure about this?" Leah interrupted, looking as if she wasn't willing to let herself believe her good fortune. "I mean, she hardly knows us. Or me anyway."

"She apparently saw enough to be satisfied," David replied. "When she asked my opinion, I agreed with her."

"Thanks for the vote of confidence," Gabe said.

"Anyone who is willing to put the needs of so many ahead of his own is a special individual," he said, "whether they're my friend or not. In any case, on the advice of the lawyer who handles orphanage business, Carlotta has signed a document indicating her wishes. She'll transfer guardianship of Rosa, Anna and José to you to become effective on her death, providing you agree to take all three."

Leah gasped then faced Gabe with something akin to fear in her eyes. "Gabe?" she asked tremulously. "As much as I'd like to say yes, I'm not sure."

He reached out and took her hand. "Like I told you before, the decision is yours."

She met his gaze, as if trying to read his thoughts, before her expression turned speculative. "David," she said quietly, "would you mind giving Gabe and me a few minutes of privacy?"

"Sure. I'll be outside when you're finished."

From Leah's expression, Gabe knew he was in for a rough ride. It began as soon as David closed the door behind him and she jumped up to pace.

For a few seconds Leah couldn't find the words to voice her displeasure, but when she did, she delivered them fiercely. "You don't seem very surprised by David's announcement," she accused.

"I am, and yet I'm not. I wondered if this might be coming."

Her eyes narrowed. "You did? How?"

"Remember the day you held Rosa and the other two

showed off their toys? Carlotta and I watched you. In her next breath, Carlotta started talking, hinting actually, about how she wanted a couple like us to take her grandchildren."

"And you didn't say anything? Didn't you think this was something I'd be interested in knowing?"

"What could I tell you? Carlotta said she wanted a couple *like us*, she didn't say she wanted *us*, specifically," he defended.

"You're splitting hairs, Gabe. Admit it. You suspected this was coming." An unpleasant idea occurred to her. "Was *this* why you wanted me to come to Ciuflores with you? To manipulate me—?"

"There you go again, giving me motives I don't have and never did," he ground out. "Like I said before, the choice to adopt is yours. All you have to do is say no, and the discussion ends here. David will understand."

She wanted to run away and avoid facing the issue, but the picture of Carlotta as she'd reminisced about her children, then her grandchildren, stopped her. *David might understand, but will Carlotta?* she wondered.

Leah didn't realize she'd spoken her thoughts until Gabe answered. "She's bound to be disappointed. It isn't like she has plenty of time to put her affairs in order."

No, she didn't. When Leah had seen the woman yesterday, she'd been much weaker than the day before.

"I only know one thing," he continued. "As much as I'd love to accept those three, I won't do it at the expense of our marriage. It took us too long to get where we are today."

Immediately, she regretted her accusations. "I'm sorry for being so sensitive and jumping to the wrong conclusions," she said in a small voice. "I know you better than that. Will you forgive me?"

"You're my wife," he said simply. "We're going to make

a mistake here and there." He paused. "Shall we call David back in?"

Don't let fear influence your decision.

"Please do."

Although Gabe seemed curious about her answer, he didn't press her. Instead, he simply squared his shoulders as if bracing himself for bad news.

As soon as David returned, Leah didn't delay in putting both men out of their proverbial misery. She met Gabe's gaze as she announced, "We accept Carlotta's offer."

"Don't do this for me, Leah," Gabe warned.

"I'm not. I'm doing it for *me*, and for *us*."

His smile immediately grew from ear to ear and the tension in his shoulders eased visibly.

"Taking on three is a big responsibility, even without the culture and language issues," David warned. "This will be a major adjustment for all of you."

"We'll handle it," Gabe assured him.

"Definitely," Leah added.

David rose. "I know you will," he said kindly, "but I had to ask. I'm happy for you both and I'm happy for the peace of mind you're giving Carlotta."

"I do have one question, though," Leah said. "What about Carlotta's son—the children's uncle?"

"No one has seen or heard from him in five years. Even if we found him, a judge should honor Carlotta's wishes. I'm not expecting any problems."

Relieved to hear that, she and Gabe headed for the door. "We'd like to thank her for her gift. No, *three* gifts."

David showed them to the door. "She'd like that. Even though I've assured her you'll accept, hearing it for herself will ease her worries. This situation, as sad as it is for her, is also a blessing in disguise for you. So, congratulations."

"Thanks." Gabe shook his hand. "Whatever you need, just say the word and it'll be yours."

David chuckled. "I'll keep your promise in mind. Run along, now, so I can take care of the paperwork to satisfy the legal eagles."

In the hallway, Leah suddenly stopped short. "Oh, Gabe," she wailed as she truly realized what they'd done. "Have we done the right thing? One child is a challenge and two is even more so. But *three*?"

"And here we thought we'd go home to a quiet existence," he joked. "Those days are definitely over."

Leah grinned, already picturing noisy days ahead. "Oh, but just think. Rosa, Anna and José will be *ours*." Her smile dimmed. "I only wish they wouldn't have to lose their grandmother for it to happen, though. I want to celebrate, but a celebration doesn't quite seem appropriate."

"I know, honey." He drew her close. "I think she'd like us to be happy about her decision, especially because her outcome will be the same whether we agree to her offer or not. At least this way she has peace about the future of her grandchildren and we're blessed with the family we've always wanted."

As Leah rested her head on his shoulder, one word reverberated through her mind. *Family.* She and Gabe would be more than a couple, they would be a family. They'd experience all the joys and trials that came with that. She only hoped she'd be worthy of the task.

Suddenly she pulled away. "Oh, my gosh. We have so much to do to get ready for them. Our house will be stuffed to the rafters."

"You always said the place was too big," he teased. "Now you're saying it's too small?"

Love shone out of her eyes. "No, our home is going to be just right."

* * *

"How is she?" Leah asked Gabe as he came out of Carlotta's room later that evening.

Gabe tugged her out of the children's earshot. "She's slipped into a coma."

She hated to hear that. She still had so many questions and knew the woman hadn't finished telling her stories. Leah hoped Carlotta had shared her most treasured memories and she took comfort in the notes she'd recorded. Those were definitely precious pages.

"How long?"

"It's hard to say. Could be hours, or days. Not more than that, I would think."

"I'm glad we were able to talk to her for a few minutes this afternoon." A lump formed in Leah's throat as she thought about the emotional scene when she and Gabe had whispered their thanks to the dying woman. Carlotta hadn't answered; she'd simply smiled and wiggled her fingers in their hands.

"I am, too."

"I don't want her to die, but I know she's suffering," Leah admitted. "And I feel selfish for wanting to take the children with us when we leave in a few days. I'd like to stay, and yet I know we can't."

"I wish we could," he said, "but we'll have to leave as soon as they unload the plane."

She didn't like the idea very much and told him so.

"Our mission goes on, Leah," he reminded her. "A long goodbye won't be possible."

"But—" She thought of disappearing from the children's lives without warning or explanation, but Anna was the only one old enough to understand, and even then, she wouldn't. As much as she hated what her attitude said about her, she hoped she could take the children when she left.

"What if Miguel isn't back?" she asked.

"We'll cross that bridge when we come to it." His grim tone suggested he'd already considered the possibility and wasn't looking forward to making the decision.

"On the bright side, the number of new cases seems to be dropping," she offered.

"Let's hope it stays on the downhill slope."

Leah agreed. While over half of the children in the orphanage had exhibited symptoms in the last two days, none of the cases were severe enough to require hospitalization. She and the staff had been able to push enough oral fluids to keep them from becoming dehydrated and with antibiotics readily available for those who'd developed bacterial complications, a lot of problems had been nipped in the bud. So far, Rosa, Anna and José—*her* three children, as she now thought of them—only had a minor case of sniffles.

He flexed his shoulders then threaded his arm around her waist.

"It's getting late, Mrs. Montgomery," he said with the heated look in his eyes she recognized. "Shall we put our hooligans to bed?"

"Yeah, but after that, what will we do for the rest of the evening?" she asked innocently.

"Don't worry," he answered with a boyish charm. "I'll think of something."

Carlotta slipped away in the predawn hours two days later. Leah could only mourn the loss and marvel in the woman's foresight at requesting Leah write down her family history. At least the three Salazar children would know a little about their roots.

Twenty-four hours after that, Hector had improved to the point where he was working again, although Gabe refused to let him take up his duties for more than a few hours at a time. However, Hector's recovery came as a relief to everyone because their plane was due and Miguel still hadn't returned. Hector might not be functioning at one hundred percent, but if he limited himself to the seriously ill patients, he could manage.

Oddly enough, she'd hated to leave but with these new developments she was impatient for the MMF plane to arrive. First, though, she had to wait for David to return from court with the children's signed and sealed paperwork.

"Would you quit watching the road?" Gabe teased. "David will get back as soon as he can. He won't make you wait a minute longer than necessary."

She bounced José on one hip. "I know. I'm being silly, but we're so close to having everything official. You don't suppose the judge will go against Carlotta's wishes, do you? I mean, David's not an attorney and the document isn't typed up nice and neat."

"I don't know how the Mexican court system works in family cases," Gabe said honestly, "but if anyone can maneuver his way through the system, it's David. Let's not worry until he gets back, shall we?"

Unfortunately, that was the problem. Leah was ready to make plans and until she could do so with the Mexican government's blessing, she would fret.

When the unmistakable roar of the twin-engined Cessna sounded overhead, Leah's heart sank. She'd privately hoped the plane would be a day or two, or even three, late, but it obviously wasn't meant to be.

By the time they'd greeted Sheldon, unloaded the plane and restocked Hector's supply room, Leah saw David's truck parked near the orphanage. "Oh, Gabe," she breathed. "He's back. I can't wait to hear what he has to say, can you?"

Unfortunately, David's expression was grim, and she didn't like his report.

"The judge went on his circuit this week," David announced.

"Which means?" she demanded.

"He wasn't there to rule on the transfer of guardianship."

"Then when—?"

"The clerk in his office said it will take him at least a month to review the case."

"A month?" She swallowed hard. She'd wanted so badly to take the children home with her now.

"Four weeks won't be so bad, will it?" Gabe asked. "The delay will give us plenty of time to get ready."

"Four weeks is forever to a child," she pointed out. "A veritable lifetime. They won't remember…" Her voice died.

"Yes, they will," Gabe assured her. "They remembered me and they hadn't seen me for several months. A few weeks will pass quickly. This is only a minor inconvenience."

She didn't agree, but arguing with Gabe and David wouldn't change the facts. They couldn't stay and the children couldn't leave. She had to deal with it.

"You're right. We'll need every day of that to get ready," she said, determined to be positive when she felt the opposite.

Gabe hugged her. "That's my girl," he said softly.

David's face remained grave. "Unfortunately, there's more."

Leah's heart sank as she watched Gabe's eyes narrow. "More what?" he asked.

"Carlotta's son Jorge is here." David paused. "He wants the children."

"But—but he can't have them," Leah protested. "Carlotta wanted us to—"

David held up his hands. "I know that. You know that,

and Jorge knows that. He believes his mother wasn't in her right mind when she made her decision, especially since she went into a coma a few hours later."

"Is he suggesting she was coerced?"

"He isn't making that accusation directly, but he believes the children belong with the only family they have left. As he's the one in particular…" David shrugged.

Righteous indignation rose up inside her. "Where has he been all this time?" she demanded. "Can he care for three young children?" Her voice wobbled. "Provide for them. *Love* them?"

"That's for the judge to decide, Leah," David said gently. "I'm not happy with this development, either, but what can I do?"

A horrible thought came to her. "Will he…will he take them away? From Ciuflores?" If he did, she was certain she'd never see the children again.

"I've insisted they remain here at the orphanage until the matter is settled. As far as the children are concerned, he's a stranger and they don't need the upheaval right now." He patted her shoulder awkwardly. "I'll keep a close eye on them. I promise."

Leah bit her lip to keep it from trembling. Thankful for Gabe's steadying arm around her, she nodded. "Thanks."

"Should we talk to this clerk to plead our case?" Gabe asked.

"The only one who needs to hear your side is the judge and he's not available. All you can do—and I know this sounds trite—is to go about your usual business while you're waiting."

Inside, she was screaming, *Been there, done that,* but David's advice was sound, even if she didn't like it. As she glanced at Gabe, she saw the same resignation in his eyes.

She managed a tremulous smile. "Then that's what we'll do. If you two will excuse me, I have a bag to finish packing and a few goodbyes to say."

As soon as she'd disappeared, Gabe spoke to David. "There's more, isn't there?"

David exhaled slowly as he ran his finger around his clerical collar. "Yes, and no. I don't have any new information, but I've got to admit, my friend, that this particular judge isn't one I've dealt with before. Rumor has it that he's a tough cookie when it comes to placing children, especially placing them outside the country."

"Then we don't have a chance?" Gabe asked.

"Oh, there's a chance. You have a lot in your favor. Carlotta's blessing will carry a lot of weight."

"Then what's the problem? The judge should understand that if she wanted her son involved, she would have arranged for it."

"According to our attorney, a lot will hinge on Carlotta's health and state of mind at the time she dictated her wishes. Medical testimony will be crucial. Unfortunately—"

"I was the attending physician," Gabe supplied, recognizing the dilemma he was in.

"If Hector had been treating her at the time she faded," David went on, "his opinion would carry more weight than yours because he doesn't have a vested interest in the outcome. You, on the other hand, do."

"It might look that way, but if Jorge wants to reconnect with family, where has he been all this time?" Gabe demanded, incensed on Carlotta's behalf. Perhaps if good old Jorge had been around, Carlotta wouldn't have worked so hard the last several years. Perhaps she would have sought treatment sooner.

"According to him, he travels a lot." As Gabe opened his mouth to argue, David held up his hands. "I know, I know. Mail goes both ways, but that's a question he'll have to explain to the judge's satisfaction. Personally, I'm hoping Carlotta's wishes will carry the most weight because she knew her son better than anyone. If Jorge argues that he's not the irresponsible man he once was, then the court's decision could rest on who has the most eloquent lawyer."

He cast a meaningful glance at Gabe. "Unless…"

Gabe understood immediately. "Unless we can prove that Jorge isn't the upstanding citizen he claims to be?"

David grinned. "I've met lots of people in my line of work and I can safely say that clothes don't make the man."

Grasping at the hope David had provided, Gabe asked, "What can I do?"

"Nothing. It's easier for me to snoop around because as the orphanage director, I oversee the home placement study." He smiled. "You'd be surprised what sort of connections I have."

"In high places, I hope?"

"To low ones, too." He rose. "I hope you don't mind if I don't see you off. I need to start making phone calls."

"Let me know if I can do anything to help."

"I will. In the meantime, expect the best but prepare for the worst."

Leah fought the tears as she hugged Anna, Rosa and José. "I'll come back," she promised hoarsely. "Be good while I'm gone. When I see you again, we'll have all sorts of fun. We'll read stories and play games…"

"*Adiós*?" Anna asked, her forehead wrinkled in thought.

"Yes, but not for long," Leah told her. "This is just temporary." She tried to think of the right word to use and came up blank. "It's only temporary," she repeated.

Those three words had become her mantra, but it was cold comfort. She had the feeling that once she left Ciuflores, the tenuous tie between her and the children would be cut.

"Adiós mi abuelita?" Anna asked.

"No. Not goodbye like your grandmother. I'll see you again, soon." Knowing the three had seen plenty of weepy people since their grandmother's death, Leah was determined to put on a bright face. Yet as she wrapped her arms around each little wiggly body and received a sloppy kiss, her breath burned in her chest.

Overcome, she glanced at Eva, one of the orphanage's staff, who immediately spoke to the children in a lilting voice that didn't quite match her red-rimmed eyes. Herding the children in front of her, the girl left the room wearing an apologetic expression, leaving Leah alone.

She sat quietly and tried to regain her composure, but the memory of those precious hugs and their baby-clean scent, as well as the moisture remaining on her cheek from Rosa's open-mouthed smooch, made it impossible.

She couldn't leave them. She just couldn't.

Acting on instinct, she dumped her clothes out of her travel case before heading toward the children's room. She began stuffing their things inside with little regard for neatness.

"Leah?"

Ignoring her husband, she doggedly continued her self-appointed task.

He stepped inside. "What are you doing?"

"What does it look like?" She brushed past him to retrieve the two small picture frames on their dresser—pictures which she knew were of their parents. "I'm packing their things. I'd buy everything new, but having a few familiar pieces—"

"Leah," he said firmly, as she stuffed the frames in the suitcase underneath a pile of clothes for protection. "What are you doing?" he repeated firmly.

"I only need a few more minutes, Gabe, and then we can leave."

"If you're doing what I think you're doing—"

She paused, clutching Rosa's doll to her chest. "I'm taking my children home, Gabe. They're mine. Carlotta passed their guardianship to us. She asked me…" Her voice caught.

Gabe gently tugged the doll out of her arms and pulled her against him. "She asked you what?" he coaxed.

The knot of emotion seemed to grow in her throat and she swallowed hard. "Before I knew what she had planned, she asked if I'd watch over them and I promised I would. I can't do that if they're here and I'm not." She met his gaze defiantly. "I won't break my promise."

"Leah," he said kindly. "I understand about promises, but we can't take them with us. Without the proper *legal* papers, we'd be accused of kidnapping."

The sane part of her brain agreed with him, but her heart didn't want to listen. "We have Carlotta's blessing," she argued. "David has it in writing. Duly witnessed. What more do the authorities need?"

"Okay," he said, sounding quite calm, as if they were discussing a grocery delivery. "Say we do it your way. Do you really want to risk the law showing up on our doorstep to haul them away and send us to jail? Or did you plan to live on the lam?"

She wanted to deny the scenario he'd painted would ever happen, but she couldn't. And yet…

"Oh, Gabe, we're so close," she breathed. "I have this feeling that if they don't come with me now, they never will."

His dark-eyed gaze met hers. "It's because we *are* so close that we can't do this. We can't afford to make an impulsive mistake and screw this up."

Logic once again warred with her emotions. "But—"

"If we do everything by the book, we stand a far better chance with the court than if we do something stupid."

"But—"

"Leah," he urged. "Think about this."

"I have, and—"

"Leah." The pity in his eyes was her undoing.

Suddenly, facing the fact she would soon be leaving the children behind, she collapsed against him and wept until his shirt was wet and wrinkled. Once the pain finally subsided, she realized Gabe's strength and support had never wavered in spite of his own heartfelt anguish.

"I thought what we went through before was terrible," she said when she could finally speak, "but that was nothing compared to this. It's worse because I've gotten to know these three—their likes, dislikes, the way Rosa sucks her thumb when she's tired, how Anna talks with her hands—"

"How José wrinkles his nose when he smiles," he finished as he continued to rub comforting circles on her back. "You're right. This time is much more difficult."

As she stole a glance at his face, his red-rimmed eyes proved he was as torn up about the change in circumstances as she was.

"The good news is," he continued, "our absence is only temporary."

"Only temporary," she echoed as she pulled away.

He rubbed away the tear tracks on her cheeks. "Better?"

"Not really." She managed a weak smile.

"Come on," he said tenderly. "Let's go home."

CHAPTER THIRTEEN

EXPECT the best but prepare for the worst.

Over the next week, Gabe tried his best to follow David's advice, but he hadn't been able to share the same counsel with Leah. If he suggested there was a chance the court wouldn't decide in their favor, he didn't know how she'd react. During the time they'd been home she'd jumped between chatting about what toy each child would like to fretting if they were eating properly, getting enough hug time and staying healthy.

Sitting on the sidelines, as David had also suggested, was impossible. Although he had plenty of faith in his friend, David wasn't the only man with connections and Gabe didn't hesitate to use them. Discreetly, of course.

But by the beginning of the second week his guilt demanded he pull Leah aside.

"I'm going to Mexico tomorrow," he told her.

Her hands flew to her mouth. "You have news?" she breathed, her eyes lighting up.

"No," he said. "I haven't wanted to tell you this because I didn't want to raise your hopes, but you deserve to know the truth. I promised complete honesty when we got back together and I haven't held up my part of the bargain."

"What are you saying, Gabe? What aren't you telling me?"

He drew a deep breath, glad she was more interested in

his news than in his moral lapse. "David is trying to dig up information on Jorge Salazar and so far he's coming up blank. I'm heading down there to see what I can do."

"I'll go with you."

"No. Absolutely not."

"Gabe," she warned. "I have a vested interest, too."

"Yes, but David says the key is to be discreet. There are places I need to go where you'll stick out like a sore thumb. If Jorge tells the judge we're deliberately trying to sabotage him…we can't take that risk."

"Then I'll stay in Ciuflores."

He shook his head. "I'm headed to Mexico City. This is a fly-in and fly-out trip. I can't work in a detour for you. I'm sorry."

She let out a deep sigh. "Okay. I don't like it, but I understand."

"Good."

"Thanks for being honest," she said. "I know it would have been easier on you to keep me in the dark, but I'm glad I know what you're doing. Just keep me posted, okay?" She grinned. "I know how much you hate to fly."

"Count on it."

Although Leah was glad that Gabe had gotten past his overly protective attitude, she almost wished he *had* left her clueless. The very thing he'd worried about—putting her on an emotional roller coaster—came to pass. Over the next two weeks he flew four more times to Mexico and on the conclusion of each trip he simply shook his head.

Her optimism was fading, but she clung to the idea that on one of his fact-finding missions he'd finally have news that would be in their favor.

And yet she watched Gabe push himself harder and harder, as if he was determined to succeed at any cost. At times she felt as if she was losing him because he became so focused on his objective, which was to bring the Salazar children home. She didn't know what to do or say to warn him about the path they seemed to be on, but the words came to her after the foundation's fundraising gala...

"You're leaving again?" Leah stared at her husband as he stripped off his bow-tie and tossed his tuxedo jacket on their bed at two a.m. She still wore her black shimmery ballgown, minus the strappy heels she'd kicked off the minute they'd walked through the door.

"First thing in the morning."

"It *is* morning," she pointed out.

"At eight," he said. "That gives me..."

"Six hours," she supplied. "That's all the notice I get? Six hours?" She couldn't begin to describe the hurt she felt. "How long have you known you were leaving?"

"I planned this trip yesterday."

"You should have told me."

"You were busy with the last-minute plans for the ball," he pointed out. "Honestly, it slipped my mind."

"It may have, but it's no excuse," she insisted. "You have to slow down, Gabe. You can't keep up this pace."

"Don't worry. I'll sleep on the plane."

"This isn't about sleeping, although you *are* burning both ends of the candle," she said tartly.

"I'm doing this for you, Leah. For us."

"I understand." She sank onto the bed and began toying with a loose sequin. "Tonight, when I saw the picture of me and the children on the screen..." Her throat closed and unconsciously she knotted her dress in her fist. She hated getting emotional and had told herself she wouldn't, but here she was, doing the very thing she'd vowed she wouldn't.

"That photo is my favorite," he said as he sat beside her.

"I don't know how or when Sheldon snapped it, but I'm grateful. He's going to give you a copy, by the way."

"Thanks," she said. Seeing the image was a bittersweet experience and would be until the Mexican court finally reached a decision. She was at the point where she was willing to propose they grease a few palms, although she could imagine Gabe's horrified reaction to the suggestion. If he'd nipped her kidnapping attempt in the bud, then he certainly wouldn't be open to her attempt at bribery.

She rubbed her forehead, wondering what her ideas said about her character if she was willing to resort to illegal activities. Then again, she was a desperate woman.

Pushing those thoughts away, she added, "The point is, after seeing those pictures, I...I need you, Gabe, here with me. Not jetting miles and miles away."

He caressed her cheek. "Aw honey, I'd like nothing more than to be here, but this trip is important. I feel as if I'm so *close*."

She held his hand to her face. "You said that last time."

"I know, but—"

"You'd tried to protect me from experiencing emotional ups and downs, but now it's my turn. Please, Gabe, don't go. I know you're trying to give me my heart's desire, but maybe it isn't your place to provide it."

"I want to, though."

She snuggled close. "And I love you for trying, but we need to step back and let David handle things." She paused. "He is still investigating, isn't he?"

As Gabe's nod, she smiled. "Then let him do his job."

He stared at her like a dog staring at a new dish. "What if David doesn't succeed? What if we lose our case?"

"I'll be crushed," she admitted, "but I won't be nearly as devastated as I will be if I lose you. So, please. Promise me this is your last trip."

He looked as if he was ready to protest, but instead he simply nodded. "Okay," he said wearily. "You win."

"Good," she said, relieved by his decision. "Would you like me to drive you to the airport?"

"Thanks, but Sheldon is tagging along so he's picking me up. Meet me when my plane lands on Monday evening?"

Greeting him at the airport when he returned had become part of her routine. She'd added it because she needed the reassurance that he'd arrived safely. The main reason, however, was because she missed him terribly and wanted to see him as soon as possible.

"I'll be there with bells on."

Leah puttered around the house after Gabe left, wanting to do something but unable to find anything interesting enough to hold her interest. She baked a cake, but when it didn't rise, she realized she hadn't added all the ingredients. It landed in the trash.

She sewed a couple of loose buttons on Gabe's shirts then discovered she'd stitched the placket closed. She ripped it out and started over.

She took their formal wear to the dry cleaner's and after arriving at the shop across town realized she had forgotten to bring Gabe's tuxedo pants.

Staying at home and reading a book was pointless because she couldn't remember what she'd read from one page to the next.

Unsettled for reasons she couldn't understand, although she attributed the feeling to Gabe's absence, she meandered again into what she'd tentatively decided would be the girls' room.

Idly, she wondered if Gabe had seen the changes she'd made in here. Granted, they'd only been small ones and had only occurred a few days ago, but for her they were a step forward.

As she looked at the space where the crib had once stood, she reflected on all the "what ifs". What if one or both of their previous adoption attempts had been successful? Gabe wouldn't have insisted she join him on his trip to Ciuflores. She wouldn't have met Carlotta or her three grandchildren.

But even before that, what if Gabe hadn't returned from his plane crash? Or what if he had, and they'd divorced?

Those ideas sent a cold shudder down her spine. Of all the people who'd come and gone in her life, Gabe was her anchor. Whether or not the Mexican government allowed her to keep her promise to Carlotta, she would still have Gabe. He was her rock and she couldn't imagine life without him.

Fortunately, Jeff had taken her announcement in his stride. He'd suspected she hadn't gotten over her husband and was glad he'd allowed her the space she'd needed to figure that out for herself.

As for the children, if fate exacted another pound of flesh and stole her dream again, she would grieve, just as Gabe would. The difference was, they'd do it together, not separately. She loved him too much to fall back into those marriage-destroying old habits. She might never raise children, but she had Gabe and she would fight to keep their marriage alive, even if she had to resign her job and donate her time to the Montgomery Foundation in order to see him.

Strangely enough, her decision chased away her gloom. Over the next twenty-four hours nothing spoiled her good mood or her inner peace—not even what Jane had affectionately termed "another shift from hell".

Fortunately, she was able to leave the hospital promptly

at six p.m. on Monday. Forty minutes later, she'd been cleared to wait on the tarmac near their plane's hangar, where she polished off the bottle of soda she'd purchased from a vending machine. Finally, the familiar plane with its red and black markings appeared overhead, and a few minutes later taxied to a stop in front of her.

She stood, eager for Gabe to open the door and descend the stairs. He'd been gone less than forty-eight hours and it seemed like forever.

Finally, the door descended, but no one exited.

"What's taking so long?" she muttered impatiently as she stared at the empty opening.

No sooner had she spoken than Gabe appeared. She strode forward, determined to meet him at the bottom of the steps. "Gabe," she called, waving to capture his attention.

His answering smile was broad. Apparently his trip had turned out better than he'd expected because he seemed happier than he had on previous returns.

She watched him step out, but then, before he carefully descended the stairs, he hoisted a small figure onto one hip. Her steps slowed. What in the world…?

Behind him came a larger child wearing a floral print sundress. This one painstakingly took each step as she held onto the railing with one hand and clutched a familiar doll in the other. Sheldon brought up the rear, carrying another child—a boy.

Leah froze in her tracks as the group come forward. Gabe looked positively ecstatic and the children's eyes were filled with wonder as they took in their surroundings.

The crowning moment came when Anna saw her. A huge grin spread across her little brown face and she ran forward, crying *"Mamacita!"*

Mommy. Leah swore her heart skipped a beat, probably several. Could it be?

She crouched down to hug her. "My goodness, you've grown," she told the youngster in a tear-choked voice. "Gabe?" she asked, hardly able to believe the reality of the little girl in her arms.

Her husband's smile stretched from ear to ear. "Hi, honey. We're finally home."

The look of awe and pure joy on Leah's face made everything Gabe had gone through worth the effort. Gifting her with the Hope diamond wouldn't have made her this happy or been this satisfying.

"Gabe?" she said again as she rose, reaching out tentatively to stroke Rosa's hair, as if afraid the children were only an elaborate hallucination.

He bent his head to drop a swift kiss on her startled mouth. "How do you like the presents I brought?" He held out Rosa, who immediately dove into Leah's arms, confident in Leah's quick reflexes and ability to catch her.

"They're fantastic," she told him, "but how was this possible? Are they here for a visit? When do they go back? Where's David? Did the judge finally hear our case?" Then, *"Why didn't you tell me?"*

He laughed at her rapid-fire questions. "First things first. Let's get these monkeys in the car."

"But we don't have three car seats," she wailed.

"Yes, you do," Sheldon piped up. "As soon as we knew we were bringing them, I called the office. Loretta found three and stuck them in my car."

It took a while to make the transfer, but she and Gabe soon had everyone buckled into the safety seats and they were on their way. Corey would deliver the rest of their things later.

The children were clearly tired and fussy from their experience, so Leah's questions had to wait. All except one.

"Are they ours, Gabe? To keep?" she asked as he drove out of the airport.

Determined to chase away the fear in her eyes, he nodded. "They're ours. No refunds allowed."

She let out a long, deep, heartfelt breath then turned the most brilliant smile on him as moisture glistened in her eyes. "Thank you," she said as she squeezed his elbow before she looked into the back seat for the tenth time in as many minutes.

Leah smiled at the children behind her. Rosa and José were dozing and Anna was fighting to stay awake, but soon the car's motion lulled her to sleep, too.

The nap during the short drive home completely restored their energy. They were more than ready to eat the crackers and sliced apples she hurriedly assembled before rushing off to play with the toys she and Gabe had purchased beforehand, in anticipation.

"We need an emergency grocery-store run," she informed her husband. "I don't have kid-friendly food in the house."

"I'll go," he advised her. "Or, better yet, call Loretta and give her a list."

She didn't think shopping for groceries fell under the duties of an office assistant, but the woman was a grandmother and under the circumstances, would most likely be thrilled to do it.

"Okay, tell me what happened," she demanded when the youngsters were entertaining themselves with both their old and new toys. "And talk fast because we have a thousand and one things to do."

"After we landed in Mexico City, David called to tell me the judge was holding a preliminary hearing. I wanted to be there to state our case and answer his questions, so we immediately flew to Ciuflores. As it turned out, the investigators David hired had turned up some rather damning information about Jorge. Once the evidence was presented to the court—at the eleventh hour, I might add—the judge ruled in our favor. I thought about waiting until we could bring them home together, but David thought the children would have a difficult time with another separation, even a short one. So, here we are."

"Why do I sense there's more to this story than you're telling me? And where did David find the money to hire an investigator? His services couldn't have been cheap."

Gabe shrugged innocently. "I heard he received an anonymous donation to help defray those costs, but it's purely a rumor. Of course, it would also be pure speculation to guess the identity of the man who personally called in a few favors from some of his own contacts."

"I should be upset with you for leaving me out of all the fun, but I'm not." She stood on tiptoe to swiftly kiss him. "I'm glad you're back, Gabe. If I forgot to tell you this, welcome home."

His midnight-black eyes reflected tenderness. "I know things will be crazy for a while, probably years," he tacked on wryly, "and we may feel harried and hassled, but I'll always make time for us."

She wrapped her arms around his chest. "I intend to hold you to your promise."

The sound of raised voices caught Leah's attention. Clearly, José and Anna were having a difference of opinion. "You may want to rethink your stance on work-related travel," she advised. "A trip may be the only time you experience peace and quiet."

"It might," he agreed, "but peace and quiet can't compare to having a family who needs me."

"And we always will."

2 FREE BOOKS
AND A SURPRISE GIFT

We would like to take this opportunity to thank you for reading this Mills & Boon® book by offering you the chance to take TWO more specially selected books from the Medical™ series absolutely FREE! We're also making this offer to introduce you to the benefits of the Mills & Boon® Book Club™—

- **FREE home delivery**
- **FREE gifts and competitions**
- **FREE monthly Newsletter**
- **Exclusive Mills & Boon Book Club offers**
- **Books available before they're in the shops**

Accepting these FREE books and gift places you under no obligation to buy, you may cancel at any time, even after receiving your free books. Simply complete your details below and return the entire page to the address below. You don't even need a stamp!

YES Please send me 2 free Medical books and a surprise gift. I understand that unless you hear from me, I will receive 5 superb new stories every month including two 2-in-1 books priced at £5.30 each and a single book priced at £3.30, postage and packing free. I am under no obligation to purchase any books and may cancel my subscription at any time. The free books and gift will be mine to keep in any case.

Ms/Mrs/Miss/Mr _____ Initials _____

_____

Surname _____

Address _____

_____

_____ Postcode _____

E-mail _____

Send this whole page to: Mills & Boon Book Club, Free Book Offer, FREEPOST NAT 10298, Richmond, TW9 1BR